PICKING UP THE PIECES

PAULA VINCE

Even Before
Publishing®

Picking up the Pieces

Published by Even Before Publishing; Christian books by Wombat Books.

P. O. Box 1519, Capalaba Qld 4157

www.evenbeforepublishing.com

www.wombatbooks.com.au

© Paula Vince 2010

Second Edition

Original edition published by Golden Grain Publishing, SA.

ISBN: 0-9585523-4-7

Design and layout by Even Before Publishing

ISBN: 978-1-921633-16-4

National Library of Australia Cataloguing-in-Publication entry
National Library of Australia Cataloguing-in-Publication entry
Author: Vince, Paula, 1969-
Title: Picking up the pieces / by Paula Vince.
Edition: 2nd ed.
ISBN: 9781921633164 (pbk.)
Dewey Number: A823.4

Publisher waiver: Any opinions expressed by the characters are not necessarily the opinion of the publisher. Any relation to real people either living or dead is purely circumstantial. This book is a work of fiction. As the issues presented may be sensitive to some we have provided resources on the website for support: www.evenbeforepublishing.com/pickingupthepieces.html

Picking up the Pieces is the best book of its kind I've read in ages. A well written novel about relationships with characters that live on long after you put it down. *Picking up the Pieces* bravely examines issues that are so often swept under the carpet.
Rosanne Hawke, author of Wolfchild.

I loved *Picking up the Pieces*. Paula Vince's characters really came alive for me and gripped me from that first page – so much so that I ended up burning the midnight oil because I simply had to find out if, and then how, she reconciled the terrible things done to Claire. The ending came together so beautifully it made me laugh, cry, but overall rejoice that we have such a wonderful and loving Heavenly Father who can 'make all things new' with forgiveness and love.
Mary Hawkins, author of Return to Baragula

I started reading *Picking up the Pieces* yesterday morning and couldn't put it down. It was amazing. I was left breathless at the end – literally! It was such a beautiful example of the amazing forgiveness of our Father and the way He can totally transform lives. Wow, I tell you the honest truth – I was left breathless!
Martha Mugamu, New South Wales

I couldn't put *Picking up the Pieces* down. It just seemed to get better and better as I was reading. After I'd finished it, I didn't know what to do with myself because nothing that I could do seemed interesting.
Kristy Lynch, South Australia

Picking up the Pieces was a delight to read. It touched me so much. Even now that I've finished, I still find myself thinking of Blake Quinlan and Claire Parker.
Deborah Moffatt, South Australia

About the Author

Paula Vince lives in Mount Barker, South Australia, with her husband and three children. She enjoys her lifestyle of writing and educating her children at home.

Paula values her faith, family and fiction. She believes nothing has more power to delight and inspire people than a good story with lovable characters.

Paula Vince is a talented writer of fiction and "Picking up the Pieces" is Christian fiction at its best. It's a contemporary drama that had me absolutely riveted from the first page. I was hunting for excuses to sit down and read some more. I feel that PUP rivals the best there is in the same category of comtemporary drama, romance.

The story tackles the sensitive issue of sexual assault as the main theme. Secondary themes of dealing with self-image in the lives of the physically and emotionally abused brothers also has the readers asking all those difficult questions over again; but Paula Vince handles the answers in a mature, realistic and satisfying way.

I'm totally committed to seeing this novel and this writer taking a secure place on the Australian Christian fiction bookshelf. Australian readers will be proud to know that Paula Vince is one of our own.

Meredith Resce, author of the Green Valley series, For All Time and The Schoolmasters Bride.

Prologue

Claire was already seated on the bus before she saw him. She had not noticed him among the crowd waiting to board, or she would never have got on. She sat with an empty seat beside her, waiting for Angela, who lingered near the front exchanging pleasantries with an old friend. That was when she saw his face. He was sitting across the aisle, two rows ahead of her.

Claire's throat instantly tightened and she could hardly swallow. It was him! Blake Quinlan. She had not seen him for seven years, but she would have recognised him anywhere. Her knotted insides made her queasy as she tried desperately to control the shaking.

His appearance had changed. He was now a man instead of a boy. He had lost his adolescent gangliness and filled out a little. He had the same slender face, with hollow cheekbones and strong features. His hair was thick and dark, with the hint of a wave at the back of his neck. Claire had never denied Blake Quinlan's good looks, even seven years ago. They did not assuage her dread. She felt as if she were facing a monster.

She wished that she dared tug the emergency cord and demand to be let off. Of course it was unthinkable. How could she explain herself to the camp administrators without blurting out the bitter truth? What would the bus driver think? They might refuse to let her disembark, and everybody would think she had gone crazy.

A tight fist of fear formed in Claire's stomach, and all at once she was back there, sixteen years old again. She felt a wild hope that he would not recognise her, and knew it was wishful thinking. He would soon recall, and he would surely remember when he heard her name. Would he expect her to pass the time of day with him, as if they were old friends?

As if he felt her eyes bore into the side of his face, he turned his head and caught her eye. Claire watched his large, dark eyes fill with recognition. His pupils dilated with shock, until his brown eyes appeared inky black. The colour drained from his face and his lips parted, slightly. Claire broke eye contact and stared at her tightly clenched hands.

Her mind whirled with anger. A person like him had no right to attend a Christian camp! Why hadn't he attended the information night a week ago? If she had seen him there, she could have darted out of the auditorium far more easily than she could jump off a moving bus.

Blake sat chilled to the bone. He could not have moved a muscle for a million dollars. He had carried Claire Parker's image in his head for seven years, so he could not possibly mistake another girl for her. Her delicately chiselled profile had first caught his attention. Her eyes were still as clear and as inviting as deep pools, and her skin transparently pure. She wore a teal blue T-shirt with a triangular cut collar, and her smooth, white neck looked slender and fragile. His blood curdled anew at the thought of what had happened.

Although his body was still, his brain teemed with plans. He had no place on this bus with other Christians. When they made their first rest stop, he would leave and work his way back home. There was no way he could face Claire Parker. What would he say? "Long time, no see!"

She studiously avoided his eyes now, but her startled gaze had cut his heart to ribbons. She had looked at him as if he were a noxious disease. He felt like a grimy and despicable youth again. It was just an illusion that he could ever forget his past. It would always hover over his life like a black cloud. He felt even worse to think that it would also loom over Claire's.

However would he get himself out of this fix?

PART ONE

Chapter One

Claire had met Blake Quinlan only twice, but those two meetings had tainted the rest of her life. When she moved with her parents from Melbourne to a lovely home in the Adelaide Hills, nobody could have anticipated the event that had almost broken her. If William Parker had imagined what awaited his beloved daughter, he would never have considered the move.

Initially, it had been a happy change. Claire's father liked the new position in the Adelaide branch of his company, Claire fitted into her new school easily, and her mother, Kate Parker, was anxious to renew a friendship with an old friend who lived only two blocks away. Claire was with her mum the day she first paid a call on Rowena Quinlan. Rowena and Kate had clung to each other and sobbed glad, noisy tears, while Rowena's three sons regarded Claire bashfully in the background

Claire sat at the Quinlan's solid pine table eating Rowena's delicious apricot slice and listening to old school reminiscences. Rowena O'Shaughnessy and Kate Ferris had been the best of friends all through High School. Their paths separated when Rowena visited relatives in Ireland and met her future husband, Gerard Quinlan, a young farmhand who had swept her off her feet. She returned to Australia with Gerry the year after her first son, Sean, was born, but by then, Kate had drifted to Melbourne as a secretary, and there she married her own husband, William Parker. This was the first time the friends had laid eyes on each other in twenty years and they laughed and chatted like a pair of magpies, often interrupting each other, and often dabbing their eyes.

Rowena's youngest son was a chirpy eight-year-old with a pointed elfin chin. He liked new faces, and tried to interest Claire in a game of toy cars on the floor. She knelt down to indulge him but her attention wandered to his two older brothers. They were twenty and eighteen years old, and at sixteen, Claire was keenly aware of young men.

They sat shoulder to shoulder across the table, politely listening to the women's conversation. Sean, the oldest, was rugged and blonde. He had just returned from football training and his cheeks glowed. While the others sat in pullovers, he wore a T-shirt, and Claire saw that he had hard, smooth muscles. As fragile Rowena was nothing like her son, Claire guessed that his father, Gerard, must be a big man.

She merely stole the occasional peep at Sean, because he kept gazing directly at her with a friendly smile. Claire felt embarrassed if she caught his eye and did not know where to look. Aware that she was the object of his scrutiny, she wondered if her hair was tidy after the windy walk with her mother. She hoped so, because there was no way she would raise her hand to check.

She liked Sean's face. His hazel eyes were frank and direct, and his smile was pleasant. However, at the age of twenty he seemed out of her league, and she was somewhat daunted by his sheer size.

She could inspect the other brother for as long as she pleased because he never once raised his eyes. He stared at his clenched hands on the table and only looked up if he were spoken to. Only then did she see that Blake's eyes were dark brown and hard to read. He was more slenderly built than Sean, but looked as if he possessed a wiry strength of his own.

Claire hardly knew what to make of Blake. Although only two years younger than his brother, he seemed much younger in his quiet confusion. She wondered if he were merely bashful, or sulky at being there. Whenever his mother tried to draw him out with a question,

Blake's smiles seemed forced and his comments were soft and short. Perhaps he would rather be somewhere else. If so, she wondered why he did not just get up and leave.

She half decided to dismiss him as uninteresting. There was still a trace of the pimply, gangly schoolboy about him. However, there was something she liked about the depth of his eyes. She would not set aside Blake Quinlan as an object of interest just yet. She returned her attention to little Mikey's cars and tried to determine which of Rowena Quinlan's two older sons she preferred. Solid Sean or awkward Blake? Maybe neither of those. There might be someone better waiting for her than either of them.

Claire was romantic. Ever since she was twelve years old, she had been addicted to love stories and dreamed about her own prince charming. Some of her school friends had career ambitions, but Claire cared only for romance. As she scrambled to her feet to join her mother out, she gave a small sigh. Being sixteen was OK but she would give her eye teeth to look into the future to see who God had in store for her. Always below the surface lurked the dread that there was nobody special waiting for her at all. She hoped he would hurry up and come.

Rowena Quinlan sniffed as she washed the evening dishes. Seeing Kate again was wonderful, but made her feel sadly nostalgic. It transported her back to their school days, when they were closer than sisters. All the sleepovers, cups of hot chocolate, giggly secrets, and crushes on boys they had shared. Rowena wept for the merry, scatter-brained girl she had once been. She wept silently so the boys would not see.

Kate looked lovely. The years had treated her well and she obviously hoped that Rowena would be happy to resume their old intimacy where it left off twenty years ago. Rowena wished it could be so but she knew better. She would have many cosy chats with Kate, but time and circumstances had formed a great gulf between them. She had a dark, painful secret she could never share with Kate, or anybody else. The boys knew too well but they would never tell anybody. They knew their family honour was at stake. They all owed it to Gerry to keep hidden the atrocities he was capable of when he was drunk.

When dour, self-driven Gerry Quinlan hit the bottle he became a different man. He could stretch his periods of sobriety for over a month but the lure of the bottle always gripped him eventually. It was not only beer, but also hard spirits like whisky and gin. Gerry was not a happy or sentimental drunk. He was a mean one. He would lurch through the door like a snarling beast, poised to tear apart the first person who got in his way. Rowena knew Gerry could not help it. It was the drink that did it. In her heart she knew that it was not his real self.

For fifteen years he had been the same, and she did nothing because she loved him. Whenever she looked into his disillusioned, weary eyes, she saw the resolute young battler who had stolen her heart when she was twenty-one. Gerard had huge problems even back then. His mother had died giving birth to his younger brother and his father had cared nothing for the boys. Gerry and young Patrick had spent their miserable youth being buffeted from one uncaring relative to another.

When Rowena met him he had been a ragged menial, shovelling manure on a farm in her neighbourhood. She had been the only person who had ever brought love into his life. When Gerry swore at her, drunk to the bloodshot eyeballs, she reminded herself that he was not responsible for his underprivileged past. When he hit her, she remembered how he had once stroked her hair and whispered that he was not good enough for her. She had insisted that she never wanted anybody but him, and she stuck to it. If ever she were to leave him, it would be Gerry's undoing. Besides, he would kill her and the boys.

When he threw missiles and screamed at her, she reminded herself that he did not behave this way when he was sober. When he flung her against a wall, she anticipated the way he would weep with remorse in her arms the following night. Perhaps he was right when he accused her of ruining him; that she should never have convinced him to try their luck in Australia. Gerry had made the move, full of eager optimism, but quickly discovered that nobody wanted a bar of him on that side of the world either. Watching his hope dwindle and die had been a painful thing.

Rowena loved the man she believed he could have become, had life treated him better. She knew he loved her despite how he behaved when he was drunk, and she was proud of the three strong, healthy sons she had borne him.

The thought of her boys brought two more large tears which made small, fizzing holes in the suds. She had tried to help her sons understand that their father was not really a beast but she did not know whether she had succeeded. She hated it when Gerry attacked the boys instead of her. She had chosen him, after all, but they had no say about being born. The boys seemed to have a knack of provoking him. When Gerry was drunk even the drop of a pin could make him explode.

She let the water gurgle down the sink and looked at the kitchen clock with a sense of foreboding tightening her chest. She and the boys had long since finished their meal, and Gerry's waited in the oven. When he was this late home from work it meant only one thing. Rowena drew a deep breath, to fill herself with a degree of composure before his inevitable homecoming. Her heart warmed as she looked at her sons' three bent heads, two fair and one dark.

Sean hunched by the television enjoying the replay of a football match, and Blake and Michael sat at the table, where Blake had just repaired one of Mikey's toy cars. Blake was quite clever with his hands. Everything appeared warm and cosy, but the atmosphere was already charged with unspoken friction like the calm before an electrical storm. The boys knew what to expect as well as Rowena did.

She saw their heads flick up. They all heard the heavy shuffling footsteps characteristic of Gerry when he could barely place one foot in front of the other. Still, they all knew that disorientation would not stop him from using his fists and feet with devastating accuracy if he got hold of a person.

The door swung open, bounced off the rubber doorstop and belted back into his arm. Gerry let loose a string of foul curses and kicked it shut with a force that rattled the windowpanes. Rowena chewed the insides of her cheeks. It was going to be one of those nights. With a very slight movement of her chin, she gestured to her oldest son to stop his noise. Sean had already switched off the TV and waited by the wall with his brothers.

Gerry felt a ball of red-hot anger rise in his chest. He hated the way they herded close together like frightened sheep when he entered. They were his family, for pete's sake! If they thought he was the big, bad wolf, he was all set to give them what they expected.

He glared at his wife, whose eyes were the largest and brightest of all. "Where's my tea?"

Rowena winced and dashed to the oven. "Here it is. It's roast beef." She never stopped hoping that one night, if they did everything to placate Gerry, he would contain his rage. She gingerly set the plate on the table and stepped back, awaiting his next move.

Gerry stared at the congealing mashed potatoes, cool carrot rings, and the dried out edges of his meat slices. With a sweep of his hand he knocked the plate off the table and watched three peas roll beneath the stove. The faces of his family registered nothing but blank resignation.

"What sort of rubbish is this?" he barked. "It's overdone!"

"It was ready three hours ago. I expected you home then," Rowena said simply.

"Get me some sausages!" he bellowed. "And make it snappy!"

The colour fled from Rowena's cheeks. They were in for it now.

"We have no sausages and the shops are shut." She braced her limbs for the blow that would surely be forthcoming.

Gerry did not hesitate. He swung his open hand against his wife's face, and she reeled against the fridge. As he stepped back, something crunched beneath his boot, and evoked a sharp cry from young Michael. "That's my favourite car! Blake fixed it for me, and now you've squashed it!" He burst into tears.

"Stop that noise!" Gerry hollered. "What a fuss about a stupid toy. Shut up or I'll deck you one."

Mikey clamped his lips shut, but his chest heaved. A flood of silent tears welled over his eyelids, and that was enough for Gerry. He clutched one of Mikey's shoulders, and began a fumbling attempt to loosen his own belt from his pants. "Don't wriggle away, you little newt. I told you to stop your fuss, but you didn't, so now you'll get a good walloping."

Sean and Blake stared meaningfully at each other over their mother's head. It was Blake's turn to intervene. Several months earlier they had made a pact to take turns to distract their father whenever he was set to hurt Rowena or Mikey. Blake licked his dry lips and wondered what would work this time. Their ingenuity often ran dry. If he or Sean simply commanded Gerry to stop, he would certainly continue even harder, to prove that nobody could tell him what to do. Sean and Blake had to invent diversions of their own and it was not always easy to catch his attention.

Blake had not a second a spare. He looked at Mikey's blotchy, streaming face, which had been smiling and happy ten minutes earlier. Something in Blake snapped. He seized Sean's football from an armchair and directed it at Gerry's precious soccer trophy, high upon the bookshelf. The trophy cup hit the slate floor with a clatter, bounced once and came to rest with a dent in its pewter side.

Rowena gasped, and even Sean stood stunned. Gerry had won that cup as a teenager in Limerick. It had always stood upon the shelf because its hallowed presence represented Gerry's only proud moment. Sean clutched his mother's hand, and his heart thumped. He would never dare do such a thing. He did not doubt that Blake's scheme would work. He feared that it would work far too well.

Gerry dropped Mikey's arm, the younger child forgotten. For a moment he blinked, bewildered. Then he charged at Blake with a bellow. "You imbecile! Why did you do that?"

Blake stood his ground, trembling. He gazed his father straight in the eye. "I was knocking the football about and it just happened. I'm not as accurate as Sean. Bad luck." His voice was so low, he could hardly hear himself over his pounding ears.

Gerry did not miss Blake's gleam of defiant hatred. "You did it on purpose!" he ground out. "You'll regret that, you mongrel!" He felled Blake instantly with a swing of his beefy fist. He fell upon his second son, whacking at any piece of bare flesh he could find.

Blake struggled to ward off his father's blows. He heard his mother's screams and his own panting, sobbing breath. He always suffered more than Sean in these combats. He was no match for Gerry's drunken, frenzied sixteen stone, and he knew it. His ribs ached with each breath he drew, and his head hurt. He felt his eyes sting with bitter tears. They were not tears of pain, but futility and contempt. He would give anything to be able to strike back at his father, but he couldn't.

Blake's nose began to bleed, and Gerry shoved him aside at last, with a kick of the boot. He was often appeased by the sight of blood. He taunted Blake with the choicest jibes he could think of. It wasn't the first time such phrases had come out of his mouth in a verbal assault. "You're a pathetic weakling and a no-hoper," Gerry mocked "You'll never manage to get a girlfriend or hold a decent job. I don't know what I did to deserve a wimp like you for a son. You couldn't fight your way out of a wet paper bag. You couldn't even look a girl in the eye without stuttering like a nincompoop." Gerry paused and Rowena hoped that he'd finished, but he went on with one last insult. "If I had any decent sons I might not feel the need to drink away my sorrows." Blake hung his throbbing head and sniffed. He had no comeback for his father's taunts, for he believed every word of them.

Finally Gerry hunched over the wreck of his precious thirty-year-old soccer cup and wept as if he were mourning an old friend. Blake crept off to his bedroom and flung himself onto the bed. He buried his face in the pillow, because he did not even want to speak to Sean if he should follow.

Gingerly he pressed his battered ribs, and concentrated intensely on how much he hated his father. Blake wished Gerry would drop down in one of his drunken stupors and never get up again. It was an unpleasant wish for a son to have about his father, but there it was and Blake could not change it. He was not sure he wanted to change it even if he could. Gerry deserved his hatred.

Mingled with Blake's impotent rage was a hollow feeling of loneliness. He knew the rest of the family did not share his hatred. Sean was often on the receiving end of Gerry's wrath too but he held no rancour in his heart. Sean seemed to regard their father more as an object of pity than a menacing animal, but then he had his own great ambition to grip his thoughts. Sean wanted to be a state football player and he was just big enough and skilful enough to make it someday. Sean tolerated his father's abuse because in his case, it was unfounded. Blake was excited for Sean but also a little envious. He had no aspiration to focus on and wished he had.

His mother and little Mikey actually loved Gerry. That was what Blake could not possibly comprehend. Both Rowena and Mike lived for the times when Gerry was approachable. They treated his drunken frenzies as temporary inconveniences. When Gerry was ever in a rare good humour, Mike adored him. That was why Blake's heart ached in protest when his little brother was set upon.

He never forgot his own early memories of the countless times his father had chased him and Sean through the house, raging like a mad bull, when they were smaller than Mikey. When he caught them, he would thrash them with the metal buckle of his belt until their little bottoms bled. He had lambasted them for the slightest imagined grievances and deliberately destroyed their prize possessions to punish them. Blake set his teeth and vowed that these things would not happen to Mikey as long as he had the power to distract their father. He was glad he had knocked down Gerry's trophy. He would do it again, a million times!

If ever Gerry thrashed Mike the way he used to hurt him or Sean, Blake would do whatever was necessary to put an end to the tyranny. He would tell the police. He would accuse Gerry of murdering somebody, if necessary. Anything to have him put away. He refrained for the time being, for the sole reason that his mum and Mikey loved Gerry, and they would be badly hurt if he did. Blake folded his arms across his chest and scowled at the door. He yearned for the day when Gerry would get what he deserved. When that day came, Blake hoped he would have something to do with it.

Chapter Two

"Claire, would you like to go to a work dinner with my son Blake on Friday?" Rowena asked quite out of the blue.

She had chosen to visit Kate that afternoon. When Claire returned from school, she helped her mother to fix the coffee and slice the cake. Rowena's eyes were drawn to the fascinating girl, for Claire moved gracefully with the quiet assurance of youth. Rowena was unfamiliar with young girls. She was proud of her three sons but envied Kate for a having a daughter. Claire's clear, fresh complexion reminded Rowena of innocent pleasures of long ago. She would never have a daughter now, and looked forward to someday gaining a daughter-in-law. Rowena began to cherish hopes of pairing Kate's daughter with one of her own sons and Blake was closest to Claire's age. Besides, by securing him a date for his annual work dinner, she would be doing him a service. Rowena saw that the girl was lost for words.

Claire flushed to the roots of her hair, and gave a confused laugh. Finally she looked up at Rowena. "Would he like me to go with him?" She sounded surprised.

"I'm sure he would. He's been working with the bottling factory for two years now and he's the only lad who had no partner last year. He's always been very shy about approaching young ladies but I know he'd love to take you."

Claire nervously flexed her fingers. She looked enquiringly at her mother, and Kate gave a smile and a nod. "What do you say?"

Kate liked the idea of Claire seeing one of Rowena's sons too. Her only regret was that it would not be the big, handsome, athletic one. Kate had liked Sean's looks straight away but guessed he must have a girlfriend already. It would be strange if he didn't. Still, Blake might be nice too. She had not paid him much attention.

Claire's heart fluttered with excitement at the prospect of going on her first date. She sensed that she would always be disappointed if she passed up the chance for the experience. "I suppose I wouldn't mind going, if Blake would like me to." It would be a first for her, so she did not mind which brother took her out.

Rowena's face broke into a beam. "Thank you. You'll be doing him a real favour, I can tell you." She turned to Kate. "I'm beginning to worry about that boy," she confided. "I have to push him to say 'boo' to girls, and he's eighteen. Sean was never like that."

"Give him time, Ro," Kate advised. "I wouldn't worry until he's into his twenties. My own brothers were very backward about coming forward when they were teenagers and now they're both happily married."

"Sean never has trouble attracting girls," Rowena repeated proudly. "He's an excellent athlete, just as Gerry was when I first met him in Ireland. Claire, if you can help boost Blake's confidence, it might be the making of him."

Claire smiled back but began to feel a trifle uneasy. She swirled the particles of tea leaves in the bottom of her cup and wondered what she was letting herself in for. She was a bashful girl herself. What would "boosting Blake's confidence" involve? If he were going to sit there without a word to say, she would be stumped. How would she last out a whole evening? Perhaps she should have said no, but she could not change her mind without offending Rowena, who she liked.

Claire steeled herself to go. It would be only one evening out of her life. If she did not like him, she would not go out with him again. It would be no big deal and she would gain an idea of what to expect from future dates.

———

Rowena faced a battle royal at home that evening. Blake was horrified that she poked her nose in on his behalf, but Rowena had expected as much.

"Muuuuuum, mind your business and let me find my own dates."

"Well how were you going about it?" she asked mildly.

He sighed. "Taking my time," he admitted, "but I might've got around to asking somebody." He knew very well he wouldn't have. He didn't even know any girls since leaving school, and he wouldn't have asked any even if he had. "I'd rather not go than have my mother ask a girl on a date for me."

Sean and Mikey sniggered behind him and made Blake more defensive. "You two belt up!" he flung over his shoulder. His blood grew cold at an extremely unwelcome thought. He could hardly force himself to ask. "Mum, does she think I asked you to ask her, by any chance?"

"Oh no, no, no," Rowena assured him. "She knows it was all my idea. I made that very clear."

Blake was only slightly mollified. "Well, what sort of ass she must think I am, when my own mother doesn't trust me to find a date?" Although he knew Rowena meant to help him, he felt hurt by her lack of confidence in him.

"Just the ass you are!" Mikey piped up. He thought the whole conversation was a huge joke.

Blake shot him a withering glance. "Who asked you? Wait until you start looking for dates."

The eight year old shook his head loftily. "I'll never be interested in girls, ever. But Claire's great. You should go with her."

"Well, I won't go now. It'd be too embarrassing."

"But she'll be disappointed!" his mother cried. "She's looking forward to it."

Blake stared. It struck him as strange that this should be so. Claire

Parker barely knew him. "Why would she be?" he asked suspiciously. It was probably one of his mother's little white lies.

"Perhaps she is," Sean put in. "She kept staring at you the day they visited here. She's a nice looking little bird." Sean's only problem had always been letting girls distract him from his training schedule. He sympathised with Blake's dilemma but felt smug about his own popularity with the opposite sex. He had decided to take a break from girls to focus all of his energy on football.

He sounded so serious, Blake felt a strange thrill of hope creep up and down his spine. "Did she really keep staring at me?" he ventured.

"Yeah. You had your eyes riveted on the table, or you would've noticed. Gee whiz, Blake, the first step to go about getting a date is to notice when a girl might be interested."

Blake kept his head lowered because he felt colour seep across his face.

"If I were you, I'd take her," Sean went on. "Go ahead with this plan of Mum's. Claire said 'yes'. That's the important thing. Even though Mum asked her for you, Claire was not obliged to say 'yes'."

"That's true," Blake conceded. His chest filled with a warmth which filtered slowly through him. He had dared take only a few fleeting glances at Claire, but they had been enough to show him how pretty she was. He had been struck by her shining blue eyes and the soft curves of her cheeks, but then he had forced himself to think no more about her. It did him no good to moon over what he could not have. Dad was right. Blake always clammed up around girls. The more he tried not to, the more he couldn't seem to help it. Well, perhaps his luck was about to change.

"What time is she expecting me?" He took pains to keep his voice casual.

"Seven-thirty." Rowena's voice rang with victory. "The ball starts at eight, doesn't it?"

Blake glowered at her. "It's a dinner-dance, not a ball!" Mum always stuck her foot in it. He wondered what hair-raising disclosures she had made to Claire and her mother about him. "I hope you didn't say how desperately I need help, or any rubbish like that."

Rowena carefully chose her words. "No, nothing like that." She quickly crossed her fingers beneath the table. It was an old superstition she had never outgrown since girlhood.

———

When Blake cleaned his teeth later, he took a good, thorough inventory of himself in the mirror. He decided that even after generous allowances were made, he was nothing to boast about. He was pretty skinny and his mouth and nose were too prominent, like his father's. Blake hated to have to admit that he resembled Gerry in any way at all. He gave a rueful shake of the head. If he were a girl, he would not go out with himself.

Still, if Sean was telling the truth, Claire Parker had kept staring at him, and then said 'yes'. If Mum had told him that, Blake would have been sceptical, but he had no reason to doubt Sean's words. Perhaps Claire did like him. Blake turned hot all over again, to the tips of his ears. His heart pounded so that his chest felt as tight as a drum. Deep inside himself he felt a tiny hope stirring.

He had daydreamed about how wonderful it would be to have a girlfriend. The fellows at work flaunted their affairs at him like trophies. Daryl and Larry discussed their sexual exploits at length. Blake suspected that they embellished their stories but he listened anyway. He could not help listening when they all stood working at the same bench. *I can't tie knots in my ears, or switch off my hearing, can I?* He couldn't help it if their lurid stories were more fascinating than the inane talk back programmes which blared from the radio in the corner.

He also poked his nose into the centrefold magazines that filled their lunch corner. Robbo brought them from home. The more Blake browsed through the pages, the more he appreciated what he saw.

He had not seen any harm in it, excusing it with the justification that everyone read them.

To Blake's disgust, he and Todd Robertson had been voted the two least likely to attract women. In Robbo's case it was easy to understand why. He never washed his hair, cleaned his teeth or changed his clothes. The others smelled him coming a good few minutes before he appeared. Blake had been singled out for a different reason. Larry and Daryl had dubbed him Birdman. Blake puzzled over the nickname until Larry could no longer contain his priceless wit. "If a beautiful woman moved toward Quinny-boy here, he'd turn and fly in the opposite direction." Mark and Robbo had laughed so hard, they almost capsized their vat of olive oil.

Blake swallowed down the hard lump of resentment in his throat, and clenched his fists. He did not know what he had done to give the guys at work the same impression his father had of him. He longed to cram their hurtful words back down their throats. Perhaps if he ever found the right woman, he could prove that he was not the hopeless wimp they all expected him to be. He wanted somebody special in his life. Somebody to hold and caress. Somebody to … yes, somebody to love! That word was nothing to shy away from. His mother had loved his father once. She had told the boys she adored him. *If Dad could attract a lovely woman, why couldn't I?* Blake reasoned mentally.

He had several brushes with attractive girls who accosted him in the street or school-yard to interrogate him about Sean. They had been too bashful to approach the handsome football player directly, but seemed happy to use his brother as a go-between. "Hey, Blake, is Sean seeing anyone…Blake, what's Sean's favourite colour…Blake, will you tell Sean that I'm available…Hey Blake, what turns Sean on?"

"How should I know?" he had scoffed in reply to the last question. Carolyn Backet had asked it. She was a pretty brunette in Blake's own year level at school. He had been attracted to her himself, not that anyone ever knew. He had been wise to keep his feelings concealed as it turned out, for Carolyn had a crush on Sean, like dozens of others. It was high time Blake found a girl who liked him for himself.

With nervous feelings in his chest, his thoughts returned to Claire Parker. He went to bed and daydreamed about her in the safety of darkness. He had wanted to daydream about Claire all along, but common sense had prevailed. Gerry said Blake would never have a girl. Perhaps his grim predictions would prove to be unfounded, after all. Still, Blake found himself wondering about Claire's intellect, or if she needed glasses! At the very least, she couldn't be too choosy. Why would she choose to stare at him, when he had been sitting right beside Sean?

Whatever the reason, he found himself looking forward to Friday evening with breathless anticipation. A stab of fear struck his heart. What if he should make a fool of himself and become tongue-tied?

Although it was late, Blake switched on his bedside torch without waking Sean. He dug a notepad and pen out of his drawer and began to jot down one-liners he could use if the conversation lapsed. It was best to be prepared. He was careful to slip the paper deep between his mattress and bed frame when he finished. If Sean ever discovered it, Blake would never live it down!

―――――

At seven fifteen on Friday evening, Claire sat waiting with a churning stomach. She had eaten nothing since her light lunch and wondered if her slight queasiness was caused by emptiness or nervousness. Probably a bit of both. She had boasted to her school friends that she would be going out with an eighteen-year-old boy and she knew they would expect a vivid description on Monday morning.

At seven thirty precisely, she heard a car door slam and rose to her feet. She smoothed her dress and drew a deep breath, to appear more confident than she felt. She was pleasantly surprised by her first sight of Blake. He was much nicer looking than she had given him credit for when she first saw him. He wore a smart blue shirt, his dark hair was neatly combed back off his face, and he smelled like soap and aftershave. Once again, she liked his eyes. Tonight, he looked quite his age, if not older, and Claire wondered if she would be able to hold his interest. She flashed him a wide smile. That must be a good start.

Blake opened the passenger's door for her with his heart in his mouth. She was a knockout. He felt himself breathing fast and shallow, and consciously slowed down. None of the girls who'd ever accosted him to enquire about Sean were as pretty as Claire. A strand of her soft hair brushed against his wrist as he held the door handle, and his pulse raced.

He was certain he would never hold her interest, so as soon as they set off he blurted the first question he had jotted on his list. "Do you like living in Adelaide?" Not very original, but fairly safe.

Her soft lips curved into another sweet smile. "I love the Adelaide Hills. It's so beautiful here. Much nicer than the middle of Melbourne was."

He thought of saying something about how much more beautiful the Hills were now that she was there but decided it would be far too corny. "Do you like school?" That was his second question.

Claire's nose crinkled. "Not really. It's a bit of a drag. I'll be glad to finish."

"What will you do then?" he asked.

Claire had to think quickly. "Anything to do with creative writing, I think. Maybe journalism, or freelance writing." She made that up on the spur of the moment, because English was her best subject. There was no way she would tell him that she really only wanted to be a wife and mother.

"Wow, that'd be great," Blake offered feebly. He ignored the dismay coursing through him. He felt outclassed. She was a girl with brains. What would she think when she discovered that he'd left school the moment he'd turned fifteen to let his mind stagnate in a boring factory? Generations of Quinlan men had always held menial jobs and Blake's father constantly said they could never do any better; that is not unless Sean made good with his football.

Blake also realised that he had almost galloped through his entire list of small talk and it had taken less than five minutes. He swallowed and chewed his lip.

Claire broke the lengthening silence. "This is a work dinner, isn't it?" He nodded.

"Where do you work?" She regretted it as soon as she asked. It must sound so dumb. She accepted an invitation to his work dinner and did not even know where he worked.

"Golden Harvest Fine Foods," he told her.

Claire asked the question he had hoped not to hear. "What do you do there?"

He attempted to hedge the point. "I might rise higher. I'm still one of the juniors right now. I help label jars, stuff envelopes, stir the occasional pot, that sort of thing." He spoke quickly, aware of her delicately chiselled profile beside him. He felt miserably conscious of the ink stains deep in his fingertips which he could never completely scrub away.

Claire's thick eyelashes flickered at him. "How far away is it?"

"Not far now. The hall they hired is just ten minutes from here."

As he turned to her, she smiled at him again. Blake cautiously smiled back. He had never met a girl like Claire before. She was wonderful. She did not seem to mind his fumbling attempts at conversation. She must be one in a million.

———

Blake sized up the situation when they entered the hall. The company directors and sales representatives filled most of the floor-space. Blake's own factory colleagues had been relegated to the corner furthest from the bar and the door. He had not taken long to work out that everybody at his workplace was class conscious and stuck to their own type. He shepherded Claire to his crowd and introduced her to Daryl, Mark, Larry, Robbo and their girlfriends. He did not miss their astonishment when they laid eyes on Claire but sincerely hoped she did. None of Blake's mates had believed he would find a partner.

"Hello Claire. What can you possibly see in old Quinny here?" Larry joked.

For her part, Claire felt euphoric. She saw nothing but acceptance and friendliness on the faces of Blake's friends. It made her feel warm inside. Perhaps they thought she was older than she actually was. She shook her hair over her shoulders and decided to enjoy the night for all it was worth. She shot Blake an arch smile and told his friend, "That's for me to know, and you to find out."

She was pleased with the general merriment her comment caused but a good look at Blake's face might have warned her to tread carefully. His plans were moving far faster than hers. Had she studied his eyes, she might have seen the dawning of a sheer adoration she was not ready for. What she intended as light flattery he lapped up like a starving dog ready to fall at her feet.

Claire had no idea of the deep feelings that were stirring inside him, so she gave him another playful smile. With no hesitation at all this time, he smiled shyly back.

Several hours passed before it dawned on her that she could get in too deep. She had spent the evening copying the other girls' behaviour. When they leaned against their partners over dinner, she shuffled closer to Blake and made eyes at him. She helped herself to a few glasses of the fruit-punch at the table, but quickly decided it made her head feel light and funny. She stuck to straight orange juice after that and nobody commented.

Blake kept drinking from the punch bowl like the others and also bought himself a few different drinks from the bar. Sean had kindly suggested that just a little more alcohol than normal might enhance Blake's social skills. Blake found that he no longer had to struggle for something to say. He heard jokes and wit stream from his mouth like a waterfall. His work friends gaped as if they had never seen him before. Blake marvelled at his new, confident self. Claire's dazzling smiles coupled with a little alcohol were all it took to make a comedian and a genius of him. He felt ecstatic. It was the best night of his life.

Claire could not help noticing the change in his behaviour as the evening progressed. His tongue had loosened, and he no longer seemed so shy of her. In fact, he began to ramble on about all sorts of crazy things. Claire began to find him not so likeable. She wondered uneasily when her parents would expect her home. Blake was not as pleasant and polite as he had first seemed that evening. He had become loud, irritating and boring.

After dessert the lights dimmed and couples paired off for slow, intimate dances. Blake's friends held their girlfriends tight and began some erotic swaying on the floor. Blake gave a bleary smile and moved toward Claire although he could barely walk a straight line. She suddenly felt sick and revolted, then fearful. Her heart pounded and she wanted to get far away from him. But he clutched her arm with a forceful familiarity she did not like.

"C'mon, let's dance," he slurred. Blake felt as if his old, quiet and uncertain self must have been an illusion. How could he have behaved like a dope for so long when this exciting, powerful hero existed just below the surface?

Claire numbly let him steer her on to the floor, but she wished for more distance between them as Blake's hands began to creep further and further down her back. They hovered lightly over her hips, and felt burning hot through the thin, cool fabric of her dress. She raised her hands and pushed him away. "No!" She shuddered with distaste.

Blake blinked at her. She watched a tinge of hurt dawn in his large pupils. "Why not?" he asked thickly.

"Because this is only our first date. I hardly even know you." Her voice must have carried further than she expected for somebody leaned behind them and tapped Blake's shoulder. It was his friend Larry, with an idiotic grin.

"Tough luck, Quinny. The little chick hasn't sussed you out yet. Can you blame her?" He and his girlfriend Pam broke into a fit of giggles. Claire's eyes welled with tears. Their smiling faces no longer appeared friendly as she had first thought, but derisive, and primed for a jibe at anybody's expense. She longed to be home. The crowd in the hall was far too hot and raucous, and Blake was the dumbest, most ostentatious person in it.

He still gripped her shoulders possessively, although he now held her at arm's length and searched her eyes beseechingly. "But don't you like me?" Something disturbingly familiar was jarring its way into his newfound paradise: rejection.

She jerked herself out of his grip. "No!" she yelped. "I mean, I don't know. I'm not ready for this."

By now, all of Blake's friends pressed close, curious, to enjoy the scene. In their predictable lives, such spectacles were too few and far between to miss. Mark gave a twisted leer and mimicked, "She's not ready!" in a piercing falsetto. He flicked the back of Blake's head in a harsh gesture that seemed intended for fun.

Blake lifted Claire's chin with a rough thumb, and pulled her close against him. His heart thumped fast like the pulsing of loud music, although he was just standing there. "Just try it!" he half-demanded and half-pleaded.

She found herself suffocating with the now sickly odour of mingled drink fumes, smoke and perspiration. Claire did not hesitate. She mustered all of her strength and shoved him hard against the nearest table. The plates and glasses jangled.

Blake swayed foolishly, then lost his balance in his confusion and fell on to the floor in a puddle of spilled drink. Claire's heart lurched into her mouth. She had not meant to be quite so forceful. Now the crowd of onlookers swarmed around him like sharks closing in for the kill. They leered down at him and laughed mockingly.

Larry gave him a hard shove with his boot. Daryl's girlfriend, Tina scoffed, "Did you really think she was interested in you? She was just using you to get to your brother." Tina knew Sean from school days.

For the first time in several hours, Blake's arsenal of ready speech withered up. He hung his head in shame and wanted to die.

"I'll bet he wouldn't even know what to do with a girl," cried Robbo, who had come with no partner. "If a gorgeous genie popped out of a bottle and offered herself to him, Quinny's mouth would drop and he'd say, 'I'd rather take the money!'"

The other's roared laughing and Blake found his eyes burning.

He scrambled blindly up, and bashed his hip against the side of the table again. "Ish no' true. I'd know what to do!" He was humiliated to hear tears in his voice.

Mark hooted. "Now he's gonna cry. What makes you think you could hold a girl when you can't even hold your drink?" He turned to Claire, who stood shrinking on the outside of the circle. "Forget about him. He's a dead loss. We'll set you up with someone else."

"No! She's with me!" Blake made his way toward her again but Claire gasped and acted out of sheer panic. She did not wait to see what would happen next. She turned and fled toward the door, her heels clattering across the parquet floor. Elbowing her way through the condescending stares of the company giants, she finally burst into the cool, crisp night. There was no way she would get back into Blake's car with him. He would tear her to shreds. Especially after the way his so-called friends had treated him. Too late, she realised that she had made the mistake of her life in going with him.

As she clattered along the pavement, a stitch tore at her side. She hunched over to regain her breath. The huge black silence of the sky made her ears ring. Finally, when she was able to straighten, she decided to find the nearest telephone booth and phone her dad to come and get her. She was not familiar enough with the district to know her whereabouts but she would look out for street names.

Claire felt a measure of reassurance knowing that her father would rescue her from this fix. She began a staggering jog because she longed to see his familiar, bespectacled face.

Blake gaped at the spot where Claire had been. What had he done wrong? Nothing he had not thought she would expect and welcome. His right elbow throbbed from its forceful contact with the parquetry. The others crowed with relish to witness his humiliation.

"Nice going, Romeo! She doesn't think much of you, does she, Quinny? Where did you pick up such a wet little goody-goody, anyway?"

Angry and embarrassed, Blake couldn't stay any longer or he would break down and really give them something to crow about. He hurried to his car, resolved to catch up with her and thrash it out. Blake was familiar with rejection, but even he had never known pain quite like this. He felt hard, uncontrollable sobs rise from deep in his chest. Above all, he felt a red hot rage which made his mouth taste bitter.

If this had been Claire's attitude all along, why had she agreed to be his date? Why had she flirted with him and lured him with her provoking eyes? He hadn't wanted to take her in the first place! He hadn't pushed himself forward to invite her! It had been arranged totally by his mother and Claire herself. Claire helped to arrange his life for him and then treated him like dirt! He had not asked her to come and trample his dignity beneath her heel. He was so upset he could have exploded.

He fumbled with his key in the dark. He could not find the keyhole for the life of him, so he swore and kicked his tyre savagely. It didn't make him feel any better but hurt his foot, so he let out another string of foul expletives. With each moment, she was getting further away from him and he was determined to let her know exactly what he thought of her.

At last, the door creaked open. Blake roared out of the car park with a squeal of his tyres, accompanied by the smell of burning rubber. He did not usually thrash cars that way, but he was beyond caring what he did that night. Only one thing mattered now and that was finding Claire.

Chapter Three

He caught up with Claire a few blocks away, and squealed over to the curb beside her.

"Hey, get in!" he ordered peremptorily. "I have something to say to you."

"Go away!" she cried. "I don't want to hear what you have to say."

"Get in!" he repeated louder. "You're my date, and I promised to take you home."

"You're drunk!" Her voice was filled with tears of disgust.

"I am not!" he yelped. It seemed he would have to drag her in, so he climbed out of his car and did just that. Claire writhed to free herself, but Blake pressed his fingers deep into the flesh of her upper arm and did not release her until she panted, momentarily beaten, on the seat beside him.

"Let me go, you creep!" She hunched shaking, with her face averted from him.

"First, tell me this. If you don't like me, why did you come?" he demanded.

"Stop the car and let me out. I'll never bother you again. I never want to set eyes on you, ever. I don't care if our mothers are friends." Although he was driving quite fast, she fumbled with the door handle. He leaned over and jerked her wrist back.

"Don't be a moron! You'll kill yourself!" he yelled.

"Stop the car, then!"

He pulled over beside a quiet, dark reserve, while a chill of despair swept through him. He supposed he would have to let her go if she insisted. No sooner had the wheels stopped turning than she flung the door open. Something in Blake suddenly snapped. The evening had been a mess and if he didn't do his best to salvage it, she would never look at him again. She was so beautiful and he knew she had liked him at the start. He had seen it in the way she smiled at him. Another burst of red-hot fury erupted in his chest, this time against his friends. If they hadn't stuck their noses in and degraded him, he might have still had a chance with Claire.

He impulsively clutched her against him, as he had longed to do all evening. "Give me a hug. Just try it," he pleaded. "You might like it. You'll see." The car windows seemed to spin around his head. Tall trees and street lights bounced like pogo-sticks and Claire's bright, alarmed eyes blazed into his senses, but he could not focus on her face. Everything outside of his own head was a queer blur. Grasping her even tighter like a life buoy, Blake briefly closed his eyes to quell the dizziness. He had a fuzzy notion that if he could prove to Claire that he was manly and desirable, he would feel strong and capable again, as he had before. He had to make her like him. He would never find another girl like her. He was not going to let his only opportunity for happiness slam the door and run away from him. He still felt invincible, and felt he could please her. In fact, he knew he could.

By now, Claire clawed at him, properly terrified. "Let me go!" She kicked him hard in the shin with her shoe heel. He tensed with the pain but kept his vice-like grip on her. She managed to scratch the side of his neck with her thumbnail, and he cried out in rage and frustration. Pursing his lips tight he forced her flat across the bench seat of his old car.

"That's enough from you," he grated between his teeth. "Just be quiet and let me do this for you. You'll like it, I promise!" He smothered her with his entire weight to stifle her struggling. Claire could no longer raise her weary limbs to ward him off. Her arms felt like paperweights, still she filled her lungs and screamed at top pitch. Blake reacted quickly, covering her mouth with his own. Claire moaned with the revulsion she felt. The reserve was far from any homes and nobody heard her scream. She knew that Blake had lost his capacity for rational thought entirely. She cried silently for God with all her might, but God did not seem to hear her.

Blake's veins buzzed with exhilaration when his hand touched her bare thigh, soft and warm like velvet. Now he would discover what intimacy felt like. *Quinny wouldn't know what to do with a girl!* Robbo had taunted. Blake would prove him wrong. He would show them all. Hadn't he listened to three years worth of Daryl and Larry spouting off their mouths? Hadn't he read all those articles in Robbo's magazines? He knew exactly what he should do. Emotion bubbled up in him like torrid lava and buried his feeble misgivings as if they were flickering cigarette butts. Years of rejection, pent-up frustration and pain poured out of him and he could not possibly stop until it was spent.

———

At last Claire struggled no more. She drooped her head and her cries subsided into muted, devastated gasps. Another stab of sobriety tried to pierce its way through Blake's heart. He gently shook her, white with fear. "Claire?" He placed his hand around her chin and tried to prise open her eyes.

She looked nothing like the sweet, smiling girl he had picked up from her home earlier that night. Her eyes were red and swollen and strands of sticky hair clung to her cheeks. He began to tremble and his stupefied mind tried to fumble for a way to undo his damage. "Claire, I'm sorry."

She leaped out of her torpor and rammed him in the chest with her knee. This time, he did not stop her from flinging open the door. "You're a pig! A filthy, disgusting pig!" she sobbed.

With that, she stumbled from the car as fast as she could. She instinctively knew he would not follow her this time. It would make no difference if he did now. He couldn't do anything worse than he had done already. The fresh air cooled her sore face, after the close, stuffy atmosphere of the car. Claire gulped great mouthfuls into her burning lungs and almost choked. She shuffled aimlessly on, aware of excruciating pain in her midriff.

She saw a landmark she recognised and suddenly knew where she was, so she could work her way home. She would not phone her father now. She could not bear him to see the state of her clothes and person. Her mind struggled to find a way to tell her parents what had happened to her. Claire's teeth chattered so hard that her chin ached. Mum and Dad might blame her, for being in a position where such a thing could happen to her. Perhaps she could have prevented it somehow.

Oh, she had screamed and flailed with all her might. If she had been strong enough to beat off Blake Quinlan, she would have. Yet if she had behaved differently in the first place, he might not have done it. Claire let out an anguished sob. She should have refused to go out with Blake. She shouldn't have been so interested in dating a boy. Blake had accused her of leading him on. Claire's heart burst, but she had to admit there might be some truth in that. She had been free with her smiles and she had been far friendlier than she would have been if she had known what he was like.

All her life she had loved God. She had been taught that He always listened to cries for help. But where was He when she screamed for help? Either He did not exist, which she did not want to contemplate, or He stood back watching because she deserved to be in her fix.

Oh God, if only I had behaved differently. Did I over-react when he tried to dance with me? Perhaps I shouldn't have pushed him over. Maybe I shouldn't have run out of the hall. Then he wouldn't have got so angry. I feel so dirty! So bad and stupid!

When she reached home, she stood outside her lounge-room window like a fugitive, and watched her parents by the television. It was long past their normal bedtime but she knew they would be waiting for her. Her father's arms were folded across his chest and her mother wore a slight frown of concern. Claire was their only child and they loved her dearly. They expected her to breeze in and announce what a wonderful time she'd had. She dissolved into tears again.

She could not bear for them to see her crumpled, torn clothes or swollen face. Worst of all, there were a few spots of blood upon her dress. If Kate and William saw their daughter's shame, she would crumple up and die. Claire tiptoed inside through the backdoor and upstairs to the bathroom. She locked the door, peeled off her clothes and turned on the hot shower tap full bore.

Her knees buckled, and she hunched in the corner of the alcove. Her skin turned bright pink and she feverishly scrubbed herself with soap until an inch of lather coated her. She longed to be clean again but the filth and dirtiness penetrated deep inside where no soap could touch.

She heard her mother's feet mount the stairs. Kate tried the door handle and then knocked. "Claire, can I come in?"

Claire dried herself fiercely and wriggled into her towelling dressing gown. She could not bear to have another person look at her disgusting flesh after what had happened. Not even her mother. She unlocked the door.

Kate blinked in the steam. "When did you get back?"

"A little while ago." It was the first time Claire had spoken since she last screamed at Blake. Her heart pounded with alarm because her voice sounded so different to her own ears. It was hoarse from screaming and shouting. She felt sure her mother would guess the sordid truth just through hearing her speak!

Kate was puzzled. "Why didn't you come through and say hello? We didn't hear Blake's car. You knew we would be waiting for you."

"I just wanted a shower!" Claire heard herself snap. After what had happened, she could not bear the sound of any reproach.

Kate placed a tentative hand on her shoulder. "Are you O.K.? Did something happen?" Her brow knitted with concern.

Claire focused on the blue, mosaic tiles beneath her toes. She could not look her mother in the eye, but Kate found her chin and raised her face.

"You've been crying!"

That drew another storm of tears from Claire, like a tidal wave breaking through the weak spot in a dyke. She supposed there would be tears below the surface for the rest of her life. She wept onto her mother's shoulder.

Kate held her close and rocked her gently. At last she asked, "What happened? Did you have a bad time?" She felt helplessly idiotic. It was obvious that Claire had a bad time.

"Yes, but it's OK now," Claire gulped. "I never want to go on another date. That's all." She could not burden her mother with the truth.

"Didn't Blake treat you nicely? You can tell me. Nothing can be as bad as all this."

Couldn't it? Claire thought. *Mum has no idea.* "I just didn't like him. That's all," she hedged.

Kate's heart ached for her beautiful daughter. She stroked Claire's hair and crooned, "Let's get you into bed. It's all right, Baby. You don't have to go out with him again. You tell me about it when you feel like it. Tomorrow, maybe. I'll fix you a nice hot drink." She felt like a chattering fool. *If only I knew!*

Claire's stomach recoiled. "No thanks." She doubted if she could ever stomach food or drink again. She collapsed between her sweet smelling sheets but continued to tremble until her very bones rattled. Soon both her parents stood at the foot of her bed together and stared down at her.

"Mum says you had a bad time. Tell me what he did, so we can fix it." William Parker's fists were already half-cocked, ready to fly into a temper. Claire had never been on the receiving end of one of his rages. The cross words she'd had from William had been for nothing more serious than failing a Maths test. She did not want to see him lose his cool now.

"Nothing. I just didn't like it," she lied glibly.

"That's not good enough. Tell us why."

Claire's nerves snapped. "It's none of your business, Dad."

"Let's leave her to herself. She's had enough for one night," Kate said quickly. "She's very tired. There'll be time enough to find out tomorrow. We love you, Sweetie."

William stood seething, staring at the curve of his little daughter's high, white forehead. His stomach knotted as he tried his utmost to remain calm. He had treasured his baby girl from the moment he first touched her warm, round head. He had never forgotten the feathery dark hair, and little rolls of skin, as if her tiny skull still had to grow into it. He also remembered how she would nestle into his arms for a bedtime story, as if it were yesterday.

She was only sixteen and he had hated the idea of her going on a date, anyway. It made his blood boil to think that the Quinlan kid might have hurt her in any way. He wanted to tear at his hair in frustration because she would not tell him. William mustered all the patience at his disposal. Claire was hurting and Kate was probably right. He would wait until tomorrow, but he would not sleep a wink.

He forced his voice to sound even. "Yes, we do love you. Remember that." With that, he followed his wife out of the door. William had never been one for touching people but that didn't mean he didn't care. He cared far more for his family than they would ever know.

Left alone, Claire's shoulders shook with more sobs. Her father had sounded so curt. She felt he was angry with her already and he didn't even know. He would go off the deep end if he ever did find out. He would have a heart attack. She understood her father, and loved him deeply. There was no way she would be responsible for killing him. How she hated Blake Quinlan but she had to keep it locked in her own chest. She had never felt so lonely.

———————

Blake did not wake up until the crack of dawn. He wondered why he could not stretch out, then realised he was still in his car. He could not understand the great weight of dread that pressed down on his chest. The shirt he had worn to the dinner-dance was thin and he shivered, because he was icy cold. Blake gingerly stretched his cramped joints and sensed that something terrible had happened. Then with a cold shudder of horror, he remembered. It was the worst moment of his life.

What have I done? For a moment he desperately hoped it had been a bad dream. That happened to him sometimes. He woke, heart thumping, from a nightmare, to discover that the trauma had been imaginary. Not this time. Sickness surged up his gullet again. He remembered Claire's beauty, his own humiliation and fury, and his brief illusion of power and exultation. Blake rested his throbbing head on the steering wheel and groaned.

With a tight band pressing his temples, he drove home. What else could he do? He knew nobody would have waited up for him and he found the little house bathed in the fresh stillness of dawn. The frosty morning air stung the insides of Blake's nostrils and one scarlet little bird on the trellis whistled a lilting tune, yet he felt sordid and depraved.

Blake slid between his sheets fully dressed and peered around the shabby little bedroom in the grey light. There was Sean's sleeping face in the bed across from him. Sean always slept with his mouth half open and breathed heavily. Blake watched his brother with a wistful ache. He would give anything he owned for Sean's clean conscience and cheerful nature. Sean would be waking up soon to begin his morning jog. Blake would cram his head beneath the covers then and pretend to be asleep.

He kicked a heap of shirts off the foot of his bed. He had tried them all on the previous evening, longing to impress Claire. The contrast between the happy optimism he had felt and the despicable guilt upon him now was too great. He knew he would have to rush to the toilet or he would be sick in bed.

When he returned to his bedroom, Sean had woken up. He was lacing up his jogging shoes and looked up at Blake with a grin. "Man, you must've got in late," he whispered. "Tell me everything. How was your date?"

Blake discovered tears coursing down his cheeks. "Terrible," he croaked and climbed back into bed. He felt sick again as he watched Sean's face sober with sympathy he knew he did not deserve.

Sean walked to Blake's bed and gave his hair a ruffle. "Hey, don't take it so hard. There are plenty of girls out there. You'll have better luck next time. If she didn't like you, that's her loss." And Sean left to begin his morning jog.

Blake heaved a deep sigh. Sean's compassion would soon turn to repugnance when he found out. Mum would be devastated. A queer thought shot through Blake's mind. *At least Dad will have no reason to belt Mum and Mikey now. I've given him reason enough to attack me for the next ten years.* He faced the fact that he was far worse than the violent father he had grown up hating. In all his years, Gerry had never done such a vile thing as Blake had just done to Claire Parker.

At the thought of Claire he broke out in a cold sweat. How beautiful she was, and how her eyes had sparkled with shy mischief early in the evening. Blake buried his face in his pillow and wept gallons for Claire. How must she be feeling now? What had he expected of her, for heaven's sake? Of course she would be reluctant to have him paw all over her. No wonder she did not wish to go home with him. Where had he left his brain? What had he been thinking? How could he have been screwed up enough to force himself upon her? He leaped out of bed and made it to the toilet bowl in time to be sick again. Blake hunched there shivering with his lip hanging over the bowl. As the full realisation dawned, he felt only utter hopelessness and self-contempt.

How could he ever apologise or make amends for what he had done? There was no way. He had violated her in the worst possible way, and he was prepared to face whatever he deserved. Not for one moment did it occur to Blake that he could wriggle out of the consequences.

Chapter Four

Blake was astounded when Saturday passed without any word from the Parker family. He spent the morning in bed, sick with the hangover and disgust with himself. Each moment he expected to be summoned out in disgrace but it did not happen. Rowena often appeared to offer him food, but Blake turned away, moaning. He thought he could never face food again. She scolded him for having a hangover after his date with that sweet little Claire. Blake closed his eyes in pain. When she found out about him he would get more than a tongue-lashing.

Sean bounced in and urged him to get up. "You'll feel better if you get moving, and do something."

Blake couldn't.

Gerry poked his head in and scowled at him. He was sober for the time being and deep in his usual depression. "Did she give you the old heave-ho? What do you expect? Just take a good, hard look at yourself."

Blake stayed in bed. He did not take a good, hard look at himself. He knew what he would see.

Finally, Michael perched on the foot of his bed and gazed on him with pity. "Are you feeling sick?"

At least Blake could be honest. "Yeah, I'm feeling real sick, Mikey." Of course it was not the sort of sickness his little brother meant, but he appreciated Michael's sympathy.

He dragged himself out of bed early in the afternoon and tinkered with Rowena's broken alarm clock which his father had knocked off the shelf. Usually Blake found it easy to get engrossed with the working of machinery, but this time his mind wandered. His nerves were badly on edge with waiting and he began to wish the Parkers would hurry and confront him.

Night fell, and there was still no word from them. Blake hardly knew what to make of that. He went to bed but did not sleep. He steeled his nerves for the postponed abuse he must face the next day. Claire's parents must have needed all day for the bombshell to sink in.

All Sunday morning, he still heard nothing. By now Blake's nerves were in pieces. The slightest noise made him jump out of his skin. He was almost relieved at two o'clock, when he looked from his window and saw Kate Parker opening their front gate. Blake sank on to the bedroom chair because his knees would not support him.

Mrs Parker's relaxed manner suddenly struck him as strange. She walked with a spring in her step, and lifted her face to admire Rowena's jasmine creeper. Did she know what had happened to her daughter? Blake caught sight of his confused reflection in the mirror. What the heck was happening?

With trembling hands, he opened his door a crack to hear whatever Claire's mother had to say. It was as bad as he had begun to suspect.

As they made themselves comfortable, Kate began, "Ro, I hate to stick my nose in, but have you any idea what happened on Friday night? Claire is quite upset and she hasn't told me anything."

Blake's stomach lurched. *Why not?*

"I don't know any more than you." His own mother sounded perplexed. "Blake has been a bit miserable too. Moping around all week-end."

"Well, Claire's locked herself away, crying. I've heard her." Kate's cup jangled on her saucer. At last, she sighed. "William and I are very worried about her. Rowena, if you do find out..." Her voice trailed off.

"I'll let you know," Rowena promised. "Blake usually keeps

things to himself. It's a shame things didn't work out, for whatever reason. Do you think Claire might give him another chance? He's really a good boy."

Blake clicked his door shut and buried his face in his hands. He couldn't bear any more. He moved back to his window and stared out, churned up and utterly bewildered. Why on earth would Claire keep such a despicable thing to herself? How she must be hurting! Did she wish to keep her family from being hurt too? Did she feel as if she were somehow at fault? Did she find it too terrible to put into words? He found his heart pounding so hard his chest ached.

For the first time, a wild possibility darted through his mind. *If Claire's prepared to forget it, why shouldn't I?* Blake felt like a fish that had been jerked off the hook and thrown back into the sea. He sank on to his seat again, weak in the knees. The heady relief felt similar to the course of alcohol through his body. First it hit his shoulder blades, then trickled through his limbs and finally settled in a warm, tingling ball in his solar plexus. Claire was not going to tell! He would not be in trouble. Blake felt giddy with thankfulness.

———

Despite his relief, Blake woke the following morning feeling more terrible than he had before. He wondered why his stomach still churned with worry since his deed had not been revealed. Yet the guilt still pressed on his chest like a millstone. Whenever he had indulged in too many sweets as a child, the sickly waves of nausea would eventually subside but he knew the heaviness of his shame would not go away. In fact, it grew stronger with each passing hour.

It was Monday morning but he could not face work. The thought of standing before the cruel and inquisitive eyes of his friends made him cringe inside. He phoned in sick and reasoned that at least he was telling the truth. He was sick in his heart. He wandered aimlessly through a shopping mall and did plenty of hard thinking.

He realised why he still felt scared. Claire was staying silent now but Blake had no guarantee that she always would. If she ever blurted the truth to her parents in the future, the consequences of his deed would catch up with him. Just because he had got away with it for now did not mean that it would last forever! Blake's heart thumped hard against his aching rib cage.

He returned to his car, hid his face in his arms and wept. He was now a cry-baby, on top of being a rapist. Blake had no idea what the penalty for rape was. He never would have imagined he would need to know such a thing. It was probably several years in prison. His scalp prickled with stark fear. He did not want to be put away with desperate criminals, like murderers, paedophiles and other rapists! The ugly word hit him hard like a cricket ball between the eyes. *He was a rapist!* For as long as Claire kept her secret, he would never bring himself to own up either. He felt far too scared. He could not face the punishment which would surely be meted out to him.

———————

The days of the week passed slowly until it was Friday again. Blake had spent all week away from work, but none of his family knew. In the evening, he ran blindly down his street. He could not stay still with his teeming thoughts and Sean always said that a good jog was incredibly mind clearing. Blake should have guessed that his own mind was cluttered with too much filth and dirt to be cleared. At least he could allow the tears to flow freely down his face and let the wind dry them.

If he and Claire both kept quiet, would life carry on as before? Would their mothers keep visiting each other? Would they expect Claire to greet the boys over afternoon tea? He knew that was ludicrous! When she could not force herself to do it, would they demand to know why? The sordid truth could not be concealed forever.

Huge raindrops began to fall, but Blake hardly noticed he was getting wet. He stayed out until long after dark, then returned home soaked through, to shower quickly and retreat to his bed.

He jerked awake at 3.00 am, gasping and perspiring. He glanced across and saw that Sean was still sound asleep. Blake's lucid dreams had been full of Claire. The freshness of her skin, the softness of her lips, the frail slenderness of her arms which he had handled so roughly. He gazed up at the ceiling and felt the beads of sweat on his brow turn cool. He remembered how Claire had struggled and writhed and how her heart had hammered against him like a trapped bird's. The sound of her terrified screams for help still haunted him.

Blake gave a low moan and scrambled stiffly out of bed. He hunched up on the window chair and rested his chin on his knees. He knew how badly Claire must be hurting. He had heard her mother say so. For some reason of her own, Claire was keeping silent, but perhaps it would be far easier for her if she would open up. Her parents seemed like decent people. Mrs. Parker in particular, appeared to be friendly and caring. If they knew what their daughter had gone through, they could help her to recover from any false sense of shame she might be carrying. He ought to admit his crime for Claire's sake. After what he had done, that was the least he could do for her. It might help to ease his own load of guilt.

Violent shudders wracked Blake's body yet he was not cold. He wrapped his arms around his chest and his teeth chattered. He wanted to wake up his mother and get his confession over and done with but it was only 4.15 am. He would have to wait three more hours. He would tell Rowena everything and leave her to decide what to do about Claire's parents. It would be a heavy burden to put on his mother but Blake felt that he could not possibly approach the Parker family himself. Telling Mum would be hard enough.

He chewed his bottom lip and prepared himself mentally to face prison. It would be no more than he deserved. He knew that being drunk was no excuse for what he had done. It pierced his heart like barbed wire to imagine the pain his mother, Sean and Michael would feel. Blake sat and watched dawn roll in over the distant hills. He no longer felt like crying. Now that he had made the hardest decision of his life, he felt strangely calm.

———

Before breakfast, Rowena looked up from setting the table. There stood Blake, with dark furrows beneath his tragic, hollow eyes.

"I have to talk to you, Mum." His voice was firm but his eyes welled with tears.

She could see from his face that it must be something very serious. Rowena pulled out a chair for him, then stroked his hair as she used to when he'd grazed his knees. "Whatever it is can't be all that bad." Blake did not miss the edge of apprehension in her voice and he felt her pulse throb through her fingertips.

"You'd better sit down too, Mum. You're going to hate me," he said bleakly.

"I'd never hate you! You're very precious to me." It was true. She had a special spot in her heart for each of her sons and Blake was her little "pain boy". He had always taken the most out of her. She had the longest, most difficult labour with him, and he'd never stopped draining her with his little traumas ever since. He was the one who would lie awake, crying softly at night because he imagined Gerry would murder them all in one of his drunken rampages. He was the one who would clutch her arm like a life buoy and plead with her not to leave him at school because he was convinced the teacher and other students hated him. She could never forget his tear-streaked face, or the way his thin shoulders would finally slump with acquiescence.

It was Blake who needed an emergency appendectomy when he was six. Then he suffered a series of kidney infections the following year and needed another operation. It was Blake who required two sets of braces on his teeth when he was fourteen. He was the one who had brought home a string of wild pets, then howled when Gerry carelessly killed them. Rowena was relieved that young Michael seemed to take after sunny, dependable Sean, and not Blake, who always took everything so hard.

What can it be this time? His look of total abjection broke her heart.

"I love you, and nothing can ever change that," she repeated.

Blake licked his lips and lifted his face resolutely. "Try this, then..."

Two hours later, Rowena stood on Kate's veranda and paused to steady her breathing. Her head spun and her eyesight was fuzzy with grief. She still could not believe that one of her beloved boys had sat before her and admitted something so atrocious. She thought she knew her sons. Rowena had grown hysterical. She had yelled at Blake until her voice grew hoarse. He rose quietly and withdrew to his bedroom, leaving her to sit at the kitchen table and sob until her stomach ached with the effort.

Rowena had very nearly given up the idea of going to Kate's house. Although she was disgusted with Blake, it shook her to the core to imagine him in jail. Whatever he had done, he was still the little boy who had loved snuggling up to her for bedtime stories. He had spent hours messing around in the backyard alone, happily playing with toy cars or digging holes in the dirt with his plastic shovel. He had cared deeply for tiny, defenceless creatures. He had always been so shy and sensitive to pain. If they informed the police it would kill her. She had been tempted to carry on with her washing and ignore the issue.

Then she thought of Kate and Claire. They had done nothing to deserve such heartache. Claire seemed such a sweet girl, and Rowena had always loved Kate like a sister. She knew that if she had a daughter of her own she would fiercely resent such terrible news being kept from her. Kate ought to be told, that was certain. Rowena felt duty bound to go out of loyalty to Kate.

She had poked her head into Blake's bedroom and huskily told him her intention. He kept his face buried in his pillow and gave no indication that he heard. Walking out of the front door was one of the hardest things Rowena ever had to do.

Now she stood outside Kate's door, shaking. She would repeat Blake's story and then she would appeal to Kate's own feelings as a mother. She would kneel on the carpet and plead, if necessary, that she and William would take no action against Blake. Claire was Kate's baby but Rowena would remind Kate that Blake, however corrupt his deed, was still one of hers. At last Rowena raised her hand and knocked at the door.

Kate opened it and greeted Rowena with a smile but it quickly died when she saw the tears streaming down her friend's cheeks.

"Kate, I'm so sorry. So very sorry!"

Kate's head spun with dread as she led Rowena to the couch. "It can't be that bad," she heard herself trying to soothe her friend. She guessed that it must be desperately bad but a part of her wanted to postpone hearing it.

Rowena wiped her hand across her eyes. "That's what I said!" she wept, "but believe me, it's far worse than we could have imagined."

Sean Quinlan drove home from his football match and yawned with weary delight. He turned the volume of his crackling car radio high so he could sing along to the rock and roll. He had a lousy voice but nobody ever heard him in the privacy of his car.

His team owed their victory to him. He had soared up for the stunning mark of the match just before half time and kicked five great goals. He could still hear the wild cheering ringing in his ears. In the changing rooms, his coach had whispered that several interested parties were keeping an eye on his progress. Sean's only regret was that he had wasted so much time trying to study at school. He should have concentrated on football from the time he was old enough to kick. There were many talented players far younger than twenty but Sean would do his best to make up for lost time.

He dreamily re-lived the afternoon highlights. Football was so easy for him. When he got out on an oval he felt as if he could fly. So much energy pulsed through his muscles; he thought he could touch the clouds. It felt wonderful to break through a crowd of intimidated opposition like a hot iron rod cutting through a block of ice.

He wished his dad had been there to see the match. Sean knew a moment of bitter frustration. Dad should be proud to watch him play football but he preferred to stay shut up in his smoky pub, grumbling to his friends. On Friday night, Sean had to distract him in one of his foul, drunken tempers. He had done it by drop kicking his football so repetitively against the pantry door that Gerry's nerves snapped and he yelled at Sean to stop.

"You play football!" he had ridiculed. "What a joke! You haven't got the gumption to stick to anything. Stop wasting your time."

Sean felt the familiar surge of anticipation tingle in his fingers and toes. He lived for the time when his dad would be forced to eat his words. All his life, Sean had longed to make Gerry proud of him. He wanted to give his father something to live for. So far, nobody had succeeded.

He had to admit Gerry had good reason for his opinion. Sean had never stuck to anything in the past. He had been a poor student. Sitting in a classroom while the sun shone and the wind blew stifled him. Dry facts and figures flowed in and out of his head while he pined to exercise his body. He cared nothing for book learning but he would stick to football. He knew it in his bones.

He imagined the money he could earn. Of course, the game itself was what counted. Money was just a bonus, but it was a good bonus. He would buy Dad a new car, and watch his face glow with pleasure for a change. He pictured Mum's joyful beam when he gave her a new washing machine. And he would be able to afford a shiny five-speed racer for Mikey. How his little brother's eyes would pop out of his head. Sean laughed happily at the thought of it. But by far best of all, he and Blake could visit Ireland.

Ever since the two boys were small children, they had longed to visit the land of their ancestors together. The same Celtic blood coursed through their veins. They were as different as could be, but they shared a bond of closeness that nothing would ever break. Sean had many football buddies but Blake was his best friend.

Only Blake understood how thoroughly Sean lived for football. Every moment he had to spend at work sorting potatoes on a conveyer belt, Sean counted the hours and minutes until footy training. He never felt totally alive without the adrenalin surging through his body and cheers ringing in his ears. He liked these weary moments after a game, when he felt wrung out but knew he had played his very best.

He was still on a high when he swaggered into the kitchen and took a few gulps from his own personal ice-water bottle. "Hi Mum, I played well today." Then he noticed Rowena's face.

Sean replaced his bottle in the fridge with an arm as heavy as lead. "Mum, what's wrong?"

Her face crumpled. "Sean, it's something terrible!"

His stomach gave a queer lurch. "Dad?" he breathed.

Rowena shook her head. "No, it's Blake," she said numbly.

Sean's stomach gave a nastier lurch than the first. "What happened?" His mouth turned suddenly dry, despite his drink of water.

He clutched his mother's hand and listened as she told the story. The further it progressed, the more emphatically Sean shook his head. "No way! Blake would never do such a thing!" He even jerked his hand away. He was annoyed with Rowena for believing such a preposterous lie. She should know her own son well enough to support him.

"Mum, how could you believe it for one second?"

"I wouldn't have believed it, except that I heard it from his own mouth!" Two large tears slid over her eyelids.

Sean still sat and shook his head, which was now pounding like a drum. "No!" he denied again. "You must have heard wrong. He couldn't have done that. Not Blake!"

Rowena just watched him tragically, waiting for him to adjust to the news as she had done.

"Where is he?" Sean grated at last. His disbelief gave way to intense hurt and red-hot fury.

Rowena tilted her chin back. "In your bedroom," she murmured with a twinge of guilt. She had been unable to face Blake since she had heard his story, and still did not know how she ever could.

Sean stalked in to find Blake lying face down on his bed with his feet hanging over the edge. "Tell me it isn't true!" he demanded without preamble.

Blake stayed silent for a long moment. "It's true," he muffled at last, with his face pressed deep into his pillow.

Sean slammed the wardrobe door with his foot and his face burned. "Well, what sort of animal are you?" His own voice was thick with tears of disgust. "What were you thinking?"

"I don't know what I was thinking. I was drunk."

For the first time ever, Sean longed to pound his brother to pulp as fiercely as their father would. "That's no flamin' excuse!"

"I know it's no excuse! I'm not excusing myself!" Blake's voice was high and crackly.

"Well, what are you going to do about it?" Sean yelped.

"What do you suggest I do?" Blake shot back.

Sean angrily paced the length of the floor. His room was far too small to contain the grief and shock that swelled in his big heart. "Even Dad never did such a foul thing when he was drunk!" He could hardly articulate his choked words.

"Do you think I don't know that?" Blake's chest heaved and fell. He felt like scum from the dirtiest pit but spoke on anyway. He had always shared things with Sean, although he expected that to end after this day. "If I could change what happened on Friday night, don't you think I would? Sean, do you think I'm proud of myself? I wish I could do something to make amends. Anything!"

"You're pathetic," Sean managed to hiss. "I can't believe you!" He had nothing more to say. He had to stalk out of the room or he knew that he *would* hit his brother. Sean had enough self-control left to know that it would be counter-productive. Although he was tired, he started to jog feverishly around the block. Every footfall set off a sharp twinge in his head. Sean let his tears flow unchecked at last.

He was shocked to his core to think of poor Claire Parker. He was unhappy for his mother, who did not deserve such a disgrace to her family name. Most of all, he was deeply hurt and disgusted to discover such an ugly side to his brother who he loved. A side he never imagined existed.

"Why didn't you tell us what happened?" William Parker's voice bounced off the walls, and made his own ears ring. He watched his daughter cringe, and felt a stab of compunction. He had not realised how loud he was.

"Don't yell, Dad!" Claire sobbed. "I didn't tell you because I knew you would be mad, like this." Her father's head was a terrifying sight. It had turned bright red from the neck up and angry purple veins bulged out like ropes.

She could not tell him the total truth, which was that she had felt too grimy and repulsive to admit it to anybody. If only Blake Quinlan had not blabbed to his mother. Claire's chest tightened with resentment. If he had left the matter alone, at least her degradation would not have to be dragged before her grieved parents. She could not bear to face them.

"I am mad!" William fumed in a quieter tone. "I'm furious!"

"Not at you, though," Kate added quickly, and tightened her grip around Claire's shoulders.

"Did you think we'd blame you?" William demanded. "How could you think such a thing? I'm furious with that mongrel of a boy." He rounded on his wife. "I told you Claire was too young to be dating, yet you sent her out like a lamb to the slaughter."

"Don't shout at Mum!" Claire pleaded. "She didn't know what he was like. None of us did."

"I'm going to kill him," William seethed.

"Leave it, William," Kate gasped. "Don't get violent." Her chalky face contrasted with his crimson one.

"I won't get violent. We'll call the police and have him put away," William blustered.

"No!" Claire yelped. "I don't want the police to know. I want to forget it ever happened." She had suffered enough without having the matter dragged out so more of the public would know about her shame. She turned to Kate. "Please Mum, tell him."

Kate felt that she was now the meat in the sandwich. "William, let's leave the police out of it for Claire's sake. For Rowena's sake too. She's devastated by what her son did and begged us not to take it any further."

Kate had chosen the wrong tactic. William pounded his fist on the table. "I don't give a damn about Rowena! It isn't her daughter who was raped. In fact, I don't want you to have anything more to do with her. Don't speak to her. Don't even set eyes on her, ever again."

"I won't," Kate promised. Although she did not hold Rowena responsible for Blake's action, she could not face her friend again. She loathed the boy as much as William did for what he had done. Claire had never hurt anybody in her life, and Kate wanted to scream her anguish out before God. She would do so later. Right now, somebody had to contain William's wrath.

"Telling the police won't undo what's been done," she urged. "Claire's had enough. Let's leave it between the families. I promised

Rowena that none of us would inform the police about Blake. Bringing them into it will only prolong Claire's agony. I'll never see Rowena again, and not taking legal action will be my last favour to her. Please leave it be, William."

She could tell by William's face that he was listening.

"I hate him to get away with it," he growled at last.

"He won't get away with it. His parents will deal with him. Rowena promised me that."

William changed the subject abruptly. "Claire has to see a doctor, anyway."

"No!" blurted Claire. Her cheeks were blotched from crying and she could hardly form her words, but she faced William and cried, "I don't want to, Dad."

He knew she thought he was cruel and turned away in hopeless pain. "You have to be examined. We have to know the extent of any damage."

"There's no damage. I'm O.K. now." Claire felt sick. She could not bear to have another man invade her privacy. Wasn't it enough that Blake had done it? If it happened again, she would die.

William was inexorable. "We have to be certain he hasn't given you some... disease. If he's raped you, he might have raped other girls." He could not believe he was talking this way to his gentle and precious little girl. Last week, Claire had been an innocent child, and now her red-rimmed eyes were shaded with too much knowledge. William had not missed the way she studiously avoided his eyes and it cut him to the quick.

Her shoulder blades flinched as if she had been stabbed with a knife. That thought had not occurred to Claire, and she sank into an armchair and wept.

"I'm sure you have no disease!" Kate cried. "Rowena says her son never had any girlfriends. Claire was the first date of his life." Her eyes shot signals of alarm over Claire's head to William, to say no more.

"Don't make me see a doctor, then," Claire croaked.

William's mouth tightened and he clenched his fists. She was so distraught he decided not to force her to see a doctor yet, but a man could not be expected to stand by and hear that his daughter had been raped without doing something. He decided to take matters into his own hands somehow or he would go mad.

———————

Claire retreated to her bedroom, locked herself in and huddled between her fresh, clean smelling sheets. She could not escape from the frightening thoughts which whirled through her head, even in bed. Just because Blake's mother believed he had never raped anyone else, it was not necessarily true. Now she felt like a time-bomb with something dark and mysterious lurking in her body but she was too terrified to go and find out for sure. Her pastor had always said that nothing was too great to take to God in prayer. If ever Claire had a chance of putting that to the test, it was now.

Oh Heavenly Father, why did you let this happen to me? Perhaps I didn't behave quite right in the hall that night but surely I didn't deserve this! At the very worst, I might have something which will kill me, and at the very least, I won't ever get married and have any babies. No man would love me now and I don't even think I would want to be loved, in that way.

Claire's face flamed, and she admitted what she had felt ever since the night in Blake Quinlan's car. *I don't see how anyone could do... that... even in love. It's the most horrible, painful thing. I could never fall in love with anybody now. All I ask is that you please help me to forget.*

She knew that she was asking God an impossible request. The pain and shame were branded fiercely into her for life.

Chapter Five

William Parker huddled in his car across the street from Gerard and Rowena Quinlan's house. Their home was right at the bottom of a small deep valley, so he had a good view of the comings and goings from their driveway and front door. He had been waiting there late every evening for the better part of two weeks, but the person he waited for had not shown his face. William heaved a grim sigh. He could not keep up the cloak-and-dagger business for much longer or the Quinlans would recognise him and call the police.

He managed a short bark of a laugh but he was not amused. He never would have believed that he would resort to sneaking around in the dark waiting to attack a youth. He doubted if the police would approve of his taking matters into his own hands but he'd convinced himself that any father would do the same. He had suffered at work with throbbing, tension headaches. He could not sleep at nights, for his anguish sought release in action. He had tried pounding a pillow and pretending that it was Blake Quinlan, but that did not help. It had to be the real thing or he would burst.

God help him if his pastor ever found out. It occurred to William to wonder what Jesus would say about a mature, respectable businessman thirsting for revenge, but he snapped his mind shut. *Jesus never had a daughter who was raped!* Sometimes, a man just had to do what a man had to do.

He pulled his duffle coat closer around his throat and shivered.

The longer he waited in his cold car, the testier he became. It was as if the kid guessed William's intent and avoided him deliberately. *Doesn't he ever go out, like normal boys?* William reminded himself with a scowl that Blake Quinlan was anything but normal; but didn't he poke his nose out after dark ever?

William had often seen the bumbling lout of a father lurch up the steps. Gerard Quinlan appeared to be a habitual drunk. William's mouth puckered in disgust. *What sort of family are they?* He had seen the woman. He had seen the older son, the strapping blonde one. He had even seen the little boy dart out of the door but never the only person he wanted to see.

He squinted at his watch in the moonlight. It was close to midnight and Kate and Claire thought he was working late all week. He would have to go home frustrated again. William thumped his steering wheel and hurt his fist. He was a fool to be sitting out watching his windows mist over, probably contracting pneumonia, while Blake Quinlan was cosy in bed, oblivious to the ulcers William was giving himself. He ground his teeth and prepared to start his car.

Then something happened. William could not believe his luck. The Quinlan's front door opened, and out stepped the very person he sought. Blake sat on the steps, rested his chin on his hands and appeared to ponder the night sky.

He must be cold, in just pyjamas and dressing gown. Perhaps Blake couldn't sleep. Perhaps he wanted a breath of air at 11:57. For whatever reason he was out, William was exultant. He slipped out of his car and tiptoed down the Quinlan's driveway, feeling twenty years old again.

He paid no heed to the misgivings that began to roll through his brain. *What will happen when the kid starts to yell? It will wake the neighbours, and somebody will call the police. Worse still, it will arouse Blake's father and brother, and all three men will assault me.* William tightened his jaw and pushed these thoughts aside. He did not care. This was his moment of retribution and he was doing it for

Claire. *Hang the consequences.*

He stood behind a thick daisy bush only two metres away from Blake. He could see the parting of his hair and even the veins in his wrists, because the full moon was so bright. William's time was now. He cleared his throat and stepped forward. "You have some nerve," he growled.

The boy almost jumped out of his skin. He looked at William with one large, shiny eye, because the other was swollen shut. William could see now that the kid had suffered. He was pale and wan and looked as if he had lost weight since the evening William met him, when he'd come for Claire. Blake had no spare flesh to start with, either. William felt his first surge of gloomy satisfaction. Blake deserved to suffer.

He watched the boy's good eye dawn with guilty recognition. "Mr Parker," he mumbled thickly.

William stepped closer. "Tell me what sort of depraved animal you are, to rape an innocent young girl?"

Blake's lips parted and showed a glimpse of white tooth. It appeared vulnerable and boyish. How deceptive appearances could be.

"I'm sorry," he breathed. Blake hung his head. He knew that was pathetic.

"Sorry?" William hissed. "I'll give you sorry!" He no longer cared if he alerted the father and brother. In fact, he rather hoped he would. He was so angry he felt as if he could easily take on all three of them and win.

He curled his fist and gave Blake a swift belt on the jaw. William's knuckles vibrated. He psyched himself up for the uproar he expected but the kid just gave a soft gasp and clutched the side of his face.

"You've got no idea what you've done, have you?" William choked. "You've ruined my daughter. She was happy and well-adjusted, willing to like whoever she met, and now she's a nervous wreck. Her self-confidence has been slashed to ribbons. She's scared of people and she cries all the time. She'll never be the same again, but you had your fun! You must feel happy."

The boy was in tears too. He shook his head. "I don't feel happy."

"No?" William asked. He glared pointedly at Blake's black eye. "You've been set upon already, I see. Who did that?"

"My dad," Blake whimpered.

"Did he? So he damn well should! Did he do this too?" William slammed Blake hard against the brick wall until his teeth rattled. Blake doubled over in pain and shielded his face, but still made no noise.

"This one is for Claire." William gave Blake a final cuff near the side of his head. Then he let loose a string of despicable language he recalled from his youth, language such as William had never used before and had forgotten he even knew. He hardly knew where it was coming from and almost shocked himself. Blake slowly sunk down the wall. He hung his head and took it without striking back.

"Don't ever let me see your face again!" William concluded. "You're lucky I didn't kill you. You might as well have murdered my daughter because you've destroyed her life." He wheeled around and stalked back up the steep driveway without a backward glance.

In his car, William let his guard down. He rested his forehead on the steering wheel and sobbed deep wrenching sobs. Attacking Blake Quinlan had not made him feel better about Claire. Kate was right. Another act of violence could not undo the damage that had already been done.

He expected the house to be dark when he returned home, but Kate was awake. When she heard his footsteps she flicked on her bedside lamp and blinked at him. He could tell by the brightness of her eyes that she had not slept a wink. Her features were etched with fine lines that William had never noticed on his wife before. The days of grief had taken their toll on Kate, too.

He instinctively turned from her scrutiny, like a guilty schoolboy. "I thought you'd be asleep," he managed to mumble.

She sat up against her pillow. "I can't sleep with you somewhere out there thinking about who knows what," she murmured. Kate was close to tears. She hated the evenings now. She and Claire sat in the family room together while William's absence hung between them like a grim spectre. Claire blamed herself. She thought her father was too uncomfortable to be in the same room with her anymore. Kate looked at his hunched back and could not bear to tell him that to add to his misery.

As he slowly undressed, she slipped her arms around his waist and squeezed him gently from behind. "William, have you really been at work? If not, where have you been?"

Her tenderness was his undoing. William found himself sniffing like a baby. He told her. He let out his secret like an uncorked champagne bottle. He had kept it bottled up for almost two weeks, but he could hold it in no longer. He poured out the whole story of how he had confronted Blake Quinlan, and all he had said and done. At the end, he sighed, "Now that I've done it, I won't need to wait there anymore. You'll have me at home again, for what it's worth."

He turned, and saw that Kate's eyes were round and glazed with horror. "William, how could you attack an eighteen year old boy?"

He thought she was rebuking him for picking on a youngster and jumped to his own defence. "He's as tall as I am, and probably much fitter. He was strong enough to rape our girl. He could have defended himself if he'd wanted to."

"That's what I mean," Kate exclaimed. "You're middle-aged and hardly ever exercise. You could have been badly hurt."

He turned his back on her again, feeling somewhat deflated. He thought he should take offence at her neat assessment of his masculinity but he was too tired. Instead, he pulled Kate's head against his shoulder and closed his weary eyes. As he lay between sleep and wakefulness, he pondered Kate's words. For the first time, it struck William as strange that Blake had not attempted to strike back at all. He had not even opened his mouth to make a sound.

William turned over and grunted. *So he knew he had it coming to him. So he damn well should!*

———————

Claire had to excuse herself from the table again. Her mother's vegetable soup used to be her favourite but now she could hardly bear the sight of it. Just the smell of it turned her stomach. She hunched over the toilet bowl and breathed deeply to clear her head. She had been a wreck since the night of the date and hoped she would have been able to put it behind her by now. Not only did she have no appetite, but she always felt queasy, as if she were fighting off some stomach virus.

Claire's neck prickled, as a terrible thought struck her. *Could I be...? No!* She could not possibly be pregnant. If she had not felt so terrible, she would have laughed. Sixteen-year-old girls did not fall pregnant! Not very often, anyway. Claire had always wanted a baby but not now!

It could not be possible. Her own parents had been unable to conceive a baby for many years. Claire knew all about that. They had consulted a string of doctors and undergone several tests. They were very lucky to have had Claire. She had been that one-in-a-million, and the specialist said they would be unable to have any others. That was why William and Kate called her their miracle baby. That was why Claire grew up feeling so treasured and special; so much a gift of God. With her parents' history behind her, how could she have fallen pregnant so easily?

Of course it was impossible. That ugly tussle with Blake Quinlan in the front of his car could not have produced a baby. She had tried her hardest to fight him off with scratches, pushes and shoves. Only people who loved each other had babies. Claire splashed cool water over her face and crept downstairs. Surely her mother would reassure her.

Kate listened as she washed the dishes and Claire languidly wiped them. She did her best to reassure Claire but her pallor and shaky voice belied her words. Claire felt anything but reassured. Kate sounded as if she were trying to convince both of them.

"It's natural that you should still feel sick, after that awful experience. You're still so young, your monthly cycles probably haven't regulated themselves anyway. You'll feel fine soon. But I think Dad was right. We'd better take you to see a doctor, just to be absolutely certain you aren't pregnant. Don't worry; you won't have to see a man. We'll take you to a lady doctor. Will that make you feel better?"

Claire nodded with resignation. If consulting a doctor would make her feel better again, she would have to go through with it. "As long as I don't have to get undressed. I don't want to be examined."

"You won't need to get undressed for a pregnancy test," Kate quickly assured her.

———

The following morning, Claire sat in the surgery waiting room beside her mother. Some small children played noisily with a basket of toys near the magazine table and the receptionist spoke cheerfully on the phone. Claire's eyes stayed fixed on the carpet flecks as she willed her churning stomach to settle. It seemed the harder she tried, the crazier it lurched. She might be sick all over the doctor's desk which would top off her humiliation nicely.

Her name was called in a pleasant, female voice. "Claire Parker."

She scrambled awkwardly to her feet, while her mother's hand steadied her as if she were an infant learning to walk. Claire took one quick, comprehensive gaze at Dr Yvonne Tan, and then her lashes flickered down to her cheeks again.

Dr Tan was a young, pretty Asian woman with a fragile build. She wore a tailored suit and exuded the smell of exotic perfume. Claire felt angular and awkward in her windcheater and jeans; every inch the callow schoolgirl.   •

She wondered what the doctor would think when they told her they needed a pregnancy test. Would she assume that Claire was a naughty girl who had got into trouble with her boyfriend? Claire swallowed the aching lump in her throat and resigned herself to face the scrutiny. It did not matter what the doctor thought as long as she did not discover the dreadful truth that Claire had been raped. If she could get through the ordeal without bursting into tears, she would consider it work well done.

Kate and Claire sat tensely behind the doctor's desk, awaiting the result of the urine test. Dr Tan peered down at it with a wing of dark hair shielding her face, so they could read nothing from her expression. It took a long time and although Claire sat sedately with her hands folded in her lap she wanted to fidget and urge her to hurry. Her eardrums felt as if all the oceans in the world were pounding on them. Suspenseful silence could kill a person!

Dr Tan brushed back her hair. Claire wildly assessed her face and her senses reeled. The doctor didn't need to say a word. Her sad, apologetic face told the whole story.

"I'm so sorry, Claire. I take it this is an unwanted pregnancy? I'm sorry, Mrs Parker. The test is positive. You've been very unlucky. Don't despair because you are still in the early stages."

Claire's mind could take in no more. She fazed out, while bits and pieces of the doctor's dialogue filtered through her senses. "I assume you would like to finish school and put this episode behind you? We can terminate it... that would be best. We'll admit Claire into hospital... general anaesthetic... won't feel a thing. In fact, we can have her out again the same day. Won't that be good?"

"You're talking about abortion!" White-faced, Kate managed to get the words out.

Dr Tan flushed slightly as if she did not like the word. "Well, perhaps it would be the most sensible option for Claire...I promise you, the embryo is still in the very rudimentary stages of development... Just a quick, painless procedure.... Of course, I was just assuming... If you want to keep the baby....

"Claire, think it over very carefully. Discuss it with your parents. There are institutions set up to help teenage mothers...and adoption agencies. I'm sure you'll come to the right decision."

Kate's lips were grey. She clutched the arms of her chair and knew she had to say something. "This is a huge shock. We have to go home and discuss it with my husband. You'll hear from us." The only thing Kate wanted to do was to pull Claire to her heart and never let her go. She stood to her feet and forced a polite, obligatory smile of goodbye, as if the news had not rocked her to the depths of her soul. She reached for her handbag with one hand and seized Claire's hand with the other.

Claire shuffled blindly after her mother. Kate crooned, "Don't you worry, Daddy and I will fix everything." She had not referred to William as "Daddy" for many years, and Claire felt like a little girl again. She longed to believe that her parents could fix everything, but her mother's hand felt as cold as ice.

———————

"She has to have the abortion," William decreed.

"I want to keep the baby!" Claire pleaded. She had done plenty of thinking before her father arrived home. She had come to terms with the idea of being pregnant. She remembered all she had learned from her parents and pastor about the sanctity of human life. Children were a gift from God. For the first time since that horrible night, Claire began to feel thankful toward Him. God might be blessing her abundantly to make up for what had happened. Babies were special gifts. She had always wanted one.

Now she recognised the inexorable tightness of her father's jaw, and Claire felt a wave of panic surge in her chest. "Please Dad, I have to keep it."

"No, you can't!" he cried. If only Claire would yield to common sense, it would be so much easier for him. Why couldn't she understand that keeping the baby would be a disaster? He had yielded to her pressure not to see a doctor in the first place. He refused to yield to this.

"I will! It's my baby," she yelled.

William wanted to hit her but held himself back. Some ironic code of ethics deep inside told him it was wrong to strike a pregnant woman. He shook his head clear. Claire was no woman. She was a child, and a disobedient one, too.

"Don't be ridiculous. You don't know what having a baby is like. It isn't a toy. It's another life that will tie you down for the rest of yours. Children are demanding. They sap your energy and then break your heart." His voice crackled.

Claire understood the implication that she was breaking his heart and bristled with the unfairness of it. "It's not my fault I was raped!" She lowered her voice and appealed to his higher self. "Dad, you've always stood against abortion. You know how hard it was for you to have me. You know how precious babies are, and now you want me to throw mine away."

William tried to interrupt but she raised her voice again. "It's murdering the innocent! It's an abomination. You told me that."

"Not in this case," William overruled. "The doctor said that it's still in the very early stages. You'll have the abortion, and that's final. You didn't plan for this pregnancy. You were raped."

"That's not the baby's fault!" Claire shot back.

"Well it has to be done for the baby's sake too!" William's eyes blazed. He could not believe he had to argue the point. "You aren't fit to be anybody's mother, yet. You're only a teenager and the baby would have no father."

"I'd love it," she squeaked. "I'd look after it."

"You couldn't look after it. You have to finish your schooling, and

Mum and I can't take care of it for the rest of our lives. You would never find a decent husband with an illegitimate child in tow." William silently kicked himself for putting his deep objections to words. They sounded so ugly when they were brought out in the open. "I only want what's best for you," he excused himself.

Even Kate's eyebrows rose at this. "William!" she reproached.

He wheeled on her furiously. "Support me, for heaven's sake! Tell her it's all for the best." The truth was, he strongly objected to having a child fathered by that repulsive Quinlan boy in his household. At least he had not blurted that out.

Claire turned her blotched and crumpled face to Kate too. "Mum, you know I'm right. "We could take it to an adoption agency." It was crucial to convince her parents to let her carry the pregnancy. If only she could get past that first hurdle, they would have nine months to make the next decision. "Please don't make me kill it."

William stood to show that the conversation was finished. He had to make himself look like the villain of the piece but was convinced that the quick and easy way would be best for his family. "Our minds are made up. Abortion is the right thing to do this time. You're too young to make your own decision. If you did your heels in and oppose me on this, you'll have to leave this house. That would break my heart but there would be no other option. I can't have you living under this roof pregnant. That would break my heart even more. You're going to that hospital, and you will have that operation. That's the end. You'll thank me, some day."

Her coppery hair clung in wild tendrils to her wet cheeks. "I won't! I hate you. I won't go." Claire was beyond trying to reason with him. She screamed whatever diatribe came to her. She called him a hypocrite, and an uncaring murderer. She hated Blake Quinlan for getting her pregnant and she hated her father, whom she had adored all her life, for wanting to end it. Claire pounded the wall until her fists ached, as if that would mend matters.

William pulled her back and his chest heaved with emotion.

"You'll go to that hospital if I have to drag you there!"

Claire looked at his face and turned limp. She had never prevailed against her father before when he had his mind set fast. She doubted she had the strength to begin now. She curled up on the sofa, and although she was exhausted, the tears just flowed down her face.

Chapter Six

"It's fantastic, Blake. Watch me ride it! Watch me go!" Michael had never had a motorised go-kart before and he steered it up and down the driveway with a grin from ear to ear.

Blake had spent a month making it from bits of old machinery and timber he'd managed to lay his hands on. He had examined enough engines to be able to improvise a crude go-kart motor of his own. The vehicle looked rough but it worked and made Mike happy. That was the main thing. Now that he had finished it, Blake did not know what he would do with his time.

"I'm gonna take it to Jamie's house to show him," Michael announced.

"Did Mum say you could?" Blake felt deserted. He wished Michael would stay with him instead of going to show his best friend. Only Michael still loved him, because he was too young to understand what Blake had done to Claire Parker. The others avoided him like the plague.

"Yep! As long as I'm back in time for tea. See-ya. Thanks for the go-kart." Michael cruised down the footpath leaving Blake alone with the silence he had grown to dread.

He had ended up quitting work completely because he could not face his companions. Blake crept around the house avoiding his parents. He had kept his thoughts at bay by working on Mikey's go-kart but now that was finished. There was nothing but the languor of self-disgust he had built for himself. He supposed he could seek another mind-numbing job. He ought to get on with his life but what sort of a life was it to get on with?

He walked past his mother cooking in the kitchen and she did not turn around. She pretended not to see him. Blake went along with her act and pretended he did not know. He did not blame her for having nothing to say to him. There was no way she could ever forget what he had done.

He wandered aimlessly into the bathroom and suddenly the medicine cabinet behind the mirror caught his attention. Blake slowly opened it and stared at Rowena's jar of sleeping pills beside her cold cream. She battled with insomnia, and a jar of tablets had always sat on the bottom shelf since he was old enough to remember. He had thought nothing of them... until now. Blake's cold fingers wrapped around the jar and his heart pounded.

What if he ended his miserable existence and took them all? He would be no great loss to society. Instead of doing it then and there he took the jar outside to think it over. He leaned against the huge old plane tree at the back of the yard where he and Sean had always gone to talk or think things through. When they were very young, they would be up in the branches swinging, or escaping from Dad.

Blake rattled the jar like a maraca and then unscrewed the lid to look inside. Mum had finished half of them, but there were plenty left. He could never bring himself to slash his wrists or stab himself because he did not have the stomach for it, but how easy this would be. He could swallow them down with a glass of water, then sink into a deep sleep from which he would never wake up. Blake stared at the innocent looking white circles and shuddered at their potential. His pulse began to race with panic now, but if he took them it would slowly peter into nothing.

He half scrambled to his feet, then leaned back to watch his last sunset. The pink evening sky faded to grey and still he sat thinking. He should not do it in his own backyard where Mikey might come home to put his go-kart away in the shed and find him. Blake felt a wave of sickness at the thought. He loved his little brother and would never do that to him. He should walk down the road to the reserve and do it. What on earth was stopping him?

He let his fingers slacken and the jar of pills fell onto the grass beside him. Blake drew a deep breath and cursed to himself. He was not going to do it. Deep down, he knew he never would. He began to tremble with an odd relief, shocked that he had even half considered the idea. He was in a mess but the harm he had done to Claire Parker would not be mended by his inflicting violence upon himself.

If he swallowed the sleeping pills, he would be remembered by Sean's and Michael's descendents as the good-for-nothing relative who had raped a girl, then killed himself. That was not how he wanted Blake Daniel Quinlan to be remembered for posterity. At least if he stayed alive he might be able to live it down in another sixty or seventy years.

Besides, he was too unsure about the afterlife to risk committing suicide. He might find himself worse off than he already was. Blake's family had never been religious. His dad had been in some mighty brawls in the fervour of Catholicism as a boy in Ireland but Blake knew there was no real strength of conviction to back it up. His father never mentioned the name of Jesus unless he was swearing. Blake never wanted to be involved in anything Gerry approved of anyway.

He wished he knew whether the stories about God and Jesus, heaven and hell, were real or made up. A private sanctum of Blake's heart longed for a good God to make sense of life. He used to ask Sean what he thought but Sean cheerfully shoved it into the 'too hard' basket, to work on when he was older, or if he ever got around to it. Sean never wondered about God as much as Blake did. He did not think he had the need.

If you exist, please let me know, Blake pleaded to God in his heart, as if scum like him had a right to ask anything of God. If He did exist,

He certainly kept a low profile. He had never gone out of His way to look out for Blake. That was why, most times, Blake supposed God was not true at all.

Either way, he buried his face in his hands, thoroughly despondent. Even if heaven existed, it was not for the likes of him. If he committed suicide he would face either hell or oblivion and Blake did not like either possibility. He had to stay and keep facing the music, but would Claire Parker ever get over what he had done to her? The thought of Claire was still enough to bring water to his eyes almost seven weeks later. He could never undo what he had done. There was no turning back.

—————

When Sean returned home from footy training, the heavy pall of gloom latched on to his shoulders again. When he was out on the oval, he allowed himself to forget what Blake had done for a few hours. It was never long enough. Sean still found the knowledge impossible to come to terms with. *How could Blake have done it? How could he?*

Sean felt remorseful because he knew his brother was hurting but he could not face Blake for a proper talk. Not yet. They spoke about neutral topics, such as whose turn it was to take out the garbage, and pretended that was enough. They no longer even kept tabs on whose turn it was to bait Dad. There was no need to anyway because when Gerry was drunk he lunged at Blake every time. Blake seemed prepared to bear the brunt of Gerry's rage.

Sean pursed his lips and walked out to the backyard to clean his muddy football boots. He vowed he would talk to Blake when he could trust himself to speak without saying something harsh that he might later regret. Sean hated the estrangement but his distaste for Blake's action was still too great to face. The younger brother he thought he knew was a lovable, shy, sensitive character, as kind-hearted as he could be. Not a rapist. If Sean could ever reconcile the new Blake with the old one, he might be able to face him again.

He stopped short when he reached the backyard. There sat Blake with his back to him, hunched beneath the old plane tree. Sean unlaced his boots quietly by the door, hoping Blake would not hear him. Normally, he would have yelled, "Hey, watcha doing?" Now, they were like strangers.

Sean's heart wrenched with guilt again when he saw how thin and dejected Blake's slumped shoulders looked. The family had been rough on him and Blake was feeling it. Now, Sean intended to walk into the house and pretend he had not seen him again. He knew Blake was not really fooled when they all found other things to do than talk to him.

Perhaps Blake really was oblivious to his presence this time. His head was on his knees. From idle curiosity, Sean craned his head to see the object on the grass beside Blake. He focused on the bottle of sleeping pills and his heart leaped into his throat. In that instant, Sean paid dearly for the shabby way he had treated Blake for six weeks.

He was over there in three long strides. "What the hell are you doing?" Sean snatched the bottle and unscrewed the cap. He broke out in clammy sweat when he saw half the bottle empty. Sean could hardly breathe. He lived a million years in the next two seconds.

Surely Blake would never be so reckless and stupid! But he had never thought Blake would rape a girl either. There was no telling what the new Blake would do. In fact, perhaps it was like the old Blake, to feel so deeply wretched for having alienated his entire family.

"It was just an idea." Blake sounded embarrassed.

"You took half the bottle!" Sean choked. He clutched Blake's shoulders with shaking hands which could not move fast enough for him. He loved his brother and nothing could change that. Blake was still Sean's confidante and friend. He still meant the world to him. That fact hit Sean in the solar plexus like a missile. If he lost his brother he would never recover. Not ever.

His mind whirled to find a solution. He needed to make

Blake sick. They had to phone an ambulance. He tugged Blake's hand. "You're coming with me. You're not going to die."

"Sean, I didn't take any!"

"You're lying!" Sean babbled like a hysterical clown. "Half the jar is gone! Why, Blake, why?"

"Sean, I didn't take any!" Blake had to snap Sean out of his panic. He seized his brother's shoulders and looked him in the eye. "There was only half a bottle to start with. I thought about taking them but changed my mind. That's the truth."

Sean began to weep like a baby and Blake's spine prickled; he could not believe it! His tough brother never cried! Even when they were little boys, only Blake would burst into tears. Sean would just sniffle quietly even when Dad belted him really hard.

"I honestly didn't take any," Blake repeated. He looked at Sean's crumpled face and his own mind spun with relief. How sad his family would have been if he had gone through with it. He ached to think of the pain it would cause. One wrong deed would not cancel another.

Sean poured the little white pills onto the grass, and fiercely ground them to powder beneath his boot. He flung the jar against the iron fence and then sank onto his haunches, trembling. Blake squatted beside him and placed a nervous hand on his brother's shoulder. "Hey Sean, I'm O.K.," he said, and flinched. He half expected Sean to belt him for the scare.

Instead, Sean reached out and pulled Blake close to him. "Oh man, I thought you were gonna die!" He wanted to put his grief into words. He wanted to say how terrible he felt about his own part in driving his brother to the verge of suicide. He should never have withheld his acceptance and forgiveness. All he could manage was a broken, "I'm sorry."

Now Blake patted Sean reassuringly on the back because Sean seemed to need the most comfort. "I promise I won't ever do anything like this again."

———

Late that night as Blake lay awake in bed, the door creaked open. His mother tiptoed in and stood by his bed, gazing down at him. He squeezed his eyes shut and pretended to be asleep because she expected him to be. Rowena sniffed softly and he knew she was crying. Blake guessed why. Sean and Rowena had talked quietly in the kitchen while the others watched TV. Sean had naturally told her all about Blake and the sleeping pills.

Rowena drew the boys' chair to Blake's bedside, and sat down. She began to comb her fingers through his hair and Blake froze, stunned. She used to do that to him and Sean before she switched off their light each night. He had forgotten the old ritual. Now he was glad she thought him asleep. He felt too embarrassed and tired to explain his actions to his mother but he was pleased that she loved him. After six long weeks with nobody to talk to but Michael, that was good to know. He would prepare himself to face her in the morning. He realised he really was exhausted. Waves of sleep stole over him and his last impression was that she was taking a long time.

Rowena Quinlan watched her son by the light of the moon for an hour. He looked so young and fresh in sleep, as if he had nothing on his mind. She thought about the first time she had studied Blake, almost nineteen years earlier when he was born. It had been a dodgy pregnancy. She had battled with toxaemia and spent the last few weeks with her feet raised in bed. The labour itself was long and exhausting but how soft and warm he felt in her arms. She had watched her baby's every breath, thinking how close she had come to losing him.

Rowena looked at the long, thin form of her teenaged son beneath his blankets and knew she had almost lost him again. She was horrified, as Sean had been, to realise that her attitude might have driven Blake to kill himself. She buried her face in her hands and then leaned down to kiss his forehead. If he had died, she never would have forgiven herself.

Her behaviour to her son had been appalling. She had torn strips off him with her tongue, then treated him like an outcast ever since.

She felt ashamed of herself for failing to consider how hard it must have been for him to come to her and admit what he had done. The more she thought about it, the more self-reproach she laid on herself. Blake had done the bravest thing a boy could possibly do. She was proud of him.

———

Blake was first to wake up in the morning. When he went to clean his teeth, he saw that the medicine cabinet had been stripped almost bare. Only Mum's hair clips and cold cream, a bag of cotton balls and Dad's old dentures remained. All the pills and medicines had disappeared.

He could not help grinning. Mum and Sean had good intentions but how simple they were. If he really wanted to do away with himself, he could walk to the corner chemist and buy himself some type of pill to do the job. He wondered if that had occurred to them.

It was certainly good to know they cared. Blood was thicker than water. He loved his family, so as he was not going to kill himself he ought to make an effort to find some new work. Blake flicked aimlessly through the employment section of the morning paper. It did not matter much what sort of repetitive factory work it would be. He was not qualified to do anything else and it was all dull and boring, anyway.

He circled a few of the advertisements that looked most likely. His family might care what became of him but he did not give a damn. Ever since the night he had raped Claire Parker, Blake had lost his self-respect. Whenever he caught his own eye in the mirror, he was thoroughly disgusted with the person he saw there. Mum, Sean and Michael still loved him, so he would keep his true estimate of himself from them. It would only upset them.

They might forgive him for the rape of a beautiful girl, but he would never forgive himself.

"Claire! Claire!"

The voice seemed to come from miles away and she wanted to sleep. It was like Mum waking her up for a school morning but far worse.

"Claire, it's all over, honey." The nurse's cheerful voice was abrasive. She evidently required some sort of response so Claire flickered her eyelashes and managed a moan. Waves of nausea swept over her, and her head spun. She did not know if the sickness or the giddiness felt worse. The combination was gruesome.

So the operation was over. There was no going back. She couldn't stop it and she couldn't change it now. Part of her began to grieve, and she knew she would feel even worse later. The grief would have to be postponed until she felt herself again. If only her head would stop spinning and her stomach would settle, she could get her bearings.

"Just relax, now. It's all over. You did fine."

She didn't do fine! She didn't do anything but lie there counting backwards as the anaesthetist had asked her to. She remembered getting as far back as ninety-seven. Now it was finished. The last time she was awake, she had a little baby growing in her. Now it was gone. Claire felt herself break out in perspiration.

The nurse approached her bed again far sooner than she was ready for. "We'll wheel you out of recovery now. Your parents are waiting to see you."

As the bed was wheeled along, Claire concentrated on breathing deeply to counteract the waves of illness that threatened to erupt at any moment. She was taken to a small, private room and lifted on to the bed there. William and Kate had been sitting down and they rose to their feet to greet her. Claire managed to groan her request for a bucket in the nick of time.

Afterwards, Kate stood stroking Claire's damp hair back from her brow. "Are you all right?" she asked tenderly.

Claire could hardly talk. The nausea was still there. "Mmmmm," she breathed. She tried to lift her head, but the room spun, so she lowered it to the pillow again and closed her eyes. She felt as if she were on a relentless carousel.

Oblivion struggled to claim her again and she wished it would. It would take her away from the sickness. Unfortunately, the sickness was too severe to phase out. She managed to rest a hand upon her stomach. It felt concave. She had lost plenty of weight, because her appetite had been so poor for weeks.

William stood staring down at her face. Claire focused on his thick moustache, and its familiarity comforted her. She could not muster the effort to be angry with Dad any longer but perhaps she would renew her resentment when she had the strength.

William did something unusual. He reached down to touch her cheek, and his eyes were sad. For the first time Claire saw how tired and washed-out they were. He cleared his throat, and tried to speak soothingly. "It's all over now. You came through wonderfully, as we knew you would. We're proud of you." His moustache drooped.

Now she felt the flicker of anger re-ignite. *I didn't have much choice, did I?*

"We can put it all behind us now." Dad smiled at her. "You can get on with your life. You'll soon be stuck into your schoolwork again and things will be just as they used to be."

Claire managed a feeble nod. "Mmmmm," she said again.

Just as they used to be? Would they really? Could she pick up the pieces and carry on as if nothing had happened? Now that the little growing baby had been scraped from her womb, could she forget how terrified she had been in Blake Quinlan's car, or how he had hurt her? Could she forget that Dad had forced her to have an abortion and instructed her to keep it secret? Or that now her own child would never see the light of day or have a chance to know her?

Claire's eyes welled with tears. People kept telling her that her baby was far too small to know a thing but she couldn't escape the knowledge that she'd committed the most culpable crime to somebody who never had a chance. She had acquiesced to her father's will but he had no power to make her forget. Claire couldn't possibly forget if she tried.

Chapter Seven

S ean sprinted home from football training, flapping his precious slip of paper. His car had broken down, but he did not mind running, although he was bursting with his news and longed to tell his family. The letter he clutched was the culmination of all his dreams. It was from a new coach, and next season he would be recruited to a brand new, higher profile team.

Darkness had settled but the evening was still early so he supposed Dad would not be home from the pub. There would be only Mum and Mikey to tell, because Blake was out listening to a free lecture on the Middle Eastern crisis with a friend from work. Blake had become interested in current affairs and Sean knew he would arrive home upset by what he heard. Although Sean was jubilant with his own victory, he shook his head. Poor Blake. Sean would not change places with his brother for the world. He pitied anybody who could not play football. Let the rest of the world sort itself out.

It was not that Sean didn't care about the people of war torn nations but there was nothing he could do for them. He preferred to feel grateful for his own good fortune. Blake spent too much time dwelling on situations that did not concern him and could not be changed. He thought far too hard

Sean crested the top of his hill, and saw that his dad *was* home, because his car was parked beneath the carport. He instantly forgot about Blake's gloomy lifestyle. For once he was delighted that Gerry was home early. He could hardly wait to see his father's face when he heard the news.

He heard Dad's strident voice before he opened the door. Gerry obviously had enough time to get himself raging drunk. "What did you do with the money I gave you on Monday? I don't bust my boiler all week to let it slip between your fingers!"

"Mikey needed a new pair of shoes!" Rowena cried. "He's worn holes through the toes of the old ones." It was one of the rare times when neither of her two older sons was there to defend her.

"So my hard earned cash goes on peoples' feet!" Gerry scowled at Mikey, who cringed against the wall. "Take better care of your things, you little runt!"

"He's had them for two years. His feet have grown out of them." Rowena never lost hope that one day Gerry might listen to reason.

"I'll wear the old shoes, Dad," Michael cried, anxious for peace. "They're still comfortable. We can take the new ones back."

Sean threw open the door and saw Gerry clutching Rowena's face beneath the chin and shaking her. For once, he did not pause to invent a diversion but burst into the fray and seized his father's shoulder. His news would be diversion enough. "Stop hurting Mum and listen to me."

Gerry scowled at him and jerked his arm back. "You mind your business!" he flared.

"I got drafted, just like I expected," Sean crowed, and waved his letter beneath Gerry's nose. "I start next season. Aren't you gonna congratulate me?"

Gerry stood stunned out of his temper. He blinked at Sean. "You're pulling my leg."

"No, I'm not," Sean grinned. How he had anticipated this moment. "Here's the letter from the coach."

Gerry fumbled for the paper gingerly as if he expected it to disintegrate beneath his fingers. He focused on the untidy scrawl and muttered, "I can't read it. You read it for me."

"I'll read it, Sean!" Mikey cried, eager to take part in any good news.

Sean ruffled his little brother's hair. "OK, read it loud and clear so Dad can understand every word." He bounced onto the sofa and relished the wonderful words that were already emblazoned on his heart. The letter had been in his possession for only two hours. He had never memorised things at school so easily. He folded his arms smugly across his chest when Michael finished. "Well?"

Gerry wondered if he was having a good dream which he would wake from at any moment. No, there was the spaghetti sauce stain above the clock. He had flung his plate there a few nights ago. He would not notice such a minute detail in a dream. He opened his mouth, unsure of what would come out.

"Well you'd better not slacken off. This is a chance in a million to prove your mettle. Don't blow it." He had spoken gloomy words for so many years he could say nothing else.

Sean threw back his head and laughed. He was like a breath of fresh air in the family. His father did not need to say he was proud. Sean read it on his face. "Don't worry, Dad. I won't blow it."

"See that you don't," Gerry managed weakly. He watched Rowena tumble forward, laughing and crying, to hug their oldest son. Then Sean hitched Michael up, as if he were no heavier than a feather pillow, and spun him around. Gerry allowed himself to let satisfaction infuse him for the first time in years.

He had been throttling Rowena when Sean burst in but Gerry was hard pressed to remember why. He sat on a kitchen chair and started on the chocolate pudding she'd cooked. Rowena made good chocolate pudding, but Gerry hardly tasted it. He was too busy studying Sean. He could not remember the last time he had taken a thorough survey of any of his boys.

Sean was a head-turner; stocky and barrel-chested. He had a good crop of blonde hair and open, pleasant features. He was a fine, Irish-looking lad. A fierce pride welled up from deep in Gerry's chest. Sean looked similar to the way he had looked at twenty, or how he might have looked had he been given a fair go. Gerry approved of football. It was a good, rugged sport for a man.

His other two sons were of little interest to him. Blake was a sullen, complex character whom Gerry could never fathom. The boy had become an embarrassment. Whenever Gerry glanced at Blake he saw a loser who was good for nothing. He had raped a girl, and nothing he could do would redeem him in Gerry's eyes after that. Thankfully, the lass's parents had been as anxious to hush it up as the Quinlans so at least none of Gerry's friends found out. Still, the sooner Blake was off his hands the better.

Gerry had never forgotten the first time Blake humiliated him, over ten years ago. When his two older boys were small, he liked to take them to entertain his pub friends. He had Sean to boast about, for he had been an athletic, attractive boy even then, and Blake to laugh at. It had been funny to watch Blake's pitiful attempts to mimic his brother. The fellows would almost roll off their stools when Gerry belittled Blake, for their benefit.

One afternoon the seven-year-old decided he'd had a gutful. He burst into tears, then let loose with string of angry revelations about Gerry's personal habits. The other men roared with laughter again but Gerry was on the receiving end. He belted Blake as soon as he got him to the car, but the damage had been done. His friends often teased him over what the child had said and Gerry lost face with them. Perhaps his grudge against Blake had lasted ever since.

As for Michael, he was nothing more than a household nuisance. Gerry knew the little boy loved him but he cared nothing for the affection of an eight-year-old at his stage of life. Michael had been a mistake, anyway. The last thing Gerry wanted was another mouth to feed for ten years after Sean and Blake grew up and left home. Michael's incessant energy wearied him and his prattling voice made his head ache. Gerry was too old to have a little kid always underfoot like a pesky dog.

Sean was his number one son and Sean would rescue him from his rut of depression. Gerry felt a twinge of annoyance for not having attended more of Sean's football matches in the past. *How could I have known the lad was really any good?* Sean had done plenty of boasting but Gerry thought it was just hot air, the same as he used to do himself. Gerry had been the king of wishful thinking.

He would appreciate Sean from this moment on. He licked the last crumbs of pudding from his lips and began to fantasise about having a famous sportsman for a son. He planned what he would say to his cronies when he saw them again. Gerry would live through Sean, as he should have been doing for years.

————

Claire sat in the centre of the school auditorium, and gnawed deep holes into the end of her pencil. Her Maths exam was almost blank and all her answers had been guesswork anyway. There was still an hour to go and she would fail dismally. Tears began to slide down her face, and she pushed the paper aside, so they would land on the desk. She did not want her teachers to see round smudges and guess how distraught she had been.

She had been unable to catch up with her lessons ever since she returned to school after her rape and abortion. She could barely even concentrate on her English novels, and that had been her best subject. Maths, Science, Geography and History were a write-off. Especially Maths. When she sat in class, Mr Cluzek might as well have been speaking another language as far as Claire was concerned.

She could no longer make facts and figures stick in her head. Her personal pain was still so fresh after several months, it all seemed pointless. So much for her dream of attending University. Her father would be disappointed again. Her father thought she should have put her ordeal behind her by now. The abortion was supposed to have mended matters but nothing would ever be the same again.

Claire no longer lived in reality. She measured time with an anguished *if only* calendar she carried in her head. If only she could have fought harder, convinced her dad to let her keep the baby, it would have had little hands and feet, by now. Its facial features would be evident. It would have been kicking her and its unique personality would have been forming. She would have been getting thick around the waist. Sometimes Claire lay awake at night and quietly belted her own flesh as punishment for giving in to Dad's pressure. She felt that she deserved to hurt as much as her poor baby might have hurt when it was torn from the soft safety of her womb. Sure, the doctors all assured her it would have felt nothing at such an early stage but how was anyone to know for sure, except for God?

She felt so despicable she did not even bother trying to take care of her personal appearance. Claire's once gleaming hair hung limp and lustreless. Her eyes had lost their sparkle. She was as guilty of the baby's death as her father. She should never have given in. She could have carried her defiance a step further and run away to some teenage mother's shelter, if she had not been so weak. She had assented to the death of her own innocent child.

A hand clutched Claire's shoulder and made her jump. She swiped her cheeks and looked up at the watery image of Mrs Rice, the head of the Maths department. The teacher's eyes were full of compassion. She leaned close to Claire's ear and whispered, "Come with me."

Claire stood to her feet, electrified. She tiptoed down the aisle after Mrs Rice, past the hunched backs and scribbling pencils of the other students. She appreciated Mrs Rice's sympathy but wondered how much she knew. Nobody was supposed to know Claire's secret. She had made that clear before she returned to school. Blake Quinlan had once attended Claire's school too and if anybody discovered what he had done to her, she could never look them in the face again. Her mother and father had promised to keep the scandal quiet but they might have let something slip. Claire had learned that what her parents said and what they did were two different matters.

In the corridor, Mrs Rice slipped an arm around Claire's shoulder and said something astounding, for a Maths teacher. "There are more important things than a Maths test, Claire. Don't you worry. Whatever your trouble is, you have your whole life ahead of you. Things will look up."

———

Late that night, Claire huddled on the bottom of the stairs listening to her parents talk in the lounge-room. Their voices carried easily through the frosted glass door because they made no attempt to keep them low. They thought she was sound asleep.

She did not feel at all guilty for eavesdropping. Mum and Dad had sat closeted with the headmaster for an hour while she lay in the sickroom, and then emerged to tell her that she could leave school until she decided to return. Claire had been glad of that, yet she wished they had asked her opinion before they made the decision. She was tired of having her life arranged behind her back as if she were a baby.

"We should let her rest at home for as long as she likes," Kate was saying. "The month that she missed was obviously not enough. She's still grieving."

"Well, how long will it take?" William could not keep an edge of impatience from his voice. "I think we let her mope at home for too long. If she hadn't missed a whole month of school, she might have caught up quicker." He hated feeling so infuriatingly powerless. Sometimes he longed to shake his daughter and command her to feel happy again. Most of all, William hated the niggling hunch deep in his heart that he was partly responsible for Claire's ongoing misery.

"It might take several months, this time. Let's not rush her," Kate said. "Shall we leave her to do as she pleases?"

"Which won't be much," William interjected gloomily. He knew Claire would keep to her bedroom, trying to hide her tears.

"Or encourage her to try to find work?" Kate concluded as if he had not interrupted.

"I wanted better for our daughter than shop-work," he muttered.

"Whatever she chooses would only be temporary. There's nothing wrong with shop-work, anyway." Kate had worked in shops herself before she married William.

"I just want her to snap out of it!" he growled.

"Don't snarl at me, when you told me there was no other choice - it's your fault!" Kate regretted her words as soon as she said them. She clamped her lips shut but the damage was done. William's face clouded with hurt.

"She's still grieving over the little baby. We shouldn't have forced her to abort it." Kate said "we" to soften the blow, but they both knew the decision had been solely William's. Kate had urged him to consider the possibility of adoption, but his mind had been made up.

William hid his face and started to sob. Kate's spine tingled. She had rarely seen her proud, self-reliant husband so hurt and vulnerable. At once, she moved into his arms.

"I thought I was acting for the best," he said brokenly. "I thought the abortion would be the kindest thing for Claire."

She kissed the top of his head. "I know. We could have explored our options. We could have done some research. But we can't go back now."

"It's just that I didn't feel we had time to wait and talk. With each day, that baby was growing bigger. I just wanted things back to normal." William groaned and sank his face into his palms. He pulled his wife closer and appreciated the familiar clean flannel scent of her nightgown. Instead of bringing their lives back to normal, he feared he had lost his daughter's love for ever. When Claire's beautiful, clear blue eyes looked at him, he saw a smouldering resentment for his decision, and disillusionment for his double standards. All her life he had defended the rights of the unborn. Now, he was a murderer and a hypocrite in Claire's eyes.

William bitterly regretted his action. He hated to be alone, because accusatory thoughts gnawed him like relentless mosquitoes. Claire's baby was gone now, but perhaps it would have had her wonderful bright eyes and the slow, warm smile he had not seen for so long. The baby had been part of the Quinlan boy, but it had also been part of Claire. It had been his grandchild. Perhaps if he had let her carry it to full term she might have recovered quicker than having had it ripped from her womb. Why to God hadn't he listened to Kate and Claire? Why didn't he even ask God?

William knew the answers deep in his heart and they disgusted him. He had closed his ears to Claire's pleas because he did not want to deal with an unwanted pregnancy and have the neighbours witness their shame. He did not want to face any tricky emotional ties the baby might bring. Was all of this an excuse to justify murder? The accusation loomed before him, stark and ugly. William hated Blake Quinlan because his action brought out an ugliness in himself that he found despicable.

"I wish I hadn't made her do it," he confided to Kate.

That was enough to infuriate Claire, listening on the steps. She could no longer contain the anger that had been simmering against her father for months. His useless remorse was enough to boil her over. She flung open the glass door and confronted him with blazing eyes.

"You did make me do it! It's too late to wish you didn't. You forced me into something I didn't want to do, so at least you could stick to your guns!" Now that she had started, she couldn't stop. "And why don't you ever ask me what I want to do? I don't want to stay here at all. I want to get away. I can't stand it here."

Besides being so angry with Dad, she hated to live so near to the Quinlans. She had never seen any of them since that terrible night, but that did not mean she never would. She dreaded the thought of facing any of the Quinlan family and Blake in particular.

William stared at her, white to the lips. For once, he was too cowed to rebuke her for coming out of bed. "All right, we'll find somewhere for you to go," he acquiesced huskily and turned away to hide the tears misting his eyes.

Claire gaped. She had not expected him to give in so easily, but it was a hollow victory. If only he had given in to her demand when it really mattered. She did not know what he would arrange for her but she did not care. There was nowhere she wanted to go. She wished she could find it in her heart to love her dad again, but she couldn't. Not yet. Claire trudged back up to bed, but she had never felt so lonely.

Chapter Eight

Sean Quinlan tilted back his head and drained the last few drops from his can of light beer. He and four friends had found a great spot for a barbecue in an overgrown, bushy reserve. There was a run-down tennis court and an old flying fox over a wide, deep creek bed. Only a thin ribbon of water trickled between the jagged rocks on the hot November day. The young men had set up their portable barbecue and cooked all the chops and sausages they had brought.

Kookaburras swooped to the branches of the gum trees above their heads and scolded the human intruders with their quaint cackles. Sean was happy with life. He leaned his head back against a warm lichen-covered rock and stretched, soaking in the sun before deciding how to exercise. Sean was too energetic to rest for long.

John screwed the lid onto the tomato sauce bottle and stowed it back in the esky. "Who's for a game of cricket on the tennis court?"

Sean sat up, grinning. "Me, but first I'll try that flying fox."

"Me too," said David.

"Me first," Sean insisted.

Simon laughed. "You guys are clowns. It's a rusty old rattletrap."

Sean was already on his feet, dragging the heavy handle of the flying fox through the powdery dry dirt to the end of its cable. "Here goes." His shoes pelted the ground hard and fast, raising a cloud of dust, and he took off with a whoop of joy. A mild breeze ruffled his hair and he watched the shapes of the trees whiz past. This was what it was like to fly.

Thwack! He hit a build up of calcification in the middle of the cable and stopped moving. He was stuck. Sean lifted his head, and saw how rusted and frayed the cable was. It had not occurred to him to check, before. He felt compelled to gaze beneath his dangling feet and the hair on his neck prickled. There was nothing but jagged rocks at least ten metres beneath him. Sean's muscles began to quiver.

He instantly tightened them. It was not time to panic yet. He could hang on for as long as need be. "Hey, you guys give me a shake, to get it going again!" He did not dare crane his neck to peer back at them but hoped they heard him loud and clear.

John's voice reached him, as a thin cry. "Hold on Sean, we'll give you a bit of a shake!" They had not heard his call. Sean's ears detected an edge of panic in John's voice. It was most unpleasant to be stuck high in the middle of nowhere.

An itch started behind his right shoulder where he could not scratch and drops of sweat trickled into his eyes. Sean found himself desperate to reach the other side of the creek bed. When he got there, he would tell the others not to bother using the flying fox. Simon was right. It was an old heap of junk.

He felt himself sway gently. The fellows were shaking the cable but it was not enough to budge him. Sean pursed his lips and bounced himself, to no avail. "Harder!" he yelled between clenched teeth. His head filled with blood and made his temples pulse.

"Try again, Sean!" the others hollered. They made no attempt to disguise their sheer fright.

Sean felt a moan escape from his lips. He gave another feeble bounce, knowing it would be useless. A strange, desperate plea shot out of his mouth. "God, help me!" He had never called on God before but where else could he turn? If he crashed on those rocks he could die. God, he was not prepared to face death.

He forgot about the friends behind him and thought of the people he loved most, Mum, Blake, Michael, even Dad. He longed to see their faces, hear their voices. Strange, buried memories came to mind. He had teased Mikey as a toddler by hiding his favourite teddy bear. He had broken a window with his cricket ball and blamed Blake. He had never admitted his guilt for either of those but if he got off the flying fox alive, he surely would.

Suddenly the unthinkable happened and Sean watched with horror. The cable three feet in front of him snapped. Still gripping the handlebars of the flying fox, he plummeted down and pelted with full force onto the rocks. All of the air exploded from Sean, and something deep in his body snapped. Hot, sharp pain seeped through him. Sean looked at his fingers, still curled tightly around the handlebars of the flying fox. He blinked at a startled coppery lizard on a rock three inches from his nose.

He closed his eyes and felt deep, intense thankfulness. It was all over and God had heard him. He had no further to fall, and he was still alive. Then another wave of grinding pain surged up from his midriff and made him dizzy. He released the handlebars at last. He heard the metal clink on the rock beside him and a whirlpool of black and grey sickness claimed him.

Blake was helping Michael with his homework when Mum went to answer the phone. He was trying to explain an easy way to remember the nine times tables but Mikey could not grasp it. Blake talked himself blue in the face trying to make it sink in.

"If you just remember that ten nines are ninety, then it follows that ninety nine must..." His voice trailed off. His mother stood in the doorway, white as chalk. Blake leaped up to support her, because she looked ready to crumble. He caught Rowena beneath the elbow and eased her onto the sofa. She gripped his wrist with surprising strength. Her pressure burned his skin but Blake barely noticed.

"Sean's been hurt!" she gasped. "He fell onto some rocks from a flying fox. They're taking him to hospital. Oh God." She buried her face on Blake's shoulder and he felt her tears trickle down his neck.

Michael howled on the other side of him. "Is Sean hurt badly? Is he gonna die?"

Blake wanted to burst into tears too but he couldn't. Not yet. Somebody had to keep his head. "I'll drive you to the hospital, Mum. I'll leave a note for Dad." His voice was steady but he felt sick to the stomach, as if he had wolfed down a meal too fast. He had often felt the same way as a little boy on the way to school, frightened to face the class bullies.

"We'll leave you next door with Mrs Lester," Rowena told Michael.

"No! I want to see Sean too!"

"You can't!" she snapped. Rowena knew her nine-year-old would prattle non-stop, demanding to know what was happening. She could not handle that now. Michael was terribly upset, but she had to close her mind to him. All her energy was focused on Sean. She had only enough room in her heart to worry about one son at a time.

Blake squeezed his brother's shoulder. "We won't be able to see Sean yet. I'll phone you as soon as we hear how he is," he promised huskily.

Blake and Rowena drove to the hospital alone, and he kept his arm around her shoulders as he led her to the right ward. Rowena could not speak to a soul. She sobbed quietly. They found a doctor who explained that Sean had done some spinal damage. He could not say how serious it was until the operation was over. He assured them that Sean's life was probably not in danger and Blake let go of his mother for long enough to phone Michael and tell him that much.

A few hours passed while they sat in the waiting room. Blake brought Rowena a hot cup of coffee and held her hand. Eventually Gerry shuffled towards them, with a bright red nose. Blake's stomach instantly knotted with tension. They could do without Dad's mindless drivel.

"What's happened to Sean? What's he done? I told him to be

careful and now he's done something stupid!" Gerry's voice boomed like a megaphone and heads swivelled to look at him.

Rowena broke down again when her husband appeared, and Blake said, "Dad, we don't know how bad he is yet. They're still operating." The tears that he had held back for hours were dangerously close to the surface.

Gerry strode across the floor. "I want to see him. Where have they got him? I have to talk to him."

Blake grabbed his arm. "Dad, they're operating. You can't barge in to see Sean. Don't be stupid."

Gerry was furious. "Keep your hands off me, wimp. It should have been you in there, not him. You don't have a great career to start."

"Well what's most important to you? Sean or his career?" Blake shot back. He knew it was a mistake to bait Dad when he was drunk so what happened next was partly his fault.

Gerry snatched his shoulders and shook him. "That's enough from you, you pathetic loser. I'm fed up with your abusive mouth. Sean's twice the man you are. If he dies, it will be all your fault." He did not care how absurd his claim was. Gerry needed a scapegoat to load his grief and confusion on.

Two burly orderlies came to Blake's rescue and hoisted Gerry off to some other room to dry out. The waiting room was silent again, and Blake stared at the floor. The tears that he had held back for so long streamed down his cheeks and he wiped them away with his hands. If he had not been far too bitterly humiliated to look up, he would have seen that some of the glances cast his way were sympathetic.

Angela Powell was on duty when the new patient was brought into hospital. She assisted the emergency team of surgeons who worked on him. He was a blonde lad of about her own age, or perhaps a few years younger. It was hard to tell because his face was contorted with pain, and although he clamped down upon his ashen bottom lip with his teeth, he could not hold in his hoarse cries of agony.

Angela's heart sank as she heard his injuries described. She had nursing experience enough to know that this type of accident was often very serious. She gauged from the tones of the doctors' voices that Sean Quinlan was in a bad way.

They snipped away his jeans and T-shirt and shaved him all over. Angela steeled herself to do her part of sponging the grimy smears away from his face and body, although the patient's moans intensified. He squeezed his eyelids shut but she saw the tears force their way out from between them. Angela set her own jaw and battled with the usual waves of heartache and sympathy that threatened to swamp her. Sean Quinlan's arrival helped to reinforce the decision she had just made.

Earlier that week, she had quit work with two months notice. She saw so much pain and sickness in the hospital that she would cry at the drop of a hat. She never got used to it. Her colleagues could detach their minds from their work but Angela found it impossible. Her health suffered and sometimes she had to force herself out of bed in the mornings.

She had no doubt that nursing was her ideal career. God had planted the drive to nurture and heal deep inside her heart years ago. Working in the hospital had been a big mistake but Angela chalked it up as a rich learning experience. Now she felt the Lord gently prodding her to seek work as a private nurse. She had a caring heart and longed for a deeper relationship with one patient instead of brief, harrowing encounters with many. Angela was an outgoing and sociable girl but had nobody to call her own. Her parents had died in a car accident and all her other relatives lived in England. Angela did not really need her hospital employment for the money she earned. When her parents died, she had received a comfortable inheritance. She wanted to nurse for the love of it. She had no idea what lay ahead of her but she would let God direct her path, as He always had.

Angela looked at Sean Quinlan's broken frame again. He had the physique and muscle tone of an athlete. Now Dr Forbes poked his arms gently with a sharp prod. "Can you feel that, son?"

Sean winced, and his eyes flew open, bright with hope. "Yes, I feel it," he cried.

The doctor directed the point further down Sean's body. When it reached waist level, Angela saw that Sean's face registered nothing. She bit her lip and tried not to let the tide of pity drag her under. "Did you feel that?" asked the doctor.

Sean gulped. "No. No, I didn't." All the way down his thighs to his toes, he felt nothing. Dr Forbes straightened, and Angela read the meaning behind the grim line of his mouth. Her heart began to palpitate with something like claustrophobia. She would be released when Sean was wheeled to theatre, but she could not just walk to the cafeteria and forget about him. She would be unable to swallow a thing.

"We'll operate on your spine, Sean," Dr Forbes said. "Tell me what you've eaten within the last six or seven hours."

Sean slowly described the barbecue he had enjoyed with his friends prior to the accident. He nervously moistened his lips and ventured, "Can you tell me how soon I can expect to get better? I have to play football next season."

The doctor sighed. "I think you can forget about football. For the moment, at least, and probably for a long time to come." Even blunt Dr Forbes could not bring himself to tell Sean that he might never walk again. "I can't tell how serious your injuries are until we've looked at your spine."

Sean's face crumpled again and his shoulders shook. He bit his lip and nodded with resignation. His hazel eyes moved from one face to another, and Angela bunched her hands tightly in the folds of her skirt. He was trying to grasp what he had been told, lying on his back circled by strangers, alone and overwhelmed.

"Do my family know what happened?" he asked huskily at last.

"Your family has been informed. They're on their way. They might be here already. You can see them after your surgery." The medical staff had to stay kind but detached or they would go crazy with the grief of strangers.

As Sean was wheeled away, Angela took her last glimpse at the back of his head and then she was free to leave. She leaned against a wall in the corridor and drew deep, fresh breaths. In a few hours her working day would be over. Tomorrow she would learn the outcome of Sean Quinlan's surgery. But already she battled with a sinking sensation, for she guessed what it would be.

"Lord, please comfort his heart," she breathed. Angela made a habit of praying quick prayers for her patients. "Nobody can do it but you. I know nothing about Sean Quinlan, but he needs you. Only you know the full extent of his injuries. You can work miracles. I pray that he will regain the full use of his legs and be able to play football again. But whatever the outcome of the surgery, please keep your hand on Sean's life."

Chapter Nine

"Claire, I'm over here!"

Rachel's bright voice carried through the train station. Claire had not seen her vivacious cousin for over a year. Rachel bounced over to relieve Claire of one of her cases and then hugged her fondly. "The car is this way. The others are waiting for us at home."

Claire was tired after sitting up all night in the Overland Express and stared wearily at the familiar, crowded roads of Melbourne as they crawled through. Just over a year ago, she had been so excited to leave teeming, metropolitan Melbourne to live in the Adelaide Hills. Now here she was, back where she started. It was like a bad dream.

When she had demanded to leave her parents, it still did not mean she could make her own choice. She had just turned seventeen and had nowhere to go. Kate and William arranged for her to stay with William's sister, Tessa, and her family. Kate hoped the youthful spirits of Claire's cousins would rub off on her and cheer her up. Apart from Rachel and her brother Steven, Auntie Tessa had six-month-old twins. They were the children of her new de-facto husband, Russell Timms. Auntie Tessa had not seen Uncle Henry since he'd left her three years ago.

Rachel chattered incessantly as they drove. "I'm glad you came. I'm sorry to hear about your family situation. Uncle William told us over the phone. He sounded so sad."

Claire instantly felt torn by guilt again. "I'm glad you can have me." She felt responsible for the upheaval with her parents. She never stopped wondering if being raped had been partly her fault, or whether she had treated her mother and father badly by demanding to leave. *Perhaps Dad was right, and I should have shoved the incident behind me long ago. Dragging out the pain does nobody any good.*

"Your family would have to be in dire straits to be worse than ours." Rachel bitterly described how she and Steven hated their mother's new boyfriend, and could not accept him as a stepfather. "And Steven won't talk to Dad, for walking out on us and the babies cry day and night. Sometimes I don't know if I'm coming or going."

"Perhaps you don't really have room for another person to stay," Claire ventured slowly. She might be making things worse for both families by refusing to stay with her parents. It sounded as if her Auntie Tessa had enough on her plate without a troubled niece thrusting her way onto the scene.

"No, I wanted you to come," said Rachel. "I insisted. I wanted to help you out."

Claire forced a smile of thanks for her cousin but wondered if Auntie Tessa and Russell wanted her to stay equally as much. She felt lonely and burdensome.

They arrived at Auntie Tessa's small timber-frame home in the Dandenongs and a din hit their eardrums the moment they left the car. A stereo thrashed out some heavy driving sounds and Auntie Tessa stood to meet them with two screaming babies, one on each hip. Her eyes were heavy and her hair was frizzled and unkempt. She gave her niece's cheek a soft peck and said, "Welcome, Claire."

Cousin Steven glanced up from his study at the kitchen table, with law textbooks and loose sheets of notepaper strewn around him for a radius of two metres. It was he who had the stereo blaring near his ear. "Hi Claire," he mumbled, and quickly lowered his gaze to his work again to hide his flushed face.

Claire felt her own cheeks burn. She guessed that Steven felt awkward because he knew she had been raped. Her parents must have told Auntie Tessa the whole sordid story and now her secret was an open book for the whole family. She had been raped and had not recovered. She wanted to bury her face beneath a cushion and never re-appear.

Piles of mess lay everywhere, like islands in a sea of carpet. Nappies and squeaky toys, text books and shopping bags, shoes, belts, magazines and dirty plates. Claire wished she had not come. There was no room for her and nobody really wanted her there. It was all her own fault, for insisting that she leave home.

"I've been trying to cook a special meal to welcome Claire, and the sauce is burning but the babies won't belt up," Tessa told Rachel. "And your lazy brother won't lift a finger to help."

"I have to finish this assignment by Monday," Steven scowled defensively.

"Rachel, will you give it a stir?"

Rachel clicked her tongue moodily and moved to the stove. "When will Russell be home?" she grumbled, with narrowed eyes.

"When he's finished fishing," Tessa snapped. She was on her knees changing baby Ryan's nappy while Cindy wailed on the floor.

"Can I help?" Claire asked tentatively, and stooped to lift the baby girl. Cindy filled her lungs and screeched louder. Claire did not know what to do.

Tessa jerked her chin to indicate a bouncinette in the corner, covered with books. "Put her in there. You don't have to help on your first day here." She could not smile because she held a safety pin between her teeth. "Relax, while you can. We'll find plenty for you to do in the morning." She spoke as if she were half joking.

Claire placed Cindy down to remove the books and then wriggled the baby into the bouncinette. It made no difference to the noise level.

"Go and unpack if you like. You'll be sharing with Rachel, through there." Tessa gave another nod of her head in the direction of the bedrooms.

Claire found Rachel's bedroom in a bigger mess than the lounge-room. Clothes, make-up, books and jewellery were piled on the unmade bed and trailed across the floor. One corner had been swept free of clutter to make room for a small stretcher bed and Claire eased her two cases onto it.

She opened the wardrobe door a crack and Rachel's clothes bulged out of it. Claire sank down beside her baggage. It was all very well for Auntie Tessa to say unpack, but she could not cram one thing into the wardrobe. There was obviously no extra room in the small house for a boarder. Claire's head spun. She wished Tessa had told her mum and dad straight out.

Quarrelsome voices reached her from the living area. "Mum, Russell never pulls his weight with Ryan and Cindy and they're his babies too," Rachel said.

"Steven, turn that noise down!" Tessa bellowed.

"I have to keep it loud because the babies won't shut up, and I'm trying to study."

Claire found herself trembling. She had jumped from the frying pan into the fire. At least her own home was quiet and orderly, with plenty of breathing space. She drew a breath and stashed her cases beneath the stretcher bed. She would have to live out of them as they were. She even forced a faint smile. She had made her own bed and now she had to lie in it.

———————

Blake sat on the sand-hills overlooking Brighton beach, sobbing. He had cried gallons since they learned the extent of Sean's plight. He cried even more than his mother and Michael, though he usually did it in private.

Sean had severed the fourth and fifth vertebrae in his thoracic spinal column. It would curtail the mobility in his chest and legs permanently. He was a paraplegic. Gerry had screamed at the doctors, demanding that they do something, but the surgeon sadly shook his head. Sean was undergoing physiotherapy and rehabilitation, but what was the use? Nothing would help him to walk again. When he left hospital, he would be confined to a wheelchair forevermore.

In many ways, Blake had been closer to Sean than the rest of the family because of their similar ages. His memories of a lifetime with Sean crowded his head with pain but he could not stop them. He squeezed his sore eyes shut to avoid the white glare on the sand, and remembered jogging along beaches like this during holidays while Sean's feet cut in the sand ahead of him, strong and steady like machinery. Blake's legs always tired first until he had to lag behind, but Sean jogged on until he became a distant blur.

He remembered Sean's arm reaching down to haul him higher into the branches of the old plane tree to escape from Dad. Sean's legs clamped tightly around the thick boughs, and he showed Blake some hair-raising, hanging acrobatics which Blake never dared to copy. They used to skateboard down their steep driveway together and Sean practiced his fancy stunts until he had them to perfection.

In later years, Sean set off for his evening jog every night he did not have football training. It had become a ritual with him. When he played a game of football, he would leap high for the ball, giving himself completely to the game while Blake sat watching with pride in the spectator's stand.

Blake buried his face in his folded arms and his shoulders shook. Sean would never recover from such a blow, ever. Sport and fitness had been his whole life. Blake grieved for his brother as if he were actually dead and not just injured, for without his power of motion, Sean might as well be dead. His physical prowess had defined his personality. Without it, he would wither by slow degrees. Blake dreaded Sean's heartache and loss of dignity. The pain crowded in on his chest so he could hardly breathe.

Self-reproach struck him like a blow. He thought of his moments of jealousy, when Sean outclassed him in whatever contest they attempted. *It isn't fair. Sean doesn't deserve this. He never did anything to hurt anybody. I'm the one who raped Claire Parker. If anyone deserves not to walk, it ought to be me.*

He was relieved that he had escaped with nothing but a few bruises from Claire's father, but Blake still baulked at the injustice of getting away with what he had done. He must have ruined Claire's life and he should have suffered more. Instead, he had found a new job and carried on as before. He was working for the Social Security Department. He had sat a Public Service exam expecting to fail dismally, but the questions were amazingly easy. Now he set off to work in a neat shirt and tie instead of his old ragged factory clothes, but that was the main difference. The work was still dead boring. His hands were still covered with calluses and ink stains from sorting jam-packed files and stuffing envelopes. Still, at least he was earning his board.

Blake kept aloof from his fellow workers, because social mingling did not come easily to him as it did to Sean. Sean made dozens of friends with his smiling face and outgoing disposition, but Blake could not overcome his natural reserve, no matter how hard he tried. He had made only one friend, a young Italian named Joseph Giordano. The others shunned Joseph because of his difficulty speaking English and Blake was drawn to him. Their language barrier did not stop them chatting fairly well together over lunch each day. Joseph understood English far better than he could speak it.

Joseph invited Blake to some free lectures on world current affairs, and Blake was willing to attend. He liked to learn about history being unfolded, hoping it would help him to determine the meaning of life. Instead, he came away feeling confused and upset by what he heard.

Blake let sand trickle between his fingers. Nothing made sense to him. All over the world, people were starving or at war, and closer to home, Sean, the best fellow to be found, was crippled for life. He never even had his chance to play proper league football. He was struck down at the outset of a promising career.

Blake's fury against God surged up, as he knew all along it inevitably would. He could no longer sit still. He scrambled to his feet and flung rocks bitterly towards the surf.

You aren't fair. Why did it have to be Sean? If you created the Universe, why don't you keep it in better shape? Why am I standing here talking to you, when you probably don't even exist? If you were totally good and totally powerful, you'd surely do something to help people.

Blake strode along the foreshore from Brighton to Glenelg with his hands wedged into the pockets of his jeans. He breathed in a great lungful of salty air and watched the white, frothy caps of the waves. They were so beautiful, he felt more confused than ever. If God did not exist, why was creation so lovely? He shook his head, feeling tired to his very bones. He could no longer think straight. He would go to visit Sean. Blake was convinced that sociable Sean must always need company and hate to be alone.

———

Sean lay awake in the early hours of the morning, trying to wriggle his toes for the millionth time. His feet just poked up beneath his sheets like a stiff pair of bookends. He could not even tell if they were warm or cold. Last night, his mother had remarked, "Your feet are chilly," and carefully covered them with the blankets, but she needn't have bothered. Cold feet meant nothing to Sean.

At first, he had hoped for a miracle but he had been incarcerated in hospital for so long, he supposed the doctors were right. He had damaged something in his spine and nothing could bring back his leg movement.

Sean's chest heaved and fell angrily. The surgeon's description of his spinal damage had never sunk in. Even his mum and dad did not understand it. Only Blake could grasp the detailed explanations and diagrams. He tried to explain it slowly to Sean later, but Sean shook his head and gave up trying to follow. He had never been able to keep up with Blake's ramblings, anyway. The only thing he understood was that he would never walk again.

People said he was bearing up well. Rowena was proud of the way he handled the mind-numbing repetition of sponge baths, three daily meals, hours of television, physiotherapy and rehabilitation sessions that did no good. No fresh air, no changing scenery, no chance to run. The list was endless.

His family were supposed to watch his exercise regimes so they could look after him when he went home, but Mum was too easily distraught and Dad was too impatient to take it in. Nobody knew how frustrated Sean felt. He clenched his teeth and longed to shake his parents or rattle their heads together. He wanted to scream, "Concentrate, for Pete's sake, so I can get out of this joint!" Blake was quick on the uptake, but that was not good enough. They told Sean his brother could not be expected to be always on hand to take care of his needs. He needed a competent caregiver always nearby.

Nobody knew how close Sean came to flying off the handle but he set his jaw and seethed inside. He was a man. At least, he used to be a man before he became a useless slab of meat. He had to keep a brave face because his family was already devastated by his accident. He did not wish to make them feel any worse. His plight was nobody's fault but his own.

Being trapped inside a powerless body with his thoughts was living hell. Sean had always shied away from thoughts and chose action, but now there were nothing but torturous thoughts to fill his time. The bitterest one of all was what a rash and stupid fool he had been.

The flying fox accident would never have happened if only he had used a little common sense. If only he had thought to check the strength of the cable before flying recklessly out. If only he hadn't been so anxious to show off. If only he could turn back time and return to the moment when he had just finished eating his barbecue lunch. It was too late. He could not turn back.

Sean wanted to throw something but there was nothing nearby but his pillow. He gritted his teeth and flung that. It hit the wall with a soft thud, but the futile action didn't help him to let off steam. All he had done was leave himself even more helpless, now with no pillow. Sean lifted the stark white sleeve of his hospital gown and wept bitterly.

He let himself go, because it was 3.30am with nobody to disturb him. He drained himself of the supply of tears he had dammed up for hours, but no doubt there would be more the following night. He did not know that nurse Angela Powell waited outside the door of his private ward with her fists bunched against her mouth.

She longed to zoom straight to his side but hesitated. He thought he was alone, and she did not wish to make him feel ashamed. She wanted to preserve his sense of manhood and dignity. She decided to wait until his storm of tears was spent and then go to him. Angela bowed her head and returned to the nurse's station.

She had grown to know Sean well as she cared for his needs. She admired him more with each passing day. He always behaved with stoic fortitude around others and treated Angela herself in a courteous manner. While she attended to his charts or helped him through his muscle exercises, she tried to get him talking about himself to cheer him up. It seemed his life revolved around football. As he spoke freely of his training sessions and the friends on his team, she knew he was still living in denial. He was bottling up his grief as he tried to come to terms with his accident, and Angela knew he would have to snap sometime. She wondered who would be around to help him pick up the pieces.

Sean was very handsome. She had not noticed at first because he looked terrible the first day she saw him. He scrubbed up well, that was for sure. His lips were full, his mouth wide and generously proportioned. When he smiled happily and spontaneously Angela noticed and was moved to the point that she thought he must have been truly something before his accident. Sometimes she detected a flash of warmth deep in his hazel eyes, in the rare moments when she managed to interest him in something outside of his accident. *What a sight he must have been on the football field! What a waste.*

She sternly rebuked herself for thinking in that manner. God had other plans for Sean. Nothing that He ever allowed in a person's life had to be a waste. Angela wondered if Sean was a Christian. He never alluded to God in any of their conversations so she guessed he probably wasn't. How she wished she could help to change that. If anybody needed to understand the depth of God's love, Sean did. Angela would be leaving the hospital soon and wouldn't have time to help Sean. She wished she could. She liked him very much.

She pushed her record book aside and stood up, certain that she'd given him enough time to weep himself out. As she walked back to his ward, she decided there was only one thing she could do to help Sean Quinlan. Prayer, and plenty of it.

———

Though Sean was wrung out and exhausted, he still could not sleep. He stared up at the ceiling and heard Angela's footsteps in the corridor. Hers were lighter and quicker than those of the other nurses. He had weeks behind him to learn such things. He was surprised to feel a strange anticipation stir up from the depths of his heart.

Angela Powell was unique. She was not predictable like the others, and his only entertainment was wondering what she would come up with next. She had already challenged him to a crossword competition, had a special cake delivered to him, bought him some football magazines and told him most of her own life story. He appreciated her efforts to cheer him.

Still, after his unmanly flood of tears he did not trust himself to speak. He closed his eyes and pretended to be asleep. He really liked Angela. If he still had his legs, he might have done more than like her secretly. Sean had always been confident about approaching girls because they never left him in doubt of their attraction to him. But those days were finished.

He knew Angela liked him too. She had complimented him on his fine muscle tone, and fitness. "You've looked after yourself very well, Sean," she said once. "You'll recover much quicker than other trauma patients I've seen." Her vivid, kind green eyes had smiled into his, set off by the cute map of light freckles across the bridge of her nose.

She treated him like a friend instead of a patient. Sometimes instead of leaving work, she came to visit with him. He knew that she was twenty-two years old, two years older than he was. She still bore the charming traces of a British accent. Her parents died several years ago and she had nobody. Sean heard how she had chosen nursing for her career because she wanted to help people, and how her only boyfriend had walked out on her for another girl.

That fellow must have been nuts to leave her. Angela is so attractive. Sean had always fancied blonde women, although he had been drawn to the noisy, giggly, empty-headed ones. Not smart, capable, strong girls like Angela Powell. In fact, Sean had never realised there were capable, strong girls like Angela.

He waited in the dark while she stood beside his bed. She stretched out a soft hand and stroked the hair that had begun to grow back over his forehead. Sean felt another surge of warmth from deep within his body which staggered him. It proved he was still at least half a man after all.

Angela sat quietly in the chair beside him, and she was so close that he felt her soft breath on his hand. Then she started to whisper a prayer.

"Lord Jesus, please help Sean to know that you still have a wonderful plan for his life. He's still so young. He still has his whole life ahead of him. I want him to understand that you can bring good out of his paralysis because you can bring good out of every situation."

Sean felt his ears begin to burn but Angela could not see them in the darkness. He was shocked by what she had said. Her voice was so sincere; he knew she meant every word she spoke. She thought he was asleep, so she had no reason to say empty platitudes which she did not really mean. She spoke as if she knew God in some special way.

Finally, she stood and briefly touched the top of his head. The gesture felt personal, somehow. His rush of adrenalin was almost too great to bear. Surely she must be violating every nurse-patient relationship rule, and tomorrow she would return to her normal self again. When she tiptoed out, he finally flickered his lashes and stared straight ahead of him. He drew a deep breath, flexed his fingers, and even found himself smiling wanly. At least she had given him plenty to think about now, besides his own misery.

Chapter Ten

Angela waited for Sean's brother. She knew Sean expected him, and she had something to say to him first. She had only two days left to work so this might be her last chance to catch him alone. Sean's brother was no good for his morale. He made Sean miserable without even trying, and Angela wished he would not come so often.

Sean's defeatist parents depressed him too but Angela had no heart to rebuke them, as she suspected they were too old and set in their ways to change. The little brother was no problem. He was chatty and cute, like a small parrot with tousled feathers, and her heart went out to him. When she looked at Michael, she saw how Sean must have looked as a child. *The biggest pain in the neck is the eighteen year old, who ought to have enough sense to know that his attitude hurts his brother,* Angela thought crossly.

Whenever Blake visited, he never tried to hide the fact that he was heartbroken by Sean's accident. He always looked pale and washed-out, as if he had just come from crying bitterly. He could not bear to sit still beside Sean's bed, but paced the floor while Sean watched him with undisguised envy, hating his own immobility. Sometimes Sean found himself in the position of trying to placate his brother instead of vice versa. All this infuriated Angela.

What she objected to most were the unhealthy seeds of doubt against God's goodness which Sean's brother planted into his mind, without even thinking. "It should have been me, instead of you. What sort of God would let this happen to you? If God could sit back and allow this, that's the finish of Him and me."

The more Angela dwelled on it, the crosser she became. She was sure she would not be able to find a more dismal, morbid youth.

At last he came striding down the corridor. She darted out of the nurse's station to detain him and seized his wrist as he breezed past. "Excuse me, Blake, isn't it?"

He halted with surprise, and nodded.

"Could I have a word with you, through here?" She led him back to the station and turned to find him blinking with alarm.

"Is Sean OK?" he rasped.

"Yes, he's fine," she assured him, and wondered how to begin. She had not planned a tactful way of making her point. As usual, she would have to plunge in, regardless. The worst he could do was tell her to mind her business but she would reply that her patient was her business.

"I just wanted to tell you that you aren't doing Sean any good by your negative attitude. Why don't you try to cheer him up instead of bombarding him with gloom? Will you stop telling him that God doesn't care for him?" She wondered whether she had offended Blake, but did not really care. Sean was the important one.

Blake flickered his eyelashes down, thoroughly contrite. "I didn't realise I was so bad. You're right! I should be more sensitive. I never meant to make him unhappy." He felt horrified to think that he deserved such a reproof. "I'm sorry. From now on, I'll keep my opinion about God to myself." He turned to leave, hating himself more with each step he took.

His response was all she had hoped for, but Angela suddenly realised it was not enough. "Blake, it isn't God's fault that Sean launched out on a faulty cable."

He turned again and his gaze fell on the thick, patchwork covered Bible on the desk behind her. In a flash, Blake realised that Angela was the nurse Sean had spoken of, the young and pretty blonde who was also a Christian. The sight of her Bible caused a faint flicker of hope to rise from somewhere deep inside of him. This girl might know something about God that he didn't. If so, he earnestly wished he could learn.

"But He's supposed to heal people," he heard himself reply. "He has the power to heal broken bodies but He won't heal Sean. What's the point of believing in a God who heals, if He won't heal?" He could hardly believe he had launched into a theological discussion with a girl he barely knew.

Angela did not detect Blake's desperate, unspoken plea to learn more. She looked at his tense jaw, his probing brown eyes, and her own lips tightened. She believed she had him sized up. She had seen his type before. He was a cocky, profane young cynic who thought he was smart to knock the faith of others. If he wanted a dispute, she was more than happy to oblige.

"I'm not God. Why do you ask me?" She was unaware of the defensive edge in her voice. "Nobody can know God's mind. If we could explain His actions or place Him in a box, He wouldn't be much of a God. His ways and purposes are far beyond ours." Her green eyes flashed with each word she uttered.

Blake winced at her passionate energy and his heart sank. He would not learn much from her. She must be one of those over-zealous fanatics with her mind set so rigidly on what she was taught that she could not tolerate a word of honest doubt.

He straightened to his full height of six feet, cast her a sad smile and shrugged. "Well in my opinion, if He wants to keep Himself so inaccessible and mysterious, He's not much of a friendly God. Especially if He's happy to let a healthy athlete stay paralysed." He hardly knew why he kept on. Let her keep her rosy, fatalistic little philosophy. He had come to visit his brother. He squared his shoulders and turned to leave again.

Angela felt summarily dismissed. It was not supposed to be that way. He had no right to look down at her with that disdainful grin as if she were spouting baby talk. She was the one who had taken him aside. She was older than he was, she had years of tertiary study behind her and she was a registered nurse. Besides, she was in the right and did not want him to have the last word.

"Wait! Who says that being able to use your legs is everything, anyway? I can understand why Sean is broken-hearted not to be able to play football, but there's far more to life. He could have been a quadriplegic. He still has his arms, and his mind. He could have died. He still has his life."

The deep brown eyes of the gloomy youth raked her sadly, as if she were still speaking fairy tales. He slowly shook his head. "Football was his life. Now he can't even move. It'll kill him. He's lost everything of any value to him."

"Well if you really believe that, then I pity you more than I pity Sean." With that, she swept past him. Angela held her chin high but her spirits ebbed down to her shoes. She did her rounds feeling riled and upset by the encounter. She had let him ruffle her feathers. Instead of displaying God's love to Sean's brother, she had shown herself to be petulant and snappish while he stayed cool and distant.

Most aggravating of all, she suspected that Blake Quinlan found her simple and narrow-minded. Although she had had the last word, she did not feel victorious. She suspected that her crusade made such little impact on her adversary that he did not even care that she had won. Angela found that hard to swallow.

———

Claire covertly watched Rachel and her boyfriend, Peter, during the interval of the folk dancing evening. Peter was a natural gentleman. He pulled out Rachel's chair for her and waited until she was seated before he took one himself. Rachel's mouth moved fast, chattering non-stop as usual. Claire wondered whether Rachel appreciated Peter or whether she took his scrupulous attention for granted. They had been together for over two years.

Claire watched Peter intently to see if she could detect a chink in his armour. She could not. His eyes glowed as he stared intently into Rachel's face with a smile on his lips, taking in her every word. He was quite handsome, with smooth shaven, regular features, and a crop of thick brown hair.

Claire's own world began to slowly brighten, as if a dark cloud had drifted away. At last she had seen a young man she could admire after a terrible year of mistrusting them all. Peter Lennox was living proof that not all men were like Blake Quinlan. Perhaps there might be a man like Peter for her, even yet. Her heart stirred with hope and anticipation for the first time since she was raped.

Mingled with this was the usual envy of Rachel she had battled since her arrival. Her cousin had everything a girl could long for. She attended university, with the prospect of a good career ahead of her, and had the love of an affectionate boyfriend. Claire sighed. It made her feel happy in some perverse way, to see things work out for Rachel. Fairy tales came true sometimes, even if not for her.

When Pete leaned across to kiss Rachel, Claire flushed and stopped watching them. She looked around the dance hall instead. She was enjoying the evening of folk dancing. It was more like an aerobic workout than a dance and she did not have the threat of needing a partner, for they were all circle dances. She rotated briefly from one young man to another. Claire could handle that. Her mother would be pleased to hear how she was finally emerging from her cocoon of pain. Only once that evening had she reflected that she would have been nursing a helpless, warm little baby if things had been different.

She did feel guilty for tagging along with Rachel and Peter, as if she were a child to be mollycoddled, but if Peter resented her presence he was polite enough not to let it show. Pete was willing to go along with whatever Rachel asked of him.

"Hello, can I sit here?"

Claire started. She had been so pre-occupied, she did not see the round-faced, stout young man approach her. She remembered him from the dance-floor. He had warm, moist hands.

"Yes, it's not taken," she said uneasily.

He sat down and dragged his chair closer to hers until his knees were a mere inch away from hers. Claire's skin began to prickle ominously and she flickered her gaze to her toes. When she looked up again, she saw that he still gazed steadily at her face. A jolt of alarm shot through her.

"My name is Robert," he announced.

"I'm ... Claire," she mumbled.

"You're really pretty, Claire," he breathed softly.

Although she had never met him before, there was something disturbingly familiar about the expression in his eyes. Claire felt sick as it dawned on her. Blake Quinlan had watched her with the same intense, admiring scrutiny, when he thought she was unaware. Claire swallowed against the sour lump in her throat and rose to her feet. She could not possibly stay beside him.

"I'm thirsty. I need a drink," she stammered. She felt dizzy and hot.

Robert rose too, and pushed her shoulder firmly back into her seat. "Please, let me get one for you." He was off before she could protest. Claire drew a deep breath and chewed the inside of her lip, trying to figure out what she should do when he returned.

Robert returned with a glass of lemonade and Claire moistened her dry lips with a sip. He was so close, she could see that his hair was receding rapidly, and he combed the light coloured wisps over the top of his head to conceal the fact. His breath smelled like the pretzels he had been eating and she did not find him at all appealing.

"You're a good dancer," he smiled.

"Thanks." She hoped the brevity of her reply would help him to lose interest in her.

"You're Rachel's cousin, aren't you?" he persisted.

Claire nodded.

"I know all of Rachel's family. I go to uni with Steven." He smiled confidently and said, "Would you like to come to the pictures with me?"

"No thanks," she said instantly. Claire hoped she could escape without offending him. She had offended Blake Quinlan, and that had been the biggest mistake of her life. "I'm not looking for anybody to date, just now," she added politely.

"Why not?" chirped a bright voice behind her shoulder. "Give it a go, Claire. It'll be good for you. Robert's a nice guy." There stood Rachel, with Peter by her side.

Claire began to feel dangerously hedged in by their three smiling faces. The pulse in her neck raced and as she spoke, she searched for a way to escape. "No, I'm just not interested." She hoped they would not persist or she might burst into tears. If Rachel's sole aim was to set her up with a fellow, they were all wasting their time.

By now, Robert shuffled with embarrassment. "She doesn't have to, Rach."

"She should!" Rachel said sharply. "She needs to have some fun. Take a risk, Claire. You came to stay with us so that we could help push you out. Robert is a really nice guy. I can vouch for that. He won't hurt you like that other creep did."

Claire's face flamed furiously. Rachel had a mouth like a flapping tent. She might as well broadcast to anybody who was interested that Claire had been raped. Claire glared at Rachel for putting her in such an awkward position. "No!" she repeated, behind clenched teeth.

Rachel tightened her lips and stared reproachfully back at her. Then she turned to Robert, with an apologetic shake of the head. "Give her another few weeks. She's had a rough time. It's nothing personal, is it Claire?"

Claire could take no more. "Mind your business. I'll make my own decisions." The burning tears she had held back gushed down her cheeks like quicksilver. She groped for a hanky, ashamed of herself for grossly over-reacting, but she could not help it. Poor Robert backed away, thoroughly regretful for ever having looked her way.

"I'm going over there," Claire said tersely, and brushed past Rachel. She retreated to the opposite wall and leaned against it, trying to control her jerky breaths. Every smothered gasp hurt her chest like a tight band. So much for enjoying an evening out. She was nothing but a dopey misfit who let her Melbourne relatives down as well as her own parents. She had made a spectacle of herself and now she was still clutching the glass of lemonade Robert had brought her, and it had overflowed and wet her toes.

There was no way she could possibly take part in the dancing when it started again. She longed to march out of the building and find her own way home, but her stomach churned at the foolhardiness of it. That was what she had done on the disastrous night with Blake Quinlan. She doubted if Robert would follow her in a rage and assault her, but the possibility made her skin crawl. She preferred to wait safely in the crowd, looking like a sook, until Rachel and Peter were ready to go. She guessed she would be unpopular with them on the way home.

Somebody gently cleared his throat and she looked through a sheen of tears to find Peter standing there with a regretful smile. "Hey Claire, I agree with what you told Rachel," he said softly. "I'm sorry about all that happened back there. She can be quite... overbearing, but I know she means well." He forced a self-conscious laugh. "I s'pose that's why I love her. Anyway, please don't feel too bad. I think you were in the right and I don't blame you for what you said."

He saw that she was too overcome to make a reply and he did not expect one. Instead, he smiled again and said, "I don't really want to stay for the rest of the dancing myself. If you give me a few minutes, I'll round Rachel up and we'll get going." He turned on his heel and left.

Claire blinked after him, feeling pleasantly surprised. It was uplifting to know that somebody did not disapprove of her. After all that had happened, she was astonished to find herself feeling slightly better.

Sean leaned against his pillows and listened to the conversation being bandied back and forth across his bed. Angela sat on one side and his mother and brothers sat on the other. Dad rarely came to see him, anymore. The pub suited him more than the hospital, and he seemed set to give Sean up as a lost cause now that he could not walk. Sean quickly pushed thoughts of his father aside, or he might shed some more bitter tears, in front of the others.

At least Angela came to see him regularly. This evening, she wore a slim fitting pair of black denim jeans and a red silk blouse. The colours set off her creamy complexion and snapping green eyes to perfection. Sean had been stunned when she first came to visit him in her casual clothes. Until then he had thought of her as a nurse first and foremost, instead of a person with an outside life of her own. She was even more of a knockout in her everyday clothes.

He wondered if Angela realised how pretty she was. He doubted it, because she seemed far too altruistic to bother with such superficial details. He guessed she would be shocked if she knew how he relished every curve of her neat little figure, so he kept it to himself. She pitied him for breaking his spine but probably had no idea that underneath his immobility he was still a hot-blooded male, like many others who could still walk.

Angela's eyes were kindled with the marvellous idea which had struck her at 3 o'clock one morning. The more she prayed about the notion, the more certain she felt that it was what God would have her do. *It would be perfect for everybody,* she had reassured herself. *The Quinlans need a carer for Sean when he returns home, and I have no other job prospects yet.* She was somebody Sean was used to, she knew his routine, and best of all she could keep helping him to find the love God had to offer him. Sean could be her first private job. She could stay with the Quinlan family for as long as necessary.

"Mrs. Quinlan, I'd love to take care of Sean for you," she cried.

"It doesn't matter how small your house is. I can fit anywhere. He needs a carer and I need a new job so we'll be doing each other a great favour. I'll teach you slowly, step by step, how to do his exercises with him until you understand. I know how overwhelming it is in the hospital when everybody talks at you so fast."

Sean suppressed a grin and he noticed that Blake and Michael shared the joke. Angela chattered at the rate of a firing machine gun herself. She had no idea that poor Rowena stood in as much awe of her as she did of anybody else. Mum's head was probably spinning.

"Well what do you say?" Angela stopped for a breath at last and waited confidently for Rowena to jump at her offer. After all of her prayer and planning, it hardly occurred to her that the Quinlans could refuse. She was not a person who could easily take no for an answer. Sean suspected it would be tough luck for Mum if she really hated the plan.

"I'd love you to come but we can't afford you," Rowena admitted painfully. She knew Gerry would be hopping mad if she hired a live-in nurse behind his back, despite the fact that Sean would certainly need one.

Angela tried to find a tactful way to reply that money was the last thing on her mind. If Rowena Quinlan was the proud, self-reliant type, she did not want to hurt her feelings. "I'm quite comfortably set up for money already, thanks. I've just quit work here and I'm out on a limb at the moment. I'd like to help Sean settle down while I work out what to do next. I'm sure I'll be happy with whatever we can arrange."

Rowena flushed again, and mentioned the lowest wage she knew they could spare. She and Gerry had discussed the matter during one of his rare sober moments. It was far below what live-in carers were usually paid but Rowena knew nothing about such things.

"I'll take it!" Angela cried. She saw Blake shoot her an incredulous stare across the bed. He knew she was selling herself short and probably wondered why. Perhaps he thought she had some designs on Sean. Angela was surprised to feel her cheeks flush. She squared her shoulders and gazed unwaveringly back at Blake until he looked away. Whatever he wanted to think was his business. He was probably too cynical to imagine that she would want to help just to be kind. Angela turned back to Rowena and beamed.

Sean's heart skipped a beat when he saw Angela's triumphant smile. She behaved as if slaving her fingers to the bone for him would be a privilege. He twitched his shoulders and smiled back. The plan suited him too. He was fed up with being cloistered in the hospital with its bustling noise and antiseptic smells. He supposed his father couldn't be blamed for staying away from him. He pined for his own home with his familiar belongings around him. He had not seen the inside of the house for months, ever since that morning he had packed his esky, whistling cheerfully, and set off for his barbecue.

He still wanted Angela in his life too. She made him feel brighter than anybody else could because she treated him like a man, and not like a patient. When she was not around he chafed and squirmed, at a loose end. Her chirpy greeting always touched something deep inside of him. His only grievance was that having such a lovely girl always nearby would remind him of his blasted uselessness. He was crippled for life. In the past he might have thought of developing a deeper relationship with her but it was impossible now. He wondered what Angela would think if she knew that such a thought had crossed his mind. She might be appalled.

Sean wriggled his head back into the hollow it had moulded in the pillow. He wearily closed his eyes. He'd had enough of such ridiculous regrets. He had not been interested in settling down with a girl anyway. If only he could walk, run and leap, he would not give Angela Powell a second thought. His disability was all that meant anything to him, after all. He did not care if it was Angela or the devil himself who would come to look after him

Chapter Eleven

Sean lay in bed with his arms folded, and glowered out of the window at his backyard. Though he had longed to leave the hospital, being at home seemed to cause more anguish than he had expected. In hospital he had coasted along on the waves of unreality, like a nightmare he would wake up from. At home, it struck him like a blow that he was a paraplegic for the rest of his life. All around him were traces of the old Sean who was dead and buried.

The posters of his football heroes on his wall had been tactfully removed by his mother but everything else was the same. There was the good old plane tree he had so often swung and climbed from, still strong and tall in the backyard. There were the clothes in his wardrobe, each with its own clear memory. The blue, diamond patterned T-shirt he had worn when he'd won his school hurdling competition. The pair of green board shorts he'd worn just weeks before his accident when he'd gone wind-surfing at Victor Harbor. Even the dingy factory overalls he had wriggled into so reluctantly each morning made him weep. If somebody gave him the chance to stand by a conveyer belt and sort potatoes again, he would think he was in heaven.

No doubt Mum and Angela would eventually sort out all his clothes but there were other reminders of his old self they could do nothing about. He could still see marks from his grubby fingertips on the ceiling of his bedroom, where he had so often leapt to see how high he could reach. They would remain a perpetual memorial to his first glorious twenty years.

Sean closed his eyes in pain. In his dreams he still sprinted, leaped and kicked a football, but those escapes from reality were not worth the pain of waking up again. All day long his brain teemed with bitter thoughts. How stupid he had been to launch out on that crummy flying fox. How rotten life had treated him. How he would rather be dead than live like this. How he wished he could do as Blake had almost done once, and walk into the bathroom to pilfer Mum's sleeping tablets. Only if he were able to walk in and get them, he wouldn't need them.

Sean pounded his mattress hard. He hated being so infuriatingly helpless. He still tried to keep a lid on his bitterness, but it was like a seething cauldron which had to spill over sometimes or he would he burst like an over-inflated football. *Dammit,* he still could not stop equating everything with football.

Poor Rowena bore the brunt of his flashes of temper. Her nervous incompetence used to make him feel loving and protective but now it bothered him like an itch he could not scratch away. When her trembling hands jangled his bottles of painkillers or she fumbled while tucking his sheets around his legs, he almost ground his teeth down to stumps in his frustration. Sometimes he yelled at her. He did not want to but could not seem to help himself. "Go and find Angela or Blake! Anybody who knows what they're doing!"

Then her chin would drop and she would scoot out of the door like a frightened rabbit. Sometimes Sean heard her crying softly when she thought she was alone in the lounge-room and his heart smarted with regret. Especially when she crept in to see him next time, skirting around his bed as if he were a savage wolf ready to leap at her jugular vein. Then he felt guilty as well as deeply depressed. Sean's own temper alarmed him. He had lived for twenty years not knowing his mean streak even existed and now he could not control it.

Michael irritated him with his chatter and Sean often ordered his little brother to leave almost as soon as he came in. That hurt Michael but Sean thought it far better to send him out before his patience snapped and he bellowed at him too. He even yelled at his father. Sean had always pitied his father's dreary, wasted life but now he despised him. Anybody who had never been robbed of the use of his legs ought to have made something better of himself than Dad had done. Sean had had a gutful of Gerry's maudlin tears of self-pity.

Gerry had changed. He was still a pathetic drunk, but Sean's accident seemed to have filled him with a sluggish despondency. Sean had not seen him belt his mother or the other boys since his return home, although he still abused them with his vicious tongue. He had become a deflated heap of a man. Sean's lips tightened. That was the only positive thing to have come out of his accident but if losing his legs was what it took to stop his father's rampages, it was far too high a price to pay.

One day Sean's entire football team visited to cheer him up. They filed to his bedside, filling the room with the smell of their healthy sweat. They fidgeted with their fingers, and gazed at different spots around the room. Anywhere but down at his face. They made inane remarks, like, "Hope you're feelin' better," as if he were a frail old man. Sean had longed to snap, "What do you think?" but of course he did not. That was not what they wanted to hear.

Only Simon Smith made a brave effort to joke with him, as if he were still the same old Sean. He let his eyes follow after Angela as she walked out, and gave a dreamy smirk. "Will you set me up with your nursemaid, mate? She's a knock-out."

Sean felt his hackles rise. He was surprised by the black clouds of resentment that surged up from his chest, making each breath tight. Simon thought him a useless invalid who had lost his virility when he lost his legs. *Nursemaid indeed!*

"I know she is! Do you think that just because I can't walk, there's something wrong with my eyesight?" He winced as soon as the words came out. He had meant to think them, not say them.

His friends were too embarrassed to respond. They shuffled on their feet, each waiting for the others to fill the awkward gap. It tore Sean to the heart. It was never like this before. He could sense their relief when they trooped out again, and they had not returned since. He was happy enough not to see them. He simply couldn't deal with the jealousy their visit had evoked. He had been a fitter, more talented player than any of them and it was unfair that his career was reduced to ashes while theirs could carry on.

The only person he longed to see was Angela. She still had a knack of treating him like an attractive young man instead of a cripple. She was deft and skilful when she administered his medicine or took him through his daily exercise routines. She was the only person he knew who could not compare him to his former self and see what a sorry wreck he had become. And yes, she still brought him the occasional burst of sunshine, when he had to smile despite himself.

He often lay awake and dreaded the possibility of losing Angela. Sometimes he had to bite the insides of his cheeks not to blow up at anybody while she was present. She thought he was a nice, amiable guy, and he was determined that as long as he had any willpower left he would do nothing to destroy her illusion. If he drove her away he would be a total mess.

Angela sat in her little bedroom which had once been Rowena Quinlan's sewing room and chewed her nails down to the quick. It was a bad habit from her youth that recurred whenever she found herself unsure of what she ought to do. Thankfully it did not happen often. Angela had rarely found herself at a loss, until now.

She had gone to the kitchen to wash the afternoon tea dishes while Rowena went to the shops to buy a few things Sean asked for. Angela stumbled over Gerard Quinlan, stretched full length across the kitchen tiles in a drunken stupor. One of his feet still wedged the back door open, so he must have fallen flat on his face when he lurched up the back steps.

Angela rolled up her sleeves to shake him gently. She patted his face. "Mr. Quinlan, Mr. Quinlan, wake up." All she elicited was a deep groan.

She placed her hands beneath his moist armpits and tried to tug him to his bedroom but he might as well have been a ten-ton sack of potatoes. Angela pushed a strand of hair behind her ear and settled on her haunches to think. Then she felt the toe of her sandal grow wet and her stocking sopping. Angela gaped at the floor and leaped back with a gasp of horror. A large puddle seeped out from beneath Gerry Quinlan's midriff.

Angela fled to her bedroom. She had dealt with many such accidents in the hospital but Gerard Quinlan was the head of the family, in his own house! She had expected better of Sean's father. She scrubbed her foot but still felt upset and soiled, as if she needed a good bath. When she closed her eyes she could still see Gerry's iron-grey sideburns, with him lying in his own puddle, his mouth hanging open.

She knew what she would do. She would prop a pillow beneath his head and drape a blanket over him. She ought to clean him up so his family would not see his shame, but it was too late. The front door banged open and shut, and she peeped out of her door crack to see Michael spring inside, swinging his satchel over his shoulder. He had been at a friend's house for tea and now he would find this. Angela's throat tightened. *The poor little boy.*

Michael stepped into the kitchen and leaped over his father as if he were a huge basket of laundry. He poured himself a glass of milk, gulped it down, and then bounded exuberantly over his father again. He hurried into Sean's bedroom, proud to be the bearer of news. "Hey Sean, Dad's at it again, dead drunk on the kitchen floor."

It sounded to Angela as if the child rather admired his father's exploits.

"Where's Angela?" Sean asked tersely.

"I dunno. I haven't seen her." Mikey sounded crestfallen. "Around the place somewhere, I s'pose."

"Well when Blake gets home, send him straight in to me," Sean ordered. "You go and watch for Angela. Keep her out of the kitchen because I don't want her to see Dad like that."

Michael heaved a deep sigh. "O.K." He trudged dejectedly out of his brother's room. Sean wore his grim, preoccupied expression. Michael guessed he would not want to hear about his day at school.

Angela stayed put. Before long, Blake was home from work and went to see Sean.

"I want you to drag Dad to bed," Sean said.

"Why?" Blake exclaimed. "He'll only rant and rave if I wake him up. Best to wait until he sobers up a bit and let him find his own way to bed." He sounded as if Sean had taken leave of his senses.

"It doesn't look good," Sean persisted.

Blake gave a short bark of a laugh. "Of course it doesn't. When has he ever looked good? If he wants to get plastered and fall on the kitchen floor, that's his problem."

"It wouldn't look good if Angela found him. She'd get a shock. I don't want her to see his true colours and think badly of us."

"We can't keep his true colours hidden forever," Blake sighed. "But I understand."

Angela watched him stride into the kitchen. He squatted beside his father and grunted in disgust. "Filthy old coot's wet himself," he mumbled, and braced his muscles to drag his father, none too gently, over the kitchen threshold. Gerry left a smeared trail on the tiles behind him.

"Whosh going on?" Gerry grumbled. He rolled his red eyeballs, trying to work out what was happening. Then he looked up at his son and called him such a foul name, Angela's cheeks flamed. Blake merely sighed and chewed his lips. She guessed it was nothing he had not heard many times before.

"I'm taking you to bed, and I hope you rot there," he panted.

"I'm sick as a pig. I need a doctor." Gerry's mouth frothed. "You don't care, you hard-hearted ignoramus. Get me that little nurse of Sean's. She'll fix me."

Angela's toes tingled and she fought an urge to spin around and escape from the window.

"No," Blake said shortly. "She's here for Sean, not to worry about you." His words showed plainly the scorn he felt. Then Gerry's bedroom door closed and Angela heard no more.

She stood and stretched, then looked at her pale reflection in the mirror, smoothed her hair and straightened her collar. Now she knew how things were in the Quinlan family, she would not be taken by surprise again. She had sensed the heavy atmosphere of gloom as soon as she had first walked into the house. Rowena had everything scrupulously neat and sparkling clean, but the sadness and fear felt as thick as a fog. Angela was sensitive to such things.

The house stood deep in a valley, surrounded by leafy European trees, so not much light filtered through the windows to brighten the rooms. That added to the heavy feeling of a shroud. At first Angela had been willing to attribute the sombre atmosphere to Sean's accident but now she realised that there was more to it than that. The Quinlan family had crept around, living with the father's drunkenness for many years.

Angela's heart flooded with something stronger for Sean than the admiration she had felt for many weeks. *He must be truly remarkable, to have lived for so long with this and still grown up to be so cheerful and decent as he had been.* It would have been more natural if he had become chronically agitated like his mother, or surly and embittered like Blake. Surely Sean shone with a deep inner beauty all his own.

Angela could not stop thinking about him. The strength of her feelings confused had disturbed her. Had she fallen in love with her patient? That had never been on her agenda. She had never felt this way about any man before. Sometimes as she worked with him, she wanted to cry. It became a struggle to hold back her tears. She was certain Sean would not understand her feelings for him. He had enough grief of his own to deal with. He would think she was a silly, emotional woman. She had to deny the power of her feelings for him and remain strong and steady, as she always had been. When the day came to leave the Quinlan family she would go with a smile, although it broke her heart now to think of walking out of Sean's life.

Whatever will happen to him when I do leave? Who else was capable enough to look after all his physical needs? Nobody but that dismal Blake, and he couldn't be expected to quit his job and sacrifice himself for his brother. Sean needed emotional and spiritual bolstering too, which she was sure he would never receive from anybody in his family. Angela wished she could sweep him away to live with her at her own bright spacious flat, with its cosy furnishings and cheery picture windows. He would never prosper in his parents' home, with its gloomy environment. Angela's brow knitted as she thought hard, trying to work out a way to have him live in her flat. Although she was good at orchestrating things to suit herself, she could see no way to arrange this. Not unless Sean loved her back and decided to marry her.

Angela flushed crimson again. There must be some solution. If there was one thing she hated, it was being helpless to make changes for the better.

It occurred to Angela that it would probably not do Blake any harm to move away from his parents' home either. She shuddered to think of little Michael. *How will the poor boy grow up with such a father? God has brought me to them so I ought to help them. I can start with Sean, and perhaps Michael because he is young, and Rowena, because she sorely needs it. I should begin with talking about Jesus, or maybe...*

Angela stopped short with a derisive shake of the head. She was at it again, taking responsibility solely upon herself as if God depended on Angela Powell! The Quinlan family was His to care for and He would do it His own way, with or without her help.

I rushed ahead of you again. I'm sorry. I pray for the entire Quinlan family. Only You know their hearts. I sense the sorrow I feel hanging over this house and I pray that you will meet their needs and remove it. I pray that you will use me to help somehow. I already care deeply for each member of this family.

Angela's heart throbbed guiltily as she realised this was not entirely true. She could not take to Sean's brother Blake, and it puzzled her. Perhaps it was because he was so hard to read. They spoke courteously together when they had to but for the most part, they studiously avoided each other. There was something irritating about the way he sat so quietly, absorbing everything with an inscrutable expression on his face. Angela was wary of people who built walls around themselves as if they had something to hide. There was no telling what Blake's thoughts might be, and for all she knew they could be dreadful!

She had to admit, part of her reason for wanting Sean to live at her flat was to escape from the strain of hedging around Blake, wondering if she had given him any reason to find her laughable or foolish. She hoped God would hurry and move one way or another.

———————

"Will you take these little brats away from me? There's a good girl." Russell Timms looked Claire up and down approvingly and his narrow eyes lingered over her longer than necessary.

"O.K.!" Claire hastily strapped the twins into their tandem pram and obliged, just to get away from him. The gleam in his eye when he looked at her made her palms sweat apprehensively. She did not like him a bit and it was not the first time she had noticed his scrutiny. With hot cheeks, she wondered if Auntie Tessa had told him all about her rape. Perhaps that was why Russell stared at her with the expression of bold curiosity she found so offensive. Claire wished Auntie Tessa had never met him.

At least Russell spent several hours away from the house, drinking or fishing with friends. When he was home Claire instinctively made herself scarce. She was polite when he spoke to her, but other than that she resolved to ignore him as much as possible. Perhaps then he would stop ogling her.

She took the twins for a walk to the library. Claire, who never had anything to do with babies before, had grown fond of these two. Ryan peeped at her behind his blanket, with a throaty chuckle, and she laughed back at him. He squeezed his little eyelids tightly shut, playing a game of peek-a-boo with her. He was a lovable baby with a single dimple that popped out whenever he smiled.

Cindy's lip began to tremble and Claire quickly shook a rattle to distract her before the cry erupted. The baby girl was far more fractious than her brother but Claire had mastered the art of soothing her more quickly than anybody else. She could not help feeling smug. The others would see that Claire was good for something.

She had not intended to love those twins as much as she did, because it hurt like a knife twisted deep in her heart. Whenever she looked at their soft faces she thought of her own baby, which would have been going on one year old by now. It would have been making gurgling, cooing noises of its own. She wondered if it would have crawled as fast as Cindy. It might have even ventured walking by now. *Would it have been a boy or a girl?* How Claire would have loved her own baby. The twins were not really hers to love because she would not live with them forever. Ryan and Cindy had revived something deep and undeniable in her heart which had been crushed when she was raped. Claire yearned to love and nurture. *If* Dad had let her keep the baby, there would have been somebody.

She saw that both babies' heads had lolled onto their chests. Claire moved to relax on a park bench. It was rare for both twins to sleep at the same time and she would make the most of it.

Sometimes she wondered why she chose to stay at her aunt's house. Claire did all the cleaning and cooking while the others were out so it suited them to have her there, but it was no fun. Her stretcher bed was creaky and cold. Her daytime obsessions carried over into sleep and she was plagued with recurrent dreams of a silent infant that looked at her with knowing, reproachful eyes. Claire often woke in the night with a gasp, listened to Rachel's heavy breathing and wished for her own bed at home. She pressed her tightly closed eyelids into her pillow until the urge to sob receded.

Not being able to talk about the abortion was hard. Holding in her grief made her feel like an over-stuffed cushion. If Tessa and Rachel knew about Claire's baby, perhaps they would understand why sometimes her eyes watered dismally for no apparent reason when she cuddled Ryan or Cindy. Living with those two babies always nearby was a kind of torture, but she stayed in Melbourne because what might await her in Adelaide could be even harder to face.

The threat of meeting any of the Quinlan family still loomed large, although the oldest son would not be going anywhere. Mum had written that Sean Quinlan had had a serious accident, and lost the use of his legs. That depressed Claire when she remembered the fit and glowing athlete she had met. She had nothing against Sean, except for being saddled with such a creep for a brother.

Mum and Dad would expect her to resume her education when she returned, because she had been a good student. Claire still could not think straight. Not about Maths, Science or History, anyway. She could barely concentrate on reading novels. She did not want to return to school as one of the oldest students. Most of all, she still resented her parents too much to return. Especially her father. She had lavished her childhood love on him but he had snuffed it out like a candle flame by his harsh decision. William had assured her that not everybody was like Blake Quinlan, then he had insisted on committing murder! Claire often thought of her dad's face, his blue eyes and thick moustache, hoping to fan an ember of love into flame again. She found nothing but simmering resentment in her heart for him.

Once she had almost decided to return home, but over-heard Tessa discussing her family with a friend over the phone. "My brother William has always been the self-righteous Christian but when trouble hits his family, he's quick to call on me. I really think he can't bear to have his daughter around to remind him what happened. I don't mind. Claire can stay for as long as she pleases." That settled it. Tessa was right about Dad but she only knew half the story.

Before she left Adelaide, William had pulled Claire aside and asked her to tell nobody in Tessa's family that he had made her have an abortion. Knowing his former anti-abortion stance, his sister would never stop rubbing it in. Claire nodded grimly but Dad must have read her contempt for his hypocrisy in her eyes for he turned away, abashed. The fact that he felt ashamed of himself made Claire feel no better.

She wished there was somebody in Tessa's family to like, other than the babies. Auntie Tessa always complained about noise and disorder while she was the noisiest and most disorderly one of all. Steven still shunned Claire and hardly spoke to her, but she was happy to return the favour. Rachel annoyed Claire by counselling her how she ought to behave, as if she had all the psychological answers. Claire wondered if Rachel would have recovered any faster than her if she had been raped.

Then of course, there was her never-ending quest to avoid Russell. Claire hoped she was wrong about him. Perhaps her misgivings stemmed from nothing more than morbid paranoia. He was old enough to be her father, after all. She wondered what Tessa saw in him. He certainly seemed to have no personality, looks or charm to recommend him.

Cindy squirmed in her seat and moaned. Claire quickly lifted the little girl to her chest so she would not wake Ryan. They moved on to the library and Claire found some books full of coloured paintings. While she pored over pictures of stunning beauty, she could almost believe that God did create the world wonderfully. She saw a book of tapestry patterns and borrowed that too. She had done some tapestries at school during electives and enjoyed it. As she could not concentrate on books, it might be just the thing to while away her spare time.

She returned home, heaved the twins into their playpen and went to the kitchen for their bottles. Auntie Tessa and Rachel sat at the dining room table sipping cups of coffee. Claire thought they'd heard her move in the next room but her ears began to burn. It was obvious from their conversation that they hadn't.

"How can I tell Claire? I don't want to hurt her feelings," Rachel wailed.

"Claire will understand," Tessa said with a weary sigh. Auntie Tessa often punctuated her words with a heavy sigh, as if she were on the brink of exhaustion.

"It's become a real burden on me," Rachel complained. "We invite her to our parties and then I don't enjoy myself because I'm wondering if Claire's having a bad time, or taking offence at any fellows who take an interest in her, like poor Robert Palmer."

A sick chill shot from Claire's fingers to her toes, rooting her to the floor. Only her heart moved, pumping hard.

"I don't believe she even wants a normal life again," Rachel went on. "Uncle William is right. She ought to put the past behind her and get on with life." Rachel was chafing at the hours of enforced togetherness as much as Claire was. "I wish she'd given Robert Palmer a chance. He's a nice guy."

Claire might have made an involuntary movement or perhaps her shadow fell across the table, for suddenly Tessa and Rachel both looked through the kitchen door and saw her there.

Claire watched the colour drain from Rachel's cheeks and then instantly flood back, beet red. Rachel's eyes darted about the room as she tried to back out of what she had said. "Claire, I'm sorry! I didn't mean it. I'm just in a bad temper because I didn't finish my Economics essay as I planned. I love you to come with us."

She leaped up and flung her arms around Claire in her exuberant way. Claire stood without raising her arms but Rachel required some sort of response.

Claire nodded through her blur of tears. She did not want to cause more trouble. Although she was hurt to the core, she forced a smile and pretended not to be. "Don't worry, I'd rather stay home tonight, anyway. It was good of you and Pete to invite me but I've never been much for parties, even before I was... raped." It was so hard to keep her voice from wavering that her throat ached with the effort.

"I'm happy to stay home. Honest," she persisted. "Don't worry about me, Rachel. I'm a big girl. I can look after myself. I know you didn't mean anything nasty."

Claire broke away as soon she as she could and retreated to her bedroom. She shoved one of Rachel's piles of clothes off her own stretcher bed, sat on it and cupped her chin in her hands. So much for Mum hoping that the fun of Rachel and Steven would rub off on Claire. Claire had tried to make an effort to please people. If she had her own way she would not have gone out with Rachel so often at all. She blocked her ears to the noise the twins had begun to make and squeezed her eyes shut. She had failed with her Melbourne family too. Another tidal wave of loneliness rolled over her and her heart ached.

Chapter Twelve

One day, Blake arrived home from work and saw Michael trying to clean the garden shed. He trudged in and out, lugging heavy tools and machinery behind him to clean on the grass. Blake sat in his car and watched Mikey, as if he had not seen him for months. It was unlike the chirpy little boy to drag his feet so lethargically, as if his spark had been extinguished. It hit Blake like a bolt that Michael had been neglected for weeks. Sean's accident must have made a huge impact on the nine-year-old but the family swept him aside, ordering him to hush. Blake was as guilty as the others. Adapting to Sean's accident seemed to have swallowed up the needs of anybody else.

Blake wondered if Michael cried as bitterly as he did himself when there was nobody to hear him. *Of course he must! He's only young.* Michael's face was pale and his mouth a straight line of doleful concentration. Blake's stomach twisted with sympathy. He should have thought!

Blake joined Mikey by the shed and leaned on the old brick barbecue. "Hi! Nice job."

Michael turned and Blake saw a flicker of surprise before he ducked his head. "Hi! Thanks," he mumbled and bent down to wipe mouse droppings from the lids of the paint pots.

"Did Dad ask you to do this?" Blake asked.

Michael shook his head. "Naw! I thought I'd do it because it needs doing and Sean always did it best." His voice trembled. "I thought it might make Dad feel better. I even dusted the cobwebs between the spokes of the bikes."

Blake's throat tightened because Michael's hard work would be unappreciated. The last thing on their father's mind was the state of his shed. Gerry was either sobbing over Sean or drinking himself senseless.

"Don't go to too much trouble because he probably won't notice... much."

Mikey looked at him. "I know," he said quietly, "but he'll notice if it doesn't get done, and then he'll be upset about his messy shed and yell at us."

"That's true," Blake admitted and another wave of guilt swept over him. He should have thought of that himself instead of moping beneath his own gloomy cloud, letting Mikey shoulder the entire load. He seized an old t-shirt and began to dust cobwebs from the high corners which Michael could not reach. "I'll give you a hand."

Michael stared. "Haven't you got something else to do?"

Blake shook his head. "Nothing else." It was true. All he ever did was daydream, tinker with old machinery or try to cheer Sean up, which never worked. It hurt him that Michael was so surprised he was willing to help.

"What have you been up to?" he asked as they worked.

"Nothin' much." Michael chewed his lip.

Such a short reply was odd for the little boy who used to chatter like a wind-up toy until somebody stopped him. Blake's spine prickled with the same sick dread he felt when he first heard that Sean would never walk again. Mikey's tongue was as essential to him as Sean's legs had been. Had he lost both brothers to strangers? A panic-like spasm gripped Blake's throat. He suddenly felt desperate to make Michael smile and prattle again like old times.

"How about school? Do you and Jamie still collect basketball cards? Do you still play cricket at lunchtime? How about those Art lessons you enjoy so much?" He stopped to draw a breath. He was supposed to be making Michael chatter, not doing it himself.

Michael dropped his rag and looked up with a fearful appeal in his eyes which Blake could not understand. "In Art yesterday, me and some other fellows made Sean a book to read while he's sick in bed. It's a get-well story, full of funny pictures we drew. I thought of the story and Jamie did the writing, 'cause he's real neat." Michael's eyelashes flickered briefly. "Sean hasn't looked at it."

"I'm sure he will," Blake said. "He still hasn't got used to not being able to walk. He's not interested in many of the things he used to like but give him time. He'll be happier some day soon." Blake felt like a prize hypocrite because he was not at all certain that Sean ever would be happier.

Michael sniffed and swiped the back of his hand across his nose. "Are you lying to me, Blake?" he asked directly. "Is Sean gonna die?" With that, his face crumpled, he buried his head in his knees and sobbed.

Instantly, Blake dropped the rag and knelt beside him. He pulled Michael close to him, tightly. "No! He's lost his leg movement, that's all! He's not going to die. What made you think such a thing?" Blake felt sick to the stomach. How long had Michael imagined that, with nobody bothering to find out and correct him?

Michael's fingers gripped Blake's shoulders tighter. His hands were still so small. His tongue loosened and he poured out his burden of several weeks. He spoke faster than a machine gun to make up for lost time. "The teachers don't punish me anymore. They punish Jamie for talking and muckin' around, but let me get away with murder. Darren Cooper reckons it's 'cause they feel sorry for me, 'cause of Sean's accident. Darren said Sean'll prob'ly die."

Michael rubbed his face against Blake's shoulder and choked on the rest of his story. "He thinks that's why we need Angela. Nobody needs a private nurse unless they're so sick they might die. Nobody can lose their legs and keep living for long. He reckons the hurt will seep up from Sean's legs all the way to his heart and kill him in just a few years." Michael could speak no more. He wept so hard Blake's shirt grew as damp as his knees, from kneeling on the cold earthen floor.

Blake held his little brother until the storm of tears subsided. "No way, Mike. That's a load of rubbish. You tell Darren Cooper he has no idea. Sean's spine and his legs are hurt but the rest of him is still fit and healthy. He's not going to die. That's the truth." Blake swallowed hard. "I'm sorry we let you keep thinking that. Why didn't you ask one of us, before?" He guessed Michael had asked, in a timorous, indirect way, and none of them sensed his need.

"I was scared," Michael mumbled. "I thought you were all keeping it from me and that's why nobody wanted to talk to me."

Blake ruffled Mikey's hair. "You can talk to me anytime you like, about absolutely anything. I'll always listen. I promise."

Michael squirmed and gulped once, twice. "I'll tell you something else, then. I once told Sean that I really miss him teaching me football in the backyard, and Mum told me to leave him alone. I didn't mean to say anything wrong but I miss kicking the football with Sean." Michael gave Sean's leather football a hard shove, then changed his mind and gathered it close against his chest.

"I'll give you a few kicks, if you like." It was not the same, but it was the best Blake could do. "I know I'm nowhere near as good as Sean was, but show me what he was teaching you."

Michael looked up at last and offered a watery smile. Even his eyes shone brighter and clearer, as if they had been washed. He looked like a new boy after only ten minutes of undivided attention. He pulled himself away with a grimace, remembering that he was going on for ten years old, and cleared his throat gruffly.

"OK! Thanks Blake."

––––––––––

When Sean's self-control finally snapped he was sitting in his new wheelchair beside his bedroom window, looking out at the backyard. Rowena had just brought him his tea before the others were served. She always cut his meat into bite-sized pieces as she had done when he was small and it annoyed Sean. Didn't she know he was quite capable of handling a knife and fork?

He had no appetite anyway. He watched Michael working by the shed and saw Blake come home and go to talk to him. Eventually they brought out Sean's football, which he had not set eyes upon since his accident. At once they had his full attention. He craned forward and watched their game with tense fascination.

Burning tears rolled down his face. His very own football, and he had no reason to ever touch it again. He wept for the person he had been, and the end of all his hopes and dreams. It hurt so hard he could barely swallow.

His grief gave way to fury, black as thunder. Michael beamed as he used to when Sean taught him and his happy voice penetrated through the closed window. Blake looked cheerful too and Sean's temples throbbed until he thought his head would burst. How dare they look so bright and happy while he was chained for the rest of his life to his bed or chair? Sean knew it was unreasonable to expect others to remain miserable because he was, but he could not help it. Their sadness had done him no good but their contentment made him feel even worse.

To cap it all off, they were not even playing well! Michael had forgotten all Sean had taught him and did some truly terrible, uncoordinated kicks. Blake tried to teach him but he was not much better. Blake handled the football with a natural awkwardness, yet he thought he could take over and teach Michael some skill. They were making a mockery of the game and it was not fair. Sean was the only one who could have made something of himself, yet he was the one who was paralysed.

A band of pain tightened around his chest and collar-bone and he let out some deep, hoarse sobs.

Rowena was first to scuttle over to his side. She wrung her hands and cried, "What's the matter?"

Sean gestured through the window with his chin. "I can't stand watching that."

She gasped. "I'll tell them to stop."

Something in Sean snapped. He seized his plate of food and flung it against the wall. "Do you think that will fix things?" He rolled his hands into fists and punched his useless thighs savagely, as if that would bring back their feeling. He attacked himself so fiercely that if he could have felt anything he would have been in agony.

Suddenly Angela was there, trying to snatch his fists with her small hands. Her face was pale and terrified, and the band of freckles across his nose stood out like the Milky Way.

"No Sean, don't!" she begged. "I know you feel bad but you mustn't injure yourself. You have to punch a pillow, instead."

"Fat lot of good that will do!" He raised a hand and shoved her away. With a startled cry, Angela spun against the wall.

"I don't care if I injure myself," Sean croaked. "I want to die. You don't understand, Angela. I don't need you always around. You think you've got all the answers but you can walk. Why do you keep staying here? Why do you put up with me? I don't know why you don't go and get a life of your own!"

She made no sound but he watched her face crumple. Tears sprang to her eyes and she turned away before they overflowed. In that instant, Sean knew how much he loved her. It was true. He loved Angela. She was wonderful and special. She was bright and lightened his day whenever she was near, and he adored her. Now he knew, but he had just hurt her to the core. *Now she will never stay.*

Throwing back his head against the chair he yelled in mental anguish. He did not know how it happened but the chair capsized. He found his nose upon the carpet and began to beat the floor with his hands and face. If he pounded himself unconscious, he would be relieved.

His brothers quickly came inside to witness the scene too. They had either been summoned or heard the commotion for themselves. Michael hid his face on Rowena's shoulder and sobbed but Blake knelt on the floor and tried to grab Sean's arms. He was the only one who might be strong enough to stop Sean's frenzy. Neither Rowena nor Angela had any chance.

"Sean, stop!" Blake cried.

"You keep away." Sean tried to free himself with a shove. He had always been more than a match for Blake in the past but not this time. Blake forced Sean's arms back against the floor and leaned over them with his entire weight. Sean had no way of fighting back with the rest of his body so he was helpless.

"I don't want to see you hurt yourself," Blake puffed.

Sean scowled up into his face. "Don't you know how hopeless you and Michael are with the football? I was watching you. I couldn't stand it."

"I know," Blake told him.

"How do you think I felt?" Sean demanded. "I want to die. Why did this have to happen to me? If it had to happen to either of us, I wish it had been..." He stopped writhing and broke out in a sweat, horrified by what he had been about to say, and even more stunned that he had meant it.

"You wish it had been me, instead of you," Blake finished softly.

That was what it took to end Sean's turbulence. He turned limp, squeezed his eyelids shut and wept again, spent and exhausted. Rowena, Angela, Blake and Michael circled him, touching him and trying to soothe him. Sean could not talk. He knew they thought he was still weeping with self-pity but they were wrong. This time he cried because his accident had shown him what a selfish, warped creature he really was, and he loathed what he saw.

––––––––

Sean was eased onto his bed to watch his little television but he fell asleep, spent with emotion. The others quietly waited for him to wake up. Angela would normally have chosen to wait near his bedside but after what Sean had yelled at her, she doubted if her face would be the first he would choose to see. She let Rowena wait in Sean's bedroom and sat silently in the lounge-room with the other boys.

She could not get over what Sean had told her. He did not want her anymore. Her time to move on had probably come but how could she wrench him out of her heart now? Part of her dreaded his waking up because she expected him to repeat what he had said before. He did not need her and thought she should get a life of her own.

Angela couldn't hold back a stifled squeak and looked up to see if Blake and Michael noticed. If they did, they gave no indication. They both sat wrapped in their own thoughts.

It grew late and Rowena poked her head out of the boys' room long enough to tell Michael to have his bath and go to bed. For once, Mikey obeyed instantly, without words. Blake stretched and Angela squirmed. She found her tongue because she suspected that if she did not break the lengthy silence, she would begin to cry. She did not want Blake to see her so vulnerable, so she opened her mouth not knowing what would come out, and not really caring.

"You shouldn't have been playing football out there for him to see." Although she had not used her voice for over an hour, it sounded raspy and hoarse. "How insensitive can you get? Michael is just a little boy so we can't blame him, but you should have known better."

Blake drew a breath and cleared his throat. "We weren't doing anything wrong, Angela," he said quietly. "*Michael* needs some attention as well as Sean. I think we were all insensitive to *him*."

"Well you could have chosen a better way of showing Michael attention than kicking the football right under Sean's nose."

Blake's eyelashes flickered down. "Maybe you're right. We didn't know he was watching. We didn't think...but there's no point in laying blame now, is there? It won't make Sean feel better, no matter whose fault it was." He looked at her again.

Angela chewed her bottom lip and stewed. She felt that Blake was forever trying to catch her behaving pettishly, to prove that she was not a good Christian after all. He always seemed to stare her out whenever she behaved in an unchristian manner, and it infuriated her. She would not give him the satisfaction of arguing with him and supplying more ammunition.

She sighed to herself. He was probably right, anyway. She was being unfair. It hardly mattered any more whether he liked her or not, for she would probably not be living with them for much longer.

At last Rowena tiptoed in, smiling. "Sean's awake, and he feels much better." She whispered, as if he were still sound asleep. "He'd like to see you, Angela."

Angela's heart lurched into her mouth. She stood up on trembling legs and managed to force a quick smile for Rowena, on her way past. She knew her face would be a map of raw emotions for Sean to read. She had cried all her make-up off and her eyes were swollen and puffy. She must look a fright and he was probably going to suggest she ought to leave. She would do her best to make it as easy for him as she could.

Angela found Sean propped against his pillows and he looked more rested than she had ever seen him before. Her heart raced. His outburst might have done him some good and released pent up pressure.

Sean watched her hanging back, with large, sorrowful eyes, and she had never looked more beautiful to him. He stretched a tentative hand to her; desperately hoping he had not ruined everything. How harsh and ungrateful he must have sounded after all her work for him. He moistened his lips and cleared his throat. He hardly knew how to phrase what he was about to say but nothing had ever been more important to him.

His eyes blurred, and her image swam before him like a shiny apparition. "Angela, I'm sorry for what I said. I don't want you to leave." He curled his fingers tightly, until his knuckles were white.

"Let me come clean. It hurts me to have you around sometimes because…I think you're beautiful. It tears me up inside to look at you. Before my accident I would've…I would've wanted a girl like you in my life someday. Now that I'm a useless cripple, I know I'll never have anything to offer anyone." The remainder of his speech rushed out like the last bit of air from a deflating balloon. "I think you're a wonderful nurse and you do a great job. I hope you won't hold what I said against me. And I hope you'll stay." He wouldn't blame her if she packed her suitcase that very night.

He still couldn't see her clearly through his misted eyes but he heard a strange, choked cry. She rushed to his bedside and seized his hand in both of hers.

"Sean, haven't you guessed? I'm crazy about you! Do you think I could be around you for so long and not love you with all my heart?" She could say no more because she started sobbing. Angela rubbed her hand across her eyes, tried to change it to laughter, then gave up and shook her head.

Sean's body jolted to attention. He even forgot about his paralysed legs as he gaped at her face. Amazement and joy surged through him and then she was in his arms. He held her close and rubbed her back tenderly. He felt the nodules of her strong little spine and breathed in the sweet scent of her hair which he knew now he could never get enough of. She was like a breath of heaven.

"I'm sorry," he murmured brokenly. "I'm sorry for pushing you. I never will again."

She made a strange noise between a laugh and a cry, and kissed his cheek. Her wildest dreams had come true. He truly loved her. She could feel it in the fervent way he held her close.

"Will you forgive me?" he asked. His throat had such a tight lump, he could barely swallow. He wondered how long she had loved him while he had been feeling too sorry for himself to appreciate the treasure she was.

"Sean, I've got nothing to forgive."

"Will you stay with me always? I want you close," he breathed. "I never want to be without you."

The droplets in her eyes shone like stars. "I'm here forever if you want me to be." She could hardly believe how unhappy she had been ten minutes earlier.

"How can you live with me, like this though?" Sean gestured to his paralysed legs. He had to think of practical matters. He longed to have her close to him but he was scared.

Angela gave an incredulous laugh. "Sean, don't be crazy! You might not be able to walk but you're still a man. An attractive, stunning man."

He pulled her shoulders down closer to him. "You'll have to help me believe that. You're the most amazing woman I ever met. Do you know that?"

Then he kissed her, as he had sometimes imagined kissing her in his wildest dreams and never imagined he really would.

Eventually, Sean got around to the other burden on his mind. "Will you send Blake in to see me?" He rubbed a tendril of Angela's hair between his fingers. "I said such a terrible thing to him, too."

Angela straightened and nodded. "I'll get him." She had forgotten the existence of the rest of Sean's family in those blissful moments and he pulled her back to earth with a thud. Angela flushed to recall her behaviour in the lounge-room. Not only did Blake exist, but he might tell Sean the accusatory things she had said. She hoped he would have the decency not to repeat them. She sent Blake in and retreated to her own room to bask in her joy.

Blake stood beside Sean's bed and nervously clenched his hands. "Hi, how're you doing?" He supposed Angela was not the only one who considered him the villain of the piece.

"I'm OK now." The sight of his brother's apprehension filled Sean with shame. "Blake, I'm sorry about what I almost said before." Sometimes words seemed hopelessly inadequate.

Blake smiled with relief and bounced upon his own bed. "Forget it, Sean. I understand. It's only natural for you to wish it hadn't been you. I'm not mad, or anything."

"But I can't forgive myself," Sean explained. "I won't forget it. It showed me how... how dirty I am inside to wish... this on you, or anybody else." He hung his head and admitted, "I feel like scum."

Blake shook his head vehemently. "You aren't scum, Sean. I think you're terrific. You must know how much I've always admired you." He flushed with embarrassment, but kept on. "I always wished I could be like you, and I always will."

Sean's ears burned with the praise he felt he did not deserve. It made him feel no better. He felt worse, if anything.

"I'm the one who's scum!" Blake reminded him. "Think of what I did and don't feel bad about yourself." He turned away to hide his tears.

Blake rarely spoke of what he had done anymore and Sean knew how much it cost him. He had guessed that Blake carried his deed on his mind like a heavy weight each day, and he would never forgive himself or forget it. Sean felt overwhelmingly sad for his brother. He supposed if he had raped a girl, he would feel just the same way.

But was he really any better? He mulled over Blake's words and felt dirty to the core of his heart. Perhaps Blake could forgive what Sean had said but Sean could not forgive himself. Blake had raped Claire Parker because on the spur of the moment, he was there with the opportunity. Sean knew that if he had the opportunity to let Blake or another hang on that flying fox and suffer in his place, he would have done so. There was no point in deluding himself and pretending that he wouldn't. He would rather someone else suffered than himself, if he had the chance. Wasn't the attitude as bad as the actual deed? He had put his football career ahead of the people he loved, and now it broke his heart.

Chapter Thirteen

Claire decided to go to church. At a loose end, she had caught a train into the city to wander one Sunday morning. Claire had to either work or walk compulsively to stave off the dismal thoughts of loneliness and failure that otherwise beset her.

The church she saw was a fine old stone building with arched stained glass windows, which were some craftsman's expression of his appreciation of God's beauty. Perhaps the windows drew Claire inside. Something deep in her soul always responded to anything beautiful. The large congregation was packed as far as the back rows, so she was able to slip in unobtrusively. When Claire edged into a pew at the very back nobody glanced her way. The people were singing, for the service was well under way.

Claire had not set foot in a church since her arrival back in Melbourne. She still felt disappointed with what God had allowed her to suffer. Added to that was guilt for flirting so openly with Blake Quinlan the night she had been raped, not to mention destroying her baby. Over a year had lapsed and it was still the focal point of her life. She remembered all other events in relation to "before" or "after".

Claire missed the closeness she used to enjoy with God. When the preacher stepped behind the dais she listened as carefully as her scatty mind would let her. He was a plain looking, middle-aged man with greying sideburns and a kindly face. She missed his name and did not know if he was the usual pastor or a visiting speaker. Whoever he was, when he started to speak she found herself riveted to her seat.

"Are you filled with pain because of something which happened to you?" he asked the sea of faces. "Perhaps you can't voice your grief for others to understand. You feel isolated, but God is still with you. He is sufficient. He understands how you feel and He longs for you to lay your hurt and pain at His feet."

Claire craned forward. Her shame had been branded into her like a hot iron. Her family had sympathised with her but they all expected her to leave her pain behind, and she knew she had disappointed them when she couldn't. On top of the trauma of being raped and having an abortion, she lived with the misery of knowing she could please nobody.

"Do you feel responsible for some event in your life? Perhaps you wonder with all your heart if things would have been different if only you had behaved differently. I tell you the truth. God does not want you to live with yesterday's garbage on your shoulders. There is no way to turn back time and undo what has been done, but He wants you to move on. That is why He's given you tomorrow.

"Nothing happens outside of His perfect plan for you, anyway. When harm befalls you, it is not because God deserted you for one moment. He doesn't turn His back and let things filter through without His knowledge. He certainly doesn't wish to punish us or watch us suffer. He allows hurt to happen to a person only when He knows He can turn it into much greater good. The good might not be evident immediately, or maybe not for years, but it will be there somewhere. God loves you dearly and He never makes mistakes."

Claire felt a gentle heat seep through her bones. She thought she was sitting in a patch of sunlight but blinked, surprised to find herself in shadow with no window nearby. She could not understand the phenomenon but settled forward to enjoy it, not wishing to miss a word.

The speaker leaned on his dais and cast his eyes over the people before him. "God allowed His own Son Jesus Christ to be made perfect through suffering, so we mustn't be stunned and resentful when suffering comes to us. He loves you and He knows what He's doing. He's doing a wonderful work in you."

Claire's eyes stung with tears. The preacher stepped down and the musicians took their places. She slipped outside because she knew she had heard what God meant for her. That stranger would never know how God had used his words to give her the touch from Him she needed, but God knew.

She passed a fragrant bakery and stepped in to buy herself a cake. For the first time in months, Claire felt genuinely hungry. She sat on a bench, gazed into the clear, blue winter sky and pondered. The preacher had said that God would turn her bad experience to good. *What good has being raped done me?* Claire shook her head. Perhaps she would never learn until she died but she had to choose to trust God that there was good somewhere.

There had been some positive changes in her outlook. The longer she sat thinking, the more of them she could see. She had had a bad experience but God had brought her through it. She remembered the frivolous girl she had once been, who looked to other people to fulfil her deepest needs. Perhaps God had used the last year to show her that other people could not supply what she had expected from them. Only He could understand her deepest self. She was aware of a strength deep inside she never knew existed before. The hollow loneliness showed her that only God must be relied upon for refuge. It had taught her to seek peace and contentment in the quietness of her own heart. Perhaps she would not have learned those lessons any easier way.

Claire returned home in a daze and greeted her aunt with a warm beam. Tessa gazed after her, astounded. Claire had not smiled like that since she had come to them, and what a difference it made to her face! There was a tranquillity about Claire, some radiance in her clear skin and bright eyes, which Tessa envied. It shone forth clearer than ever when the girl smiled. Tessa's own daughter Rachel was bubbly and lovely to look at but lacked Claire's intriguing mystique. At least, Tessa thought so.

She clicked her tongue and returned to scrubbing her sticky kitchen floor, cross and tired. She had just finished a raging argument with Russell for spilling his beer and refusing to mop it up. Steven and Rachel were out and about, and the babies had almost finished their only half-hour nap of the day. When they began to howl, she would jolly well ask Claire to fix them up. William had sent his daughter for them to help but Tessa believed she needed far more help than Claire. Nobody bothered about her!

———

Sean's eyes were closed and his head rested on Angela's lap. He enjoyed the caress of her fingers in his hair. They were alone in his room by the cosiness of a gas heater, and if he had not had so much on his mind he might easily have fallen asleep. Since he could not escape from his thoughts by running now, he found himself wondering a great many things he had never wondered before. He hoped that Angela, with her faith and wisdom, could help him learn.

Since the evening he had seen Blake and Michael play football, then yelled those terrible things, Sean was convinced of his own depravity. He discovered a hunger to know more about God deep inside of him. He had never felt anything to equal it. In the past, Sean simply never felt the need for God. He had so much going for him with his all-consuming football career and the occasional date on the side, God never fitted into the picture.

During their talks at night, Blake had sometimes asked him what he felt about God. Sean would brush him off with a shrug and a laugh. He could not have cared less then but now things were different. He remembered his life-changing moment, when he hung on that flying-fox and prayed for the first and only time in his life. When he faced death, he instantly called upon God as the giver of life. He recalled how he had crashed upon those rocks, severely battered but not killed, and thanked God that his life was still intact.

Nobody knew better than Sean how a wonderful life could turn sour in a matter of seconds. When he had his strength and talent he breezed through life, good-natured and likeable. It took losing all of that to show that he was really selfish, bad-tempered and hateful. It disturbed him to wonder if God had taken away the power in his legs to show him the true state of his heart.

"Why would God give me the talent and desire to play football, then sweep it away from me like this?" he murmured to Angela. "I don't understand." Yet, deep in his heart, he thought he understood a little. God needed to show him that people were more important than football. He grimaced. *Couldn't God have used a far less destructive way?*

Angela combed his blonde hair between her fingers. "I don't know, Sweetheart. All I know is that God never makes mistakes. Maybe you're privileged, Sean. Things like this don't happen to many people and God might want to do a very special work through you." She would never have dared suggest such a thing a few weeks ago but a gentle, approachable light shone from Sean's eyes that had not been there then.

He swallowed, and looked up at her. "Tell me about God, Ange. Tell me about Jesus. I never cared before but now I really want to know." He gave a grim laugh. "With nothing to do but lie or sit, I have nothing else to think about."

Angela's heart quickened. Now was the moment she had waited for. She had longed to plunge into such a talk many times before but always sensed that the time was not right. Now she was glad she had waited. Sean would not have been ready to hear it, before.

"What do you know already?" she ventured.

"Only bits and pieces Mum has told us, over the years. Jesus was God's Son and He died on the Cross for us almost two thousand years ago." Sean wrinkled his forehead. "I've never understood why something that happened so long ago should mean anything to us."

Angela drew a deep breath and found the words to tell him. She explained how every person sinned and fell short of God's standards because sin was so deeply rooted into every human heart. She watched Sean nod intently, as if he knew through bitter experience. Angela told him that Jesus was the only perfect person who never sinned once, because He was also God's own Son. He allowed Himself to be born as a human being just so that He could take the punishment others deserved upon Himself.

"It's because He loves us so much. He doesn't want to see us get what we really deserve. No matter how bad we are, all He wants is for us to accept that He died in our place so we won't be judged for our sins. He wants us to set our hearts on Him and know Him so well that He can live in us and help us grow more like Him all the time. We can have His heart of love and joy and peace."

Sean wiped his moist eyes and nodded. Now that he was rooted to one spot and had finally bothered to listen to the gospel, he accepted it as truth. It never occurred to him to doubt it. He knew it must be true because it struck a chord deep inside his heart.

"I would never have done what He did," he said bleakly. "I could never have given my life voluntarily to die for people who hated me. When I was hanging onto that flying-fox, I would have done anything to have got down. I would rather it had been anyone else in my place." His eyes blurred with burning tears again. "Even my own brother. You heard what I told Blake. I would rather it had been him than me. Angela, I'm a rotten sinner." Unable to keep on, he turned his neck to bury his face in his pillow.

She rubbed him softly between his strong shoulder blades. "We all are," she whispered, "but He loves us. He understands and He wants us to let Him bear it. That's why He died."

"Will he really take away all my guilt?" Sean rasped.

"Yes! You just ask Him to." She clutched his hand.

Angela prayed for Sean and then he added his own incoherent, heartfelt prayer, only the second of his life. His surroundings were still the same. Sean held the grey, woollen edge of blanket beneath his chin and watched the gas flame flicker. On the surface nothing had changed, but a reservoir of excitement began to make itself felt deep inside of him. It reminded him of the happy surges of energy which used to make him want to sprint and jump, while he still could. Sean kissed Angela's palm, then pressed it to his cheek.

She watched his face intently and sensed again that God had something far more special in store for Sean than playing football.

————

"No, I can't!" said Blake. If his friend had asked anything else of him he would have obliged, but not this. Joseph wanted him to take his sister on a few dates, because she was new to the country.

"She spik good Eenglish," Joseph persisted. "Better den me."

"That's not the reason I can't," Blake told him. "It's to do with me, Joe."

He had met Joseph's sister twice. Rita was pretty, with thick, black shiny hair and snapping black eyes, but Blake had vowed never to date anybody ever again after what had happened the first time. Sean thought he should put the past behind him and get on with life, but after what Blake had done to Claire Parker he could never forgive himself. If he ever found another girl who liked him, she would be repulsed when she discovered what he had done. He could not keep such a thing secret for the rest of his life.

Joseph's own dark eyes narrowed. "Whatsa matter witt you, Blake? You no like weemen?"

"Yeah, I do, but... I shouldn't, for reasons of my own which I'd rather not discuss." Blake was getting in deeper water with every word he spoke. Joseph, with his strong code of moral ethics, would be aghast if he knew what Blake had done. "I'm not the right sort of guy for any girl."

Joseph still stared at him perplexed, and Blake lowered his gaze.

"You're a nice guy," Joseph said at last. "Rita be nice for you. She's a good girl, and very beautiful."

"I know she is." However, Blake could not help comparing every pretty face he met with the delicate skin, shining eyes and shy, sweet smile he would never forget. He always flinched with self-disgust when he caught himself still thinking about Claire. He had no right to, but he could not stop himself.

"Joseph, I think Rita will have no trouble finding a date of her own without you needing to set one up for her," he said. "Somebody planned a date for me once, and it was... terrible."

"It's de right family ting to do," Joseph replied curtly.

Blake backed down. "O.K.! I don't have a sister so I don't know much about a brother's duties."

Joseph stood and shoved his chair back. "You stay een your comfort zone. You're right. She'll find anotter." He spoke with forced evenness but his nostrils flared. He took Blake's refusal as a snub to his family.

Blake returned to work feeling thoroughly upset. The last thing he wanted was to offend Joseph, but he felt cornered. He refused to either agree to the request or explain the true reason why he could not. He hoped he had not ruined their friendship, but if he had there was nothing he could do about it.

He tried to switch his mind to pleasanter thoughts. Sean was getting married and his high spirits were a burst of sunshine. Blake realised how thoroughly the whole family had always counted on Sean's good cheer. When he was sorrowful and angry they wilted as one, but when he started to smile again, they lifted their heads and bloomed in response.

Blake always guessed that Angela was determined to get whatever she wanted, and she had clearly wanted Sean from the outset. Sean had a way with women, even when he lay paralysed in hospital! Blake grinned to himself. He wondered if Angela had ordered Sean to marry her as part of his healing process. He would not put anything past her.

Next month there would be a wedding in the family, the last thing anybody had expected. Sean was supposed to have been in the thick of football playing, but instead, he was getting married. Angela had almost finished having her own flat adapted to suit the needs of a paraplegic. Two doors were widened, and ramps and bars added. It would be all ready for Sean to move into. He would be married in Angela's church in his wheelchair, and Blake would stand beside him as best man.

Sean's new religious belief stunned Blake most of all. He had felt certain Sean would never recover from this cruel blow, yet Sean turned to God. That was the last thing Blake ever expected him to do. Sean had always shunned anything spiritual, but now he seemed to have the sort of deep-seated faith in Jesus that Blake had always longed for.

At first, Blake wondered if Sean latched onto Christianity merely to please Angela. He decided there must be far more to it. Sean was still paralysed. He knew he would never walk again. His lifelong hopes and dreams had crashed around his ears. Wanting to impress Angela could not explain the new light that shone deep in his eyes. Although he still had moments of bitterness and frustration, they seemed to be temporary setbacks. Blake wondered if Sean's new attitude could possibly last forever. He fervently hoped so.

One thing was certain. He would have to learn about God from Sean, not Angela. Sean thought God was working in his life and Blake longed to know what made him sure it was God and not his own imagination.

Whenever he ventured the subject to Angela, she turned instantly thorny and defensive. Angela thought that Blake aimed to belittle Christianity but it was not true. He only wanted to know more about it, but there was no telling her that. Sometimes he wondered if she found his questions threatening because she was not as deeply rooted in her faith as she pretended to be.

Blake shrugged sadly. He knew Angela did not like him much, and wondered if Sean had told her what he had done. He liked her well enough. He thought she was cute and spunky. He liked her forceful way of giving her opinions and admired her for loving Sean deeply enough to marry him with his handicap. Blake wondered if he unconsciously tried to rile Angela to get a bite out of her. No, he honestly did not think so. He would not bother. It was too easy to get a bite out of her without even trying.

Anyway, he would ask Sean about Jesus. Blake finished writing his last address and looked up to see Joseph's head bent grimly over his work across the room. Joseph's rigid posture indicated that he was still offended, and Blake's grief came rushing back. Even if he found out how Sean knew Jesus, it would be no good for the likes of him. Nothing could ever change what he had done and end the guilt he still felt whenever he thought of Claire. Blake wanted to shrivel up and die.

Chapter Fourteen

Rowena Quinlan sat on the front pew of the little church between Gerry and Michael and clenched their hands on either side. Her eyes were fixed on Sean in his wheelchair at the front of the church. She was convinced there could not have been a more handsome groom and watched him as he smiled spontaneously and lovingly up at his bride. Rowena's eyes brimmed over with happiness.

Throughout those long, awful months following his accident, she never expected to see him smile like that again.

Angela's radiant face glowed, with the tresses of her golden hair swept back into an elegant twist laced with sprays of gypsophila. She was like an angel sent for the whole family. Rowena and Angela had shared many late night cups of tea at the kitchen table, long after the men had gone to bed. They discussed many things. Rowena had suffered so long for lack of female company in her family and at last God had given her a daughter. But how could Angela help loving Sean?

Rowena's head spun to think of all Sean had been through. He had never caused a moment of worry before his accident and she had always counted on him as her most sturdy and reliable helper from the time he was a small boy. Rowena never considered that she favoured any of her sons, but perhaps she had been unduly proud of Sean. He was the last person she would have expected to suffer such a traumatic accident. If it had to happen to any of her boys, she would have expected it to be Blake, who had always attracted trouble.

The hardest time for Rowena had been those weeks when Sean rejected her every attempt to care for him as she longed to do. She was either too slow and fumbling or too quick and jumpy to please him. He would upbraid her because she could not read his mind and guess what he wanted at a particular moment. Rowena understood how hard it was for independent Sean to learn to adjust to his paralysis.

She had wept many bitter tears, as if her healthy, cheerful son had died. Now she looked into his face and knew that he was back again. He still had a long way to go, but the strength of his buoyant personality was too great for him to be held down for long. She felt prouder of him this day than ever. Prouder than if he had become the great football player he had expected to be. Her boy would adapt. He always had before. Perhaps it was even providential that it had happened to Sean instead of Blake, for Rowena believed Blake would never have recovered.

She looked at her second son, standing beside Sean's wheelchair, and her face clouded. He had never recovered from his terrible action and she feared he would let it taint the rest of his life. Others did not notice Blake's instinct to turn and flee whenever he heard the name of a pretty girl, but Rowena did. She was his mother. She knew he detested himself, and she had no idea how to change that. Blake's shame cut to his bones.

She felt responsible for her own part in arranging his date with Claire Parker. She hoped God would forgive her culpability for she could not forgive herself. She had been an interfering and manipulative mother. If she had not pushed her son out before he was ready, he might have found his own match in his own good time. The chances of that happening now were slim. Blake needed a special girl who would probe beneath his walls of shyness and insecurity to see the tender and sensitive heart that beat beneath. Rowena doubted if the most wonderful girl in the world would be able to penetrate the fortress of his reserve now.

Her thoughts wandered to Kate Parker and their broken friendship. Rowena had expected Kate to provide the female friendship she had yearned for, but it was not to be. Rowena had almost collided with Kate behind their supermarket trolleys a few months ago. It had been highly embarrassing, for Kate looked as awkward as Rowena felt. They both sensed without words that it would be foolish to try to renew their friendship, after what Rowena's son had done to Kate's daughter. They passed each other with mumbled greetings and Rowena read the regret in Kate's eyes which must have mirrored her own.

At least God, in His grace, had given Rowena a daughter in Angela. Many of their late night discussions had centred on God. Angela had spoken of her own lonely yearning for the mother she had lost, and her conviction that God cared for her. Angela easily led Rowena to renew her own faith in Jesus. Rowena had always believed in Jesus but somehow her faith had been pushed into the background by her tempestuous marriage. Now it was solidly grounded again. Jesus had given her a daughter, Sean a wife, Angela a husband and a mother. Rowena faced the future with courage and hope.

With God, there was always hope. Perhaps there was still a chance of happiness even for Blake.

———

Gerry slouched beside Rowena and let her clutch his hand without returning the pressure. He saw her tears of genuine pleasure and thought, not for the first time, what a simpleton his wife was. He could hardly wait for the farce of a wedding to finish so he could escape. Gerry felt cross and tired. Sean was not supposed to be getting married. He was supposed to be playing football. Any Tom, Dick or Harry could get married but few could play football as well as he'd convinced himself Sean would have done.

That thought did bring water to Gerry's eyes and Rowena looked at him and squeezed his hand harder, not knowing they were tears of self-pity, and not sentimentality, like hers. When he could disappear without making a scene, he would sneak off to the pub. His bar mates treated him like a hero; for they understood what a blow it had been for him to have his son break his spine. Gerry appreciated the attention but wondered how long it would last. Not as long as the glory would have lasted if Sean had done something great with his talent. Gerry felt a tight knot of frustration deep in the pit of his stomach. Only several drinks could help him to loosen it for a few hours.

He squirmed on his seat and blinked at his knees, for he could not bear the sight of Sean's broad shoulders in that wheelchair. He rarely talked to his favourite son any more because it hurt too much. He knew one day he would lash out at Sean for being such a careless fool as to ruin both their lives. Luckily for Sean, Angela was taking him out of his father's clutches. Gerry closed his eyes and gave Sean up as a lost cause, as if he had died. His bowed head made it appear as if he were praying.

He had nothing to centre his hopes on now. He looked at Blake, and quickly looked away again. Blake had always been a write-off. Gerry turned his head to peer at little Mike, seated on Rowena's other side and squirming with bottled up energy. Gerry's mind ticked with an idea. Perhaps he could pin his hopes on this one now. No, he felt too old and tired to wait for another son to grow up, and Michael would surely let him down. No man would be lucky enough to have two sons of Sean's calibre.

Gerry's life was full of shattered dreams and he knew he must be jinxed. He had heard many superstitious tales as a boy in Ireland. His elderly relatives had believed in being cursed from birth. Old Auntie Mary with the fuzzy top lip set great store by such things. He had not thought of her in years but he sat bolt upright in bed after a drinking binge a few weeks ago and remembered all she had told him. It hit him like lightning; his rotten luck had been mounting since he was a wee lad, smaller than Michael. Teachers, employers, bank managers, even fate, seemed to unite against him. It could not be mere coincidence.

Gerry gaped at the image of the Cross which hung over the church dais and his stomach lurched. He wondered why the building did not crumble to ruin around his ears, for somebody up there surely hated him. Sean's accident must have been inevitable, because that someone knew how Gerry had counted on him. Suddenly Gerry broke into a sweat beneath his collar and found himself trembling with fear.

Rowena and Sean had both begun to jabber about God's endless love. *They've listened too long to Angela. Where was this great and almighty God when Sean dangled off that flying fox, for Pete's sake?* Sean had let the trauma of his broken body addle his head.

He really was well and truly lost to Gerry. At one time, Gerry would have been annoyed enough to thrash Rowena for her gullibility, but now he could not be bothered. What was the use of violence? Since Sean's accident, a heavy weight of lethargy held him pinned to the floor until he could hardly motivate himself to lift one foot after the other.

"I'd like to present Mr and Mrs Sean Quinlan." The pastor's triumphant announcement broke through Gerry's thoughts and he stood to receive them as the others did, although he could not make the effort to paste a false smile on to his face. At least the whole nauseating ceremony had passed quickly.

He did not know how much of his jinxed life he still had to live, but he would spend it gravitating between work, home and the pub, but mostly at the pub. *What else can a man do, when God is out to get him?*

————

"I'm certain that God allowed this pain to happen so that He could work good through my circumstances," Sean said, as he watched Blake wire up the new contraption he had brought. It was a switch device that he connected to the radio, television and light, so that Sean could operate each of them from his bedside.

Blake moistened his lips, unsure if he should continue his line of questioning while Sean was clearly much happier than he had been before. He certainly did not wish to make his brother unhappy. He knew Angela would disapprove. It had been almost impossible to steal a few moments alone with his brother without Angela hovering around his elbow like Sean's guardian angel. Even now, she was only in the kitchen, showing Rowena the layout of their flat. Blake decided to plough on and he hoped Sean would have good, convincing answers for his questions.

"How about suffering animals, who have no personality to work through? Why does God let them go through it? How about sick little babies who end up dying? What is the point of the pain God lets them experience for the short time they're alive?" He couldn't look at Sean, but instead at his own fingers, because he did not want Sean to see quite how passionate he felt about the subject.

Sean faltered. "Well... I dunno. It does seem a bit... pointless."

Blake heaved a ragged sigh. That had not been what he wanted to hear.

"It's too deep for us to understand," put in Rowena, who had just entered with a tray of tea-cups and biscuits. "I'm sure God does protect many people from harm. I hear cases of divine intervention often."

Blake straightened. "Why doesn't He do it all the time, Mum? Why does He help some people but let others keep suffering in the same circumstances?" He clenched his hands. "Why didn't He stop me doing what I did, that time?" he asked in a low voice. He would never have kept on had he known that Angela followed close on Rowena's heels with the teapot and the milk.

She instantly set her jaw. She did not understand his last reference but realised that she could not leave him alone with Sean for one minute. *How dare he try to undermine Sean's newfound faith with his perpetual pessimism?* Just because Blake insisted on walking beneath a gloomy cloud, she refused to let him pull the others down. She swept in with her chin held high, intent on rescuing them.

"God isn't in the business of being everybody's personal bodyguard, Blake. He treats us as individuals and does what He knows is best at the time. It may not look right to us with our limited perspective, but this life is not the be-all and end-all. Heaven is a much nicer place and what we can't understand here, He will explain there."

Blake gave a wry smile. He was up against the over-zealous Angela again. There was no way he could corner Sean for a private discussion anymore. He knew he would get himself into hot water now but he might as well keep on and hope for the best. "That's what you believe Angela, but where is your proof?"

Her chest tightened as she felt herself put on the spot. "It's in the Bible, and that's God's revelation to us," she said tritely. "Besides, if He rescued people all the time, everybody would want to become a Christian just to be looked after."

"Well, what's wrong with that?" he asked. "God wants us to be Christians, doesn't He?"

"Not because of what we can get out of Him," she retorted. "But because we love Him!"

Blake slowly shook his head. He was back to square one. "How does He expect us to love Him if He won't look after us, and lets bad things happen when He could stop them?"

Angela bit back a sharp retort. She told herself that Blake wanted her to lose her cool, and appear foolish in front of Rowena and Sean. She hated the way her heart sank when she found herself with no reply. No doubt she would think of a pithy comeback later but that would not help her save face now. Angela would have been aghast if she realised that she had begun to regard her disputes with Blake as a contest of wills instead of a chance to speak up for Jesus.

"If you have eyes to see, the evidence of His love is all around you," she snapped. "In my career, I've met people who've had terrible things happen to them, and they still praise God because they learn to recognise Him speaking into their hearts. He's spoken into my heart, and shown me He cares when I've had troubles!" She folded her arms across her chest, daring Blake to challenge her statement.

Angela's defensive tone was evident to all but herself. Sean and Rowena exchanged glances of trepidation behind her back. Neither Angela nor Blake purposely tried to bait the other but any room where they were together buzzed with tension. Sean often wished he were able to get up and walk out until it passed over.

Blake pondered Angela's words and felt even more hopeless. If Angela felt God speaking into her heart, he had no reason to doubt her or call her a liar. He had forfeited any right to earn such a thing himself. He ignored the sinking weight in the pit of his stomach and gave a brief nod. All he had learned for sure was that God wanted none of him. He supposed he would have to live with that.

"You study world history," Angela appealed to him. "Can't you see God's hand working through it all?"

Blake slowly shook his head. "All I've seen are centuries of bloodshed and fighting and waste. I've tried reading the Bible, and also the Talmud and the Koran and some existentialist authors, but none of it has proved anything to me." He had borrowed the philosophical literature from Joseph, who was just as confused in his mind as Blake.

Angela closed her eyes and her head spun. "Why do you have to read all that twaddle?" Never had she studied any religious doctrine other than Christianity so how could she possibly refute what was in them without sounding narrow-minded and intolerant? She began to fear that Blake was more than a match for her.

No! Surely not! She struggled for something else to say to save God's name, but Rowena spoke up and changed the subject.

"Sean, are you getting tired, sitting in the chair? Angela, when should he do his exercises, before or after we have afternoon tea?"

Angela forced a smile on her face, although she knew Rowena was trying to rescue her from her fix. It felt unpleasant to think she might be vanquished. "We'll do Sean's exercises after we have afternoon tea," she said tightly.

Blake watched her, with an expression of mingled regret and shame. "Angela, I'm not trying to make trouble. I just want to find out." Her back was turned to him and he could see by the slump of her shoulders that she was deeply offended.

"Perhaps you shouldn't speak to me then," she heard herself snap and began to rub Sean's ankles between her hands. Angela had already forgotten that she'd decided to do Sean's exercises after tea. In her mind, she cried, *He's telling me I'm not good enough to trust. After all the years I've been a Christian, after all the years I've trusted you, Lord, why couldn't I have a better come-back?*

Later that night, Sean and Angela lay in bed listening to soothing music. She brushed the hair back from his brow and he leaned his head against her shoulder and enjoyed the rhythm of her soft breathing. Sean was surprised each week to discover how many little moments of contentment lightened his life, although he could not walk. Perhaps they were moments he would never have even stopped long enough to notice in the helter-skelter pace of his old life.

He quietly thanked God in his heart for the cosiness of it all. Angela had suggested that Sean look for some small blessing to thank God for each day. He tried it, and it worked.

She stirred drowsily and murmured, "It's late! I'd better turn off the music."

Sean reached out his hand to detain her. "Wait, let's try this thing Blake set up for me." He flicked a switch and the music stopped. "Pretty good, eh?"

Angela examined the small gadget by the light of the small lamp. "Quite ingenious," she said, with the grudging respect she often felt for Blake, much as she disapproved of him.

"Yeah, he's pretty bright, although it's never got him anywhere," Sean mused.

Angela cocked up an eyebrow. "Why not? Why doesn't he try to forge a decent career he could be proud of?"

"It wouldn't work." Sean vaguely wondered why he felt so certain and fell back on the reason he had heard so often from his father. "Quinlan men have never gotten anywhere in life. We don't usually have what it takes."

Angela leaned up on one elbow and glared at him. "I never expected you to take up with that defeatist talk your father carries on with. What's wrong with Blake, anyway? He should find himself a girlfriend. He's not bad looking."

Sean quickly shook his head. "He's had... a pretty grim experience on his very first date. He won't risk it again. I know him well."

"Come on! Is he going to let one bad experience ruin his whole life? That sounds typical of Blake."

"What happened was pretty bad," Sean said awkwardly.

Angela's green eyes glinted with curiosity. "What did happen? And what did he mean this afternoon when he asked why God didn't stop him doing what he did?"

Sean hesitated, and then regretfully shook his head. "I'd like to tell you but I don't think I should. It's his own business. Sorry, Sweetie." He kissed her cheek.

By now Angela was truly intrigued, but thought it unwise to push Sean. Let him keep his brother's confidence for now. She would find out another time. "O.K.! I still think the way to mend a broken heart is to try again but I doubt if any girl would fancy a guy as glum as Blake, no matter how many brains he has."

Sean managed only half a smile. Angela and Blake were two of the people he loved most in the world and it grieved him that his wife had formed such a skewed opinion of his brother. Sean knew that Blake could be both fun and happy. He could have rattled off a string of wild pranks they had shared in their boyhood but doubted if Angela would believe him.

It hurt him to think that Blake's happiness had been snuffed out. Sean would hate to see Blake become more and more like Dad, for now that Angela had drawn it to his attention, he had not seen a genuine smile cross Blake's face for a long time. Suddenly Sean longed to call his brother back as soon as he could, to try to cheer him up. Blake had always been there for him when he was low.

"You don't like him much, do you?" he asked Angela sadly.

She was glad the room was dark so he could not see the pink glow that suffused her cheeks. She knew she ought to try to hide her negative feelings better. "I don't dislike him. It's just that I always have trouble dealing with gloomy people, determined to doubt God. I don't like to argue but when he starts, I don't know what else to do." She did not add that she suspected Blake disliked her. He probably thought her talk empty and shallow. Angela even wondered if Blake resented her marrying Sean and taking him away.

"I think we should pray for him," Sean suggested softly.

"Pray?" Angela echoed, with a guilty lurch of the heart. Prayer for Blake Quinlan was the last thing that had crossed her mind but of course Sean was right. She should have thought of it first.

"Yes, because he's really anxious to know God, but he thinks too hard. He needs to let go and let God swallow him up in His love, as He did for me," Sean said slowly. "I'd love to see Blake find peace in his heart."

Angela squeezed Sean's hand tightly. Here she had been regarding Blake as her adversary, some sort of cross to bear, a threat to be overcome. She had to remember that he was Sean's brother and Sean loved him. Angela knew how close the two boys had been. She should learn to love Blake as a brother but she did not see how she could. As with everything else, she had to relinquish it to higher hands than hers.

Angela swallowed. "You're right. Let's pray."

Chapter Fifteen

Claire sat cross-legged on her stretcher bed and worked on her tapestry. She was looking after the twins as usual, for Tessa and Rachel had both gone out with friends. Claire had implicitly become the family housekeeper, cook and live-in babysitter. Russell was home but nobody ever expected him to lift a finger and he always met *those* expectations. Claire wished she had friends to go out with. Once she had enjoyed a blossoming social life but since coming to Melbourne, she seemed to have lost her knack for making friends.

She realised she was tussling with self-pity again and snapped it out of her head. How insidious her bitterness was, but she was dealing with it at last. She had started to attend a small church near Auntie Tessa's home and none of the family commented. Whenever she finished the work, they were happy to let her do as she pleased. Claire gasped and shook her head. Already she was indulging in more self-pity, fast on the heels of the last lot. It had become as natural as breathing.

For almost two years, she had chosen to blame God for allowing her to be raped instead of searching for the good which He could work through the rest of her life. "Why me?" she had demanded so often. Well, why not her? God's ways were stranger than her own. There had to be a good reason why He allowed it, but just because she demanded to know did not mean He had to tell her. She wanted to be a truly faithful person who believed in God's purpose, regardless of what happened to her.

Claire craved love, acceptance and a deeper purpose for her life. Experience showed her that other people could not meet her needs. She had to look to God alone, for only He could give her life direction. She consciously took her pain out of her own hands and relinquished it to God, the only one who was equipped to deal with it. She left the pain of losing the baby with Him too. He understood. She knew that, because He said so. God had loved that baby, and He had taken care of it. He still had a purpose for Claire. Helping Auntie Tessa seemed to be His purpose for her at the moment. Although she was not entirely happy, neither was she unhappy anymore.

Watching her silver needle glide through the fabric, she thought deliberately for the first time of the boy who had raped her. Blake Quinlan. The thought of his name instantly made her go ice-cold all through but she pursed her lips and worked through it. Since she had turned back to God, Claire sensed Him urging her to face perils from her past instead of trying to smother them with daily trivia.

Claire's needle trembled as she allowed her mind to rehash, not for the first time, the dread of that night. Her feelings made it horribly difficult for her to battle through those sordid details, even before she could think rationally about her assailant. At last her pulse slowed again and her heart steadied.

Surprisingly enough, although Blake had forcefully made the biggest impact on her life of anyone, she barely knew him. Indeed, she had met him only twice. All she really knew of him was that he had dark hair, brown eyes, a shy, edgy manner and a sudden, drunken, vicious temper. She did not care to know any more of him. She despised him. She wondered if he knew how he had destroyed her and hoped he would suffer as much as he had made her suffer. The problem was that now she had renewed her Christian commitment, she felt God drawing her to forgive Blake Quinlan.

At first, Claire had broken into a cold sweat and baulked. *No way! That's too much to expect from me. It's impossible to forgive him. He destroyed my life and I loathe him.*

Then she remembered that with God, all things are possible. In actual fact, Blake Quinlan had devastated one evening of her life but he had no influence over what she chose to do with the rest of it. God said to forgive others and there was no way around it. Claire bit off a piece of thread. Although her heart clung desperately to the antipathy she had carefully cultivated, her mind *did* want to forgive Blake, for her sake, not his. The bitterness she carried was ruining her life.

Perhaps forgiveness had to begin in the mind, for it was impossible to force her heart to forgive. If she left it to God, He might be able to work some miracle. *Here I am, Lord. I don't want to hate Blake Quinlan anymore but I still do. There's nothing I can do but leave it with you. I do want to forgive him now, and when I feel the usual fury at him I'm willing to ignore it and behave as if it doesn't exist. Will you please work in my heart and help me to forgive, for I know you understand I just can't do it alone?*

She wondered what Blake was doing now. She was eighteen so he must be twenty, close to twenty-one for all she knew. How twisted his self-esteem must have been, for him to do such a thing. She wondered if he was still mixed-up inside. That must break God's heart, for He knew Blake as well as he knew Claire. She prayed again, *Please do what you need to do in his life too, Lord,* and was half surprised to realise that a part of her meant it.

A thin wail from Cindy broke her reverie. Claire put down her work and hurried to check, before Ryan woke up and added his own lusty protest. Russell looked up from his television as she passed. "G'day love," he said.

"Hello," she responded politely, and went to bend over the cot in Cindy's room.

"Hi there, Little One," she crooned, and Cindy's wobbly lip turned into a dimpled smile at the sight of her. It warmed Claire's heart.

"You little darling." As she stooped to lift the baby, a sudden hand clamped over her hip.

Claire spun around with a lurch of the stomach. There loomed Russell, so close behind her that she could see how sparse his greying hair was, and smell the odour of cigarettes on his breath. He had tiptoed in so quietly she had heard nothing, and now he smirked at her in a twisted, purposeful way that turned her blood to water.

Claire took a step backward and lunged into the bars of the cot. "Leave me alone!" she pleaded.

He clucked her beneath the chin. "That's no way to speak to your good old Uncle Russ. I'm not going to hurt you. I just want you to treat me nicely."

She tried to sidestep him and bolt for the door but he snatched her forearm. His face had lost its smile and she saw a glint of perverted malice deep in his little eyes.

Claire tried to jerk free. In the midst of her terror, her head whirled with disbelief. *Why would he do this to me?* He was Auntie Tessa's new man! He was old enough to be her father! In a flash, she knew that if he had his way with her, it would be far more ravaging than before. He was middle-aged, overweight and thoroughly unappealing. He was not even drunk! Anybody who could make such a calculating move in his right mind must be outright cruel. Worst of all, she knew what sort of treatment to expect. She had been through it once before and could anticipate every wretched detail.

Russell jerked her against him and planted a wet kiss on the corner of her mouth. Claire's stomach heaved with revulsion.

"Come on, don't pretend you don't like men," he grunted. "You're too pretty not to. Tess told me what happened to you before. I'll bet you got some poor young bloke's blood boiling the way mine is. C'mon, give me a cuddle. We needn't tell Tess or the others."

"No! Let me go!" Although she struggled as hard as she could, Claire sensed with sick certainty that he would overpower her.

She managed to writhe away but his arm snaked after her and snatched her back. Beads of sweat stood out on his furrowed forehead. "Look, my fine young woman, you owe me," he snarled. "You've enjoyed my hospitality for so long, did you really think I'd expect nothing in return?"

By now, both babies howled with all their strength but Claire was oblivious. "Let me go!" she screamed. "I won't stay any more. I'll leave."

Russell shoved her hard into a chair and stood straddled over her. "You're going nowhere until I've finished with you, and if you tell Tessa you'll regret it. Do you think she'll believe the man she loves or some little vixen who makes mountains out of molehills?"

Claire's temples pounded. She could draw no breath to scream because her ribcage felt like an iron trap around her lungs. The four walls of the room spun crazily and she cried out to God in her head, *Please don't let this happen to me again, Lord! Please! If it happens to me now, I'll die!*

Suddenly she could draw the huge breath she needed. "Help! Someone heeeelp!"

Russell slapped his thick, square hand against her right ear. Through the buzzing vibrations, Claire heard something. It was not just pounding blood but someone knocking on the door.

"Heeeeelp me!" she hollered again before Russell shoved his hand over her mouth.

The front door swung against the wall and a voice called, "Claire, where are you?" Her knees turned to jelly. It was Rachel's boyfriend, Peter Lennox.

"In here, Pete," she sobbed between Russell's fingers.

Russell instantly dropped his hands, stunned as Peter's frame darkened the doorway. The young man stared from one to another with a blank face. Claire watched it turn thunderous as he realised what he had interrupted. She rushed over to him and felt his arms automatically encircle her protectively.

She whimpered like one of the babies. "He hurt me. He was going to assault me."

"She's a lying little tramp!" Russell fumed. "I just came to give her a hand with the kids."

Peter felt Claire's heart pounding, as he held her. "Claire would have to be a brilliant actress to make herself appear this scared!" He could hardly believe the evidence of his own senses. He had never liked Rachel's shifty stepfather but had never imagined him capable of anything like this.

"Why don't you beat it! This is my house. I could have you arrested for trespassing," Russell snarled when he saw that he had been caught red-handed. Since Peter's arrival, he appeared not quite so much like a formidable threat and more like a pathetic, lecherous old man.

Peter's lip curled. "Yeah, we'll both beat it! When Tessa comes home we'll tell her exactly what happened. I was a witness." He encircled Claire's shoulders with his arm and gently shepherded her out to sit on the porch steps. He stood helplessly by while she placed her head between her knees and breathed heavily. Peter suddenly felt awkward, knowing that as Rachel's boyfriend, Claire might reject any attempt of physical comfort from him. He hoped Tessa or Rachel would return soon. She clearly needed comfort from somebody.

As soon as her head cleared, Claire looked up at Peter with large tears welling in her thick lashes. "The twins," she cried. "They're frightened."

Peter felt his heart melt. "I'll get them," he muttered. He entered the house and saw that Russell had disappeared. He must have bolted from the back door. Peter fetched Cindy and Ryan and returned to find Claire still trembling in the golden sunshine as if she were freezing. He went inside to fetch a crocheted blanket from the back of the sofa, and gently draped it around her shoulders.

He had actually come to visit Rachel and wondered where she was. Peter wished she would hurry. Meanwhile he sat as close beside Claire as he dared, hoping to show that he was there if she needed to lean on somebody. He was embarrassed to feel himself flush when he felt her gaze fix on his face.

"Thank-you, Peter," Claire breathed. She was so close to him that if she tilted her head she could rest it on his shoulder. She didn't, of course, but she appreciated his presence more than she could say. He was an honest and truehearted person, there when she needed him. Claire was certain Peter's coming at that moment had been God's answer to her prayer.

Not for the first time, she thought how lucky Rachel was to have Peter.

And he looked sideways at her wing of soft hair and resisted the urge to reach out and touch it. She was not his type of girl, of course. Feisty, energetic Rachel suited him much better, he was happy, but Peter knew he would not soon forget Claire's wonderful blue eyes, as bright as a summer sky.

Blake strolled down the street, to buy himself some tea from the fish and chip shop. Rowena and Michael were eating at Sean and Angela's flat and Angela had not indicated whether he was included in the invitation. Blake decided he probably wasn't. He hated to intrude. As happy as he was for Sean, he missed their old close companionship. Sean's new relationship as a husband had to take precedence over his old one as a brother, of course.

Blake wanted to escape from the house to evade his dad, if he should stumble home from the pub earlier than usual. Gerry was not as violent as he used to be but he still abused Blake whenever he found him alone. Blake hated to admit his cowardice but he still feared Gerry's spiteful tongue as much as he ever had.

"Hey, Quinny!" a voice called behind him.

Blake froze. Nobody had used that old nickname since his factory days at Golden Harvest. He slowly turned, to face one of his old acquaintances.

"G'day Robbo," he said quietly. He hadn't seen any of his old crowd since that dinner dance when he'd raced out after Claire. He sometimes wondered what they thought when they never saw him again. Had they put two and two together and guessed the shameful thing he had done? Blake looked at the gravel beneath his feet. He supposed there was no reason why they should. His own guilty conscience was over-active.

"How've you been keeping, Quinny?" Todd Robertson had gone to seed over two years. He looked just as Blake remembered but even more unkempt. He wore the same old factory overalls with a few more grubby stains, his hair had grown oilier and stragglier and his teeth had become yellower and more chipped.

"Not bad," Blake responded. He felt a wave of pity for Robbo, who had hated factory work intensely. As Blake briefly explained where he worked, it was good to see Robbo's chipped grin flash in the old friendly way.

"You always were a smidgin too smart for the rest of us. It's great to see you, Quinny? Are you going anywhere in particular? How about joining me for a few drinks at the pub?"

Blake hesitated. He had not touched a drop of alcohol since that terrible night because he felt so repulsed by what he had done under the influence. The mere smell of beer fumes sickened him but he was lonely, and it was good to meet an old friend. It hardly mattered what he did or where he went anyway, because God had given up on him. Angela would agree.

"O.K.! But do you mind if we don't go to the local? I'd rather go someplace else." The truth was he would go to any lengths to avoid his father. Gerry often sneered at Blake and predicted that he would not keep away from drink for long. If he were to see his son wander into his pub and already had a few beneath his own belt, he would cause a scene Blake would rather not be part of.

"Sure, I know a few decent ones closer to town."

They hopped into Robbo's old car together and drove to an old stone pub. They stepped into a noisy, crowded pandemonium with a haze of smoke as thick as pea soup. Blake felt his throat tighten. He had intended to order a schooner of beer like Robbo but changed his mind and asked for a coke.

Robbo's chin almost hit the table. "Have you turned into a wowser? Miracles never cease. You were pickled to the eyeballs the last time I saw you." He leaned back and relished the discomfiture on the face of his companion.

"I know I was." Blake began to wish he had not weakened and agreed to come.

Robbo blew a hole into the froth on his beer. His eyes glittered over the rim of the glass. "We often wondered what became of you and that frigid little sheila. Did you track her down and have your way with her? You can tell me, Quinny. I'm your old mate and it won't go any further."

Blake was annoyed to find his face flaming. He wondered what lunacy had prompted him to go with Robbo, who had always been a shameless philanderer. "What does it matter to you?" That was as close as he could come to saying, "Mind your business." He instantly knew his question was tantamount to an affirmative and mentally kicked himself.

"I thought so," Robbo crowed, with undisguised delight. "Congratulations."

A hard knot twisted in Blake's stomach. Robbo had not seen Claire's white, petrified face, or heard her shrill screams for help. He had not snuffed out her bright, gentle spirit like a fragile flame. Blake still suffered nightmares about her pain and woke sitting bolt upright, sweating profusely. Suddenly, he no longer even felt like coke and pushed his glass aside.

"Robbo, you're warped," he managed to grate.

His old friend laughed with abandon. "You're the one who's warped, Quinny. Is that why you've gone off drink and changed jobs? You're consumed with guilt. Is that it?"

Blake struggled with tears and did not respond.

Robbo suddenly pursed his lips and turned serious. "Don't let society dictate how you ought to feel or behave," he advised. "The world is uninformed, Blake. There is no black and white, no such thing as right or wrong. That's all rubbish that people try to impose on you. Every man ought to be free to please himself. So you raped a chick? Big deal."

Blake flinched to hear it stated so brazenly.

"Who says rape is bad?" Robbo went on. "Sex is supposed to be good, so you've done yourself a favour. Good on you. I'm surprised you had the guts." He leaned over and patted Blake's shoulder.

Blake felt a queer tickle begin at the base of his spine and rise to the hair on the back of his head. His heart pounded a warning tattoo. Robbo's piercing eyes scrutinised him, quite sincere about all he said, but Blake knew that his philosophy was not merely misguided, but dangerous and corrupt.

His lips were numb but Robbo waited for him to reply. Blake took a nervous gulp of coke and coughed. "If all people agreed with you, there would be total anarchy in the world! People would hurt others to please themselves every day and nobody would care a thing about it."

"To hell with others!" Robbo's eyes appeared more glazed than one schooner of beer would warrant. He must have been already slightly inebriated when he'd met Blake on the street. "Others don't care two hoots for you! Look after number one. Milk others before they milk you. Eat, drink and be merry, for tomorrow you'll be cold and stark." His twisted smile held something truly ghoulish and Blake just wanted to get away.

"All you own is yourself, so you might as well please yourself whenever you can," Robbo concluded.

"Has that attitude got you anywhere?" Blake asked. Deep in his heart, he knew Robbo was wrong. If he, Blake Quinlan, lived life focused solely on himself, he would miss all the wide world had to offer, more than he would ever dream of. Every creature had to be part of creation as a whole. People had to be responsible to one another or there would be chaos. There had to be one ultimate Creator who controlled all things, and the truth about life had to come from Him. In a flash, sitting in a smoky pub across from a crazy anarchist, Blake knew that he believed in God.

"Yeah, I'm totally happy," Robbo asserted. "My only desire is to quit my rotten job but that's a prime example of what I mean. The bosses use us all they can to feather their own nests. Do you think they give a damn about us? If the dole paid any better I'd be out in a flash."

He continued to complain about work, abusing people Blake used to know, peppering his diatribe with many choice swear words. Robbo did not notice the gaping contradiction between his grumbling and his initial statement that he was totally happy. Blake noticed, but thought it too sad to be funny.

The pub grew more rowdy and congested and three long-haired youths crammed themselves into the spare space at the table. They challenged Robbo and Blake to join them in the billiard parlour and Robbo agreed with enthusiasm. Dirty jokes were bandied about in slurred, shrill voices. Blake waited a while, then slipped outside unnoticed. He would not let Robbo drive him back, in his condition. Let him think they got separated. Let him think what he liked. The quiet night air was a welcome relief after the smoky, stale bedlam and he shook his head clear as he walked.

Blake caught a bus back up to the hills and as he walked home, he lingered in the reserve where he and Sean used to play football when they were small. The light of the full moon cast a silvery shimmer over the gum trees and the age-old rocks near the creek bed. Blake sat on the wooden picnic bench and pulled his jacket closer around his chest. He felt cold but thought how good the tangy creek air smelled.

He thought over what Robbo had said and slowly shook his head again. He could not possibly buy it. Rape was bad, because God said it was wrong to violate another person. God was the author of truth, righteous and holy, and there was no way bad could be twisted into good, however hard Robbo wanted to try.

Blake felt the last sensation that he would have expected that night, a wave of relief almost akin to pure happiness. He had no idea how he could ever relate to God on a personal level but at last he felt certain in his heart that God existed. He hungered for God, and perhaps that was additional proof that God must be real. If no food existed to satisfy his appetite, surely the hunger pangs would not be so persistent. Blake's blood buzzed through his veins and he felt both cold and exhilaration. *What a breakthrough!*

"I believe that you exist," Blake whispered into the breeze, just in case God did not mind hearing from the likes of him. He looked at the neat flower beds in the centre of the reserve. How beautiful it all was. Earlier that evening he might not have even noticed, but now it struck him like a revelation. It had been always under his nose, but he had been too blind to see. *Surely God created it all!* A total fluke might have formed something so lovely, but he doubted it.

He wondered if it was presumptuous to hope that the God who had made such an incredible world might be willing to help him get his life back on track. As far as Blake knew, sixty or seventy years of living stretched before him, so surely there might be some purpose for them. If God wanted to give up on him, He could zap him out of existence.

He would examine his Bible again. Blake had read it before with a mindset to tear it apart and zoom in on any inconsistencies he could find. If Jesus Christ was a real and living person two thousand years after His death, what an insulting way to approach Him! Blake had never treated any human friends in such a rude manner.

He had come to God demanding proof before he would believe in Him, but that had not worked. Blake stood up, stretched his limbs and vowed to step out and believe Him anyway, with no pre-conceived expectations of his own. He would believe that every word of the Bible was true and he would believe that God heard prayers. Then whatever evidence God chose to give him would be a bonus. In a flash, Blake recalled a phrase Angela had used. That was "real faith in action". Now he understood what she had meant.

Angela had been right. Who did he think he was? Blake had made a terrible mistake. He was young, sinful and ignorant, yet he had the audacity to try to dictate how God should behave before he would believe. God was God and He would rule His universe as He saw fit. How dare Blake try to set the criteria of their relationship?

"I believe you," he breathed again. He rubbed his hands together and began to jog home. When he got there he would grab his Bible and read, whether Dad was home or not. This time, he would do it very differently. He would regard Jesus as the Son of God, the one who held the secret of the meaning of life. Something told Blake that this time he was on the right track.

Chapter Sixteen

Claire placed her folded clothes in the top of her suitcase and smartly snapped the locks. There were only two more days for living out of the suitcase and then she would catch the train back to Adelaide and her parents. If only she had done it far sooner. Avoiding Blake Quinlan in the same suburb would be far easier than avoiding Russell Timms in the same house!

Claire had still been sitting on the front verandah with Peter when Tessa got home. Claire was too choked-up to talk clearly so poor Peter had to tell his girlfriend's mother what had happened. Tessa shook her head and flatly denied it. She folded her arms across her chest and towered above them on the top step.

"I'm sorry you had to be mixed up in this, Peter, but it's not true. Russell would never do such a thing. I ought to know because I live with him. Claire is a confused young woman still living in the past, and she obviously mistook a friendly offer of help for a pass being made at her."

Deep in her heart, Tessa knew Russell would never offer to help with the children but she was desperate to believe in him. She had felt the same sick sting of betrayal when Henry deserted her and she did not want to face it a second time. She glared down at her niece. "I did my best to help Claire, but she's grossly over-reacted. She must need psychiatric help."

A wild hand of fear began to strangle Claire's throat, and make her breathless. Peter had not seen most of Russell's action. He might believe Tessa's explanation. Claire would be alone and spurned.

"I'm sorry Tessa, but Claire is telling the truth," Peter said steadily. His Adam's apple bobbed as he swallowed hard. "I saw how frightened she was. I saw the look in Russell's eye." He wished Russell had been caught by Tessa's own son, Steven. Peter hated to buy into such a volatile family scandal.

"I'll tell you all the things he said!" Claire blurted out the entire encounter and watched her aunt's thunderous face twist to haggard despair.

Tessa ground her teeth and her chin turned rock hard. "You must have flirted with him," she said with the hardness of desperation. "I should have guessed. I wonder if you are as sweet and innocent as your father thinks, young lady! I've seen the way you smile! I've seen the way you carry yourself. You seduced him." Tessa knew she was talking rubbish but wanted to avoid the truth for as long as she could.

Claire turned porcelain white. What sort of nightmare had she found herself in? Tessa's accusations sickened her to her stomach, and she lashed back. "I can't stand him! If I ever wanted to encourage anybody, it wouldn't be him! It would be someone younger and more handsome. Someone who wasn't bone lazy and sneaky as an old fox." Claire pressed a hand over her mouth and stared into one of Tessa's mud puddles, with its shimmering roof reflection. She had said too much.

Tessa's cheeks were mottled with rage. Her anger brought out her resemblance to Claire's father. Tessa and William were brother and sister to the core. In a flash, Tessa lunged at her and slapped her face, hard. Claire held her burning cheek and blinked, poised to run for cover if Tessa should completely lose her cool.

"Is this how you repay me when I take you into my home?" Tessa screeched like an old fishwife. Her hair stuck out like long corkscrews around her head. "By breaking up my family and insulting us? I wish I'd never laid eyes on you! I'm going to phone your father and tell him to take you the hell back to Adelaide."

A firm arm slipped around Claire's shoulder. Peter knew it was time he intervened again. Claire had no other friends in Melbourne and he had been a witness. That made it his business.

"Tessa, this isn't Claire's fault. Russell is the only person to blame. She did nothing wrong. She was only looking after the babies as you asked her to. All she's ever done is try to help you, however she can."

The blotches in Tessa's cheeks faded, leaving them dingy, tired grey. She sank onto the steps and began to cry.

Claire's resentment changed to sympathy and she wished she had not spoken those angry words. She knew how it felt to be lonely and deserted. "I'm sorry it happened, Auntie Tessa." Her voice sounded thin and feeble. "I will go back to Adelaide, as soon as I can." Although she had given Russell no encouragement, perhaps she was to blame. If she had not been too proud to return to her parents months ago, it would never have happened.

Tessa looked up, squared her jaw, and made an effort to pull herself together. She had to face things as they were. Happiness had always eluded Tessa. She had been a desolate single mother with two teenagers. Now she would be a desolate single mother with two teenagers and two infants when she sent Russell packing. She would be better off without such a cheat.

A new thought shook Tessa to her marrow. Had it occurred to Claire to blame her for what happened? When Claire reported the incident to her parents, William would go crazy. He would curse himself for sending his precious daughter into the household of a sleazy wolf-in-sheep's-clothing, and he would lay all the blame at Tessa's door. Knowing her brother, he would buzz across to Melbourne like a mad hornet to abuse her for living with Russell. William would cause a family ruckus which would last until their dying days.

"It wasn't your fault," Tessa conceded gruffly, but could not bring herself to look at Claire's pretty face. Accusing her niece had been the last thing she should have done. Tessa and William had never been terribly close, but since the death of their parents he was the only family she had. She could not bear the idea of never being on speaking terms with William and Kate.

Tessa attempted a reassuring smile, with a lugubrious effect. "You're right, you have to go home, but promise me you won't tell anybody what happened. Your father would murder me." Tessa's children had hated Russell from the start and they too, would despise and disown their mother if they found out. She spoke quickly to beat her rising tears. "Please don't tell Rachel or Steven either. I would rather this went no further than the three of us."

"I won't tell a soul, Tessa," Peter promised readily. The sooner he could distance himself from the sordid business, the better.

"I won't either," Claire echoed. She supposed keeping silent was the least she could do for her aunt, so she ignored the heavy weight of deja-vu which rooted her to the step. Claire felt burdened with yet another shameful secret. It all started when she consented to her mother's promise to Rowena Quinlan to tell nobody what Blake had done. Next, Claire's father made her promise she wouldn't tell anybody she had been pregnant and then he made her have an abortion. Now here she was promising her aunt she wouldn't tell anybody that she had almost been assaulted by her step-uncle. Claire wanted to bury her head deep in the mud puddle and never emerge for another breath. *Is there anybody in the world with nothing to hide?*

Very soon, Rachel arrived home and found them sitting there. Tessa wiped her tear streaks and tried to appear normal. Peter whipped his arm away from Claire's shoulders and stood to greet his girlfriend with the usual kiss. Rachel's narrowed eyes proved that she was nobody's fool. She had glimpsed enough in a few seconds to guess that something was up. She demanded to know what it was and the three on the verandah made a fair show of playing dumb. However, it was not quite convincing enough.

Claire leaned her elbows upon her suitcase with a sad sniffle. Russell had returned sheepishly home and he and Tessa spent their time closeted in their bedroom with angry murmurs waffling through the chinks of the door. Rachel had not spoken a word to Claire in two days. She turned sullen, and whenever Claire approached her, she spun on her heels and walked the other way. It hurt Claire to leave on such bad terms and she longed to tell Rachel everything. However, her promise to Tessa bound her. It seemed Claire wreaked havoc wherever she went. She could not go away from Melbourne without leaving either her aunt or her cousin hostile. She sighed deeply and wriggled beneath the sheets of the uncomfortable stretcher bed. Only once more, and then she would be on the train bound for home.

––––––––––

Blake was on his way to visit Sean and Angela, and as he drove he pondered deeply all he had read. He had been right. As he read his Bible afresh, Jesus lived for him in the pages of the Gospels. Blake discovered a God-man who was vibrantly alive, compelling and good. Each word He uttered touched Blake's heart with its fresh simplicity and stark honesty. Yes, Blake believed that Jesus was the Son of God. Having made the claims He made, the only other alternatives were that He had delusions of grandeur or some twisted plan to lead people astray. The quality of His life did not fit either explanation.

Blake was relieved to know that one sinless person had existed, full of such love for all men and women that He was willing to lay His life down for them. It proved that not everybody was out solely for himself as Robbo claimed. Blake would have loved Jesus and followed Him if he had been around then. He could still find it in his heart to do so now, if Jesus was truly alive and willing to accept him as a follower.

He stopped at a set of traffic lights and thoughtfully ran his tongue over his top teeth. Not only did he believe in God, but he believed that Jesus was God's own Son as He claimed to be. *Does that make me a Christian?* He slowly shook his head. There was the rub. He still had so many questions and doubts, so much he did not understand about the way the salvation message worked.

Blake could not read the accounts of the Crucifixion without feeling a tight ache in his chest. The more he knew of Jesus, the sicker he felt to think that somebody like Him should have had to die such a brutal death for people like him. Blake's head throbbed with the futility of trying to understand why a good and loving God had let His Son go through it. How could one grossly unfair miscarriage of justice to an innocent man mean that all others should be pardoned? It did not make sense to him.

Blake honed in on some of Jesus' words. "I did not come for the righteous, but for sinners." And how gracious He had been to the woman caught in adultery. "As others have not condemned you, no more do I. Go, and sin no more." Blake tried to compare his own sin to that of the adulterous woman and came up black as soot. His case was far worse than hers. He would be willing to bet that woman had not hurt the men she was with as badly as Blake had hurt Claire Parker.

Blake reasoned that he was even worse than Paul before his conversion. For at least when he was killing Christians, Paul's mind had been deluded into thinking he was doing good. When Blake made his move on Claire, he knew very well that he was doing a vile, despicable thing, yet he kept right on doing it. Try as he might to find a loophole in the Bible to excuse himself, he could not. His guilt held him fast, like a heavy suit of chain mail.

He remembered reading something in his Bible about an unpardonable sin against the Holy Spirit. Blake did not understand what that meant but he would not be surprised if he had committed it. Claire had been fresh and beautiful, like a delicate rosebud ready to burst forth, and he might have cruelly snapped her stem so that she could never blossom as she should. *Isn't shattering another person's life and spirit unforgivable enough?*

Blake parked in the visitor's car park, near Angela and Sean's flat.

Their two front windows were cheerful squares of light to welcome him out of the dark night. It was time for Blake to push his condemning thoughts to the back of his mind. Sean had problems enough of his own without buying into Blake's confusion. Blake did not feel like putting on a bright face for a game of chess but he would make a good show of it.

He wondered if he had burdened Sean too much as it was. It seemed odd for Sean to phone Blake especially to challenge him to a game of chess. Sean had always hated chess before his accident and he could rarely sit still long enough to play. In fact, games of strategy had been the only contests Blake had ever been able to beat Sean at. He guessed that Sean was making an effort to cheer him up the best way he knew how. Blake felt bad for putting him to the trouble. He tapped on the door, resolved that even Angela would find him a model of sunshine and cheer.

The evening progressed smoothly for a time. Sean and Blake played two games of chess while Angela sat in the background with a crossword puzzle. Sean looked fit and happy, as he always used to. Blake sat across the table from him but it always came as something of a shock whenever he stood and saw Sean's wheelchair. It filled him with fresh admiration every time. Sean was one in a million, and Blake never had a bigger hero than his own brother.

Trouble erupted at the finish of the evening when nobody expected it. Blake had wiped Sean off the board for the second time, and Sean pushed his red pieces good-naturedly aside, grinning. "It's not fair. I really tried hard, that time."

"When will you ever learn, nothing is ever fair in the world," Blake commented as he folded the board. He had not intended to make a philosophical observation. He had not even meant to be morose. The remark just slipped out and he was smiling as he said it.

Angela immediately put down her newspaper, rolled her eyes and peered at him. "What do you mean?" She was sure Blake wanted to irk her and knew she should ignore him, but she never lost hope that someday she might get the better of him.

"I didn't mean anything, Angela. It was a silly thing to say. Forget it." He felt too tired to be grilled by Angela that night.

"I want to know why you think the world is so unfair," she persisted and ignored Sean's pleading eyes and shake of the head. Earlier that night he had begged her to let an evening with Blake pass without a dispute. Angela promised she would try and now she was going to let Sean down. She would be sorry later but she was convinced Blake had started it.

Blake sighed and tried to answer her question without getting in any deeper. "I haven't noticed much justice," he hedged. "If you think the world is fair, Angela, that's excellent. Don't worry about what I think." He wondered why she took his opinions to heart when she did not even like him.

Her pen slipped out of her hand, forgotten. "If you're referring to Sean's accident again, I can tell you, you needn't worry. He has accepted his circumstances and he's doing very well."

"I know you think that God has everything in the world under control," Blake told her.

Angela stalked to the kitchen and filled the kettle, turning the tap on hard. "Indeed I do! If you don't believe it, that's your problem," she called over her shoulder.

Suddenly, Blake became fed up with Angela's digs at him for daring to consider opinions other than hers. She never bothered to understand where he was coming from. She was so overbearing, she drove him up the wall. "He expected His only Son to die!" he cried hotly. "He sacrificed the only person who never did anything wrong, to forgive others. Not only does that seem unfair, to me. It seems totally crazy!"

Angela slammed the tin of biscuits hard on the counter and flinched at the noise. "It isn't as if Jesus had no say about it!" she flared. "His Father didn't force Him to lay down His life. He did it voluntarily."

Neither of them noticed as Sean, still sitting at the table, buried his face in his hands and groaned. It seemed he would have to invite his brother to visit him only when his wife would be out.

"I still don't understand how His death could save anyone else," Blake was saying. "It doesn't make sense." He despised himself for getting bogged down into this argument when he had been determined not to.

"The people who don't accept Him won't be saved," Angela snapped. "Nobody is going to force you to accept Jesus' sacrifice. If you don't like it, forget it, Blake. Just keep going the way you're headed."

Her words hit him like a hard blow. Suddenly, Blake found it all too much. Angela was right. He could do nothing but tread the same confused path he had always trod. Suddenly, the unthinkable happened and Blake could not prevent it for the world. His eyes turned misty and a few tears slipped through his lashes before he could slam up his iron self-control.

"O.K. Angela, I'll never bother you again." He strode away, disgusted with himself. What a dope he must appear and how she would laugh at his weakness. He had been in the wrong frame of mind to visit. He should have stayed home.

Angela gaped after him. Her sharp eyes had seen his tears. Her hand trembled as she gingerly placed the cup she held back on its saucer. Angela considered herself an impeccable judge of character. It was almost impossible to surprise her but Blake had just done it.

Sean shook his head reproachfully at her and Angela felt an unfamiliar regretful sensation suffuse her cheeks with heat. She realised it was shame and tried to justify herself. Blake behaved so much like a cocky smart-alec, how was she to guess that he hid a vulnerable side? One thing was clear, she ought to stop him before he escaped. For once, Angela saw herself through somebody else's eyes. It was not a pleasant sensation.

"Blake.... I didn't mean to sound harsh." She hardly knew how to apologise. With another hot surge of guilt, Angela realised it was something she had not practised much.

By now, he was master of himself again. He shrugged his shoulders and attempted a couldn't-care-less grin. "Don't worry Angela, I don't mind what you say." He looked at her sorrowful face and knew that this time, she saw through him. Blake cursed himself for being so spineless. He did not want to leave her upset and supposed he owed her some explanation.

"It's just a bit hard for me sometimes, coming to terms with what I did, you know."

She stared at him, grey to the lips. "I don't know what you did," she murmured.

Blake stared blankly at Sean. "You didn't tell her?" Now he had really put his foot in it. If Angela disliked him already, how much more reason she would have to detest him when she knew!

"No!" Sean answered firmly. "I have no right to tell Angela your business."

Blake sighed. "You might as well tell her. Then she might see why I'm scared to face God." Blake felt he might as well lay all his cards on the table now. She hated him already, so perhaps one more disclosure would make little difference.

He turned to face her and his great dark eyes burned with humiliation. "You'll really have words to say to me next time you see me," he said, with a wry smile.

Angela still said nothing but her own flickering green eyes looked him up and down as if she had never seen him before. Blake found he could not stand her scrutiny. He hurried to get out of their bright little flat into the darkness outside, where he felt far more comfortable.

————

Much later, Angela huddled in the cane rocking chair by the large window of her flat, watching the dawn of the new morning. The window faced the east, and the picture was superb, as if somebody had poured a huge tin of rose coloured paint over all the trees, roads and house tops she could see. Angela's eyes were red and swollen with weeping and sleeplessness. She and Sean had talked far into the night, then she had tossed and turned long after he lay asleep with his mouth wide open. She decided she needed to grab a blanket and spend some time talking to God in her favourite quiet place.

At first, Angela tried to rationalise her behaviour. She hated the creepy, prickly conviction that she had treated Blake badly. She had been hard on him for good reason. She'd been thinking of Sean and Rowena, trying to shield them from Blake's doubts so that their new faith would not waver. She had wanted to make the path as easy as possible for them to love God, but had known nothing about Blake's personal history, so she could not be blamed for making him feel worse.

The more Angela tried to justify her attitude, the heavier her heart felt until it seemed like a rock in her chest. She felt God urging her to be totally honest. He was the Creator of the universe and He did not need her help. He alone was responsible for guarding the hearts of Sean and Rowena. Angela knelt on the carpet and readily admitted that she had once again taken upon her shoulders too much responsibility for others. She could not understand the niggling impression that there was even more to it than that.

Come on Angela, you can hide nothing from Me, so don't fool yourself. Pull the blinkers away from your eyes and face up to the truth. Why did you really *object to Blake?*

She examined the depth of her heart and what she found made her weep with bitter shame. She had felt threatened by Blake. Angela had cleverly convinced herself that she stood for God, yet it was essentially a personal grudge. She hated to feel shown up; it was plain and simple.

Angela had been thrown on her own sense and resourcefulness for many years. She had thanked God for giving her those gifts to help her face life, yet deep down she was inordinately proud of them. She made an idol of her intellect. Then she met Sean's younger brother, a dour, self-professed cynic in a dead-end government job. Angela refused to acknowledge the possibility that he might have had more imagination and depth of thought than she. She had disliked Blake not because of who he was, but because of how he made her feel. The truth broke Angela's heart.

When she had been unable to convince Blake to follow Jesus, as she had Sean and Rowena, Angela felt like a failure as a Christian. She resented him for not believing instantly what she believed. *I might have even driven Blake away from wanting to know about you, Lord. If I'm the best example of Christianity he sees, I wouldn't blame him for wanting none of it. I'm truly sorry for any stumbling block I may have been.*

She thought of Sean's disclosure about Blake. Angela had been horrified to learn what he had done, but her initial response had not been repugnance, as he obviously expected, but shocked surprise. She had believed Blake capable of many things but rape was not one of them. She could not visualise her quiet, reflective brother-in-law turning passionate enough to do it. Angela furrowed her brow. *What could have come over him that night, to do such a terrible thing?*

As she pondered Blake in a more detached way than before, she began to perceive things which had escaped her in the past. His low self- esteem was written over every inch of him. Angela guessed that this was not just the result of his having raped a girl but also part of the cause. He must have taken the girl's rejection to heart and lashed out in anger. It was not difficult to understand. She had seen the coarse way Gerard Quinlan treated his family, and Blake in particular. Sean told her that before his accident, their father had been far worse.

It was easy to see that Gerry had favoured Sean when he was fit and athletic. Blake had a quick mind, but Angela was sure brains were something Gerard had never much banked on. He probably never even realized that his second son was quite bright. Angela wondered if Blake realized it himself. She deeply pitied the girl Blake had raped but found it very easy to pity him, too.

She closed her eyes and prayed for guidance. First, she laid her own pride down for God to strip it away in all its ugliness. An uncomfortable impression crept up on her that although this was good, God wanted more from her. She had admitted her culpability to Him, and she should also admit it to Blake.

At first, Angela baulked. *Please Lord, won't a simple apology do? I've admitted my shame to you. Do I have to tell Blake? Won't you leave me with some dignity?*

She flexed her toes restlessly against the wall. It was a silly question and she knew the answer. God had put it on her heart to tell Blake, and she would follow Him, whatever it took. It would be far from easy, but God had not promised her a life in her own comfort zone. She swallowed hard.

I'll tell him. I'm not looking forward to it, but I'll do it. She did not know when she would see Blake again but remembered his departing words to her that night. "You'll really have words to say to me the next time you see me." Angela managed a grim smile. He was right. She would have words to say to him, but they certainly would not be the words he would expect to hear.

Chapter Seventeen

It was noon, and Claire was already packed to catch the seven o'clock train to Adelaide that evening. She stood ironing the few dresses she had borrowed from Rachel, careful to leave them spotless and clean. Rachel sat by the television with her back pointedly toward Claire, buffing her nails. Nobody else was home. Claire longed to speak to Rachel but Rachel's stiff shoulders looked like an impenetrable wall, so she said nothing. How she hated to leave things as they were between them.

The telephone rang and as Rachel made no sign of moving from her chair, Claire answered it. At last she had to speak to Rachel, because it was one of her friends asking for her. Rachel swept over and snatched the receiver. Claire returned miserably to her ironing. She supposed she would be just as angry if Rachel shared a secret with her mother and refused to divulge it.

"No Carol, I won't listen to what he has to say," Rachel was saying in a flinty voice. "He's had time to make up all sorts of lies by now. Peter and I are through..... I'm free any night you like." She lowered her voice but Claire still heard her words. "I can't say any more right now but I'll tell you the whole story tonight, and why he's the prize sneak of all times."

Claire waited until Rachel hung up the phone. She knew her head would be snapped off but she was too concerned not to ask. "Why have you and Peter split up?"

Rachel whirled on her, with an angry crimson spot on each cheek. "You have a damn nerve!" Her dirty look pierced Claire like lightning.

"I'm sorry for listening in. I know it's none of my business," she blushed.

"Stop playing your innocent games with me. None of your business, indeed! You're in it up to your eyeballs. Do you think I'm stupid?"

Claire was puzzled. "What do you mean?"

Rachel shoved her aside with a hard push. She forgot about her TV and leaned belligerently in the kitchen doorway. "I know you've been seeing Peter behind my back," she said darkly. "Is he going to follow you to Adelaide or have you dumped him too?"

"That's not true!" Claire gasped.

"I caught you red handed! You all tried to cover up as soon as you saw me, but I saw enough. He was sitting there with his arm around you! Mum came home and caught you both kissing and cuddling, didn't she? Then the three of you hashed it out and agreed not to hurt me, as long as you went straight back to Adelaide."

Claire desperately tried to deny it, but Rachel surged on. "You had us all well and truly fooled. We felt so sorry for you and all that time you were such a hypocrite. Then he had the cheek to stand up and kiss me as if nothing had happened. The two-timing jerk!" Rachel burst into tears.

"It was nothing like that!" Claire wanted to kick herself for not guessing how bad it must have looked. Instead of grieving over Rachel's coldness to her, she wondered why her cousin had not clobbered her. Claire was aghast to think that for four days, Rachel had believed such a preposterous misconception.

"Didn't you ask Peter?" she blustered. "He could have told you."

"Of course I asked him," Rachel sniffed scornfully. "He clammed up and denied it, just as you are doing now. He said he's not free to tell me the real story but he loves me deeply and wants me to believe him." Rachel's lips puckered, as if she were sucking a lemon. "What does he expect me to think?"

Claire understood. Peter had stuck to the promise Tessa extracted from him. Although he stood to lose his girlfriend over it, he did not weaken. Claire's heart was sick of deceitful cover-ups. Peter had saved the day, and it was unfair that he should suffer, while Tessa and Russell saved face.

"I'm going to tell you the truth," she said quietly. Claire did not care that she was breaking her own promise. She did not care if her aunt would be angry for she was leaving that evening, anyway. She needed to do what she thought was right.

It was difficult to tell Rachel what Russell had done to her but Claire managed. Although her throat ached, her voice remained steady. She was doing it for Rachel and Peter.

She moistened her lips at the end of her story. "I'm sorry I had to tell your mother's secret, but it's not fair to you or Peter to leave things as they are." At last Claire wiped her sleeve across her sore eyes.

She looked up, and saw from the concerned shadows over Rachel's face that her cousin believed her. Claire's knees trembled with relief. Rachel slumped into a chair, every trace of anger gone. "Claire, I'm.... sorry."

"Don't worry about me. I'm OK." Claire was astonished to realise she meant it. She was OK. "You'd better phone Peter and tell him that I told you. Tell him you believe him."

Rachel bowed her head in her hands. "I can't. I said such horrible things to him. I called him some disgusting names. He won't want to speak to me ever again."

"Then I'm going to phone him for you!"

"You can't." Rachel spoke hesitantly but her eyes brightened, clearly hoping that Claire would.

Claire was already leafing through the pages of Rachel's crammed address book. "Peter is great, and he loves you." She punched in Peter's number while Rachel hovered anxiously near her elbow, all four nails of her right hand between her teeth.

"Hello Mrs Lennox, this is Claire Parker, Rachel's cousin. Could I please speak to Peter? Thank you." Both girls waited breathlessly, until Claire's hand tightened around the receiver, and she spoke again. "Hi Pete, it's Claire. Rachel told me what she thought and I set her straight. She's sorry for doubting you. She wants you to forgive her. Would you... speak to her?"

Rachel's heart plummeted when Claire said, "OK, Peter," and hung up the phone. "Didn't he want to speak to me?" she moaned.

"No, he didn't want to." Claire's back was turned to Rachel, but when she spun around, her face shone. "He said he's going to come around here right now, to see you in person."

Rachel squealed and bounced on her toes. She threw her arms around Claire and squeezed her hard, then stood back with a watery smile. "Thanks, heaps," she said.

Claire laughed and hugged Rachel again. It was the first time she had impulsively touched another person for two years. Now that she had only a matter of a few hours before leaving, she felt closer to Rachel than she had in all the previous months. It was almost worth being suspected of foul play, for the delight of being able to put things right.

———

It was quite dark at the railway station when Claire said goodbye to Rachel and Peter on the platform. Rachel hugged her and Peter gave her hand a firm, warm squeeze. "I hope things go well for you in Adelaide," he said with a regretful edge to his voice. Claire could not hold his gaze. She hastened to duck her head and step onto the train.

She found her seat and peered out of the window, to see them still standing, with their arms entwined. She smiled, with a glowing feeling inside her chest. It was pleasant to know that she had helped to make peace instead of trouble. Rachel had cried and hugged her mother with pity, so even Tessa was not angry with Claire for spilling the beans. Peter had thanked her profusely for setting things straight. What a good looking couple he and Rachel made. Claire sighed, satisfied with their romance.

The train started and she watched the fences and light posts of Melbourne whiz past her. She wished she had a boyfriend like Peter, who would love and treasure her. Claire felt empty and forlorn, but somehow it proved that her heart was healing. She had shied away from thoughts of romance since she had been raped, but now she longed for it as she used to. Sure, there were many men like Russell Timms at large, but there had to be several Peter Lennoxes too.

She leaned her head against the headrest and flexed her toes. She would be sitting up in her seat all night, so the sooner she reached Adelaide the better. Claire found herself longing for the city where she had suffered the worst night of her life. After so long apart, she could hardly wait for her first glimpse of her parents' faces. How they must have missed her and worried for her. Claire would show them that she was fine, and ready to stretch her wings and embrace life again.

She leaned her chin on the window and gave a surprised chuckle. Her mother had been right all along. Living with Auntie Tessa's family had done Claire a world of good.

Blake sheepishly tapped on the door of the flat. He had kept a low profile for as long as he could, but at last Angela, not Sean, asked him to visit. She said she had something important to tell him which could not be done over the phone. Now she opened the door, grabbed him by the shoulder, propelled him to a kitchen chair and pushed him into it. The kettle had already boiled and Sean was nowhere in sight.

"You sit and drink your coffee, and don't say a word until I finish what I have to say to you," Angela ordered.

Blake nodded. That, at least, would be easy enough.

Angela placed a piping hot cup of black coffee by her own elbow but never looked at it. Blake, on the other hand, compulsively sipped often, in his customary way when he felt nervous. While his fingers curled around the cup, his dark eyes watched her curiously over the rim.

Angela moistened her lips. "I shouldn't have said the things I said. Not just last Wednesday night, but ever since I've known you. I've taken every chance I could to jump down your throat. I never gave you an inch. I've been thoroughly obnoxious, and you must have found me a pain in the neck."

Blake inhaled quickly and seemed about to speak, but remembered his promise and kept quiet.

"I've worked out.... well, I think God has shown me, why I behaved so badly," Angela went on. "I was proud. I felt bitter to think that you might be as smart as I was, when I was older than you and had years of study behind me. I resented you for not wanting to instantly jump on my bandwagon. I thought I must look shallow or stupid in your eyes, and I hated you for it."

At last, Angela raised her cup of coffee. She needed to shield her burning face.

"That was a terrible attitude. My arrogance was inexcusable. I was in the wrong, Blake, and I don't blame you for feeling as you felt. I hope you can forgive me." For one who was unaccustomed to making apologies, Angela could not help thinking she had done a pretty good job.

Blake's pupils were huge with wonder. He did not know what dumbfounded him more. The fact that Angela thought him smart or hearing her admit it to him. "Am I allowed to talk yet?" he asked quietly.

She cleared her throat and nodded, with a forced smile. "Permission granted."

"I never thought you were shallow or stupid," he said earnestly.

"I did think you were a little inflexible at times, but I never meant to belittle your beliefs." He swirled the last inch of coffee around in his cup and kept his eyes fixed upon it. "For what it's worth, I'm sorry too. I envied you, for being so sure of what you believe."

She nodded slowly. "Sean and I had a long talk. He told me how you used to badger him to know his thoughts about God, at a time when he didn't even care. He said that all you ever wanted was to learn. I believe that now."

"Did Sean tell you.... what else I did?" Blake managed to utter. He could hardly bear to look at her but he had to.

"He told me," she said, almost inaudibly.

Fresh firecrackers of guilt and shame snapped in his head. "Well don't you think I'm a no-good rapist?" he croaked. He was amazed that Angela could face him at all, let alone apologise so humbly.

"I think you were that night," she replied steadily. "I don't think you are now. The best thing about a past, Blake, is that you can put it behind you and move on." She struggled to say what she felt on her heart without sounding like a know-all, again. "I know you'll never forget what you did, but I'd hate to see you let one rotten action ruin your whole life."

He had finished his coffee but still fiddled with the cup, needing something to occupy his fingers. Every move displayed his shame and insecurity, and she wondered why she had never noticed such things before.

"But what if I've destroyed... that girl's heart?" He almost brought himself to say the name Claire Parker, but when it came to the crunch, he could not utter it aloud. It would be the finish of him.

"God loves her as much as he loves you," Angela said gently. "All you can do is leave her to Him, and work out what He wants for your own life." She flushed. "I hope you don't mind my talking about God. I really believe in Him very strongly."

"I know you do," Blake said. "I've decided I believe in Him too, and you've just helped me believe in Him without a doubt."

Angela's jaw dropped. "How did I do that?" She found her heart thumping.

"By admitting what you just told me." He managed a slight smile. "I know you well enough to know you'd never say all that off your own bat. You must have heard from Him, as you said."

Angela tilted her head back and laughed. She had been so ashamed to face Blake with the truth and that was the nicest thing he could have said to her. "He will speak into your heart too, if you ask Him to," she cried.

"How can I do that?" he asked anxiously. "Tell me Angela, because I really want to know." At last he was getting somewhere with her.

Angela briefly closed her eyes, and breathed a quick prayer for guidance. Blake was such a complex person; she had to say the right thing. "I think you should learn to simply believe that God's words are true instead of always gauging life by your own feelings," she began. "Feelings are unreliable guides, and God has said that He loves you and will forgive you if you ask Him to. Just because you don't feel loved or forgiven by God, doesn't mean it isn't true."

Her expression softened. "Just because it seems ludicrous to you that Jesus would be prepared to die for you, God has said that it's true. He doesn't expect you to bend yourself backwards and try to make up for what you've done, because you know that's impossible. He just wants you to believe He's taken care of it for you, and repent of what you've done. Then, He will live inside of you and guide you by speaking to your heart through His Holy Spirit. It's that simple, because He said so."

Blake sat quietly, but she saw that he seriously considered every word she said.

"Shall I pray for you?" Angela ventured.

He flexed his fingers self-consciously and nodded. "I'd like that," he said briefly.

Angela clasped her hands and said a simple prayer that Blake would come to learn the depth of God's love for him. "He's repented of his sins many times, and you know that, Lord. He wants to turn around and give his life to you. He wants you to live in him and fill him with your desires and your thoughts. You can make Blake into a brand new man and I pray that you will help him to believe it. Thank-you because you want him to be a precious son of yours, and you love him."

She looked up at his bowed head. "That's all, Blake. You pray the same thing for yourself." She knew she had got to the crux of his problem. "You needn't make God's love out to be more complicated than it is. He loves you for who you are, so you believe it."

Blake straightened his bent shoulders, and nodded. "You're right, Angela. I feel no different to before, but I will believe it. I think it must be true, just because God said it is." He realised that he did sense something new. A light impression of relief, and muted excitement filled him.

Angela proffered her hand. "Friends?" she asked.

Blake grinned shyly, then awkwardly shook her hand. "Friends," he echoed.

A wave of unexpected affection for her pensive brother-in-law surged through Angela. How ridiculous she had been to regard him as an enemy all that time.

"Where's Sean today?" Blake asked, as if his brother's absence had only just occurred to him.

"In the bedroom, watching TV. I wanted to speak to you alone."

Blake laughed. "Does he always do as he's told? Who wears the pants in your family, anyway?"

Angela laughed with him. She was willing to accept his gentle teasing in the light-hearted manner it was meant. A shaft of sunlight shining through the kitchen window helped to make her feel clean and bright inside. "You go and tell him he can come out now, if he likes."

Angela began to clean her stove top vigorously and hummed while she worked. Resolving her feud with Blake had given her a boost of energy. How exhausting it had been to cling to her inner competition with him. It would be a pleasant change for everybody, to see her on good terms with him. She looked forward to it. Yes, she was sure Blake would be a good person to have as a friend.

————————

Later as he drove home, Blake's mind was whirling with a number of impressions. *Wow, what a morning!* He grew increasingly more excited to dream of being accepted by God. And what a surprise package Angela turned out to be!

Blake could not help noticing the intimacy she shared with Sean, in their holding hands, the fond smiles they exchanged, the way her hands caressed his muscles when she took him through his daily exercises. He found himself wondering about their most intimate moments. Although many of Blake's memories of the night with Claire Parker were hazy, there were some details he would never forget. Had it been easy for Sean to make the transition from bachelor to husband with his handicap? Blake flushed and felt ashamed of entertaining such thoughts.

Was his mind naturally quirky, or did all people think along those lines sometimes? Could God really love him, in spite of it all? Blake quickly shook the returning doubt out of his head. God did love him. Angela had only reinforced what was in the Bible. Nobody was unworthy of God's love.

Angela is very pretty. If she had never met Sean, Blake wondered, *what would she have thought of a guy like me?* Although Angela was very bossy, and four years his senior, a girl like her might get along OK with him. This time he gasped, truly horrified with himself. He would forget he had ever thought such a thing.

PART TWO

Chapter Eighteen

The craft shop had closed for the night, and Claire was busy shifting the merchandise displays to set up the circle of desks for her tapestry class.

"Claire, Love, I'll leave these two packets of biscuits for your group's supper tonight," said Pam, her employer.

Claire gave a dimpled smile. "Thanks, Pam." She thought for the thousandth time what a kind boss she had. When Claire had started working on tapestries to kill some lonely time at her Auntie Tessa's house so long ago, she had no idea that she would forge a career out of them. Claire began by selling some of the wall hangings and cushions she produced. She researched historical tapestries and tried her hand at designing her own patterns, many with Christian themes and some like stained glass windows. She even had some of her patterns published in craft magazines. Even after four years, Claire shook her head, dumbfounded, when she thought of how quickly she had found this new direction.

She had not even applied for her job at Busy Fingers, Pam Lewis's craft shop. Pam had contacted her through one of the magazines and offered her work. Now Claire spent two days serving customers, three evenings teaching classes, and the rest of her time working on her own creations at home. It was the ideal lifestyle for her and she had never returned to school, although her parents had hoped she would.

One term, a pregnant teenager had attended her classes. Janine

Turner. Claire had never forgotten her. She'd given the girl some extra tuition after hours and Janine had confided in her, with tears streaming down her cheeks. She had been terrified at the thought of having a baby. She'd never meant to fall pregnant. Janine had almost convinced herself to visit an abortion clinic. All Claire had done was offer a shoulder to cry on. She even cried with her and spoke of her own abortion; the first time she had ever done so. Her words seemed so inadequate to her, but they seemed to be enough.

Janine had written her a heartfelt card at the end of term. She'd continued the pregnancy and was getting closer to term. She'd met a wonderful counsellor at a crisis pregnancy centre who was helping her. Janine thanked Claire for being the first person who had helped her think with clarity instead of sheer panic. That had been over a year ago. Claire often thought about Janine's little baby. *Perhaps it really had been partly because of what I said or did.* Somehow, the memory helped her feel refreshed, just that little bit closer to the baby she would not have the chance to get to know.

Pam's daughter, Michelle, sat behind the counter with her feet resting on top, leafing through a pile of catalogues. "Claire, my new church is having a study camp in a few weeks. It's a bus trip to a beautiful old function centre in Sydney and the course is aimed at finding our place in God's plan. Look at the subjects it covers."

Claire scanned the course outline. It included productive prayer techniques, powerful quiet times, sharing your faith, coming close to God's heart and discovering your own destiny. On the front of the programme was a photograph of the campsite. It showed a rambling stone building surrounded by green lawns with a rock garden, swimming pool and tennis courts.

Claire passed it back with an envious sigh. "It sounds fascinating, Michelle. You'll have a great time."

"Would you like to come with me? You see, I don't know anybody yet, and I don't want to take off for two weeks on my own. Mum'll give you time off, won't you Mum?"

Claire's heart leaped at the thought of an unexpected holiday. "I don't know if I can afford it." She had recently bought herself a small second hand car.

"Look at the cost!" Michelle cried. "It's quite reasonable for a fortnight, and it includes travelling expenses. They won't make a profit out of us. Come on, it won't break you." When Michelle wheedled, it was hard to refuse.

"At least come to the information night," she urged. "One of the speakers is going to show a video with the course overview next Thursday night at eight. Then we get the registration forms."

Claire nodded. "OK. Give me the church's address and I'll meet you there after my tapestry class." If Pam was willing to give her time off, she would at least attend the information night. It was not often she was invited on a holiday by a friend.

Michelle beamed. "Thanks Claire. I knew I could count on you. I talked myself hoarse trying to convince Tara to join me, but you know her. She wouldn't have a bar of it. Stubborn as an old mule."

Tara Pritchard, the other shop girl, snorted. "I'm not interested in that Christian baloney, but you girls have fun."

Although it came as no surprise, Claire's heart sank to realise she had been second choice. If Tara had agreed to go, she doubted that Michelle would have bothered to ask her too. Michelle and Tara had been best friends since they were ten years old so it was only natural that Claire was going to feel on the outside of a special bond, even after the four years she had known them. They were both good friends to have so she tried not to mind.... much.

Angela Quinlan watched her husband, with tears prickling her eyes. For the first time in over six years of marriage, Sean was going away without her to a conference for para-athletes. He assured her they would all be cared for and catered for fine. Although his wife would be allowed to attend, he thought it would do her good to have a break from him.

"You need a rest, to get over what happened to you last month," he said gently, "and looking after my needs is the last thing you need. I want to see you get some colour back in those pale cheeks." He raised her chin and gazed deep into her eyes with loving concern.

Angela forced a smile, although she hated the idea of going away without him. She would feel like only half a person. Perhaps her own identity had been swallowed up in years of caring for a paraplegic husband. She languidly tried to think of a holiday destination which would suit her alone, and came up blank. There was one thing she was half interested in but she could hardly be bothered to pursue it.

"If you don't need me I'll stay home here, and do lots of reading and shopping while you're away."

Sean shook his head, adamant for once. Angela usually had her way but this time he stood firm. "I don't want to think of you pining here alone. You need a totally different scene to perk you up."

She felt a cold chill at the thought that he wanted to fob her off so he could enjoy his conference without having her on his conscience. It saddened her to know that he no longer needed her always by his side. Competing in wheelchair pentathlons seemed to be enough to keep his mind off her and the baby they had just lost.

For years, Angela and Sean had visited fertility clinics, longing to start a family. Sean's spinal injuries had affected his fertility. The doctors said that his problems were natural but not insurmountable. Angela's own troubles had proved to be worse. The endometriosis and ovarian cysts she had known of for years turned out to be real barriers to conception. At last she became pregnant only to lose the baby two months later. That was only a month ago. Her surgeon said that her reproductive organs were a mess. When he suggested that they consider adopting a child, Angela had believed that was the end.

She grieved for the children she would never have. There would be no golden haired boys with Sean's amiable hazel eyes and his sweet smile. No pert little girls with her own determination to make a difference in the world. Angela's heart held a great maternal void which could now never be filled, but at least she had started to feel well in her own body again.

She wondered if she had tried to keep Sean tied to her apron strings like a substitute child, now that no baby would fill her arms. *Is this his way of trying to beg time out from my smothering love?* Perish the thought! She would go along with his plan, and she would even try to enjoy herself.

"There is one interesting camp I've heard of," she told him. "One of my old friends, Chad Matthews is a lecturer. It's tied in with his church. I knew him years ago when I was a nursing student." She handed Sean the programme to read.

He ran his eyes down the page and nodded his approval. "It sounds like your cup of tea, although it's not quite what I had in mind," he grinned. "Too much hard thinking for a holiday. You would never dream of simply relaxing for two weeks, would you?" He tugged her hair fondly.

The study aspect was what appealed to Angela the most. If she had nothing to concentrate on she would go mad dwelling on what she had lost. What better to fill her head with than thoughts of faith and God's goodness?

She gasped, with a sudden brainwave. "This course would suit Blake, too! I don't think he's truly certain of his own worth, even after all this time." If she could convince another member of her family to accompany her, she might not pine so deeply for Sean. "Would you help me talk him into coming? He'd like it."

Sean stiffened and tried to keep his voice detached. "Yes, Blake probably would like it, but he might not be able to leave work at the drop of a hat."

Angela scrambled to her knees. "That'll be easy enough. I can talk to Mr Phillips for him." An old flash of pride stirred her, and her eyes sparkled. She had secured Blake a job with a repairman from her church. Mr Phillips had wanted an apprentice and Angela convinced him to try Blake, who was already twenty-one at the time. Now Blake tinkered with electrical gadgets all day long, and he was far happier than she had ever seen him before.

Sean felt another sense of misgiving. He had tried unsuccessfully to fire her up for weeks, and he was dismayed that the prospect of going on a holiday with Blake was what it took.

"I meant for you to go on your own!" He had not intended to snap. As her eyes filled with tears, he lowered his head, ashamed. He hated to hurt her. In a way, he longed for the early days of his marriage, when Angela and Blake were sworn antagonists. He was not completely comfortable now that they were friends.

Sean felt envious because he could not give his wife the sort of mental stimulation which his brother obviously could. Angela and Blake both liked to discuss subjects he had never heard of, and they both spouted multi-syllable words as easily as if they were using baby talk. He wondered if others noticed how spirited Angela became whenever she had Blake to talk to.

"What difference does it make if I invite Blake to come?" she asked.

"Think about it!" he said testily. He was annoyed at having to explain himself. For somebody who was so bright, she could be pretty dumb sometimes. "Do you know another woman who would jump at the chance of a holiday with her brother-in-law while her husband's away?"

Angela gaped at him. Several expressions chased each other across her face. First bafflement, followed by a dawning understanding; stark shock came next, and finally hilarity. Angela threw back her head and laughed a loud, throaty laugh, as she used to. She wiped her moist eyes and gave his shoulder a gentle shove.

"Tell me you're joking. If not, you must be crazy. If Blake and I lived together we'd drive each other up the wall."

Sean watched her quietly. The fact that she was so amused mollified him slightly. "But you're always so pleased to see him," he muttered. "You rant and rave about things I don't understand. I don't know if I could understand them if I tried, but I can't be bothered trying."

She placed a hand on his knee and stared up into his face. "Sean, are you really so insecure? Listen to me; you're the sort of person God intended when He made man. I wouldn't change you for the world."

"But I wish I could be more like Blake, to please you. He thinks about so many things."

"Which drive him mad," she continued. "Blake is idealistic. He would love to change the world, but you're happy with it the way God made it. Your contentment and reliability and good-heartedness mean the world to me." She was pleased that Sean loved her enough to think of being jealous, after six years. It did her heart good, like a tonic.

He smacked a great kiss on her lips and felt a little silly for his apprehension. "You're such a treasure, any man would want you," he declared. He rubbed his face into her hair, a bright patch of warmth against his black jumper. "Ask Blake along, if you want to. It does sound like his thing." Sean was back to feeling sorry for Blake, who still had no girlfriend at the age of twenty-five, and probably never would. No wonder he was restless. Lonely Blake never knew what he was missing.

Well, perhaps he does know. Sean remembered Blake's big mistake, which had caused so much of his uneasiness around women.

"Wait until I tell him what you thought. He'll die laughing," Angela giggled.

"No, don't tell Blake." Sean felt that enough had been said on the subject. "Let's go to bed," he whispered. He was soon to face two weeks without her and it tore his heart. Although Sean was doing it for Angela's sake, it was a great sacrifice for him. He would far rather have had her close to him.

"Do you feel like some hot chocolate? I'll fix some." He rolled his chair into the kitchen and fixed the two mugs of drink at his own bench which had been fixed to suit his wheelchair height. Angela watched her well-adjusted husband with admiration, but although she was proud of his independence, she felt a pang of nostalgia for the old days when he relied on her for everything.

———————

"Have you met any nice young women lately?" Rowena asked her son.

Blake faced the same question whenever he visited her, and he rolled his eyes to the ceiling. "No Mum. Only old men." At least he would get it over with early in the visit.

"I'm sure you don't meet enough pretty girls in your line of work. Do you still go to your church youth group?"

"Yeah, but the girls and I are happy to leave each other alone. Has it occurred to you, Mum, that I'm not interested in finding a girlfriend?" It was a lie; he thought about girls far more often than he thought he should, but hoped his mother would leave him alone if she thought he was happy.

Rowena clucked her tongue. "When will you be ready? You're twenty-five years old now."

"I know how old I am, Mum. I'm not over the hill yet." He dreaded the time when he would turn thirty and still have to face his mother for this conversation.

"And you're very handsome," she added.

Rowena watched Blake's white smile flash. She admired his dark good looks. The girls were missing a treat.

He brushed off her compliment with a laugh. "Thanks for the vote of confidence but I think you might be biased. Let's talk about something different, Mum. How are Sean and Angela? Has he convinced her to take a holiday without him?"

"Yes, she's going to a Christian camp in Sydney. They're running a course about finding your place in God's plan." Rowena rummaged among her papers on the table. "Angela left this for you, because she's certain it would suit you, too. She said she'd talk to Mr Phillips for you and convince him to let you have a holiday."

"I'm sure she would, but if I wanted a break I'd ask him myself." Blake glanced at the programme. The subject matter did appeal to him, but he objected to Angela deciding what would suit him. Let her stick to organising Sean's life. Sean liked domineering women.

"We both think you should go," Rowena said. "We discussed it over afternoon tea yesterday. It would be just the thing for you. You might meet a nice girl there."

Blake shoved his chair back and wandered across the room to look out of the window. "Why do you think I need my own girl, with you and Angela always around to tell me what would be good for me?" He spoke with forced patience but Rowena got the message.

"Don't take me the wrong way. I'm not finding fault with you. I'm very proud of you." She remembered when she had arranged a date for him and what had come of it. Rowena rebuked herself for poking her nose in. Even when she resolved not to interfere, she could not seem to help it. She only wanted to see him happy. "It's entirely your own decision," she said, chastened by her reflections.

The door burst open and Michael rushed in. Now fifteen years old, he was barrel-chested and sturdy. His bushy hair was fair, like Sean's, and he wore a football uniform as Sean used to, with a pair of very muddy shoes slung around his neck by the laces.

"G'day, Blake. Wish I could stay but I'm off to a party soon." He dropped the filthy shoes at Rowena's feet. "Mum, clean these up, would you?"

Rowena instantly fetched newspaper and a scrubbing brush, and knelt on the floor to do it.

Michael switched on the television and collapsed on an armchair. "Hurry up!"

"Why don't you clean your own shoes?" Blake demanded. Whenever he visited he noticed that Michael bullied Mum as if she were his personal servant, just as Dad had always done. It disturbed him to see Michael mirror Gerry's behaviour.

Michael bristled: "I'm in a hurry, I told you!"

"Not in too much of a hurry to flake out on the couch," Blake shot back. It was time someone butted in.

Michael turned on him. "I've been busy at school all day and she sits home doing nothing. Anyway, you don't even live here anymore, so mind your business."

"I don't mind cleaning the shoes," Rowena interjected, anxious to restore peace.

Blake pursed his lips and said no more but let thoughts run through his mind instead. *If Mum is happy to be bossed around, my interference won't make any difference. It must happen continuously while I'm not around to stick up for her.*

Eventually, Michael got up to go and shower. "Iron me a shirt, too," he flung over his shoulder.

As soon as the bathroom door closed behind him, Blake asked, "Why do you let him treat you like that?"

Rowena sighed and plugged in her iron. "I'm a bit lenient with him because he's my baby, I suppose. Now that you and Sean have left home, he's all I have left... except for your father. I like to make Michael happy."

Blake could understand that. "I still think you've created a monster," he said, and leaned his chin on the back of a chair to watch her iron.

He noticed a persistent buzz and realized that it was coming from the iron. It struck him that Rowena still used the chunky old iron she'd had for over ten years. Sean had bought it for a Mother's Day present long before his accident.

"Can I have a look at that iron when you finish Mike's shirt?"

Rowena hesitated before handing it over. "Don't pull it apart. It's the only one I have."

"I'll try to control myself," Blake assured her, although he longed to fetch his tools and pull it apart. He turned it over carefully in his hands and said, "Don't use this anymore, Mum. It's so old. It could be dangerous. Probably beyond repairing. The cord looks a bit frayed and I don't like that noise it makes. I'll buy you a new one."

"Don't spend your hard earned money on me," she cried. "At least, wait until my birthday."

"Mum, I'd love to buy you a present. I wish you wouldn't worry about putting me out of pocket because I have a good wage and nobody to spend it on but myself."

Blake could have bitten out his tongue as soon as he said it. He had given her an ideal opportunity to heckle him again about finding a girlfriend.

Rowena looked up with large eyes, limpid with pity. "Perhaps one day you'll find somebody to spend it on, besides your old mother."

Blake sank down in his seat and took it. It served him right.

Chapter Nineteen

When Claire arrived at the auditorium in the dark, there was no sign of Michelle. All the other young adults were engaged in conversations with friends and she slipped into an aisle with a view of the door. She supposed Michelle was running late and kept an eye out for her.

The two lecturers, Tom and Chad introduced themselves and took turns giving an overview of the course material they would cover on the camp. They glowed with enthusiasm for their ministry and Claire found herself getting caught up in their vision for young adults. The camp outline appealed to her but she grew increasingly concerned by Michelle's absence. If her friend did not show up, Claire did not know whether she would dare venture off to Sydney alone with strangers. Not for two whole weeks.

Somebody slipped beside her as she toyed with her pen, debating whether to complete her camp registration form. "Hi, can I join you? I'm alone too, and I felt like a sore thumb back there."

Claire looked up at a pretty young woman with blonde hair pulled back into a ponytail, and a pleasant, freckled face. She looked quite a few years older than Claire. Probably in her late twenties.

"Of course," Claire cried. Already she felt less conspicuous herself.

"My name is Angela," the stranger said. "I don't know a soul here except for Chad, the brown haired lecturer. I thought I'd join the camp because my husband is going away without me and I need something to do."

Claire gave her slow, dimpled smile. "I'm Claire. I wasn't supposed to be alone. A friend from work invited me, but she hasn't come. I was just deciding whether to stay or leave when you came."

"Oh, please stay," Angela urged, as if they had known each other for two years instead of two moments. "The others all seem to be great friends and I don't fancy the thought of elbowing my way into one of their little cliques. If your friend doesn't come, we can stick together and share a dorm. I think the course will be well worth studying. I've lost touch with Chad over the years but I can tell you, he's a very powerful speaker."

Angela was intrigued by Claire's quiet serenity. She looked similar to the way Angela always imagined the Madonna must have looked.

"Yes, I think I will stay," Claire had warmed to Angela instantly. She admired people with a flair for talking. Claire's heart suddenly fired with the adventure of launching out to do something unexpected. For too long she had confined herself to the safe and narrow cocoons of home and work, reluctant to take any risks.

As others rose to file out of the theatre, Angela peered at her watch. "My husband won't expect me home for a few hours so as we've only just met, Claire, shall we go to a cafe down the road, and get better acquainted?"

"OK." Claire was willing to follow the lead of the confident and dynamic older girl. She stopped wondering why Michelle had not arrived and fell into step beside Angela.

Over cappuccinos and croissants, Claire heard Angela's engrossing love story. She had been a nurse and met her future husband when he was rushed into hospital after a serious fall. Angela had become his private nurse and fallen in love with him while she worked for him. She had managed to convince him that he was still handsome and desirable, even as a paraplegic. Eventually, he'd returned her affection. They had been happily married for six years and she had helped him realise his new ambition, of being a wheelchair athlete.

Claire thought she had never heard anything so romantic. Her gaze wandered to the sparkling wedding ring on Angela's small finger, and she hoped she managed to conceal her envy. She flushed as she briefly sketched her own history. She liked tapestries and needlework, had a good job with a lovely lady, and taught some classes. She was embarrassed that there was no more to it than it. How lame it must sound after Angela's stirring story.

Angela seemed impressed. "I love old tapestries," she cried.

Claire's occupation suited Angela's conception of her appearance. With a flowing silk gown and pointy, streamered hat instead of denim jeans and white blouse, Claire might have stepped straight out of the Middle Ages. "Perhaps I could buy a tapestry for our flat. I'd love to see them. My husband always says he never knows what I'll come up with next," she laughed.

"I suppose you'll miss him during the camp," Claire said.

Angela's face clouded. "I sure will. Every moment without him will drag, but I still haven't given up hope of convincing my brother-in-law to come. He refused when I asked him but I might change his mind yet. This course would do him good. He's a bit of a loner. He's been a Christian for five years, but can't shake off something that happened in his past." Angela had never been reticent to discuss either herself or others.

Claire's face expressed her interest. Angela's brother-in-law's story sounded similar to her own. "Was it a bad experience?"

Angela nodded. "It was a very sordid experience which happened when he was younger, but he's never put the pain behind him, although he's tried. It's put a damper over every day of his life but he's one of the nicest fellows you could meet. As generous and thoughtful as the day is long. He has plenty of head knowledge about God's forgiveness, but still needs to feel it deep in his heart."

Claire's heart warmed to Angela's relative with each word she uttered, and she slowly ventured to speak herself. "That's a bit like my story. Something.... really horrible happened to me when I was sixteen. I found it hard to get over for many, many months." Claire amazed herself for divulging even this much to a person she had just met. She usually kept the old hurt tightly locked in her chest and had never breathed a word to Michelle or Tara, after four years. There was something about Angela's kind and straightforward green eyes that attracted confidence.

Claire forced a bright tone into her voice. "Now I'm twenty-three and I only think about it sometimes. God helped me to put it behind me and move on with my life." She really believed it.

"You look as if you've come a long way," Angela said admiringly. "I think you'd get along well with my brother-in-law. You might be able to help him lay some of his own skeletons to rest."

"Why wouldn't he come tonight?" Claire was now eager to divert the conversation from herself.

Angela's nose crinkled. "Pigheadedness, I think. I thought of the idea instead of him. He didn't want to be coerced into anything by a woman. You know what men are like?"

Although Claire nodded, she didn't really know what men were like. She wished she could learn. "I hope you are able to convince him," she said.

"I'll do my best, believe me." Angela's eyes danced. "Can you believe that anyone would ever find me pushy?"

A laugh sprang naturally to Claire's lips. She liked Angela very much. She had never warmed so quickly to a chance acquaintance as now. With each moment, she was more certain that her decision to attend the camp was a good one. It would be fun, with a vibrant character like Angela along as her friend.

Claire was already half-way home in her car before she reflected that she and Angela had not even exchanged surnames.

———————

"Mr. Phillips, could I please have some holiday time?" Blake asked. He was confident that his employer would agree because in four years of work, Blake had never made such a request before. He enjoyed work, and there was never any need to take a break, so he never bothered to ask for one. Whenever he did have enforced leave, the time dragged on his hands.

"Certainly," Des Phillips cried. "Any time you like, from next week."

"Could I take next week and the week after?" Blake had swallowed his pride and decided to go with Angela. Hadn't he always wanted to find his place in God's plan, which was just the issue this course aimed to address? He hadn't been to Sydney before and he might even enjoy the trip.

"Any special reason?" Mr. Phillips asked conversationally.

Blake worked deftly on the DVD player he was fixing. "It's a Christian study camp. Sean's going off on a conference which happens to be the same fortnight, and Angela thought the camp sounded interesting so she's going. She asked me to go along too."

Angela had finally twisted Blake's arm by appealing to his sympathy. She told him she would appreciate his company to help her stop missing Sean. She rarely showed her vulnerability and Blake's heart had melted. He could only imagine the pain she and Sean must have felt when they lost their baby. He had been torn apart himself, and he was only the baby's uncle. If his presence would cheer Angela up a little bit, he would not say no. He could not forget that he owed his job to her anyway.

"Take three or four weeks if you like," Mr. Phillips offered lavishly. "We're not run off our feet this month and you're entitled to them."

Blake shook his head. "No thanks, I'll be happy with two."

"Suit yourself." Desmond studied his young employee's bent head and bowed shoulders. Young fellows were different to how they had been in his own generation. If Desmond's boss had offered him extra holiday time, he would have been as happy as a pig in mud. He would have found something to do. Fishing, golfing, or just sleeping in and going out with friends. Blake didn't mention many friends to Des, except one Italian chap named Joseph who used to work in the Public Service with him. Blake was a very private type of lad but certainly likeable enough.

Blake suddenly looked up, with a laugh. "Hey, Mr. Phillips, check this out." He pushed the DVD player across the counter. "These people had a go at fixing this themselves. They stuck the switch down with chewing-gum, then wondered why it didn't work."

Des guffawed, and asked, "Do you know how to fix it?"

"Yes, it won't take me long."

From the very start, Des Phillips could not have hoped for a better worker. Angela Quinlan had asked him to hire her husband's brother as a sort of favour to her. Des was dubious, because Blake was already twenty-one at the time and had done no formal study. However, Mr Phillips was partial to Angela, so he agreed, on the condition that Blake attend trade school part-time two evenings a week.

It was instantly clear that Blake knew his stuff. Whatever Des had been able to teach him was soaked up like a sponge. Blake only had to hear an instruction once and he stored it in his head for good. He was deft and skilful, with plenty of initiative and common sense. The boy was a godsend.

Des Phillips reflected that Blake probably knew as much as he did already. Perhaps he deserved a pay rise. Des turned back to the television set he was repairing. He would think about that later, when Blake returned from his holidays.

"Claire, I'm so sorry," Michelle wailed. "I'd totally forgotten you'd go to the information night. I changed my mind about the camp. Tara's brother, Jack showed up from New Zealand, and drove everything else out of my head. The two of us are going to take him to Kangaroo Island instead so I won't be able to take in this camp as well."

"So you forgot all about poor old Claire?" Pam was horrified by her daughter's thoughtlessness. "You left her waiting at the auditorium and never showed up?"

"Awww, Mum, it was just one of those things."

"That's OK, because I'm going on the camp anyway." Claire was neither hurt nor annoyed by Michelle's oversight as she would have expected to be. She was merely a little smug to prove that she did not require Michelle's presence to go and enjoy herself. "It sounds excellent and I'm looking forward to it."

"Good for you!" Pam cried.

Michelle blinked, quite taken-aback. She rarely thought of Claire as a person with a life outside of the craft shop.

"If it's wonderful, don't tell me," she said. "I don't want to know what I'd have missed."

————

Claire was already seated on the bus before she saw him. She had not noticed him among the crowd waiting to board. She had not even seen Angela until the last moment. Angela had seized her arm and said, "Save me a seat on the bus," and now she lingered near the front, exchanging pleasantries with Chad Matthews, her old friend. Claire waited with the empty seat beside her.

That was when she saw his face. He was sitting across the aisle, two seats ahead of her. Claire's throat instantly tightened and she could hardly swallow. It was him. Blake Quinlan! She had not seen him for seven years, and she had only met him twice, but she would recognise him anywhere. Her insides quivered and made her queasy but she could not stop shaking.

His appearance had changed. He was now a man, instead of a boy. He had lost his adolescent gangliness and filled out a little. He had the same slender face, with hollow cheekbones and strong features. His hair was thick and dark, with the slightest hint of a wave at the back of his neck. Claire had never denied Blake Quinlan's good looks, even seven years ago. They did not assuage her dread. She felt as if she were facing a monster.

She wished that she dared tug the emergency cord and demand to be let off. Of course it was impossible. How could she explain herself to the camp administrators without blurting out the bitter truth? What would the bus driver and the lecturers think? They might refuse to let her get off. Everybody would think she had gone berserk, including her new friend, Angela.

A fist of fear clenched Claire's stomach and all at once, she was back there again, as a sixteen-year-old girl. The details of that terrifying night hit her senses like a brick. Whatever would she do? How could she face him again, let alone spend two weeks in his company at a Christian outreach camp?

She felt a wild hope that he would not recognise her, although she knew it was wishful thinking. He would refresh his memory over time, and he would surely remember her when he heard her name. Would he expect her to pass the time of day with him after what he had done, as if they were old friends?

As if he felt her eyes bore into the side of his face, he turned his head and caught her eye. Claire watched his large, dark eyes fill with recognition. His pupils dilated with shock until his brown eyes appeared inky black. The colour fled from his face and his lips parted slightly. A wave of nausea made Claire's head spin. She instantly broke eye contact and stared down at her hands, bunched tightly on her lap.

She found her mind whirling with anger. *A person like him has no right to attend a Christian camp. Why didn't he attend the information night a week ago?* If she had seen him there, she could have darted out of the auditorium far more easily than she could jump off a moving bus.

Suddenly the picture clicked into place. *Angela! He's Angela's brother-in-law.* Claire nursed her aching head in her hands and groaned. *Why, oh why didn't I twig?* Angela's paraplegic husband was Sean! Blake was the brother who tried so hard to overcome a horrible experience in his past. If Claire had not been so upset, she would have laughed with scorn. *A horrible experience for him, indeed!*

She mentally prepared herself for the ordeal she must face. Angela would be back to join her in the seat, soon and what could she say? How could she extricate herself from such a horrible fix?

Blake sat chilled to the bone. He could not have moved a muscle for a million dollars. He had carried Claire Parker's image in his head for seven years so he could not possibly mistake her for another girl. Her delicately chiselled profile had first caught his attention. Her eyes were still as clear as deep pools, and her skin transparently pure. She wore a teal blue T-shirt with a triangular cut collar, and her smooth, white neck looked slender and fragile. His blood curdled anew at the thought of what he had done.

Although his body was still, his brain teemed with plans. He had no place on that bus, with other Christians. He would have driven his car, if he thought it could have made the long haul to Sydney without breaking down. He was holding off on trading it in until he could afford a decent car. Angela had wanted to catch the bus, anyway, because she liked to be sociable. Angela wanted to catch up with a friend she had met on the information night but Blake would have to leave her to it. When they made their first rest stop, he would leave the company and work his way back home.

Angela would understand that there was no way he could face Claire Parker. What would he say? "Long time, no see." If he did not leave of his own accord, Claire had every right to pull the plug on him and then the others would kick him out. It would be best to save both him and Claire the embarrassment of exposure.

She studiously avoided his eyes now but her startled, fearful gaze had cut his heart to ribbons. She looked at him as if were a noxious disease. He felt like a grimy and despicable youth again. It was just an illusion that he could ever forget his past. It would hang over his life like a heavy cloud forever. He felt even worse to think that it would also loom over Claire's.

Angela moved back down the aisle and tweaked his shoulder. "Turn around and meet my new friend. Hey, Claire, I managed to convince him to come, after all. This is my brother-in-law, Blake."

They both sat dazed and silent. Finally Blake uncoiled his clenched fingers and drew an uneasy breath that he rather wished he couldn't. He longed to pass out and wake up in his bed to discover their encounter had been a dream.

"Hi, Claire, I'm...." He trailed off. He had almost said, "I'm sorry," but how lame that would sound. He would not blame her if she flew across the aisle and tore him apart.

Claire's lips twisted into a shape which looked like hello but no sound emerged from her paralysed vocal chords. Instead, she managed a stiff nod of her head.

Angela stared at her. She noticed Claire's extreme pallor and thought she had motion sickness. "Are you OK? Do you need a paper bag?"

Claire came to herself with a jolt. "No, I need some fresh air. That's all." She caught sight of a small gap in the seat along the back of the bus and darted into it without looking back to see how they would respond.

Angela turned to Blake dumbfounded. He also seemed green around the gills. "Do you two know each other?" she hazarded.

Blake sank down onto the empty seat Claire had vacated. "Oh, Angela," was all he managed to groan.

She stared at him, and slowly the truth dawned on her. "Was Claire.... the girl?" Angela knew the answer before she asked. Blake's burning eyes told the story.

Angela suddenly remembered what Claire had shared, about a terrible experience when she was sixteen which had been difficult to put behind her. Her own heart lurched when she thought of all she had divulged about Blake. Angela had never goofed so badly before. "Golly gosh, if only I'd known, I wouldn't have told her....." She could not continue.

Blake whirled on her, fiercely. "Told her what?"

Angela cringed beside him. "I told her that you'd had a dreadful experience you never recovered from. I explained how I was trying to change your mind about coming. I even said that as she'd had a bad experience, she might be able to help you recover from yours."

Angela fully expected Blake to explode but he didn't. It was not that he was not furious, but the damage was done and his horror was too great for words. However, if looks could kill, she would have been slain on the spot.

"Good grief, Angela," he hissed, and his chest heaved.

She tried to excuse herself. "You never ever told me her name!" She felt close to tears.

He flushed redder with each second. "That's no excuse for gossiping about me behind my back, telling my life story to people you've only just met." He turned his back on her and gazed steadily outside the window. "I'm not going to talk to you anymore," he said flatly.

His protruding shoulder blades looked like sharp knife edges and Angela knew that he would keep his word. She blinked hard and fast to fight her growing urge to sob and thought about all the wounds that had been re-opened. She had no idea what the next two weeks would hold, but it would certainly not be the relaxing, pleasant holiday she had anticipated.

Chapter Twenty

B lake sat in the games room with his chin in his hands, pretending to watch some other fellows play table tennis, but his thoughts were miles away. He continued to mull over the reasons why he had decided to stay at the camp instead of turning his back and scooting home. He had sat through the opening lecture by Chad Matthews and missed every word. He rested his notebook on his knees but the page remained blank while he chewed the top of his pen to splinters.

Claire deserved to know how sorry he was. For years he had longed for the courage to tell her that he would do anything in the world if only his deed could be undone. He knew where she lived. He could have tried to face her any number of times except that he was so scared. His family had counselled him to leave her alone, and Blake did not wish to confront Claire's angry father again. Mr Parker had belted him once and might have torn him to shreds if he'd appeared on his own doorstep.

Perhaps God had brought him face to face with Claire now so that he could finally apologise. He would be a base coward if he ran away. Blake did not admire much about himself, but if he turned and fled, he would detest himself all through. After what Claire had endured that night, his own discomfort was irrelevant.

He wanted to study her from a distance, to see how she was going. She had been alarmed to see him on the bus but that was understandable. If she was happy and calm most times he could lay some of his own torture to rest. He would feel relieved beyond words if he saw that he had not scarred her for life. He could watch her for hours if he had the chance.

Of course Blake knew that his deed was repugnant in God's eyes, whether Claire had recovered or not. He wanted Claire to be happy for her own sake. He did not wish to distress her further and carefully tried to plan the best way to approach her. The more he pondered, the more he couldn't work out how to do it. He should just say what was on his heart as quickly as possible. There was no way it would be easy, but then he didn't deserve it to be.

He brushed the hair off his forehead and drew a slow, deep breath. Trying to make a good impression was ridiculous. After what he had done, how could she possibly respond with anything but withering scorn?

He set his jaw, resolved to face it.

———

Claire lay on her bunk with her face buried between her sleeping bag and pillow. She tried to calculate how much of the fortnight she could spend tucked up there, away from scrutiny. At any moment Angela might enter. They had been put in a two-person dormitory as they had requested when they'd completed their camp forms. When Claire closed her eyes, she could still see their names on the cardboard placard above the door. Claire Parker and Angela Quinlan. Yes, she knew Angela's surname very well now, and far too late.

Claire was furious with her reaction. The shock of the encounter had swept her wits away in one wave of total fear. She had showed Blake Quinlan that she was a mass of jelly, quivering at the sight of him as if she had thought of nothing else for seven years. She should have greeted him with icy disdain and let him be the one to cringe and hide at the back of the bus. Claire writhed and even her toes curled tight with mortification. What a fool she was.

Next time she faced him she would do her best to erase that dreadful first impression. She would treat him as rudely and coldly as she could manage to treat another person on a Christian camp. She would keep as much distance between them as she possibly could.

Claire could still go home. She could tell the camp organisers that something personal had cropped up. She would not need to give details. However, there was something disgraceful about conceding defeat to Blake as if he wielded power over her. If she ran like a frightened rabbit, she might resort back to the frightened rabbit mentality. She did not want to lose the ground she had won. Perhaps if she lived the next two weeks with strength and courage, she could lay the ghosts of the past to rest at last.

The sight of him made her think of the loss of her baby, which would have been a seven-year-old child by now, smiling and chattering. Claire felt her face contort with the pain of recollection and she had no power to uncrease it. It would be easier to straighten a sheet of corrugated iron. She tried to smother the choking sobs which she would have loved to give rein to. The effort stung the back of her throat.

Claire's thoughts turned to Blake. He was a Christian now. She used to wonder what became of him and now she knew. Claire tried to deny the tight fist of resentment that wrenched her stomach. What right had she to feel angry because God was helping somebody else to iron out his screwed up life? Was Blake more culpable in God's eyes for raping her than she was for aborting her baby? God had a right to forgive whomever He pleased.

Heaven forbid, God might even expect her to approve of the situation. If Blake had not raped Claire, he might never have turned to God for forgiveness. His shame and guilt might just have prodded him in the right direction. Wasn't she supposed to feel glad for every new person who turned to Jesus?

Claire flopped onto her back with a frustrated grunt. Perhaps she should not make ripples by being rude to Blake. Her hostility might send him back to the cocoon of guilt and shame he had emerged from, and then God would be grieved. Claire did not want to grieve God but if He expected her to be friendly and polite to Blake Quinlan, He expected far too much. *Didn't He?*

The door slowly opened and Claire quickly pulled her head back under the covers. She sensed Angela's shadow from her tiny breathing chink and kept her eyes closed. She had not faced Angela since she had made such a colossal fool of herself.

Angela was not fooled into thinking she was asleep. "Hi, I thought you might like some time alone," she murmured.

Claire gave a sniffle. She would have liked much more time alone but that was an unrealistic wish. "It's your dormitory too," she said.

Angela sat on the bunk with a squeak of the springs. "I'm so sorry, Claire," she said with a catch in her voice.

Claire flicked her eyelashes apart and saw Angela's own swollen and red-rimmed eyes. She felt somehow better to see that Angela was moved to tears by her plight. She must understand, at least a little.

"It seems I'm not coping as well as I told you I was," Claire admitted. "I honestly thought I had finished picking up the pieces." She felt foolish to remember what she had told Angela, on the evening they met.

"Hey, I don't blame you. You just came face to face with the guy who raped you! I think you coped very well."

Angela's gentle tone was Claire's undoing. She started sobbing again. She embarrassed herself for being so emotional over something that happened so long ago. Angela put her arm around Claire's shaking shoulders and Claire smelled the sweet scent of her perfume. She felt acceptance and sympathy in the older girl's touch.

"I hope we can still be friends," Angela said.

Claire squirmed to a sitting position and collected her wits. "So you're married to Sean?" she asked dully, anxious to deflect attention from herself.

Angela nodded, with a slight smile. "Yes. I suppose you met him once or twice."

"Only once," Claire said. "I remember him well. I thought he was very nice. I had nothing against him. I felt sorry when I heard about.... his accident."

"He's accepted it now," Angela assured her. "He'll never recover any leg movement but he's good at making the best of things. He's a wheelchair athlete. He races and plays hockey. He's even an assistant chaplain at the old football club where he used to play. The young fellows love him." Angela could talk continuously on the subject of Sean. "He's truly happy. God has healed his mind wonderfully."

"Do you think God would do the same for me?" Claire asked plaintively.

Angela's arm tightened. "I think He already has. I can't believe you handled yourself so well on the bus. Many girls would have freaked out. I don't know how I would have behaved, in your place."

"Angela, would you do me a favour?" Claire asked.

Angela's eyebrows rose inquiringly. "You name it."

"Blake is your brother-in-law. Will you keep him away from me?" Claire wished he would have the sensitivity to leave the camp himself. She would at least be able to enjoy herself without his presence oppressing her.

Angela chewed on her lips with sorrow. "I will, although I'm sure I won't have to. He's been hating himself for what he did these seven years. Claire, this might sound awful coming from me, but he's no fiend." Angela stopped guiltily. Blake was already sulking because she had talked about him before. He would be furious if he knew she was doing it again.

Angela didn't know where he had disappeared to and longed to reach out to him, but he would not let her. She wondered if he could maintain his stony silence for the duration of the camp. Angela's temples throbbed with the beginning of a tension headache. What a mess she had made of things. She had wheedled Blake into coming along, only to have him alienate himself like a hermit crab, and as unhappy as he had ever been. He probably hated her and she would never make any more plans in her life.

———————

Rowena Quinlan had finished her afternoon work, so she eased herself onto the couch with a hot cup of tea and rested her stockinged feet on the coffee table. Her relaxation CD soothed her. It played sounds of a tropical rainforest with a mellow flute tune in the background. Gerry and Michael couldn't bear it so she listened to it only while they were out. Blake had given it to her. It had been an impulse buy for him but meant the world to her.

Rowena took a sip of herbal tea and closed her eyes. God had been good to her and she was as content as she had ever been. A week earlier, Angela stunned her by blurting, "You've had such a sad life, Mum, and sailed through it all. I want you to know you're an inspiration to me."

Rowena had never thought of her own life as particularly sad. There had been some low points of course; times like Sean's accident, Blake's incident with the Parker girl, Gerry's drunken rages, and most recently, poor Angela's miscarriage. Rowena accepted them all as part of life's rich tapestry. Warped spots of pain were an inevitable part of loving people.

Each day, Rowena thanked God for giving her so many people to love. She would not change any one of her three sons for the world. Sometimes the affection she felt for them made her ache, as if her heart was bursting at the seams with the love. She was certain God honoured the simple prayers of a mother. His tender care must surround them like cotton wool, even when they were unaware of it.

Sean had a passion for wheelchair sport. That boy was not designed to sit back and spectate. His paralysis had simply been an opportunity to prove the strength of his zest for life. He lived it to the full and he was a role model for her. Blake was in a job he enjoyed, which brought Rowena's heart a peace she had not known before. His faith in God was rock solid and he sometimes surprised her with comments which showed plenty of wisdom for his age. She had not told Blake that she was proud of him for a long time. Rowena took another sip and resolved to do so when she saw him again.

A concerned frown creased her brow as she thought of Michael. He was causing most of her grey hairs now. He had grown headstrong and irresponsible and she feared he was treading the same path as his father. His sole purpose in life seemed to be to have fun with as little work as possible. He was always in trouble with teachers for sloppy work and laziness. She did not know what would become of Michael.

He had been a special gift from God, a child of her later years. After a traumatic pregnancy with Blake, Rowena resolved she would have no more children, but God had other plans. Michael had been conceived during one of Gerry's frightening rages. He was proof of God's tendency to take bitter lemons and make sweet lemonade. How that chirpy little boy had buoyed her spirits during many lonely moments after his brothers had grown up. Rowena knew her lad's heart was in the right place, but Michael lacked Sean's singleness of purpose or Blake's depth of thought.

Just then he walked through the door and flung his backpack across the kitchen floor. "Hey Mum, I have an interview for a part time job. What'll I wear?" His hazel eyes sparkled so much like Gerry's and Sean's.

"Your green shirt and good fawn trousers," she said instantly. "Where is the job, Love?"

"No time to explain," he called over his shoulder. "I'll tell you tonight if I get it." He emerged from his bedroom and dropped his shirt and pants onto her lap. "Iron these while I have a shower. They got creased in my wardrobe. You buy me too many clothes."

The bathroom door closed behind him and his strident heavy-metal music soon blasted out over her gentle rainforest sounds. Rowena set up the ironing board and plugged in her old iron. Blake had bought her a new one, bless his heart, but she decided to leave it packaged until the old one wore out. He'd told her to throw it away but she could not bring her frugal heart to trash something which still worked perfectly well. She did not mind the slight buzz and frayed cord. It had been like that for over a year. She would wait until the iron broke down completely.

Rowena draped Michael's shirt over the board and turned to pour herself another cup of tea from the pot. She leaned across to raise the iron with one hand while she held the cup with the other. Rowena stumbled over Michael's bag which he had thrown onto the kitchen floor. She gasped as the tea spilt over the iron. It made an angry crackle and a sharp jolt of pain shot up Rowena's arm. She managed one sharp cry as the shock surged through her body to the tips of her toes. Then Rowena turned rigid and crumpled to the floor. She knew no more. The accident took only a few seconds.

———————

Michael tilted his head back and sang lustily beneath the shower. He looked forward to the interview with the manager of his father's pub. They needed a young fellow to work in the drive-through bottle shop and did not know that Michael was only fifteen. Gerry had assured his friend that his son was almost eighteen. Perhaps they would take his word for it without demanding to see a birth certificate. They ought to hire him because Gerry was one of their best customers. What a laugh it would be when Mike's school friends were able to whiz through and he could sell them alcohol without anybody to dispute their ages.

Michael knew that his mum would disapprove of the job. She not only hated dishonesty, but also late nights and alcohol for teenagers. He kept it from her because he could not be bothered listening to her reproachful pleading. He always did whatever he pleased, regardless of his mother. He wanted to leave school soon anyway, and a pub would be as good a place as any to work.

Michael loved to spend time drinking with his father. Ever since he was very small, he had admired Gerry's absolute dominion in the household. He remembered how his mother and brothers would bend over backwards to placate Dad after an evening of drinking. They would go to any lengths to avoid his wrath. Gerry could make or break a mood with a twitch of his head. Michael had longed to wield such power from the time he was old enough to talk.

He respected his father far more than he respected either of his brothers. Sean had been in a wheelchair for half Michael's life, and Michael could barely remember his football playing days. It was great that Sean could still play some sport, but in his little brother's eyes he was no longer a true man. Sean pretended he was happy with his second-rate lifestyle but Michael was not interested in playing along with the act.

Blake was not the sort of fellow Michael esteemed either. He did not drink. He was not an athlete. To cap it off, he was a religious numbskull. So was Sean. Dad said they listened too much to Mum and Angela. Gerry laughed at his two older sons behind their backs and criticised them to their faces. Michael had no time for fellows who carried on with women's stuff either.

He thought he heard his mother shout.

"What did you say?" he hollered above his water and music. No answer came.

"Speak up!" Michael yelled. There was still no answer so he shrugged and forgot about her. If it was important, she would come to tell him.

He towelled himself dry and went into his bedroom to put on his underwear. "Bring the clothes in here," he called.

But Rowena did not respond. Michael muttered a swear word and stalked out to find her. "Mum, I said bring...."

He stopped short. His crumpled shirt dangled off the ironing board and his pants lay upon the floor. Beside them was his mother, with the iron by her hand. She was as still as stone. Her face was ashen and her lips grey.

"Muuuuum!" Michael screamed. He fell to his knees beside her and shook her shoulders. "Mum, wake up!"

Rowena's head lolled, and she did not make a sound. Her grey-brown curls tumbled over Michael's knees. He began a deep, hoarse sob from the bottom of his chest. "Noooo! Noooo!" he yelled, as if his noise could animate her.

He stopped for a breath. Mum's rainforest CD finished its last few birdcalls. Then there was total silence.

Chapter Twenty-One

"What's going to happen to me now?" Gerard Quinlan raised his head and stared across the room at his two sons. Sean had left his conference as soon as he'd heard about his mother and now sat beside Michael on the couch. Although he knew his father well, the question stunned him.

"Dad, don't you care about Mum?" Perhaps he shouldn't have said it, but he couldn't help it.

Poor Mike could not say a word. His face had streamed with tears ever since the medical staff told them nothing could be done for their mother. They told them what had happened. The flex cord had been frayed where it joined the iron, with a tiny piece of live copper wire exposed beneath. Rowena had spilled her drink directly onto it and the shock had been enough to kill her instantly. Michael's eyes looked like red knife gashes but still the tears came.

Gerry staggered across the floor and thumped the wall with his forehead. "I'm a jinx. Terrible things keep happening to me and anyone who's related to me." He kicked a wheel of Sean's empty chair. "That's why you're strapped to this monstrosity. Mike, you'd better watch out, because you'll be next."

Sean squeezed his brother's shoulder. "Dad!" he rebuked.

At last, Gerry began to weep. "Poor, poor Rowena. She never did anything to hurt anyone. She didn't deserve this. She was just doing her work. She was always good and faithful to me." He raked his fingers through his sparse grey hair until it stood out like a wispy halo around his head.

"I'm going out," he said brokenly.

It was one of the times Sean wished he could leap off his seat and detain him by force. All he could do was just call, "Dad, where are you going? I think you should stay here with us." But the door had already slammed shut behind Gerry. Sean shook his head, worried for his father's state of mind.

Michael found his tongue at last. "Would it have hurt her?" he croaked. He was glad he had his brother beside him. In a crisis time, Sean was much better to have around than Dad, after all.

"No, Mike, I don't think so," Sean said quickly. "Did you hear them say it would've been quick? After the first shock, she would not feel a thing." That was all the comfort they had to cling to.

"I was bossing her around," Michael muttered. "I ordered her to iron my clothes." His chin trembled so Sean could barely discern his next words. "She died thinking I was mean to her."

"She loved to do things for us!" Sean cried. "She was happy to iron your clothes. She loved you, Michael. She died doing a favour for a person she loved."

Michael's shaking fingers raked the tassels of his mother's floral curtains. "It was my bag she tripped on. I dropped it on the kitchen floor."

Sean opened his arms. "Come here."

Michael buried his face on Sean's shoulder. He was the kid brother again, seeking solace from somebody older and stronger.

"She's happy now," Sean choked. "We're the ones who are sad. We're the ones who will have to live without her." He lost his own self-control. They clung together sobbing, their fair hair merging as one.

"What'll we do?" Michael uttered at last.

Sean drew a deep breath and tried to be practical. "Tonight, I'll stay here with you and Dad." He had to live each moment as it came, or he would fall apart. He clenched his hands together. "I'll have to phone the campsite in Sydney to tell Angela and Blake." It hurt him to think of his wife and brother, enjoying the first holiday either of them had taken for years. What a horrific thing to call them home to.

The sun was beginning to sink over the garden, casting shades of mauve and pink on the moss rocks. Most of the campers were still outside, enjoying the balmy weather. Angela and Claire had returned from an afternoon of horse riding. They both felt stiff and sore, though neither of them would admit it. They sat at an outdoor table having a quiet chat with Chad Matthews before the others returned for the evening meal.

Anne, the camp cook and cleaner, approached their table. "Excuse me, you're Angela Quinlan, aren't you?"

Angela nodded with a beam. "Yes, have you come to join us before the rush? Take the weight off your feet for ten minutes and relax."

Anne broke into a smile. "I'd love to do that but I've come to tell you you're wanted on the phone. It's your husband."

Angela's beam broadened and she jumped up. "I hope he's calling to say he misses me." She ran into the building, and Claire and Chad continued to discuss the passage from Romans he had used for his last lecture.

Angela returned quicker than they expected. She came up behind them silently as a shadow, and as they looked up, she raised shaking fingers to her face. Shiny tears dripped between her knuckle joints.

Chad stood in a flash to support her. "Angela, what's happened?"

Instead of replying, she choked, "Where's Blake?"

Chad, the breezy young pastor, was evidently shaken. "He's down at the pool with some other fellows. Have you.... bad news from home?"

Angela nodded and sank onto a chair with shuddering shoulders.

Chad put his arm around her shoulders and looked meaningfully over her head at Claire. Claire understood his unspoken request. Her stomach churned like a tumble dryer as she scraped her chair back. "I'll get him," she said.

Chad did not know of her history with regard to Blake. Under normal circumstances, Claire would never have dreamed of seeking him but now she could not refuse. Angela would be far better waiting with Chad. Chad was an old friend of hers and an experienced counsellor. He was the best person to comfort Angela.

At the pool, her eyes raked the water for the dark head she sought. She couldn't see him anywhere.

"Hi Claire," called Matthew Muir, one of the other young men. "Who are you looking for?"

"Blake Quinlan." Her voice sounded thin, like a faraway echo.

Matthew noticed nothing amiss. "He just got out. He's in the changing rooms. I'll get him for you."

When Blake emerged he was still in his bathers, with a towel wrapped around his waist. His hair was plastered over his head and Claire saw that he was uncertain whether to smile at her or not, knowing her opinion of him. He risked a slow smile.

"Hi Claire?" It was more of a nervous question than a greeting. She would never seek him unless it was important, of course.

Her heart pounded like a drum. "Angela needs you. Sean just phoned. There's some bad news from home."

Fear darkened his wide eyes. He uttered a polite thanks, then sprinted across the lawn back to camp. The towel fell down and he slung it over his shoulder and kept running. Claire followed him. She wanted to help Angela in any way she could. Chad and Angela had moved into the dining room, so Claire hung back against the door in the shadows and watched what happened.

When Angela saw Blake she rushed over to him. He wrapped his arms around her. Droplets of water fell from his hair onto her face and shoulders, but she clung to him and sobbed.

Blake automatically held her closer and stroked her hair. "I'm here. Is it.... Sean?"

"No, it's Mum." Angela's words erupted as a sharp cry. "She's dead, Blake."

The colour fled from his face. An icy chill went through him to his bones, as if someone had dashed a bucket of swimming pool water across his back. Angela felt the jolt go through his body, and then he held her tighter. "How... I mean, why... what happened?"

"She was electrocuted. On the iron."

He felt sick to the stomach. "The new iron?"

"No, the old one."

"But she was going to get rid of it." His eyes darted from the ceiling to the table, from Chad to Claire and back to Angela.

"She didn't get rid of it. She was using it to iron Michael's shirt and she spilled a cup of tea on it. It killed her."

Blake's head spun. He wanted to scream and shout. He should have thrown the rubbishy old iron away himself instead of trusting Mum to do it. He should have guessed she would cling to it until its last gasp. He was the only one who knew anything about electronics. He was the only one who suspected that it was an accident waiting to happen. He should have warned her more carefully. It was all his fault.

Angela pulled herself away and wiped her wet face. "I want to be with Sean."

Blake nodded. "I know. You will be. We'll catch the first bus or train back to Adelaide." He looked toward the pastor. "Chad, would you please drive us to the station?"

Chad Matthews drew a ragged breath. "Certainly. As soon as possible." He squeezed Angela's shoulder and looked across at Claire. "Claire, will you help pack Angela's case?"

"Of course I will." Claire hurried upstairs, still reacting with horror to the news. *Poor Rowena!* Claire had not seen her mother's old friend for years but remembered her friendly, smiling face.

She hastily repacked Angela's neatly folded clothes, relieved to be helping. She could not erase the image of Angela's streaming cheeks, or Blake's bright eyes full of grief and hurt.

Claire gulped. However much she hated him, his mother had just died and she would not wish such pain on anybody. A shaft of guilt twisted her heart when she remembered how she wished something would occur to make him leave. Claire brushed a patch of dirt off her jeans, and felt grimy inside and out. *Oh Lord, how wicked I must be. I didn't mean something like this!*

Blake returned to his own dormitory to get his things together. That was easy because he had not unpacked much. As he crammed his few clothes into his duffle bag, his fingers closed around something hard and rectangular. It was the block of fruit and nut chocolate Mum had slipped in, before he'd left. "Here's something extra in case they don't give you enough to eat." She knew fruit and nut was his favourite.

Blake had grinned, "I'm sure they'll feed us plenty, Mum, but I'll take it anyway, thanks." He had no idea it would be the last time he would ever see her alive. As he stared down at the block, his eyes stung until streaming tears obscured his sight. He clutched the chocolate until it softened in his grip. Then he hunched his head into the pillow, and in the privacy of the empty room he gave himself up to crying with total abandon. Every breath caused a pain in his chest, but once he started to cry, he could not stop.

He had not said, "I love you," to Rowena for as long as he could remember. He was sure she knew he loved her but wished he had said it, anyhow. It would have meant the world to her. Instead, he rebuked her for worrying about his future. He had disappointed her by not living up to her expectations and becoming the sort of popular son she had hoped for. At least his brothers were not as reclusive as he was.

The sooner he and Angela could get home to Adelaide the better.

He longed to see Sean and Michael. He would have to face his father too. Blake had chosen to avoid Gerry for many months and he wondered how his dad would deal with the loss of his mum. It would be enough to push him over the edge.

Chad Matthews tapped tentatively on the door and entered. Deep lines of empathy etched the corners of his mouth and he placed a hand on the younger man's shoulder. "Blake, I'm so sorry about your mother," he said huskily.

Blake swung his feet off the bed and somehow managed to stop crying. *Chad has just finished supporting Angela. He doesn't need to cope with me too. Men aren't supposed to break down.*

"Thanks Chad. Is Angela ready?" he asked, in a surprisingly steady voice.

Chad surveyed him quietly. "She's ready. Are you O.K.?"

Blake nodded. "I'm fine." The lie sprang naturally to his lips and he even managed a watery smile. "Don't worry about Angela. I'll look after her on the way home." He hitched his bag over his shoulder and walked away with his head bowed.

Chad Matthews stared after him with a troubled frown. He did not see a manly and stalwart hero. He saw a troubled lad who was so withdrawn he did not know how to accept sympathy.

───────────

Blake and Angela walked inside the house, aching and tired after an overnight trip during which neither of them had slept a wink. The dark hollows beneath both Sean and Michael's heavy eyes spoke of their own hard night. Angela gave a choked cry and darted to Sean like an arrow to a target. His large, square hands went round her and they clung together sobbing.

Blake's throat felt so tight he could hardly swallow. At home, surrounded by his mother's cosy furnishings and delicate ornaments, he felt worse. He longed for her to bustle out of the kitchen with her cheery welcome, wiping her hands on her apron.

Like an underwater swimmer, he turned blindly to find Michael. Poor Michael described how he had discovered Mum lying on the floor. He thought it was entirely his own fault. Blake's hands tightened around Michael's shoulder blades and he patted him firmly on the back. His younger brother was as tall as he was, but cried like a five-year-old child. As long as he could do something for somebody else, Blake could function.

Chapter Twenty-Two

Rowena's funeral was almost over. Kate Parker fumbled with the clasps of her handbag and fished out the first crumpled tissue her hand touched. She knew she would need them, so she came well supplied.

She had been upset ever since Claire had phoned her from camp and told her what had happened. It had been quite a long phone-call, and when Kate hung up her first move was to dig out her old school memorabilia from the bottom of the old office file in William's study. She cried long and hard over the photographs and letters she discovered and was filled with an aching sadness.

She and Rowena had been inseparable friends. Rowena had been so pretty, with her thick, glossy plait hanging down her back, and her intriguing dark eyes. There had always been something gypsyish about her when she was young. Her smile had flashed so readily, and her laugh had reminded Kate of tinkling bells. She had been a good friend to Kate, knowing intuitively when she needed company and when she needed time alone. She had a knack of finding special little gifts which seemed tailor made to suit Kate. Small, strawberry smelling soaps, elegant, scalloped writing paper, dainty shell earrings, a smart folded fan from Ireland. She had never forgotten any of Kate's family's birthdays. There had never been a friend like Rowena and never would be again.

Kate skimmed through one of Rowena's letters. It congratulated her on the first birthday of precious little Claire, and described some of the funny things her own boys had done. Kate slipped it back into its envelope with tear-filled eyes. Nothing should have driven a wedge between the two of them, and now poor Rowena was dead.

Kate buried all the old memories as she put the things back into the file, and brushed a cobweb from her eyelashes. They could have weathered that trial seven years ago, if they had stood together. Neither she nor Rowena was to blame for what Blake had done to Claire. It made no sense that two close friends should have become like strangers, living two blocks from each other. *Oh Ro, I'm so sorry it had to be this way.*

Even William was shaken when he heard how Rowena had died. He had not objected when Kate declared her intention of attending the funeral. Now she sat at the back of the church, battling a mixture of heartache and feeling conspicuous. If Rowena's family saw her sitting there, they would have a perfect right to demand why she had crept out of the woodwork now, after shunning her for seven years. Thankfully, none of them turned their heads or acknowledged her.

Gerard Quinlan sat with his large fists bunched on his knees. He only vaguely resembled the handsome young man in the photographs Rowena had sent from Ireland over twenty years ago. The pull of gravity seemed to have taken a particular toll on him. His jowls sagged, his double chin hung, and his round belly rested upon his thighs. His face was etched with furrows that made him appear at least sixty, although Kate knew he could only be in his early fifties, like Rowena.

Sean looked like Gerry as a young man. His face was fresh and his hair neatly trimmed. Another stab of remorse pierced Kate's heart when she looked at his wheelchair. She had not even sent Rowena a note six years ago, to express how sorry she was when she heard of her son's accident. That would have been the ideal time to renew their friendship, but it was far too late.

Michael was an even younger version of his father and oldest brother. It was clear that he was suffering acutely. He repeatedly rubbed his eyes in the crook of his elbow, and Kate was glad to see the young woman beside him put her arm around his shoulders. Her own red-rimmed eyes did not detract from her prettiness. Kate had never seen her before, but she knew this must be Angela.

Her hardest challenge was to watch Blake, the one who had caused the upheaval so long ago. It was he who stood to give a message about his mother, on behalf of himself and his brothers. It was very stirring. He told several family anecdotes about her. Some were humorous and made the congregation titter and smile. Others showed Rowena's tender heart and made people sob. Blake's voice faltered several times but he kept doggedly on and did not break down until the end, when he said, "For as long as we live, Sean, Michael and I will always carry the warmth of our mother's sacrificial, embracing love in our hearts."

When he took his seat there was not a dry eye in the church. He clenched his hands upon his knees and bowed his head, blinking at the small, polished coffin. Kate studied him again. If he was the bad egg they had always thought him, he certainly did not sound like one, or look like one. It was quite ironic to her that he was the one who most resembled Rowena.

––––––––––

Gerard Quinlan drained his last mouthful of beer and ditched the bottle in the kitchen bin for the last time. He was leaving. After thirty years of working in the same factory, he'd handed in his notice on the spur of the moment. His boss accepted it without a murmur. There were no fanfares of farewell. Nobody even thanked him for years of good service. Gerry scowled and longed for another bottle. What did he expect? His place would be swallowed up by another, and the work would run as smoothly as ever.

He could not bear his house or neighbourhood without Rowena in it. She had been dead for two weeks but the sound of her voice still rang in his ears at night, louder than it had when she'd lay beside him in her nightgown, smelling of jasmine-scented talcum powder. He lapsed into fantasies of her whenever he could, because the void without her was too horrible to face. It took Rowena's death to show Gerry how he had depended on her to be there, to stroke his furrowed brow, massage his temples, and keep his house tidy.

The only chance he would have not to go crazy would be to head off alone to see new places and faces which might drive her out of his head. He would pick up a bit of work here and there. He was a jinx who turned everything he touched to dust, yet he still hoped to see some sights which might impress him and take him out of his lethargy.

He was almost out of the door when he remembered that he had not left a note for his sons. Gerry grumbled to himself as he tracked down a stubby pencil and the back of one of Rowena's shopping lists. He did not care what they made of his absence but had to leave some explanation for his own sake, not theirs. Otherwise they would have him registered on a police file as a missing person.

I'M GOING AWAY DON'T KNOW WHERE. DON'T LOOK FOR ME BECAUSE YOU WONT FIND ME. I MIGHT BE BACK IF YOU SEE ME. DAD. As an afterthought, he picked up the pencil again. GOODBYE, he added. He did not know whether he would ever see them again so he supposed he owed them that much.

The sliding door opened and Michael stepped inside. Gerry uttered one single swear word. If he had not stopped to write the silly note, he could have been a few streets away already, without facing any of them.

"Why aren't you at school?" he grumbled.

Michael wore a greasy old T-shirt with a red stain, that could have been either tomato sauce or blood, upon the left shoulder. There was a hole in the knee of his jeans and two crimson pimples on his chin. He looked appalling and Gerry winced with disgust. He had no sons to be proud of.

"I don't want to go back to school. I can't study since Mum died."
Michael eyed Gerry's bulging suitcase. "Where are you going, Dad?"

"I've left a note explaining it," Gerry said shortly. "I can't stand it
here. I'm going to work my way around the country."

"Take me with you," Michael pleaded.

"No, you're just a kid. You're much better off here."

Michael jutted his chin. "I'm fifteen! I don't need any more school.
You left school before you were fifteen and you turned out O.K. I'll
keep you company. I don't want to be anywhere but with you."

Gerry looked wearily at the sallow face and lustreless eyes before
him. There had not been a day that Michael had not wept for Rowena.
Gerry knew it was out of the question. He would not be responsible
for a grieving adolescent as well as for himself. Besides, Michael
reminded him too much of Rowena. He had to sever all home ties
completely.

"You'll be happier without me. You have Angela and Sean and
Blake. You'll be all right. Blake's come home here to live again. You
can either stay with him or move in with Sean." Gerry honestly did
not care, either way.

"I don't want them!" Michael's shout was the grating yelp of a
boy whose voice had not quite broken. He could not believe that Dad
had forgotten the jokes they had shared at the expense of the others.
He thought he was Gerry's favourite. Michael Quinlan's world was
falling apart. He could not bear it if his father discarded him like an
old shirt.

He began to rant, "If you don't let me come with you, I'll kill
myself. How can I live without you or Mum? Don't you care about
me?" He seized Gerry's arm and tried to look him in the eyes.

Gerry slung Michael's arm off, annoyed and somewhat frustrated.
His eyes blazed. He would listen to none of these emotional guilt
trips.

"You should have thought of all that before you killed your
mother," he bellowed. "You should have been careful where you

threw your bag. You should have thought before you ordered her to iron your clothes. You feel bad for what you've done but don't make me feel responsible! It's all your fault, so you can live with the consequences."

That settled Michael. He cowered down on the couch totally crushed by the harsh accusations and words of rejection. Gerry took his chance and left. Before he slid behind the wheel of his car, he peered through the front window at Michael just once. Mike still sat in the same spot with his head buried in his hands, the picture of a broken youth. Even the back of his neck looked thin and vulnerable. Gerry cursed himself for looking back. The image would leave a sour taste in his mouth for days.

He warmed up the car engine and backed it out of the drive. Life was too short to worry about anybody but himself.

———

Kate Parker drove home from the supermarket in Claire's little car. It was a hot and overcast January day, and was pouring with summer rain. Kate wound down the window an inch and mopped her moist brow. She hated the oppressive, humid heat.

She gaped with disbelief as she drove past a small reserve, and parked by the curb. There was a boy lying on his stomach by the gutter, getting drenched by the downpour. Kate thought she recognised the blonde, curling patch of hair, but she had to be sure.

She got out and ducking her head against the rain, knelt beside the curb. Yes, it was Michael Quinlan, Rowena's youngest son. That sweet, sunny little boy she had met briefly seven years ago. He was out cold, and she saw that he had been sick.

Kate used every ounce of strength to drag him to the car, while the rain poured and water ran down her own neck. She draped him across the back seat as gently as she could. Michael's head belted against the door going in, but he did not stir. She drove past his home but no cars were parked out the front. His family was all at work, she guessed. Kate was willing to take him home with her and clean him up. She could not leave him as he was.

Claire sat by the dormer window working on a tapestry, when her mother arrived home.

"Will you help me with something out here?" Kate asked. "You won't believe what I've done."

Claire's eyes widened when she saw the muddy passenger in the back of her car.

"This is Michael Quinlan," Kate said, with tears in her voice.

Claire stared at the boy from top to toe, and her mind flashed back to that afternoon when she'd played cars with the child on the floor. Michael now looked deathly sick. The blue veins behind his eyelids stood out like bruises against his pallid skin.

"What happened to him?" she breathed.

"Drunk," Kate said grimly. "Let's get him in onto the couch, and you can find Dad's blue dressing gown while I peel off some of these wet clothes, or he'll catch pneumonia." She hoped Rowena would know that she was caring for her boy. Kate would do her best to make up for seven years of callous behaviour.

She gently rubbed Michael's torso with a soft towel, while Claire carried his dirty, dripping clothes to the washing machine. Kate's hand lingered on Michael's hair. She knew how she would feel if he were her son, lying in the rain, drunk with despair.

At last, he moaned. Kate and Claire hunched forward to hear his indistinct mumbling.

"I need a bucket," Michael whimpered, while beads of sweat moistened his brow.

Claire rushed over with a bucket in the nick of time, and Kate held Michael's head as he used it. He wet his dry lips with a sip of water and leaned back against the cushions.

"Why, Michael?" Kate asked softly.

"My Dad's gone." He had no idea who the two women were but

felt too ill to care. It was enough that they knew his name. The words that spilled from his mouth were garbled and confused. "I killed Mum. She was ironing… my bag... the clothes on the floor. Dad said so. It was my fault." He leaned forward again.

Kate rocked him against her shoulder. He needed some motherly care. At last, he slept again. She tucked a sheet around him and peered at the kitchen clock. "His father will be home by now, worrying about him," she whispered to Claire. "We'll get him dressed, and then I'd better call."

———————

Nobody answered the phone for a long time and Kate was almost ready to hang up, but someone got there at last.

"Hello, Blake Quinlan." He sounded as if he had rushed inside.

Kate briefly closed her eyes. She had hoped Gerard would answer.

"Hello Blake, this is Kate Parker," she said in a gravelly voice. "Do you remember me? I'm Claire's mother." She had to clear her throat.

A few seconds of stunned surprise followed. "Hello Mrs Parker. Yes, I remember you," he responded awkwardly.

Kate's face flamed red, and she blurted her news as quickly as possible. "I have your brother at my house. I found him collapsed at the reserve. He.... had a few too many drinks. He was in a bad way, but he's a little better now."

"I'll come straight to get him!" Blake cried. "And Mrs Parker, thank-you."

They expected him directly but the minutes lapsed with no sign of him. William arrived first. His eyes narrowed at the sleeping adolescent on his couch.

"This is the youngest Quinlan boy. He's sick. He's grieving over his mother and I'm looking after him." Kate placed her hands on her hips. She did not know how defensive her words would sound until she'd said them. She braced herself for the sharp rebuke she expected for getting involved, but William merely turned his head away.

"I'm not going to stop you," he mumbled. "You have to do what you have to do."

"His brother is coming to get him," Kate added.

That did make William scowl. "I don't want *him* in my house."

Blake arrived before Kate could respond. He was sprinting on foot, and although he wielded an umbrella, he was wet through. "My car wouldn't start again," he apologised when Kate met him at the door. "I've been having trouble with it. I'm sorry I took so long."

Blake carefully wiped his muddy shoes on the doormat and stepped inside as gingerly as a cat. He resisted the urge to look right or left. He had only been inside that house once before and felt miserably self-conscious. He looked into Claire's big blue eyes, and quickly stared at his feet again.

When he saw Michael, it was somewhat easier for Blake to move. He knelt beside him and gently shook his shoulder. When Michael's eyelashes flickered, Blake murmured, "Come on, sport. It's time to come home."

"Is that you, Blake?" Michael coughed groggily.

"Yeah, it's me."

Michael blinked, trying to gain his bearings. He clung to his brother's familiar checked work shirt. "Dad left home. He reckons it's all my fault, and now he hates me. I drank what he left behind in the fridge. I couldn't think what else to do. I only ever wanted to please him."

Blake eased Michael to a sitting position and held him close for a moment. "I know how you feel," he said softly. "I tried to please Dad too, long ago. It didn't work for me, either."

Michael gripped Blake's wrists as if they were life preservers. "*You* aren't going, are you?" He could not conceal the desperation in his voice.

"No way! I'm not going anywhere. We'll stick together," Blake assured him. "Up you get."

He hauled the groggy Michael to his feet and wrapped one of Michael's arms securely around his own shoulders. He placed his free arm around Michael's waist.

"Are you mad at me for getting drunk?" Michael persisted, and erupted into a fit of coughing.

Blake looked across at the three watching faces of the Parker family. The thought flashed through his head that he could not possibly meet them again under worse circumstances. His kid brother was as dead drunk as Blake had been the night he raped Claire. Michael could not possibly feel sicker in his heart than Blake did.

"No, I'm not mad at you," he responded. Michael had no idea of the full story. It was not his fault.

"I want to leave school," Michael went on, as Blake helped him across the floor.

"We'll discuss that later, with Sean and Angela," Blake soothed. "First, we'll get you home to bed." Michael was a dead weight and Blake tried hard not to stagger. He shifted his brother's weight to a more comfortable position and braced his shoulders.

"I love you, Blake," Michael said hoarsely.

"I love you too, Mike." Now Blake knew he had to get out of there or he would cry. He managed a final misty look at Kate and Claire. "Thank-you for looking after him. We appreciate it. I'm sorry." He reddened with shame and dragged Michael over the threshold.

Kate realised that this was all wrong. "We'll give you a ride, won't we William? Michael shouldn't be walking home in the rain."

William hesitated, his first thought being that he would hate his car upholstery to be vomited on. He wanted nothing more to do with the drunken Quinlan family. They were obviously all tarred with the same brush.

Then a jab of conscience prodded him. He knew Kate was right. They were struggling with the death of their mother. "Yes, get him in the car," he said curtly.

But Blake had no intention of putting William to the trouble. "No thanks, Mr Parker. We don't need you to do that. It's not far home for us."

"Suit yourself." William did not know whether to feel relieved or indignant. It had cost him to make his generous offer, and Blake had flung it back in his face.

William folded his arms across his chest and watched the gate close behind them. Then he turned abruptly away. The sight of them trying to stay dry beneath their small umbrella bothered him.

Kate turned on him, with flashing eyes. "How can you let them walk home?"

"I would have taken them," William bristled. "He refused! Not me."

Kate set her jaw. "You made it clear that you didn't really want to. Didn't he Claire?"

There was no response. They both turned to find their daughter still standing by the window, watching the slow progress of the Quinlan boys down the street.

Claire's eyes were focused more on Blake than Michael. She watched him with the morbid fascination of a little girl who had been forbidden to watch a horror movie. He held the umbrella over Michael's head while the rain drenched his own head and shoulders. Claire recalled how he had embraced Angela at camp, when she broke the terrible news. Had becoming a Christian made him gentle and compassionate? Or had he been that way already?

Somehow, that thought made her furious. She preferred to keep thinking that Blake Quinlan was corrupted to the core, like a rotten apple. She had come to terms with the notion that a foul pervert had raped her. She could not stomach the possibility that an essentially decent, good-hearted person had done such a cruel thing. She wished with all her heart that he had not reappeared in her life to shake her preconceived notions of him to their foundations. It stung so bitterly she wanted to throttle him.

Chapter Twenty-Three

"Who are the Parker family?" Michael demanded for the tenth time. "How did they know me?"

Blake did not look up from the sink. "Mrs Parker and Mum used to be friends, long ago." He wished Mike would drop the subject.

"If they were friends, why didn't they keep in touch? They live only a few streets away."

"It's none of our business, Mike. Just forget about it." Blake kept his voice neutral with effort.

Michael plonked onto the kitchen bench. "I want to see them again." He had been so sick and drunk that afternoon that only a few details about the Parker family stayed in his mind. The lady had treated him kindly. She had the most soothing voice he had heard since his mother died. There was a pretty daughter too. He remembered how Claire's coppery hair fell across her face in soft wings when she leaned down to hear what he had to say. She looked as if she had stepped straight off the cover of a modelling catalogue.

"What's their address?" he asked. He had been too addled in his head to find his way back again.

"I don't know!" Blake shot out, before he had time to think better of it.

Michael flashed him a perplexed, withering stare. "You liar. You came and picked me up."

Blake flushed uncomfortably and told Michael part of the truth. Enough to discourage him, without divulging any of the scandal.

"The Parkers wouldn't want to see any of us. Something.... very bad happened long ago. That's why Mum and Mrs Parker stopped being friends." He looked at Michael. "It was nice of them to help you, but they would hate to see you again."

"I want to thank them," Michael persisted.

"I already thanked them for you."

"I want to thank them myself." Normally, Michael cared nothing for good manners.

"The best way you can thank them is not to visit them again," Blake said decisively.

Michael studied him carefully. "You know what happened, don't you? Why won't you tell me? What could Mum have done to offend Mrs Parker? Mum never hurt anybody in her life."

"I'm not going to talk about it anymore," Blake snapped.

"Whatever Mum did isn't our fault," Michael went on. "They shouldn't be mad at us. You should come with me to see them again."

Blake's shoulders stiffened and he turned on Michael. "I'm not going near there again, so drop the subject!"

"You're just chicken. Christians are supposed to be on good terms with everybody, so what sort of gutless Christian are you?" Michael knew the right buttons to push to upset Blake, but this time they had no effect. Blake stalked out of the kitchen to collect dirty dishes from the bedrooms.

Michael followed him. "If you won't tell me, I'll look 'em up in the telephone book. I remember the rough area where they live. It can't be that hard." He wasn't doing it just to annoy Blake. He yearned to see Mrs Parker again. She was kind and motherly, and she'd known Michael's mother when she was a girl. Michael had a feeling that Mrs Parker would be one of the closest links to Rowena he could find.

Blake knew when he was beaten. He pushed roughly past his brother, so Michael would not see the ragged despair in his eyes. "I know you'll do as you like, but don't blame me when they turn you away and tell you not to come back." He moistened his dry lips.

Michael knew he had won. "I'm going out," he announced triumphantly.

"Where?"

"I don't have to tell you. You aren't my parent. Neither are Sean and Angela." With that, he was gone.

Blake looked at the mound of dirty dishes still waiting to be washed and flung his sponge at the sink. He had worked for half an hour already, and the pile still looked mountainous. He had not even cooked anything for two days, yet the plates and cups stacked up with relentless speed.

He switched on the television but couldn't concentrate. He was too worried. Michael would loathe him if he found out what he had done. Perhaps Blake was a chicken, for keeping him in the dark.

He felt concerned for Claire. How would she feel to have Michael knocking at her door? A new possibility struck Blake, and a fist of fear gripped his throat. What if the Parkers told Michael the truth, to get rid of him? A prickling shudder made him dizzy. It would sound so much worse coming from them than it would from him.

No, he supposed he was safe. He drew four slow, calming breaths. Claire would have more pride than to take a fifteen-year-old larrikin into her confidence. She would hate Michael to know, as much as Blake would. The most likely outcome would be that Mike would shuffle home, confused and hurt. Blake's heart already ached for him in anticipation. It was all his fault. He would've loved to be friends with the Parker family too, if he had not done what he'd done.

What's going to become of Michael? Blake had lived back home for a month, and already he knew something about his brother that Mum had never suspected.

One day, Mr Phillips had let Blake take the afternoon off. Michael had returned to school that day, and Blake went to pick him up. He waited at the gate long after most students had left the grounds. Blake began to drive home, but caught sight of Michael, his friend Jamie and two other lads hunched behind the school canteen, smoking.

Blake tried to creep up and startle them, but one of the youths played lookout. When Blake got there, they blinked innocently up at him with no trace of a cigarette or joint. However, when Michael climbed into Blake's car, he reeked of hash. Blake had been a teenager himself not so long ago. He could recognise it a mile off.

Michael's behaviour was suspicious too. He was grief-stricken over Mum's death and Dad's departure, yet sometimes he seemed queerly euphoric. He would chatter, as he used to when he was a little boy, about airy-fairy nonsense. Those highs were always followed by bouts of drowsiness and poor concentration. Michael would lose the plot of his favourite comedies, so how could he be expected to remember school lessons? Blake told him how obvious it was that he was using pot, and Michael flared up and denied it. *He must think I'm stupid!* Blake thought to himself

Sean had pulled Michael aside for a serious talk about the health risks of drug abuse and Angela flatly forbade him to use them. Michael glibly promised not to, but his promises were not worth the stinking breath with which they were uttered.

Blake drew up his knees and rested his head upon them. He worried that Michael would turn to heavier drugs. He wondered if he would become a disillusioned school dropout. He was relieved that Michael had not gone with Dad, but how much better could he do at home?

Oh God, how can I help him? How can Angela and Sean help him? We all try. What right do I have to try to straighten him out, after what I did? He knows we love him, but our love doesn't seem to be enough. If only Mum were here for him. He needs Mum. I need her too.

Blake stared back at the overloaded kitchen sink. He wearily snapped the TV off and returned to the dishes. Everything had run down since Mum died. The house was a shambles. No wonder Michael wanted to retreat into his self-induced drug world. Blake thought he ought to keep the house as orderly as he could. He owed it to his mother's memory. Being faithful in small details was all that was in his power.

For weeks, Claire had wondered whether to follow up her friendship with Angela. They had exchanged addresses so it would be easy to do. They had shared some special moments in the few days they had known each other. Angela comforted Claire when she learned about her and Blake, and in return, Claire was able to help Angela when her mother-in-law died. Claire longed to see Angela again but decided to do nothing. How could she stay friendly with Angela and keep avoiding Blake? She supposed it could be managed, but it might be awkward.

Then Angela phoned her, to invite her for a meal. Claire had been edgy about facing Sean Quinlan, but she went anyway. He and Angela made her feel immediately at ease. Sean had a guileless, endearing manner. His enthusiasm shone from his eyes as he spoke of his sporting career and his chaplaincy. He and Angela admired Claire's tapestry portfolio and even ordered a wall hanging. They spoke freely about Rowena's death, and profusely thanked Claire for looking after Michael with her mother. Claire had a wonderful time and promised to see them again.

She sat sorting her different coloured threads at the table, thinking about the evening. Angela and Sean made her feel like part of their warm, close family circle. She had spent years searching for friends like them. The only member of their family they had not mentioned was Blake. It seemed tacitly understood that he was a forbidden subject. Claire appreciated their sensitivity, but she chewed her bottom lip to calm the flutter of anxiety in her chest. After seven years, she seemed to be faced by Quinlans wherever she turned. Was she really doing the right thing by staying friends with Angela?

A loud knock at the kitchen door startled her, and she turned to see Michael Quinlan. Claire couldn't hold back a wry smile. It never rained but it poured.

Michael looked most like Sean, now he was not drunk. She even caught a glimpse of Blake's uncertainty and some sort of desperation in his eyes, but then he flashed her a self-confident smile. All his resemblance to Blake vanished.

Michael addressed Claire's mother. "I came to thank you for taking care of me. Blake says you were friends with our mother and I've been wanting to talk with people who knew Mum."

Kate read the emptiness in his eyes, and her heart softened. "I'm making some sandwiches, Michael. Would you care to stay for lunch?"

She did not need to ask twice. Before Claire knew it, Michael sat across from her at the table, tilting back on the hind legs of his chair. He gobbled up two beef and salad sandwiches followed by two bananas, as if he had not enjoyed a square meal for weeks.

Kate told him several funny things she and Rowena had done when they were girls. Claire had not heard them either and they reinforced to her just how close Kate and Rowena had been. Claire felt sad to think that she had played such a crucial part in their estrangement.

"Why did you stop being friends?" Michael asked. "You were such good friends."

"It's water under the bridge," Kate said firmly. "I'm sorry it happened, Michael, and I wish it had been different. You're welcome to visit us whenever you like."

He beamed. "Thanks. I nearly didn't come today, because Blake reckons you'd hate to see me."

Claire's stomach lurched. "Did he say why?"

Michael shook his head. "Naw. Only that something bad happened, and you all have a very good reason not to want anything to do with us." Michael was oblivious to the pained expressions Claire and Kate exchanged. "He should've come with me. He would've liked those stories about you and Mum, Mrs Parker."

"Does your brother know you're here now?" Kate asked carefully.

"Nope, but I don't care what he thinks. I don't want to be like him. He's a wimp."

"In what way?" Claire asked. Kate looked at her, surprised that Claire cared to continue a conversation about Blake Quinlan.

Michael gave a scornful laugh. "He's super-religious. He thinks God's lookin' after him all the time. He never does anything silly just for the heck of it. He's all wrapped up in his narrow little world of fixin' things and trying to turn me into a goody-goody, just like him."

"Blake, a goody-goody?" Kate repeated, with a strange shadow over her face. "I must admit, he never struck me as one." She felt Claire's steady blue gaze, begging her to say no more.

Michael enjoyed himself when he discussed either of his brothers' shortcomings. It made him feel better about himself. "Yeah, he's a total goody-goody. He doesn't even drink!"

"Blake doesn't drink?" This time it was Claire who echoed him. She couldn't help it. "Since when?" She let out a disdainful laugh but felt anything but amused. She felt furious. She dug her fingernails hard into her palms. She wanted to pulverise Blake. For somebody who didn't drink, he was truly intoxicated the night he took her out.

Michael laughed with her, thinking that Claire could not believe such extreme fanaticism. "Not for as long as I can remember. Even Sean and Angela drink a little bit."

Kate almost suggested that Blake might have good reason not to drink, but she looked at Claire's white face and changed the subject completely.

"Michael, now that your father is away, who does your cooking?" she asked.

"Blake does. He's not too bad, when he bothers."

"How about washing your clothes? Doing your grocery shopping? Cleaning?"

"Blake does," Michael repeated. "He has nothin' better to do with his time. He don't go out much."

"Why not?" Kate asked.

Michael gave a contemptuous giggle. "I think he's scared of

women."

Claire's ears pounded and she felt her face flame. Michael clearly had no idea what Blake had done, but every word he said reinforced what Angela had told her. Blake was still consumed with guilt. Yes, Claire had seen anguish in Blake's eyes when he'd looked at her. She had often wondered if Blake Quinlan felt sorry for his action. Now she knew the answer. He felt so sorry, it had repressed every detail of his life.

She chewed her lip and felt like crying. Now that she knew he was sorry, she could not determine if she felt better or worse.

———

As she arrived home from work the next evening, a dusty car with a Victorian number plate turned into her driveway. Its door creaked open and out stepped Peter Lennox. He had become a family friend. He and Rachel had visited Adelaide several times together and when they did, they always called on the Parker family.

Claire walked to meet him. "Hi, I didn't know you were coming!"

He looked her up and down approvingly, and smiled. "Surprise," he said.

Claire peered through the window of his empty car and looked at him, confused. "Where's Rachel?"

Peter shuffled his feet. "It's a long story," he said. "It started when she finished her degree and took off on her adventure holiday to Europe."

Claire nodded. Rachel had spoken to her over the phone. She had bubbled with excitement at the chance to visit the Continent.

"We've split up. She met somebody on her tour she liked better than me. His name is Max." Peter's jaw tightened. "She dumped me for a French waiter called Max. She said she was sorry, so sorry she had to write it in a letter and couldn't even tell me over the phone." He kicked a pebble with the toe of his shoe.

Claire's heart melted. "Peter, I'm sorry."

He scrutinised the face of Rachel's cousin. Peter had thought of Claire, on and off, for five years. He remembered how he had played the hero and rescued her from that no-hoper Tessa had been hitched to. Peter had preferred Rachel's energy and spunk, but something about Claire had caught his attention.

He was still unsure whether he should pursue her now. He knew Claire had been raped. He hesitated to get involved with a girl who had such a sordid past. Still, that was seven years ago now. If she hadn't got over it, she probably never would. She looked pretty good. Her blue cotton t-shirt clung to her arms and bust. It made her blue eyes look stunning.

"That's OK. I've had a few weeks to recover," he said slowly.

"What are you going to do now?" she asked.

He leaned against his car door. "I'm going to live here in Adelaide for a while. I'm tired of Melbourne." He watched Claire and remembered how close he had come to pulling her head down on his shoulder.

She beamed slowly and dimpled. "That's great news." She found herself a bit flustered that he had come to visit her. She was Rachel's cousin, after all. He didn't have to visit her. Claire felt suddenly excited.

"So are you going to invite me inside, even though Rachel isn't here?" he teased.

"Of course. Mum and Dad will be pleased to see you again."

She was right. Peter had hardly walked through the door before Kate invited him to stay for dinner, and William discussed the day's finance reports with him. William's moustache beamed when he looked at Peter. The fact that Peter had split up with Rachel did not seem to bother Claire's father one bit. In fact, William wasted no time with condolences.

As they ate their meatloaf, he said, "Kate and I are going to Sydney for a fortnight next week. Now that you're here, Peter, you can take a load off our minds by keeping Claire company for us. She can show you the sights of the city. Neither of you will be lonely."

William was so pleased, he wanted to burst. He had noticed the soft way the young fellow looked at Claire. He'd always known that boy was far too sensible for muddle-headed Rachel. At last Peter had woken up to himself. Claire would make him a far better wife, some day. William longed to see his little girl set up for life with that sound, down-to-earth young economist. *God is just, after all.*

Claire cringed, and hoped her father was not as transparent to Peter as he was to her. She had a vague feeling that things were moving a little too fast.

Peter understood William perfectly but managed to keep his face straight. He had often heard William Parker described as being something of a tyrant. He reminded Peter more of an eager puppy-dog. "I would like that, if Claire would be so kind," he said in a respectful voice. Peter had been in Adelaide so often before, he knew all the sights there were to see, but he did not mention that.

He turned to Claire. "Would you like to go to the pictures tonight?" He would show Rachel that he could have her cousin Claire and her Uncle William eating out of his hand.

Her eyelashes flickered, startled. "Yes, that would be nice." It was only the second date she had ever accepted. She ignored the squirmy feeling in the pit of her belly. *Peter was a great guy.*

While he drove back to wherever he was staying to freshen up, Claire flew upstairs to decide what she ought to wear. It would help if she could stop thinking of Peter as Rachel's boyfriend. When she closed her eyes, she could not get past the image of Peter and Rachel sitting together, staring into each other's eyes and looking so happy. It would certainly take a lot of work.

Chapter Twenty-Four

One week later, a volley of thumps on the kitchen door disturbed Claire as she was about to climb into bed. Her heart leaped as she wriggled into her dressing gown. Her parents were away on holiday. Nobody ever visited so late. If only Dad were home, to confront the intruder with his stentorian voice.

Claire shook her head clear as she tiptoed to the head of the stairs. A normal intruder would not pound on their door, as if he had every right to be let in.

"Mrs Parker! Claire! It's me, Michael Quinlan. Something terrible's happened."

She could breathe again. "Hold on, Michael!" Claire hurried to open the door.

She blinked at his tall, lanky frame, and almost wished she could push him out again. He was just a youth but he was far taller and stronger than she. Her father would call her a fool.

As he lurched into the light, she gasped. His face was covered with open cuts and abrasions. His nose had been bleeding and there was the start of a deep purple bruise on his right cheekbone. "Are your Mum and Dad in bed?" he sniffed.

"No, they're on holiday. What happened to you?"

"You gotta help me, Claire." He touched a cut on his lip with his tongue and flinched.

"Blake got his new car last night and I took it out for a spin while he was out somewhere with Sean and Angela. I had a few mates from school over and when they left, I thought it would be fun to drive it round the block. I was doin' OK, but I crashed into the garage door comin' back in."

He sank onto a kitchen chair, and coughed thickly. "It was just an accident."

"How bad is it?" she gasped.

Michael's lip quivered. "The front is all smashed in. Blake'll kill me if he finds out. Will you clean me up and I'll walk home and pretend I don't know nothin' about it?"

"I can't do that," Claire said quickly. "You need a doctor, for a start." She could smell alcohol fumes on his breath. His eyes were glassy and she feared that he might be hurt worse than he thought.

Michael leaped off his seat to prove that he was fine. He marched into the lounge room and almost tripped over the split floor level. "I'm fine!" he sputtered. "Just a bit sore."

"You can't get away with it." Claire was desperate to make him understand. "Blake will know it was you. How will you explain your face, let alone the mangled car?"

Michael had it all worked out. "I'll tell him I walked round to Jamie's house and got in a fight with some thugs. I'll tell him someone else must have taken his car for a joyride and smashed it up. They might've hotwired it, you know. Blake knows how to hotwire a car." He'd almost convinced himself that his lies were plausible.

He actually sank to his knees and grasped her hands. "You're my only hope, Claire. If you get me out of this jam, I'll never do anything like this again. I promise."

"I'll help you," she said, and slipped her hands away from his hot, moist ones. She placed hers firmly on his shoulders. "You lie on the couch and I'll fix you up. I'll fetch some things from upstairs."

She rushed into her parents' bedroom and seized the extension phone. She would help him but not the way he expected. His family would be worried sick. She dialled Sean and Angela's number but they did not answer their phone. Claire hung up with a muttered prayer. She leafed through the telephone directory with unsteady fingers and punched in Blake's number; the last one she ever expected to be ringing.

He snatched up the phone after only two buzzes and she could tell by his voice that he was on the verge of panic.

Claire covered the receiver with her hand. "Blake, it's Claire Parker," she said urgently. "Michael is at my house. He's O.K."

"Thank God," Blake breathed. "I'll be straight there, Claire." The phone clicked.

Claire quietly replaced the receiver on its cradle, turned around and yelped with shock. Michael stood silhouetted in the doorway. He had followed her upstairs, and now he gaped at her showing his hurt at her betrayal. She felt as if she had been caught in some dirty treachery.

"Thanks for nothing." He turned and lumbered blindly down the stairs again.

"Where are you going?" she called.

"I don't know," he choked. "I'll find my dad. I won't be back."

"Michael, please stay." She seized his wrist. "Don't be silly. Your family love you."

He shook her off and shoved her against the wall. Claire bumped her hip on the stair rail and twisted her ankle on a step. Michael rushed outside, slamming the door behind him.

Claire chased him out to the street and her dressing gown streamed behind her like a wedding veil. Chip bark pressed into her bare feet, and she grabbed Michael's arm as he stepped off the gutter, narrowly missing a moving car. The driver tooted angrily as he zoomed past.

"Blake has been really worried about you."

"Yeah, I'll bet." Michael swung his arm back and pushed her onto the footpath. Claire felt the gravel graze her arm and she lowered her head, winded.

"I won't let you go!" she cried. She had grown fond of the unhappy boy. If he escaped from her sight, he could vanish for weeks. He might end up homeless or hungry, or dead. Blake, hurry up! she screamed inside her head, as she pursued Michael.

Anybody who looked out of their window would have seen a gangly adolescent trying to shake free of a fragile young woman, who clung to him like a small dog with its jaws clamped into the hide of a wolf. If he hadn't been weakened by alcohol and shock, she would have been unable to hold him.

Finally, Claire heard pounding footsteps. Blake arrived, panting. He was hunched over with a stitch and did his best to pin Michael's flailing arms down to his sides. "I know what you did!" Blake panted. "Do you think I care about the car? I'm just glad you're safe. You could have died."

At last all of Michael's energy ebbed away. He stopped struggling in his brother's arms and pressed his fingers to a tender spot on the crown of his head. "I hurt here," he groaned.

"Bring him back to my place," Claire said. "It's so much closer than yours. We can call the doctor."

Blake's eyes shone at her in the moonlight. "Did he hurt you?" he asked hoarsely.

Claire flicked her wild, flowing hair behind her shoulders and drew her dressing-gown closer around her waist. What a mess she must look, in her nightclothes with scratches up both arms. It must remind him of that night when he.... Claire felt a wave of nausea, and for a horrible moment thought she would be sick in the gutter. Thankfully, it passed.

"I care for Michael too," she said flintily. "I didn't want to let him go, in the state he was in."

Blake was lost for words but continued to gaze at her with his dark, sorrowful eyes.

Claire could not bear his scrutiny. "Come on, don't stand there like a stunned mullet. Bring him back to my place," she repeated with authority.

Blake winced and nodded, like an obedient servant.

Claire sat on her bed, pressed her fists against her mouth, and tried to steady her whirling stomach. The doctor had been to examine Michael. He said he had mild concussion and needed plenty of rest. Michael collapsed on the spare-room bed in a deep slumber. Claire had to face Blake back down in the lounge room.

She changed into a tracksuit and tied her hair back in a tight ponytail. She knew in her heart that he was essentially sound. He was not the moody, vicious youth she'd remembered him to be. She longed to forget the pain, humiliation and sickness he had caused her.

Her gaze locked onto one of the small tapestries she had sewed long ago, for her own bedroom wall. Claire had surrounded one of her favourite Scripture verses with flowers, fruit and leaves. "Whatever is true, whatever is noble, whatever is right, whatever is pure, whatever is lovely, whatever is admirable - if anything is excellent or praiseworthy - think about such things". Philippians 4:8.

She sucked her bottom lip hard between her teeth. If there was ever a time to practise that verse, it was now. Thinking of what Blake had done was no good for her. Claire stood and squared her shoulders. *I thought it was a tall order, Lord, but you loved the people who scourged and crucified you. You forgave them. I want to be a forgiving person, like You.* She walked slowly downstairs, trying to stay focused on Jesus Christ instead of Blake Quinlan.

"Would you like a cup of tea?" she asked.

He shook his head. "No thanks, but I'll make one for you, if you tell me where everything is." He could not bring himself to look directly at her. She was so petite and lovely. He could hardly believe what she had done for Michael that night. What she had done for him, in return for what he had done to her.

Claire almost refused, then decided that a cup of tea would be handy to focus her attention on, instead of him. "The tea and sugar are in the canisters, milk in the fridge."

"How do you have it?"

"Milk with one, thanks." She felt light-headed. Sipping a hot drink with the guy who had raped her was like living in a bizarre dream.

While he moved about in the kitchen, she felt compelled to speak, to break the pressing silence. "How bad is your car?"

"All mangled at the front. He ploughed it straight into the garage door. Probably thousands of dollars damage." Blake guessed that Michael had been drunk or stoned. *The crazy kid! He shouldn't have been driving it, anyway.*

"I'm sorry about that," Claire said. "You didn't have it for long."

"A day and a half," Blake sighed.

"Was it insured?"

Blake ruefully shook his head. "I was going to take care of that on Monday."

Claire understood why Michael had expected to be in deep trouble. "That's very bad luck. To have it for less than two days, after saving for months, just to have it written off before you even have a chance to drive it to work." While she discussed his car, there was no danger of moving to personal issues.

As Blake stirred her tea, he shot her a wry grin. "Go easy, Claire. Do you want to see me rush in there and grab him by his throat?"

"Michael thought you'd be furious," she said.

Blake brought her the tea and settled on the couch across from her. "I am, but I can't stop thinking how he could've killed himself." He could not suppress a shudder. "I have no idea where he might have driven it before he got home."

"He's very disturbed and unhappy," Claire said softly.

Blake studied the backs of his hands. "He needs Mum," he said bleakly. "Did Sean and Angela tell you how Mum died? He blames himself." Blake cleared his throat and raked a hand through his hair.

Claire had never expressed her sympathy to him. "I'm sorry about your mother."

Blake's eyes instantly blurred with tears. He merely nodded because he could not trust himself to speak.

"I haven't got used to it yet," he said at last. "I keep expecting to see her walk inside with her shopping, smiling and telling us about some crazy, labour-saving bargain she bought. Mum would buy things she'd never dream of having before, just because they were dirt cheap."

Claire noticed how different he was to either Sean or Michael. He spoke slower and more reflectively than they did, and seemed to choose his words carefully.

Blake stood and began pacing around the couch. "When I bought my car last Friday, my first thought was to show Mum, and watch her face light up. She had a very expressive face, Claire, like a star." His voice shook, and he had to stop. He only spoke to break the silence but he had stumbled onto dangerously emotional ground.

So do you, she thought. She was astonished by the way Blake looked at her, with mingled shyness and admiration. Claire would have expected a fellow to despise a girl he had raped. She had felt drawn to his deep, clear eyes back then, when she was only sixteen, before their date. There was no point denying that Blake's eyes were remarkable, but now it disturbed her to look at them. A thought of her lost baby flashed through her head.

"I'm sorry," she repeated huskily. She did not know what else to say.

He managed half a polite smile. She wondered if he ever smiled spontaneously and happily. Of course, Blake Quinlan did not have much to be happy about.

"Thanks," he acknowledged. Looking at Claire's delicate, smooth face made his heart ache. His mother's face had been like a star, and Claire's was more like a fresh, creamy flower petal. He struggled to find words for what he should have said seven years ago.

"Claire, I'm sorry for what I did. I've been... so sorry... all this time."

Her forehead furrowed and she pushed aside her half finished cup of tea.

"Why did you do it?" she asked abruptly. The subject could not be avoided indefinitely. If they had to discuss it, it might as well be now.

Her question hit him like a brick. He certainly owed her some explanation. All he could give was the truth, but the truth was so lousy. "I wanted you to like me," he began slowly. "I thought you did for a little while, but then I drank too much and it went to my head. I s'pose I wanted things to move too quickly, too fast. You wouldn't dance with me, then you pushed me over, and when you ran out the others laughed at me. I saw red. That was why I chased you down, but I never dreamed I'd go so far in a million years."

He looked up to gauge her reaction. He noticed the light scattering of fine freckles across her nose. All of Claire's features were so fine and pure. His blood surged like quicksilver.

Instinctively he shielded his face with his long fingers. "It was so horrible. I... can't get over it."

Claire was sorry she'd tied her hair back. She wished to hide her burning cheeks. "You're a Christian, now," she reminded him. "Would God love you any more if you hadn't done it? Do you think any sin is worse in His eyes than another?"

"I know God hates all sin equally," he said, "but I can't help judging some harsher than others. I didn't murder anyone, but..." He suddenly gaped at her. "Hey, why are you, of all people, trying to comfort me?"

"I know what it's like to feel consumed with guilt and shame," she began painfully. "I always hoped you'd feel the same, but now that I see you do, it seems so pointless." She felt very sad. His mother had died, his father disappeared and his brother had smashed his new car, yet Blake sat torn to shreds over something he had done seven years ago! What a waste.

"I wish I could do something to take it back," he said bleakly.

"I know you do, but you can't. Seeing you belt your head against a brick wall doesn't make me feel any better."

"I should've apologised seven years ago," he said.

She shook her head. "I wouldn't have been ready to hear it, then."

He looked at her with a clear question in his eyes. "Are you happy with your life now?" he asked.

Claire resisted a mad desire to laugh in his face. He didn't know the half of it! Her pregnancy and abortion, the nightmares which still plagued her sometimes, the sharp pain that pierced her heart like barbed-wire whenever she saw a chubby, smiling toddler. She did not tell Blake these things, because they were her own business.

"I'm getting over it," she said guardedly.

He watched a quick pulse dart in her slender throat.

"I felt guilty too," she went on. She supposed she could give him at least that much. "I flirted with you, that night. I led you on, unintentionally. I behaved badly."

Blake vehemently shook his head. "No, you did nothing wrong. It wasn't your fault at all. It was completely mine."

"I used to worry about dying of an awful disease," Claire said. "Some sexually transmitted virus." She hardly knew why she said that but almost smiled to see his eyelids spring apart. She wondered if he knew how easily his face could be read.

"No way! You wouldn't catch anything from me! I've never been with another girl," he blustered. Blake felt heartsick to imagine that she had had such an unfounded fear looming over her for so long.

A nervous giggle did bubble out of Claire's lips. "It's OK. I'd long since guessed that, but it's good to hear you say so, just the same."

Her sparkling smile had a devastating effect on him. She was all soft curves, but then he hated himself for noticing such things. "I'm glad you're friends with Angela and Sean and Michael," he said.

That gave Claire a good reason to turn her attention to Michael. She craned her neck to peer at him, through the spare room door.

"I don't think he's going to stir until morning. You're welcome to leave him here for the night."

Blake scratched his head. "Thanks, but you don't know what he's like when he's drunk," he said awkwardly. Heat infused his cheeks. *She knew what he had been like.* "Michael could wake up any time, dead sick, or crying and yelling. I won't leave you alone with that."

"Well you can stay too, and sleep on the couch." Claire was surprised to feel no qualms at all. In fact, ironically enough, Blake Quinlan would be the safest person to have in her house that night. "It would be most sensible, don't you think?"

His eyes gently questioned her. "I'd rather walk him home than make you feel uncomfortable."

"I'll be fine," she said briskly. She brought him a blanket and he leaned back on the couch and covered his knees. "Thank-you, but I won't be able to sleep a wink," he said, with a wry smile. "What if your father comes home early and finds me asleep on his couch? Do you think he'd bother waking me up to ask why? He'd pulverise me as soon as look at me."

Claire admitted that was true, but it was his problem. She doubted if she would sleep herself and she would be safely tucked up in her own bed. When she closed her bedroom door, she fell onto her pillow and wept a storm. She hardly knew why. Her bones ached and her body felt wrung out, like a damp tea-towel after a feast. She was so exhausted, she did drift into a restless sleep.

For the first time in many months, she dreamed about the tiny baby who'd never had a chance to live. This time, it had the large, shining dark eyes of Blake Quinlan.

Chapter Twenty-Five

"The hero lifts the crow-bar and knocks the dog off the top of the building, but turns to find the villain lurking right behind him," Peter went on.

Claire stared at the tines of her cocktail fork and tuned out from Peter's long description of the movie he had watched in Melbourne, because he was beginning to repeat himself. He knew violent movies did not interest her, so he could hardly expect to hold her attention.

It was Monday evening. She supposed the damage to Blake's car would be assessed by now. She wondered how poor Michael was faring. Her mother would have visited to find out, if she had been home. Claire would too, if she could be certain she would find Michael alone, but she would not run the risk of meeting Blake again. It was inconvenient to have to shun Michael just because she wanted to avoid Blake.

"Then the heroine arrives and pulls a revolver out of her purse," Peter was saying.

Claire had an excuse to visit the Quinlans. Michael had left his denim jacket behind on the spare-room bed. He had woken the morning after his accident without the slightest memory of how he'd treated Claire. He chattered incessantly, trying hard to impress her as usual. Angela had quietly warned Claire that Michael had a crush on her, but Claire would have guessed anyway. She could not deny that his schoolboy infatuation flattered her. If she'd had a younger brother, she would have liked him to be just like Michael.

The waitress brought their meals and as they ate, Peter filled Claire in with news of her relatives in Melbourne. Claire listened with interest. She learned that her cousin Steven had moved to Brisbane with his father, and had broken all ties with his mother's family, so Auntie Tessa felt as if she had no older son. The young twins caused trouble. Cindy was introverted to the point of being reclusive and Ryan had been diagnosed with attention deficit disorder. He was so hyperactive that Tessa had him on continual medication. Her most recent de-facto had left her because he could no longer bear living with the small boy.

Claire felt deeply grieved. "Poor little Ryan. And poor Cindy." She remembered the adorable, rosy-cheeked babies she'd loved. "History seems to repeat itself with Auntie Tessa. She's had a hard life."

"Perhaps she should stop choosing the same type of fellow and making the same mistakes," Peter said soberly. "People often stay stuck in a rut, and can't move out of it."

Claire sipped her orange juice and thought of one person she knew who had risen above his circumstances. Last week at Angela's flat, Sean had described a vivid dream in which he was sprinting over the golden sand of a magnificent beach. That type of dream was rare for him now, he'd said. In most of them he was bound to his chair.

It used to be different. As Angela had made the coffee, Sean told Claire that when he first broke his spine he used to long for sleep, because he could escape into dreams of running, kicking and leaping. Now, those dreams were the exception, not the norm. Claire recalled seeing him hunch forward in his chair with his strong hands curled upon his knees. He'd looked as if he could spring out of it at any moment. His posture rippled with life and vitality.

"I love my wheelchair sport," he'd told Claire. "I love my chaplaincy. Do you know Claire, if I still had my legs there's a good chance I might no longer be playing football. I'm twenty-seven now. I might have injured myself. I might never have shaped up as good as I expected to be. I'm in the right place, all right, and God has put me there. When I share my testimony with the young lads, they really listen to me. I'm totally satisfied."

Claire realised with a jolt of guilt that she was no longer listening to Peter. She forced her attention back, but he struck her with a name she would rather have forgotten.

"That Russell Timms is back on the scene, wanting to take Ryan fishing," Peter said grimly. "He's never shown an interest in his children before and Tessa wonders what he's up to."

Claire felt as if there were a lump of hot coal in her stomach, stirring her food and her bitter memories simultaneously. She tried to blot out the impression of the small, beady eyes, hot breath and wet kiss. She could not hold back a shudder of distaste.

"Auntie Tessa should send him packing. Ryan and Cindy don't need that sort of a father. Don't talk about him. Tell me about your own family instead." Peter's mention of Russell had cast a pall over her evening.

When he started she listened carefully. She had only met Pete's mother once, and his two sisters never. If her father had his way, they might be her future in-laws. Somehow, that prospect did not raise a flicker of excitement. She had rather hoped it would. Perhaps she associated Peter with her bleak, sad sojourn at Auntie Tessa's house. That was hardly fair of her. It was not his fault.

Peter described how his eldest sister and her fiancé had gone water-skiing. The story might have interested Claire more if she had met them. She rested her chin on her cupped hands and studied Peter, instead. He was clean-cut, with wavy, light coloured hair. Pleasant looking, rather than handsome. His eyes were frank and direct. Not as arresting as Blake Quinlan's dark eyes.

"What are you thinking about?" Peter's friendly question broke into her thoughts.

"I was enjoying your story. It sounds like fun," she lied glibly before the mantle of colour made its way into her cheeks.

He grinned at her. "We should try water-skiing ourselves some day."

"Sounds great."

Peter was easy to string along. He never guessed that she daydreamed while he talked. She would be willing to bet that Blake would have known. He seemed as sensitive to moods as a finely tuned violin.

Claire decided to return Michael's jacket to him. She wanted to know he was all right. If she was going to be friends with the rest of the Quinlan family, she could not spend the rest of her life avoiding Blake. She would return the jacket tomorrow.

————————

Claire chose four o'clock in the afternoon for her visit. She planned it so that Michael would be home from school and Blake would hopefully still be at work. There was a strange car parked beneath their carport. It was a multi-coloured, rusty old Holden with dented doors.

Claire's hands trembled as she tapped on their door. She had not been there since the visit with her mother when she was sixteen years old. When nobody answered she felt oddly relieved. She bent down to leave the jacket on the doormat. She would find out what happened from Sean and Angela next week. She straightened up just as Blake walked around the side of the house.

Claire's heart jolted, then settled back in its normal place, beating hard.

"Michael left his jacket behind," she said, hoping he would not notice the heat in her face. She had not missed the way his eyes flashed with pleasure at the sight of her before he stared at her feet. It stunned and confused her.

"I hope I didn't interrupt you," she added foolishly.

He shook his head. "Not at all. I was just watering Mum's jasmine vine." For his part, he hoped Claire could not detect how upset he had just been. He had been close to tears. Just in case she could tell, he explained, "It's the first time I remembered it since she died. Now it's almost dead and she had it growing for years. We should've looked after it properly."

Claire understood what he couldn't express. By nurturing her favourite plant, he wished to hold on to a small piece of his mother.

"Can I see it?" she asked. She followed him to the side of the house and examined the vine on the trellis. "Hey, I think you could still save it, if you trim off some of the withered leaves and stems. The main stem still seems green and healthy." She unconsciously began to pluck leaves as she spoke, delighted that Rowena's delicate plant was not hurt beyond repair.

Blake followed her example. He looked at the back of her head and her bent neck, slenderly curved like a creamy swan. His gaze swept the tops of her shoulders and the few small vertebrae of her spine that he could see. She made his heart do strange things. There was nobody he admired more than Claire. His brother Sean had long been his hero, but Claire was every bit as resilient and noble as Sean was. Blake sensed serene strength in every bone of her body. He had not broken her seven years ago. He thought he had, but he hadn't. He felt giddy with thankfulness.

She turned to look at him. "What happened to your new car?"

He shuffled and blushed, hoping she had not noticed how he ogled her. "Eight thousand dollars damage. There's no way it can be repaired so I sold it to the wrecker's yard." He surprised himself that he genuinely felt so indifferent about his loss. There had been a time, a few years back, when he could easily have skinned Michael alive. His last few months had reinforced how much more precious people were than cars. If only his mother had lived, Blake could have cheerfully sacrificed a dozen new cars.

"Where did the little car out the front come from?" she asked.

"My boss's son lent it to me. He wanted to sell it, but he'll lend it to me until I can pay him for it." Blake laughed. "Do you know it's in even worse shape than my old one was?"

Claire snapped off a few dry twigs and directed a gentle spray of hose water on the roots of the vine, still strong and supple. She studied Blake from the corners of her eyes and detected no trace of bitterness at Michael. She was relieved, for she had not wanted the headstrong boy to be in trouble. She admired Blake for that. It felt hard for Claire to grudgingly admire a person she had long hated like poison.

"Where is Michael now?" she asked.

"At Angela and Sean's. I had half a day off work to take him there. He'll live with them for a while. Angela thinks he needs some female influence right now."

Blake squatted down to pluck a few tough weeds away from the stem of the vine, which Claire's smaller fingers could not manage. "It might be good for both of them," he said. "Angela needs somebody to look after. Did she tell you how she lost her little baby?" He was getting dangerously emotional, so in a typical Blake gesture, he joked about it. "Now she'll have an irresponsible fifteen-year-old rebel to care for. That ought to satisfy her maternal aches."

Claire paused in picking off the leaves while her heart plummeted. Angela had longed for a baby and could not have one, while Claire had cast hers away as casually as if it were a stray kitten. Sometimes it seemed the passing years made the torment worse instead of better.

She watched Blake's long, sensitive fingers and his scuffed elbows. His throat rippled as he pursed his lips and swallowed. Then he stood up and towered over her. Claire tried not to feel daunted by his sheer height. Peter Lennox was several inches shorter than any of the Quinlan boys. Even Sean appeared rangy and tall sitting in his chair.

Blake raised his eyes awkwardly to the big old plane tree in his backyard. Claire saw the sky reflected in them.

"Claire, would you... like to come in for a drink?" Instantly he flushed and blustered, "Of course you wouldn't. I'm sorry. Forget I asked." How could he expect her to willingly enter his house?

"Hey, Blake," she interrupted.

He forced himself to look at her. "Yeah?"

"You didn't give me a chance to answer. I will come in for a drink."

Claire hardly believed what she heard from her own lips. She had no idea why she accepted his hesitant offer, except that she felt sorry for him. His eyes lit up with surprised pleasure, and then he smiled. With a twist of the stomach, Claire followed him inside. Her parents would hate her being here. She would have to escape as soon as she could.

The interior of the dim lounge-room still smelled of the beeswax furniture polish and pot-pourri Rowena had probably used. Blake looked around, dismayed by the clutter that spilled over to the kitchen. It looked as if a bomb had exploded within the four walls. "Excuse the mess. It wouldn't have been like this when Mum was alive."

"I don't mind messes." Claire was not Kate Parker's daughter for nothing. "I can help tidy up. I'm good at it. I stayed with my aunt and cousins in Melbourne once, and their house was worse than this all the time." As she spoke, she lifted some cushions off the floor, then seized the sponge to wipe the kitchen bench. She preferred doing something to just sitting there. She did not have to look at him while she worked.

Blake felt awkward to see her work and tried to think of a polite way to ask her to stop. She seemed content, so he decided to leave her to it. As long as she worked, she would stay there. When she finished she would probably go home. He watched her wonderful coppery ponytail bounce like something alive as she turned her head. He felt ashamed of the way his pulse raced in response to her nearness.

"I'll make a start on the dishes, then." He could not bear to stand idly by.

"I'll wipe them, if you give me a tea-towel," said Claire.

As they worked, she wondered if it would have been different if she had got to know Blake this way in the first place. Standing over a sink, instead of thrust together on a date when they had only just met. When she finished, she hung up her tea towel and noticed the ironing board set up in the corner, with a basket of creased shirts and trousers on the floor.

"I'll iron some of these, if you like." She did not expect him to object because she thought men hated to iron. She took a sip of the cold water he had poured her and raised the iron.

"No!" he yelled instinctively.

Claire almost dropped the iron with alarm. She let it clatter on the ironing board and nearly jumped out of her skin. She faced him, her eyes wide with concern, and edged toward the door. She felt like crying. She shouldn't have come.

Blake leaned on the back of a kitchen chair with both arms trembling, shaking his head.

"I'm sorry. I didn't mean to frighten you. It's just that Mum... Now the iron always makes me.... and you're drinking, like she was."

Claire's eyes misted with comprehension. She gaped at her shoes, stunned by her own insensitivity. After a moment of deliberation, she stepped cautiously towards him and put her hand on his shoulder. Claire never voluntarily touched anybody and the feeling of the warm skin through the sleeve of his T-shirt made her fingers tingle with the strangeness of it.

"Blake, it's OK to cry," she said nervously.

That was his undoing. He bowed his head and wept. He cried harder than he had at camp, when he'd first heard about his mum. He ran the back of his hand across his face and tried to catch his breath but the tears kept coming. He had not cried that way in years.

Claire pulled out a kitchen chair. She motioned him into it, as if he were a kindergarten child. Then she sat in one beside him. He did not look up but he knew because he smelled the freshness of her skin. He sensed that she was at a loss for what to do next.

He wrapped his arms tightly around his convulsing chest until he breathed more evenly. What an exhibition he had made of himself! In a low voice, he explained, "Nobody has said anything, but everybody must know Mum's death was all my fault."

"Blake! That's not true." His words made her shudder.

He nodded. Yes it was true. He, who always guarded his thoughts like treasures, poured them out to the person who already knew the worst there was to know of him. Once started, he simply couldn't stop himself; it all came pouring out.

"Do you know what I do for a living, Claire? I fix electrical gadgets. And my own mother died from electrocution. That iron was a death trap. It sat in her cupboard day after day and I'm the only one who should have known. I should've done something."

"You did do something. You bought her a new iron. You warned her to throw the old one away. Michael told me. He knows. Sean and Angela know too. It wasn't your fault."

"I should've thrown it away for her. I didn't take it apart but I could see that the flex cord was frayed and I could hear the awful buzz. I should have told Mum that even if she couldn't see any copper wire underneath, there still might be enough exposed to cause a terrible accident. Instead, I trusted her to throw it away and use the new one. I expected Mum to take my word for it but I knew how she liked to hold onto her things. I should have warned her more. I should've insisted that she use the new one. I should've pulled it apart and examined it in more detail." Blake had deliberately held his tortuous negligence back from his brothers and Angela. They were hurt enough. He could tell Claire. She did not know his mother and there was a good chance he would never see her again, anyway.

Claire cleared her throat. "I know nothing about electronics but I don't think the best repair man in the world could predict an accident before it happened." Her skin still crawled with horror for the load he had been silently carrying. "You did the best you could and it was her own decision to use the iron after you warned her not to." She found herself trembling with sympathy.

"You think it's your fault, Michael thinks it's his fault for dropping his bag there, and Sean thinks it's his fault for buying her that iron ten years ago in the first place. It's a terrible thing but none of you are to blame. Your mother wouldn't want you all to feel so bad. She would want you to remember the good times with her."

She watched his throat work. His eyelids were squeezed tight and his lips clamped shut. She had no idea whether her words made any impression. Perhaps his pain was beyond the release of confession. He just needed someone to sit with him and share the moment until he felt stronger. She never would have dreamed it would be her. She did not know if she wanted it to be her. Blake probably had nobody else that he trusted to whom to pour out his grief. She could certainly relate to that.

It dawned on Claire that she understood him intuitively. She was familiar with bottled-up heartache and guilt. Although she hated Blake, she pitied him. Well, perhaps hate was a little too strong a word to use now. It was difficult to hate a person she empathised with. Part of her still wanted to cling to the bitterness but her shoulders felt far lighter without the burden.

After a long silence, she drew a breath and risked the only thing she had left to say which might help him. "I'm willing to forget the past, if you are."

That made his eyelashes flicker open. For an instant, Claire regretted her impulse. Her teeth chattered as she remembered again the enormity of what he had done. He knew more of her than he had a right to know. He had savagely invaded her personal boundaries.

"That is, if you can stand to see me without remembering what you... all that happened in your car." Her fingernails dug small half moon shapes into her palms. She would have done better not to have mentioned it.

"Hey, Claire," he said softly. This time, it was his turn to help her. Something inside of him melted at the sight of her. He chewed his inner lip, not sure of what he would say, but she watched him, waiting for something.

He spoke in a low voice. "Don't forget, I was drunk to the eyeballs and fuming mad. I don't remember all those... details you're thinking of. They've gone hazy for me. If we were friends now, don't you think I'd try to treat you... much differently this time?"

Her brow uncreased and she managed a slight nod of acknowledgement. Blake felt himself smile back, and silently congratulated himself. He had been put on the spot but sensed that he had said the right thing. The ragged, raw grief he had just been feeling gave way to a tingle of excited pleasure he had not known for a long, long time.

Chapter Twenty-Six

Claire spooned melted butter through Angela's steamed vegetables while she listened to Angela tackle Michael's plea to let him attend some dubious party aboard a hired bus.

"You have to let me go," he wheedled. "I promise I won't do anything silly. I won't even drink much."

"Won't drink much!" Angela echoed. "You aren't supposed to drink at all. You're a minor."

"I won't drink at all, then," Michael said glibly.

Sean hooted from the table where he waited. "Of course you will. We weren't born yesterday."

"A bus full of booze is no place for a fifteen-year-old boy," Angela pronounced firmly. Claire admired her. Angela was young to be responsible for her husband's adolescent brother. She seemed to be doing a fine job. Michael appeared neater and cleaner since he had lived with Angela.

Her imperious tone had no effect on Michael. "Mum would've let me go," he pushed. "She couldn't have stopped me. You're too bossy, Angela."

Angela tried not to show how the comparison hurt her. "I'm making decisions in your own best interest, because I care about you."

"I have to go this time because I promised my friends I'd be there," he said. "Blake already gave me permission to go before I left home."

Angela folded her arms across her chest. "Did he?" she flared. "He needs his head read."

"You have it out with him after I've been to the party," Michael said smugly. "You always say we should keep our promises, and after Blake said I could go I promised my friends I would."

Claire placed the bowl of vegetables on the table and Sean shot her an expression of helpless apology. He was beet red, and Claire felt sorry for him. She knew what was on his mind. Until now, neither he nor Angela had let Blake's name cross their lips, but Michael bandied his brother's name about freely. When he stepped out of earshot, Claire would tell Sean and Angela that she did not mind much. Their lives would be easier. It must be a huge effort to behave as if Sean did not even have another brother.

She had not seen Blake since that afternoon at his house. After the ground she had broken then, Claire felt a bit like a deflated balloon and hardly knew why. She did not wish to see him again, of course, but the thought of his intense, walled-up guilt complex bothered her. Sometimes she caught herself thinking of him at night when she should have been asleep. She wished he had somebody to make him feel better.

In the kitchen, Angela opened the oven door, and the fragrant aroma of roast beef did nothing to whet Claire's appetite. Thinking about Blake made her too sad to feel hungry. She wondered what he was doing tonight, in exile, while she dined with his family.

They all moved to the table and Sean said grace over the food. It seemed that Michael had won the battle over the bus party, and while he smothered his meat with gravy, he beamed at Claire.

"Hey, how'd you like to come and watch my football game on Saturday with Angela and Sean?" Michael had a huge crush on Claire, and he always asked for whatever he wanted.

"Don't feel obligated," Angela put in, with a grin.

"I'd like to," Claire said. "I will come." She really wanted to watch Michael's game with her friends. She was fond of Michael, anyway.

Living with Angela and Sean had not made Michael's visits to

Claire's house less frequent. It never seemed to occur to him that he might wear out his welcome but Claire was glad. Michael Quinlan, with his youthful candour, was one of the few people she felt entirely at ease with.

Sometimes, Peter Lennox was there when Michael visited. Peter was as soft-spoken with Michael as he was with everybody else, but his eyes would narrow when he thought the teenage boy had stayed for long enough. Peter had a hard job to conceal his irritation sometimes, and stopped just short of being rude to Michael. Claire felt hurt for Michael's sake, and her only comfort was that he didn't seem to notice Peter's slights. It disappointed her to discover this supercilious side to Peter that she had never realised before.

She had thought of going to watch Peter play squash on Saturday, but Claire knew she would rather watch Michael play football. That did not say much for her romance with Peter. She liked to do things with Angela and Sean. They were the best friends she'd ever had, and sometimes over dinner like this, Claire basked in the illusion that she was really family to them. She sometimes studied them for signs of cooling off, for fear that she might wear out her welcome. Angela and Sean would be far too tactful and kind to tell her if she were becoming a nuisance.

"I'll play my very best on Saturday if you're there, Claire." Michael's beam of delight was certainly genuine.

Claire could not help laughing. She still could not get over the way the whole Quinlan family behaved as if her good opinion meant the world to them. It warmed a cold place deep inside of her. How refreshing it felt to be valued for herself. She felt honoured to be asked to watch Michael play.

It occurred to her that Blake might be there too. A few weeks earlier that would have been enough to make Claire shy away from the invitation, but now she did not mind the thought of seeing him again. After that afternoon at his house, how could she?

He was there. She saw him before he saw them. She had settled on the outskirts of the football oval with Sean and Angela, and when Angela returned to the car for drinks and picnic food, Claire noticed Blake's bowed shoulders several metres away. Even in his leisure moments, the slump of his shoulders appeared woebegone, even vulnerable. She saw him notice her and watched the surprise spread over his face. Then he held up his hand in a greeting and turned back to the game.

Claire squirmed on the picnic rug. She supposed Blake would have joined Sean and Angela if she had not been with them. She felt uncomfortable to think of him spending the whole match in self-imposed isolation for her sake. Claire looked at Sean beside her, and he was intent on the game. Silently Claire slipped away before she had time for second thoughts.

She crunched over the gravel to where Blake sat. "Hello," she said.

He gave a smile of bashful astonishment. "Hello," he responded. Blake's smiles resembled his brothers' friendly grins, yet there was a quality of quiet warmth that made them solely his own. "I didn't expect to see you here."

"Michael asked me to come and watch his game."

"No kidding? He's pretty persuasive." Blake would never have dared to ask Claire along to watch him, when he was Michael's age. In fact, he still wouldn't. He did not have the nerve at twenty-five that his brother possessed at fifteen. Michael had some sort of boyish confidence that people would like him. And people did like him.

"I know he's persuasive," Claire said. "I saw how he made Angela agree to let him go to a bus party."

"I'm still amazed that she agreed," Blake said. "Whatever came over her?"

"He told her you'd already given him permission, so he promised his friends he'd go."

Blake stared at her, and then his eyes sparkled. "He's a rotten liar. I told him he couldn't go. He said the others told him it was O.K."

Blake mimicked Michael. "Angela told me I could go, so I'm not going to listen to you!"

Claire tilted her head and laughed. She had not expected to be amused, but Michael's craftiness and Blake's clever take-off were funny.

"How are you going?" she asked.

If Blake wanted to be honest, he could have told her that he'd thought of nothing but her since she'd visited his house. His hopes had plummeted when he had not seen her since. He decided they could not really be friends, yet now that she sat beside him, sunshine poured into his world again. He wondered why she had asked how he was, and why she even bothered to greet him.

"I'm not bad. Work's O.K. Can't complain." That was his standard innocuous answer. The wind blew some of her hair across his face and he made no attempt to brush it away.

"Tell me, did you play football too?" She thought she ought to engage him in some small-talk before she made her way back to Sean and Angela.

"I played a bit of football but didn't really get into it much. I was never anywhere near as good as Sean. He was tops."

Claire regarded him with a slight frown. She wondered if Sean's talent was the reason for Blake's discouragement. Perhaps he gave up football, and probably other things, because he felt eclipsed. It bothered her.

———

Sean leaned forward in his wheelchair, glued to the game. He could not help thinking how superior his own playing had been to Michael's. It was not sour grapes. Just a fact. Whenever Michael asked for Sean's feedback, Sean hardly knew what to say without offending him.

Michael was almost laughable. He looked big and tough in his football uniform but his coordination was so bad, he rarely got a touch of the ball. When it did fall into his hands, he hardly knew what to do with it. Sean shook his head and breathed a long sigh through his nose. He would keep holding his tongue because none of his tips would improve Michael's game, anyway. It came down to raw talent.

Angela returned and poked him in the ribs. "Where's Claire?"

Sean did not take his eyes off the oval. "I dunno. I didn't see her go."

Angela gasped and clutched his arm. "There she is, over there with Blake!"

That was newsworthy enough to distract Sean from the football. He looked where she pointed.

"That's very mature of them both." He was impressed.

Angela's mind reeled, wondering how they came to be together and if she ought to do anything about it. There was no way she could sit comfortably beside Sean and watch Michael's game while she didn't know.

"They might need to be rescued. I'd better go see." She leaped up and went quickly over.

"Hi Blake. Hey Claire, I have the drinks if you want to come back with us."

Blake averted his eyes. "Yeah, don't let me hold you up." He sounded disappointed.

Claire made no move to rise. Blake was excluded from the invitation, and she felt another pang in her heart for him. It wasn't right. If she hadn't been there, they would've expected Sean's brother to sit with them. Yet if they all sat together there would be a distracting tension that would spoil everything. Neither she nor Blake could stand the strain.

"I might stay here for awhile," Claire said. "It's closer to the goals."

Angela was too stunned to reply. She managed a nod and fled back to Sean. She snatched his elbow off the arm of his chair. "She'll be back in awhile," she breathed.

"Good. Did you see the goal Jamie Clarke just kicked? He has skill. He leaves Michael for dead, but don't tell Mike."

"They have a lot in common, really," Angela mused.

"Who? Michael and Jamie?"

"No, silly. Blake and Claire." Angela peeled open a packet of potato chips and stared in at the contents without taking one. "They're both quiet. Both think a lot. Both idealistic. I wonder if it's really too late for them."

Sean stared at her as if she had sprouted tentacles. "Don't you stir up trouble. I know your wild imagination. If you have some ridiculous idea of setting them up together, just go soak your head in a cold bath or something. Angela, promise me." Sean saw the dangerous way her eyes glowed. He did not like it one bit.

"I suppose you're right," she said reluctantly.

"I mean it, Ange. You like being Claire's friend, don't you? Well don't start pushing her at Blake or you'll drive her away from all of us. He raped her, for heaven's sake."

Angela slid her hand into the chip packet, crestfallen. "Don't worry. I don't know what comes over me, sometimes."

Sean rolled her other hand into a ball and enveloped it with his larger one. He pressed his lips to her knuckles and thought of all the hard work her capable hands did for him and others. His little wife was pretty special to even consider that a romance between Claire and Blake might be possible. He would be nowhere without her energy and optimism.

"Whenever you feel an urge to meddle in other people's affairs, come to me and I'll kiss it out of you," he whispered. "You have the greatest husband in the world. Remember that."

———

Angela shook her head over the untidy state of Rowena's kitchen and began to tidy up for Blake while Michael sat on the bench and kicked the cupboard with his feet. He had asked Angela to drive him there to collect a few belongings but instead of moving to get them, he talked non-stop. Being back after four weeks brought the memories of his mother crashing down on Michael harder than ever, so he tried to drown the pain with chatter.

What he really wanted was to go to his friend Wayne's house to smoke some hash but nobody would be there tonight, so he tried not to long for it. Michael thought of other pleasant things instead.

"Hey Angela, we're so close to the Parkers, let's go and invite Claire home with us for tea."

Angela shook her head. "Claire came last night. I'd be happy to have her but we won't be too demanding. She has a life of her own."

"She's the most gorgeous chick I've ever laid eyes on," Michael sighed. "She's heaps prettier than any girl from school. What'll I do? I'm in love with an older woman." Michael was never inclined to keep his feelings bottled up.

Blake forced a grin, looked at Angela and rolled his eyes to the ceiling. Normally he would have poked fun at his young brother, but he always kept quiet where Claire was concerned. Blake hated to hear how Michael spoke of her but never rebuked him, in case his own feelings showed.

"Don't refer to young ladies as chicks," Angela scolded. "Claire is very pretty but she's too old for you."

"I know. She already has a boyfriend, anyway."

"Who?" Blake felt as if he had been punched hard in the stomach. Everything outside the window seemed to take on a shade of grey.

"Some dude called Peter. He goes to uni, I think. Seems pretty boring to me. I don't know what she sees in him. She probably likes him for his brains."

"What's he like?" For once, Blake was not concerned about making too much of an issue.

Michael shrugged. "I dunno. On the short side, brown hair, not real muscly. Goes on about finances with Claire's dad." He really hadn't been interested.

Blake sank onto the couch with his back to Michael. "Are you sure he's her boyfriend?" It was his final question and as he asked, he felt like the prize idiot. It had never crossed his mind that Claire might have a boyfriend. That might help to explain her serene strength. Blake had automatically thought of her as solitary and unattached, like himself. He shouldn't have been surprised. She was so beautiful, what did he expect?

"Of course." Michael realised that Peter Lennox had not been formally introduced to him as such but it was still obvious. "Why else would he hang around their house? Not to watch Mr Parker's moustache waggle. He looks at Claire like this." Michael pulled an exaggerated, lovelorn face that Blake did not find at all funny.

He flicked aimlessly through the television guide to hide his own face from Michael and Angela. He felt bitterly depressed and disgusted at his feelings. Claire offered to be his friend, but he could hardly expect her to fall in love with him. He had no right to be miserable because she loved another fellow. He should be pleased. It showed that she had recovered from what he did. Wasn't that all he had ever wanted to know? He should thank God, instead of moping.

When Michael disappeared to fetch his things, Angela watched him with her heart in her eyes. "I'm sorry, Blake," she said quietly. "I think I guess how you feel about Claire. You love her, don't you?"

He felt his face burn. Angela knew his story so it would be pointless to deny it. "What if I do? There's no hope for me and I don't want to talk about it, Angela." He had not intended to snap but saw no need to apologise. Angela's face was soft and sympathetic.

Blake did love Claire. He had always loved her. Since he had met her again, her every glance sent flames shooting through him. His pulse raced when he thought of her gentle womanliness, her warm understanding and her mysterious softness. He could close his eyes and picture her brilliant blue eyes, the curve of her neck and the firm knob of her chin. He could almost hear the precise fluency of her voice. He was head over heels in love with Claire Parker.

Angela reached out and patted his knee. She did not know what to say but felt she ought to say something. "I'll keep warning you when Claire visits, so you don't have to see her. Blake, I feel really bad for you."

"Don't feel bad," he responded. "This is nothing new for me. I've always loved Claire." The most aggravating part was that he might have had a chance with her once, seven years ago, when she had accepted his date. Now he had no hope. Blake no longer wanted to sit where his feelings could be read like an open book. He jumped up to help Michael look for his things.

Why was he so churned up? There was a good chance that Claire would not have stayed with him anyway, even if he hadn't attacked her. Seven years ago, he thought he didn't have much to offer a girl. That was still true. She wanted to be friends and he was glad. He could not stay away from her as Angela advised. He understood how a boy like Michael could become hooked on alcohol and narcotics. Claire was exhilarating, like a tantalisingly pure draught of wine. He would ache inside the next time he saw her, but that was far better than not seeing her at all.

Just before Angela and Michael were ready to leave, the door swung open and a bedraggled, ashen-faced scarecrow stood blinking at them. For a moment they all gaped back, stunned to see Gerry again after such a relatively short time. The coarse hair at the back of his neck was longer, his eyes were more deeply sunken, but otherwise he appeared just as cross and disillusioned as when he'd left. He looked sick too, like a dying duck in a thunderstorm.

Michael spoke first. "Dad!" He let his two duffle bags thump onto the floor and considered taking them back to his bedroom and moving back home again. Then he looked at Gerry's grim face and had second thoughts.

"What's going on here?" Gerry grunted. He was sick of Victoria and New South Wales. He came home dead-tired, hoping to slip into his house without facing anyone but there were three of their foolish faces ogling him the moment he opened the door. Only Sean, who was still his favourite, was missing. Gerry had allowed himself to be mildly impressed by Sean's wheelchair athletics.

"It's good to see you home, Dad," Angela said, rather unconvincingly. "Michael is living with me and Sean for the time being. Is there anything we can do for you?"

Gerry managed a sickly smile. It sounded like a good arrangement. "Yes. Just leave me alone for a few weeks. I'm not feeling well lately. There's a good girl." He turned wearily to Blake. "How about you? Still bumming about here, I s'pose?"

Blake nodded despondently.

"Well I'm home again now so you needn't stay."

Blake felt a surge of the old desolation he had known so often as a child but squared his shoulders and shook it out. He reminded himself that he was totally hardened where his father was concerned. "I have nowhere else to go now. I gave up the lease on my flat."

Gerry was already shuffling through to the shower, looking none too pleased. "Well see that you keep out of my way," he called over his shoulder.

"I will." That was the easiest promise Blake had ever made. He had no desire to stay in the same room as Gerry. Now that Dad was home, any hopes of future visits from Claire were dashed to pieces. Well, things were coming back to normal, now that old miseryguts was home.

Chapter Twenty-seven

Gerry Quinlan hated being home as much as he had hated living out on the road. Surrounded by all of Rowena's furniture and ornaments but without having her near him was pure torture. Fate, or God, was out to get him, and wouldn't stop until he was dead too. Gerry took a swig of beer and tried to listen to Michael instead.

At first Gerry was annoyed when the youngster called on him every few days. Now, he found himself yearning for any company to give him some respite from his morbid pining for Rowena. Michael's chatter, however tedious, was a distraction.

One thing did interest Gerry, and that was Michael's talk of Claire Parker. Mike told him that Claire was a friend Angela made on a Christian camp and she was a knock-out. At first Gerry doubted that she could be the same girl that Blake had raped. Later, Michael added that Claire's mother had been Rowena's best friend at school. That left Gerry in no doubt. *But why the dickens would that girl have anything to do with my family?*

"Hey Mike, is this Claire Parker friends with Blake too?" he asked one afternoon.

"Of course. Why not?" Michael had not seen them together much, but on the few occasions when they met each other in Sean's flat they seemed to be on good terms.

Gerry's lips twisted incredulously. Could the boy truly be ignorant of the family scandal, after so many years? They had kept it from

Michael when he was a child of eight, but was he still in the dark? It was the only subject Gerry had stayed tight-lipped about, not willing to broadcast the shame of having a rapist for a son. But it was so long ago now, and young Michael enjoyed a thrill. Gerry felt a sudden relish to divulge this piece of juicy gossip. Michael was family, after all.

"He raped her! That's why." Gerry always liked to see the shock sensation.

Michael stared at his father with a smile on his lips and a puzzled knot between his eyebrows. He thought his father was having a joke with him, but he didn't quite get it. He waited for Gerry to elucidate.

"Did you hear me? He raped her."

Now, Michael's chest heaved with concern. He wondered if the last several months of grief had sent his father around the twist. "Come on, Dad," he said. "Blake wouldn't rape anyone. He makes the Pope look like Jack the Ripper."

"It's true, I tell you." Gerry plonked his beer-can down on the glass top of the coffee table and craned forward. "He did it when he was about your age. No, he was a few years older. He couldn't summon the courage to ask the girl on a date so your mother asked her for 'im."

Gerry went on, embellishing the sordid event with vivid description. Initially, Michael listened to humour his father, certain it was one of Dad's trumped-up stories. Dad had always hated Blake. However, the lurid glitter in Gerry's eyes showed that he was genuine. Flashes from Michael's own memory struck him. Blake had urged him not to visit the Parker family because something terrible had happened. He had doggedly refused to visit them with him. He let Michael keep thinking that Mrs Parker was angry because of something Mum had done. Michael hid his head in his hands. He knew Gerry's story was true.

When Gerry had finished, he felt vaguely let down. Watching Michael's expression had not been the fun he'd anticipated. Instead of looking awe-struck, Michael's face was pea-green. He looked sick to the stomach, and he did something odd. He set his can of beer on the table half finished.

"I gotta go, Dad," he gasped.

Michael remembered how freely he had shared with Claire and her mother about Blake's fear of women. His forehead broke out in sweat as thick as the dew on a cold beer can. A surge of red-hot fury almost split his chest apart. He had been allowed to keep behaving like an insensitive oaf, wounding Claire whenever he saw her, just so that Blake could keep his disgusting secret!

"Where are you going?" Gerry cried. It occurred to him that Michael might spill the family scandal to his sleazy young friends. Gerry hoped he had not opened some Pandora's Box better left sealed.

"Someone should have told me!" Michael had not expected his voice to erupt as a high-pitched yelp, but it did.

"That's why I told you! Where are you going?"

Michael could hardly see through his screen of tears. "To find Blake." He was much younger than his brother but felt capable of tearing him to shreds. The fierce hurt inside of him broke out on his skin in crimson and white blotches.

As the door slammed shut, Gerry thumped his head on the arm of his chair. Perhaps he should have kept quiet, but nothing could be done now. That was the problem with his sons. There was always some sort of trouble brewing. He did not have to stay there. He could escape from it again. He had not tried Queensland yet. Gerry reflectively peeled the cap off another beer can and watched the gassy fumes waft out. He reminded himself that Michael could throttle Blake for all he cared, and drank himself to oblivion.

———

Michael hurtled down the street, wiping his face with the back of his sleeve from time to time. Only last week, when Blake was at the flat and Claire dropped in, he described how Angela and Blake were always at loggerheads when she first married Sean.

"I was only a little kid, but even I remember," Michael told her. "They jumped down each others' throats as soon as they saw each other."

"I can imagine Angela always jumping down someone's throat, but I find it harder to imagine Blake doing it," Claire had chuckled.

"Don't you believe it! You've never had to live with him," Michael bantered. "You've only seen him on his best behaviour. When you offend him, he can get really mean and aggressive."

At the time, both Claire and Blake turned red and speechless and did not seem to know how to respond. Now Michael understood why. He could have curled up like a beetle and died.

He had reached his bus-stop but there was no bus in sight. Michael could not bear to sit and wait, so he wrapped his arms across his chest and marched on to the next one like a soldier going off to war. He had made Blake promise to teach him to drive when he turned sixteen but he would be damned if he would ask the scum now. He only wanted to see Blake once, to tell him what he thought of him, and then he would steer clear of him.

Michael did not have long to wait. It was late afternoon and Blake was already with Sean and Angela when he got home. Most nights, Blake killed time to avoid Gerry. They were all three laughing and joking, and turned as one to greet Michael with a smile.

Michael ignored Sean and Angela and strode directly to Blake. His unshed tears burned like acid.

"I know what you did! You call yourself a Christian. You're a dirty, foul hypocrite of a Christian."

Blake turned as pale as chalk. "What do you mean?" he hedged, although he knew very well what Michael meant. Blake's stomach turned to water. He read the knowledge in Michael's eyes.

In reply, Michael sailed in with his rock-hard fists, blindly trying to pound Blake wherever he could. Eyes, stomach, throat, he didn't care. He just wanted to hurt Blake, the way he felt hurt. He wanted to make up for all the hurt he would have felt for seven years had he known. He heard foul names tumble out of his mouth which he would never dare use normally. Michael paid no heed to Angela's frightened yelling and when Sean tried to slide his chair into the fray, Michael seized its handles and shoved him out again.

Blake reacted instinctively in self-defence. He caught Michael's forearms and forced him against the wall. Then he got Michael in a tight arm-lock he could not wriggle out of. Blake felt momentarily surprised that Michael was so easy to tackle. Blake was no prize fighter himself, and Mike was such a tall, aggressive lad that Blake had expected him to be far more difficult to overcome. It was lucky for him that he wasn't or Michael might have seriously injured him in his rage.

Michael could not bear the final humiliation of being vanquished. He burst into tears like an eight-year-old and fought with the only weapon he had left, his voice.

"You filthy, rotten jerk! Why didn't you tell me you raped Claire? Dad told me. Why didn't you tell me?"

"It's not the sort of thing you want to boast about," Blake cried.

"I hate you. I'll never listen to you again. You tick me off for smoking pot and drinking! Last year you acted so horrified when I nicked a packet of fags from the shop, but what you did is far worse, in my books."

"It's bad in my books, too." Blake did not try to match Michael's vehement passion. He cringed to imagine the crude way Gerry would have told the story and wished with all his heart he had possessed the courage to tell Michael himself.

"I hate you," Michael repeated. "I'll never speak to you again. Let me go!"

Blake obediently released Michael's arms and watched him with great, sorrowful eyes, just like his mother's.

"Haven't you got anything to say for yourself?" Michael pleaded.

Even in his anger, he hoped that Blake would come up with some miracle to exonerate himself. Although he had often scoffed at Blake's high and pure moral values, he had always counted on them remaining intact.

Blake miserably shook his head. "No, nothing," he said huskily. "Only that I'm sorry you had to find out that way." He wondered if he would have felt any better if he had let Michael pulverise him.

Michael's lips puckered in a sneer of contempt and he wheeled around to leave.

Even Angela made no attempt to detain him. "Michael, where are you going?" she cried.

"Back to live with Dad. I won't stay here. He can stay with you." Michael was angry with her and Sean too, for keeping Blake's scandal from him. He no longer wanted to live with Gerry. Over the last few months, Dad's hero image had been tarnished in Michael's eyes. But he had nowhere else to turn.

And if he couldn't trust Blake, he couldn't trust anybody.

———————

Michael sat in a flowered armchair across from Claire and shuffled his feet. He had stormed back home and Gerry had forbidden him to live there any longer. He ordered Michael to go back to Angela's, and to not be so silly. Michael was kicked out of his own home. His tired feet dragged him to Claire's house. She was the only blameless person in the whole mess.

"I'm sorry for all the things I said which made you remember what happened, Claire, but it wasn't my fault. I wouldn't have said 'em, if I'd known."

A glow from the sunset poured through the window on to her dark hair and creamy skin. Claire looked so small and delicate, and he hated Blake with a fresh intensity for what he had done. She made a tranquil picture, which was a comfort in his despair. Michael considered asking Mrs Parker to let him live with them but rejected the notion. For the first time, he could not look Claire straight in the eye knowing what he knew about her.

"It's OK, Michael," she said quietly. "I know you'd never set out to hurt my feelings." Her cheeks burned and she longed to make him feel better. Assuring him that she had recovered from her ordeal did not seem to help him. Claire remembered that she had had seven years to get over it, but for Michael the pain was fresh, like a bullet wound.

The saddest part for Claire was the sense that something special was lost between her and the teen-age boy. She was well aware that Michael could not meet her eye. His openness had been his freshest and most endearing quality.

"They should've told me!" he burst out. "Do they think I'm a baby? Blake should've told me, instead of letting me go on hurting you with the things I said. He's a rotten coward."

"Perhaps he didn't tell you because he knew how hard you would take it, as you're doing now. He wanted to spare you the pain." Claire did not add that it had been Blake's own business, and not Michael's.

"I'm taking it hard because he didn't tell me. If he had, I would have dealt with it easier."

"Would you?" The questioning arch of Claire's eyebrows clearly showed that she doubted it. Michael would have reacted the same way, whether he'd heard it from Gerry or Blake.

"I don't understand how you can bear to see him!" Michael cried. "How can you force yourself to treat him like a friend? How can they expect you to?"

"It was so long ago now!" Claire had not expected her heart to burn with such compassion for Blake. In fact, her chest ached for him. Michael's rejection would wound him to the core. He did not need this, on top of everything else he had to deal with.

She tried hard to give an explanation Michael might accept. "Blake didn't deliberately set out to harm me that night. He got drunk and angry, and he just... snapped. I know that's no excuse, Michael, but he's no beast. He was just a boy who lost his cool and did something terrible. I can honestly say that now I've come to know him better, I understand that."

Two huge, shiny tears fell onto the backs of Michael's hands and shone like prisms. "I don't know what to think. I've never admired my brothers much, but I did think Blake was good. I always thought he treated people kindly and had self-control. Now I see it was all a big lie and I hate him." Michael sniffed crossly.

In a burst of clarity, Claire understood what Michael had not put into words. All his life, he had unconsciously placed his brother on a pedestal, and when he'd discovered that Blake had done something truly despicable, it came crashing down. Michael was lost somewhere in the wreckage, not knowing what pieces to pick up. No wonder he looked like a wild refugee.

"Michael, Blake is still your brother and he loves you. He screwed up badly once, but he's only human. We all make mistakes, both large and small. The only person who is totally perfect is God." Suddenly, reconciling those two brothers meant the entire world to her.

"I've never believed in God," Michael muttered.

Claire moistened her lips and spoke from her heart. "I know you don't, but I do, and so does Blake. Will you hear me out while I try to explain?"

Michael swallowed and nodded.

"We've both learned to lean on God's great goodness," Claire said. "He is the source of all that is righteous and good. He is totally faithful and dependable. Human beings screw up as you've discovered. You set your trust on Blake's moral standards, and now you feel that he's let you down. Blake and I learned to depend on God instead of people, and He never lets us down. At the same time, we've learned to see others as God sees us. Blake is a person who made a huge mistake but God sees through all that rubbish to his heart, and He knows it's a good heart, set on following Him. If God can forgive Blake, so can I."

At that moment, she knew she had forgiven him. Claire paused in a moment of wonderment. For so long, forgiving Blake had loomed before her like a colossal mountain. After all her strain to achieve it, she was staggered that forgiveness had crept up on her so quietly, she did not even realise when it happened.

"I can't," Michael said abruptly. "I told him he's a hypocrite and a liar. I wouldn't care if I never saw him again. I tried to belt him up like he hurt you. I would've, if I could've." Michael longed to show Claire that his heart was bigger and nobler than Blake's. He wanted to hear her say complimentary things about him instead of his brother.

"You shouldn't have done that!" Claire's eyes flashed. "Blake is all the things you always thought he was. Good and kind-hearted and sensitive. If you attacked him for my sake, it's the very last thing I would have wanted you to do."

Her voice crackled with passion but she could not control it for the world. "There's no way I can keep hating him, now I've come to know him better. Michael, you know him even better than I do, because you've known him all your life! You can't keep hating him."

Michael's heart sank, like a rock, to the soles of his shoes. This was not the sort of talk he had come to hear. How could she defend Blake, and why was she reproaching him for being sorry for her? Michael's head whirled and he remembered a tale his mother had once told, about a dizzy little fellow who found himself in topsy-turvy land, and did not know whether he was coming or going. Michael suddenly understood how the man felt.

He stood on shaky legs. He wanted to get out of there. "Gee Claire, I shouldn't have come," he breathed, and backed toward the door. He had come to condole with her but could tell from her face that she was far more upset than she had been before he'd entered the room.

She followed him and made a last-ditch effort to appeal to him. "Michael, please don't judge things the way the rest of the world does. Cut through all of that and look at the hearts of people."

He snatched one last glimpse at her clear, blue eyes, and darted away. She seemed to have no problem with having been raped, so why should he? Michael had hoped that seeing Claire would help him to feel better, but it only made him feel so much worse and more confused.

He had to crawl back to Sean and Angela. He had nowhere else to turn.

He hoped Blake had left.

Chapter Twenty-Eight

William Parker found a car-park right beside the repair shop. He sighed, and looked at the uneaten chicken sandwich and fruit salad Kate had packed for him. William did not feel a bit hungry, as his stomach churned sourly, gearing itself up for the disagreeable confrontation he was about to experience.

At least there would be no prowling near houses at midnight, as he had done seven years ago. This time, William would face Blake Quinlan where he worked, in a more civilised manner. His message was essentially the same as it had been then. *Keep away from my daughter.*

It was partly Kate's fault. It all started when she allowed the younger brother to visit them whenever he pleased. Blake never darkened their doorstep but William still expected trouble, and sure enough, trouble had snowballed. Claire had become far too fond of the whole Quinlan family.

She had stood Peter up several times lately, so she could have dinner with Sean and Angela. She did not mention Blake but William did not like the way she had started to retreat into herself as she had seven years ago. He did not like it one bit.

The final straw was last night, when the youngest boy visited Claire to talk about her having been raped. William had listened at the door in the interests of his daughter's welfare. He heard enough of the conversation to get the gist of it. When Michael left, Claire drifted upstairs to her bedroom and locked herself in. She had done that seven years ago, too. Then, her face had been tear-streaked with ragged despair, and now it was shadowed with some secret preoccupation. In both cases, William hated it. His food tasted like cardboard and migraine headaches thumped within his skull.

Last week, his doctor said that his blood pressure had skyrocketed. "Do you have something on your mind, William? You'd better do something to ease it or you'll get worse."

William had to eliminate the problem and then his health would return to normal. Unfortunately, even "normal" was a bit peaky, but he tried not to dwell on it. His holiday to Sydney with Kate already seemed like years ago, instead of weeks. No doubt, some of the damage with Claire and the Quinlans had occurred while they were away. He could not take a relaxing break for two weeks without some mischief being done.

William's intentions for his daughter were neatly laid out, like one of his investment portfolio plans. She would marry Peter Lennox and live in a respectable house, close to him and Kate. Peter would earn an excellent salary, so Claire could set up a small shop or studio where she could stitch away at her tapestries all day long, when she was not caring for the children she would have. No smutty, young social deviant was going to ruin it for her. Especially not this one.

William pushed open the glass door into the shop and the grey-haired man behind the counter greeted him pleasantly. "Good afternoon sir. Lovely weather. Have you been busy today?"

"I want to see Blake Quinlan, please." William was in no mood for small talk. Blake's boss was the affable, chatty type of tradesperson who drove him up the wall.

"I think he's gone off to lunch. Did you leave an appliance with him? Perhaps I can help you."

William could have kicked the counter and sworn. After all the mental preparation he had done, he had not expected to have to postpone the encounter.

"It's personal, thanks."

The mild surprise on the face of Blake's employer was evident. "Just a moment. I'll see what I can do for you." He turned to another, younger lad, busy over a broken radio.

"Ian, has Blake gone to lunch yet." Des Phillips had hired the new apprentice because he figured that Blake might not stay working there for much longer. He was competent enough to set up his own business and be his own boss. Perhaps they could even work out a partnership arrangement some day. None of these ideas had occurred to Blake yet, so Desmond let it ride, for now. There was plenty of work for all three of them. If Blake ever did want out, there was a good chance he would take a fair slice of clientele with him.

"No, Mr Phillips. He's still out the back talking to the blokes from the warehouse."

"Well tell him he can take your lunch-break today, and you take his, now. This gentleman would like to see him."

Ian dropped his gadgets and scrambled to his feet while William felt his stomach tighten. He could not return Des Phillips' smile for the life of him.

———

William found himself in a small, neat storeroom, with boxes piled high along the walls. Blake faced him, not managing to conceal his anxiety. William watched him flex his fingers.

Blake offered William the only chair in the room and William impatiently shook his head. He preferred to stand. Blake chose to remain standing too. William felt vexed that the lean young man stood a good two inches taller than he did. It was exasperating to have to look up into Blake's eyes while he lay down the law to him. Still, that was neither here nor there. William sailed straight to the point.

"I've come to warn you to stay away from my daughter."

He watched the blood recede from Blake's face, and read the

innocent statement in his eyes. Blake's expression said clearer than words, *I haven't done anything, this time!* William did not care.

"But Claire is willing to be my friend now," Blake mumbled at last. "She's recovered enough to... talk to me. I thought that was... nice of her." He felt as lame as a wooden duck.

"I don't know what's in her mind," William snapped, "but I don't want her getting any crazy notions about you. If you're thinking of courting her, forget it."

Blake felt his face flood with colour. Mr Parker certainly didn't beat around the bush.

"Claire feels nothing for me," he cried. "Not that way. How could she? I'm sure she's just being herself. She's friendly and kind to everybody. I was told she has a boyfriend, anyway."

William's taut bearing turned even more rigid. The strangest thoughts popped into Blake's head when he was nervous. He wondered how it was that even William Parker's moustache could resemble cold marble.

"Yes! She's seeing a decent young fellow who almost has himself a University degree. He's high principled and down-to-earth and I thoroughly approve of him. He will give her everything she deserves." William's eyes narrowed frostily at Blake. "He's knows what happened to her and he still wants her." William could rarely bring himself to voice the word "love".

Blake felt a prickling of indignation begin in his shoulders and creep down his arms to his wrists. Of course he should still want her! What happened to Claire was not her fault.

"Don't ever consider wriggling back on the scene to make trouble for Claire or you'll have me to deal with," William warned.

"I promise I'll never hurt Claire again." Blake's voice cracked with the strain.

"Merely consorting with her is enough to hurt her," William declared. "Stay away completely. I don't want her to see your face again. She shouldn't even see your sister-in-law, but I'll allow that."

That's big of him, Blake thought. He realised what was not quite right about Mr Parker. He was overbearing, as if Claire were still a child instead of a young woman, twenty-three years old. Blake felt helplessly sad for Claire. This type of aggressive over-protectiveness was new to him, as his own father never gave a damn what he did.

"Is that clear?" William asked stridently.

Blake's chest heaved. He decided that if Mr Parker could be frank, so could he. However, Blake tried not to be so ruthlessly blunt.

"With all due respect sir, Claire and I were kids back then and we're adults now. We want to put the past behind us. I think you'll make her far more unhappy if you drag those memories up again, by refusing to let her see me. I can assure you she feels nothing for me, so you don't have anything to worry about."

William's eyes probed Blake mercilessly. "And you feel nothing for her, either?"

Blake's eardrums pounded. There was no way he would let the domestic dictator read his feelings, but he could not lie, either. "Claire has nothing to fear from me. I do care for her. It's impossible to know her and not care for her, but I won't force myself on her."

"Keep away," William repeated. "No good will come of your friendship now."

Blake had tried to keep eye contact with the man for as long as he could, but his eyes wavered. There was a lump, like a heavy rock, in the centre of his chest, and it hurt him to breathe. Mr Parker was probably right. Blake thought of the turmoil that had already erupted because he and Claire were friends. Michael detested him and Sean and Angela shared the burden. Mr Parker's coming to see him was trouble enough on its own. It seemed there must be friction between Claire and her father at home. Blake sank onto the chair after all.

He looked at the stony face of the man standing before him and felt a sudden wave of compassion. He had probably ruined Mr Parker's life. If Blake were an old man with a lovely daughter, he would hate her to be friends with a fellow who had raped her too.

Blake's heart flipped whenever he saw Claire, but if she remained his friend, the poison from what he had done would inevitably corrode away their friendship. She would hate to live on bad terms with her father. Blake remembered how her wonderful, shining eyes had brimmed over with grief and pain seven years ago. He could not bear to cause that again. Not a second time.

Blake looked up at Mr Parker. "OK, I'll stay away from Claire," he said bleakly.

"Make sure you do." William turned abruptly and left.

Blake stayed in the dim storeroom, because he did not want to face Mr Phillips. He mechanically continued fixing the lap top computer he had been working on, with trembling hands. He had promised to let Ian watch over his shoulder but it was too late for that. Like a ghoul, Blake shunned the light of day or any human company. At last, he leaned his forehead into his cupped hands. The mess he had caused when he was eighteen kept following him.

Lord Jesus, he breathed. *I'm finding out how it feels to reap what I sowed. I know it's no less than I deserve, but I feel so bad.* Every part of him cried out for more of Claire, like a starving man. She was a feast to his eyes, heart and soul. Blake did not even try to do the sensible thing, and push her out of his mind. He knew he was too far-gone for that.

———

William's appetite had not returned when he sat down for his evening meal and Claire was not hungry either. She slowly buttered a slice of bread, then pushed it aside. There were shadows beneath her eyes and Kate asked if she were sick.

That was enough for Claire. If she did not release some pent-up tension she would burst.

"I'm worried about Blake," she admitted. "Michael found out about... you know what ... and tore strips off him. He says he hates him, now. Blake loves Michael, Mum. He must be feeling terrible, and I went to see him. His car was parked in the carport but he didn't answer the door. I don't know whether he'd gone for a walk or if he was hiding inside, avoiding me."

Claire stared down at the tablecloth and William saw that her lashes were matted with tears. He had no idea that her feelings for Blake Quinlan had gone so far. He should have had his talk with Blake far sooner.

Claire raised her face again. "I waited on the steps for a long time, but he didn't show up, so I left." She drummed her fingers helplessly on the tablecloth. "What else could I have done?"

"Nothing," Kate asserted. "You've done all you can. Perhaps it's wise of Blake not to see you. You'd better let it rest."

It took all Claire's forbearance not to rebuke Kate for her detachment. Mum was not to know that talking to Blake was vital to her peace of mind. Claire did not fool herself into thinking that she did not think about him incessantly, although she hardly knew why.

"Why would he want to avoid me?" she cried. "It's not my fault if his father told Michael what he did." A silvery tear slid down her cheek before she could stop it. She flipped her hair over her shoulder and snapped off a bite of bread with her teeth. "I'll try again after tea."

William could not keep quiet. "How long do you intend to hound him?"

Claire gazed steadily back. "Until he gives in and hears me out." She refused to let Blake shut everybody out and suffer acutely alone.

William slammed his knife down and uttered a short expletive. He had not intended to reveal his talk with Blake but Claire's foolishness forced his hand. "I went to see him at work today, and asked him to leave you alone. That's the best plan for both of you."

Claire bolted out of her seat, grey to the lips. "What did you say to him?" A small pulse raced in her neck, and another near her temple.

"Sit down and don't be so silly. I told him how well you were going before he appeared back on the scene, and warned him to back off. The same goes for you too, young lady."

"I wasn't going well!" she wailed. "I was lonely and miserable every day of my life. I was just going through the motions of living." She looked striking, with her eyes flashing, and her fine chin jutted out like a slender young Amazon. "Who are you to decide what's best for me?"

William stood too, looking slightly ridiculous with his serviette dangling from his shirtfront where he always stuffed it. "What about Peter? He thinks the world of you. Tread carefully with Peter or he'll turn cold on you. Forget that Quinlan no-hoper".

Claire did not fly off the handle, but it was obvious that she was furious with William. She stood rigid, like the masthead of a ship, and her eyes shot sparks at him. If they had been guns, he would have been slain on the spot.

Claire's face was white except for a splash of vivid colour on each cheek. She spoke between her teeth. "No way, Dad. You've butted in once too often. You made me lose my baby. You're not going to make me lose Blake, too."

Her own words shook her like an earthquake. She could not believe she had said that. It was as if her tongue and her brain belonged to two different people. Then the back of her throat smarted. She cared for him. She knew what had been brewing in her heart for weeks, like a subterranean volcano. How could she have fallen for Blake Quinlan?

William's hair prickled. She had not referred to that baby for years. "What the devil are you talking about?" he rumbled.

Tears gushed out of Claire's eyes like hot springs but she kept her jaw clamped, because if she loosened it, she would launch into hysterics. "You don't know what you're doing. Threatening Blake is a waste of time because he's no troublemaker. I'm going to repair the damage you've done." She snatched up her purse and keys.

William's gaze fell upon the small portrait of Claire, aged three, above the fireplace. In a rush of hot pain, he remembered delightful days when she'd followed him in the garden with her little plastic shovel and rake. She had always been ready with a wide smile for the daddy she adored. Her pearly milk teeth had gleamed. The hurt of her defiance pierced William to the core.

"You choose between him and us!" he lashed. "If you see him now, find somebody else's roof to live under!" He regretted his stinging words the second he said them and trusted that Claire would not take them seriously. He was too angry to take them back.

Claire did not hesitate. "I will do that! He's only just begun to forgive himself for what he did and if you've pushed him back into his shell, I'll never forgive you!" Her skirt whirled around her knees, and the screen door slammed behind her.

"William, whatever she does, she's still our daughter." Kate's hands were clammy with shock.

He blinked at his plate as if he had not heard her. "If you cover the casserole with cling film, we can eat some tomorrow," he muttered. William rubbed the back of his neck and adjourned to the lounge room to watch the news on television. If he behaved as if all were normal, the storm might blow over.

But deep in his heart, William knew better. He knew nothing would ever be the same again.

As Claire started her car, her skin tingled as she wondered when the germ of love for Blake had first been planted in her heart. Was it on that hot, rainy day when he collected Michael from their house and walked him home? Could it have been as far back as the camp, when she watched him hold Angela in his arms while his own heart broke for his mother? Had Claire started to love him on the bus, when his eyes turned so wide and bright at the sight of her? No, she could honestly say she still hated him then, but as she remembered his expression, her heart ached for him.

Claire knocked on the Quinlan's door. There were now two beaten up old cars in the carport, so she knew Blake's father was home with him. Claire dreaded Gerard Quinlan because she had heard some hair-raising tales about his drunken history from Angela and Sean. Normally, she avoided him like the plague, but now his presence filled her with hope. If Blake was trying to hide from her, Gerry might let her in.

She heard scuffling, and a flabby, grey-haired man in slippers opened the door. He exuded the odour of beer fumes and body odour and squinted at her as if she were a mirage. "Hello, what do you want?"

Claire felt heat course through her. Mr Quinlan recognised her. "I'd like to see Blake, please."

Gerry's eyes glittered. "Why do you want to see him?"

Claire did not falter. "That's personal, Mr Quinlan."

His face crinkled as he croaked out a malicious laugh. She could not determine if it were directed at her or his son. To her relief, he jerked his chin behind him. "Eh, Blake," he called. "Someone to see you."

A bedroom door creaked open and there he stood. Now that she knew how she felt about him, his attractiveness made her knees quiver. She had noticed it all along, of course, but some inner defence mechanism warned her to switch off until now. He wore his work shirt with the first three buttons undone, and she focused on the glimpse of his chest instead of his face. She could not bring herself to look into his eyes for fear of what she might read there. Perhaps he cared nothing for her.

"Hello, I have something to tell you." Her voice faltered. If he didn't want to see her, she couldn't bear it.

Blake's head whirled. Mr Parker had ordered him not to see her again, but how could he refuse, when she came to him? He would see her one last time, to explain why he couldn't see her anymore. Gerry leaned in the doorway with an inane sneer on his face and Blake flushed. "Would you like to come through to my bedroom, Claire?"

Instant horror froze his veins. He shouldn't have said that. He had only wanted privacy, but Claire might think his suggestion improper.

"How about Michael's bedroom?" he suggested instead, but that was not much better.

"Either one will do." She followed him to Michael's bedroom and sat on the bed. Blake flinched at the sight of a female centrefold poster on Michael's wall and opened the wardrobe door to conceal it. Claire had noticed, and looked at him with a wry smile. Blake felt sick. His own bedroom would have been the wisest choice after all. He carefully sat on the end of the bed furthest from her.

"I came to see you earlier today, and your car was here, but you didn't answer the door. Why wouldn't you see me?" she asked.

"After work? I was lying on my bed listening to music through my headphones. I didn't hear you knock," he said quickly. That was the truth and he hated her to think he was shunning her.

Relief flooded through Claire. "I thought you didn't want to see me. I know what my father told you today and I told him to mind his business."

"But he might be right," Blake suggested softly. "He has a right to stay angry with me, even after all this time. I mean... look, I ruined your life. He has good reason to hate me. I should've been put in jail to rot for ten years."

"I really don't think you're a menace to society, Blake."

Her soft humour made him look up sharply. Her eyes glimmered with the ghost of a smile, while his heart turned over in response to it. Then he remembered Mr Parker's visit and his own decision, and snapped it off like a light switch.

"Jesus died for your sin, Blake. If you don't forgive yourself for your own sake, forgive yourself for mine or I'll feel awful. I'm glad you weren't put away for ten years. If you had been, and then I got to know you like now, I would have hated myself."

Blake did not know what to say.

Claire's eyes shone with curious compassion. "Tell me honestly, if Sean had raped a girl, would you have hated him as much as you hate yourself? What if Michael did it tomorrow? Would you hate him?"

"After what I did to you, I'd have no right to hate Michael if he did it tomorrow. But if I hadn't done it, yes I probably would feel disgusted." Blake raised his eyes to her face. "Claire, shall we talk about something else?" His heart felt like a balloon ready to burst.

"Gladly." Claire basked beneath the heat from his eyes. Although they sat far apart, mutual understanding flowed between them like radio waves. They both bore scars from their experience.

"Blake, I came to say I still want to be friends."

He had to speak decisively now or he would no longer have the power. "So do I, but I can't." He spoke with hoarse resignation.

Claire tried to speak, but he held up his hand for her to hear him out. If she stayed friends with him, she would lose the approval of her own family. Surely she did not care for him the way he cared for her, anyway. She deserved far better than him.

"You'd better go home, Claire," he said firmly. "I can't see you anymore."

Her world collapsed around her ears. She could hardly believe his selfishness. The thought flashed through her mind that he spurned her because he had already defiled her completely. It quickly flashed out again. She knew Blake far better than that. His overactive conscience was at work again.

"I want to be friends!" she repeated hotly. "Just because you feel you deserve to be punished, do you think I deserve it too?"

"I'm doing this because I don't want to hurt you worse," he persisted. Her response distressed him. He was hurting her already! How much worse he would hurt her if he weakened and put her in the position of choosing between him and her family. He bowed his head and resolutely paced to the door, expecting her to follow. "Your father is right. I have to stop seeing you."

Claire snatched his elbow and whipped him around to face her. "No! You forced yourself on me seven years ago, Blake Quinlan, and I'm going to force myself on you now. I won't leave until I've told you what I think of you. You say you don't want to hurt me. Well, I feel as hurt as I ever did. Rejected and spurned. I wish I'd never set eyes on you, ever. You hurt me then by what you did, and now you're hurting me by what you won't do. Do you think hurting me now will make up for hurting me then?"

He began to wrap his arm around her but thought better of it and drew away quickly. That was the last move he should make. "You'll see it's all for the best. Your father will kill me if I see you."

Her soft lips tightened with contempt. "Is that what's bothering you?" she gasped. "When Michael accused you of cowardice I tried to defend you, but now I see he's right. You're the biggest coward of all times. Why am I wasting my time? You're in a bad way, Blake. You're one confused person."

Claire flung open the door herself. How could she feel so tender toward a person one moment, and want to throttle him the next? It was not supposed to have ended this way. His mind was made up and bolted like a safe. She wished she could wrench him out of her heart now. She swept past Gerard Quinlan to the privacy of her car, where she could let her face crumple.

She had just recovered from Blake Quinlan's first devastation of her life. How could she be mad enough to let the mongrel do it a second time?

Chapter Twenty-Nine

"It's no use, Mike." Sean pushed the broken pieces of Michael's portable MP3 player back across the table to him. "I can't make head or tail of it. You know I can't even fix things when I have instructions to follow."

"Where's the nearest repair shop I could take it to?"

Sean sighed heavily. "Why don't you swallow your pride and ask Blake to fix it?"

Michael's nose instantly creased, as if he smelled a sour odour. "No way! I'm not asking that creep for anything."

"How long are you going to keep hold of your anger?" Sean hated the rift between his brothers. Mum was dead and Dad cared for nobody but himself, so all they really had was each other. The three of them ought to stick closer than ever. Sometimes he lay awake at night worrying that Michael would never forgive Blake.

"I hate him," Michael's resentment was always simmering just below the surface and grew hotter with each passing day. It was most intense at those moments when he had almost succeeded in thinking of other things, then remembered in a rush what Blake had done.

Michael wouldn't admit it to anybody, but he deeply missed Blake's company. He sometimes thought of a funny joke to share with him, then remembered with a jolt that their friendly days were over. Blake was still the first person he thought to seek when he had a problem to share, because Blake had always been a patient sounding-board for

Michael's grievances. Not even his mother or Sean had been quite so good at giving Michael their undivided attention. He had not realised that until now, and fumed hotter than ever for having trusted the dirty hypocrite so absolutely.

Michael cared nothing for the deep furrows of worry on Sean's brow.

"Mike, he's our brother. He's still the same old Blake you've always loved, and what he did doesn't change that." Sean and Angela had been over the same ground with Michael many times, and each time he sat with his arms folded obdurately, and unrepentant. Sean was prepared to cover it one thousand times, if that was what it took to wear Michael down, and make him speak to Blake.

His hopes dwindled each day. Michael's heart was set against Blake like a flint. It had not even helped when Angela told him passionately that Mum would not have wanted them to remain on bad terms. Angela now sat scribbling her shopping list and chewing her lip. Sean worried about her, too. The boys' estrangement upset her deeply. Sean's family was the only family Angela had.

"It changes everything," Michael said. "He's a rapist and a coward. I don't know how you could forgive him, either."

"It was hard," Sean told him. "I felt the same way you did when I first found out. I couldn't believe he'd done it." Sean thought back seven years and remembered something he had not yet shared with Michael.

"I'll tell you what brought me to my senses. When he first did it, none of us spoke to him much, for nearly two months, except for you. You were so young and you didn't understand. I came home from football training one evening and saw Blake sitting beneath the tree with a little pill bottle beside him."

Sean described Blake's contemplated suicide attempt. Even Angela listened with interest, although she had heard the story before.

"You should've let him," Michael said at the end, with the same sullen expression. "He didn't have the guts to kill himself. I wish he had. Who needs him, anyway?"

Something snapped in Angela. She flung down her pen and stood up. "I can't believe you said that, Michael! I'm happy for you to live here but if I have to listen to that sort of remark, you can go home to Dad." Her features were pinched with white-hot anger.

Sean flinched. "Angela, he didn't mean it. He's angry." He did not want her to say anything she would later regret, but she looked like a wild, green-eyed cat.

"I know he's angry but I refuse to listen to comments like that about Blake." She whirled on Michael again. "Are you so good and pure, Michael Quinlan, that you have a right to sling stones at your brother?"

"At least I never raped anyone." Michael stood his ground although Angela's passion shocked him, and he wanted to cringe beneath the table. He did feel bad about his last remark but would never admit it.

"And hasn't he paid for it every day since?" she cried. "You have no idea how terrible Blake feels for what he did. His self-esteem is still rock bottom, and I won't listen to snide remarks about him from the likes of you."

Angela had never got stuck into Michael like that, even before Rowena died. In fact, she had always considered him rather a pet. However, now that her rage was uncorked, she could not stop. "You smashed his brand new car and I never once heard him tell you off. He thinks the world of you and helps you however he can, and this is your return! The first time you ever hear anything bad of him, you're ready to disown him. You're not much of a brother, Michael." Angela only stopped because she was close to tears.

"At least I never pretended to be good and spotless when I wasn't." Michael could not fathom why he felt so small and mean-spirited, when he had felt so righteously angry from the start.

"Neither does Blake. He's well aware of his shortcomings. In fact, he's one of the brightest, most highly principled people I know, with a heart of gold. If you turn out to be half the man your brother is, you'll be doing fine, Michael."

Michael turned his face away and blinked at the blank television screen as if he were glued to a movie. When he finally managed to raise his eyes, there was naked pain mingled with shame. "I didn't mean that, about wishing he was dead."

Angela's anger was spent. She wrapped her arms around Michael's shoulders, which were finally slumped in surrender. She never hesitated to touch anybody when she knew they needed it. Michael, who usually squirmed after some embarrassing rebuke, sat still and let her. He only moved to rub his sleeve across his stinging eyes.

At last, he scooped up his broken MP3 player and trudged back to his bedroom like someone with the spirit knocked out of him. He no longer stalked, scowling like a ravaging lion set to tear its prey apart. Sean's heart swelled as he noted the difference.

Angela sank to her knees beside her husband. "Are you going to tell me I shouldn't have lost my temper? Well, I think Michael needed to hear that." She pushed a strand of fallen fair hair behind her ear. "I certainly needed to get it off my chest."

"Do you know, I think you did right," Sean's pensive expression turned into a sly grin. "Blake has no idea you're such an admirer of his. He'll be flabbergasted when I tell him the nice things you said. You've certainly changed your opinion of him over the years, haven't you?"

Angela was still fired up enough to tilt her chin. "A woman has a right to change her mind. I don't care if you tell Blake. I meant every word I said." She always prided herself on giving credit where it was due.

Sean wrapped his arm around her shoulder and pulled her close. "As long as I'm still your favourite fellow?"

She let out a giggle. "You? I think you're sweeter than Michael and Blake combined."

He pretended to pull a face. "I don't think sweet is the most flattering compliment you can pay a man, but I'll accept it for now. Gimme a hug."

Claire's first move was to break up with Peter. Although she had no future with Blake, she could not see another man feeling the way she did. She had flinched from facing Peter with the truth, but he made it easier than she'd expected.

Indeed, she detected a flash of relief pass through his eyes before he managed to control his expression. Claire could not blame him. She supposed she had been too preoccupied to be much company for him. Peter had probably thought she was still brooding over her past.

"I hope it's nothing I've done," he said.

"Not at all," she hastened to assure him. "The reason has nothing to do with you, Pete." She was glad their relationship had not progressed further than it had. Peter had never done more than kiss her cheek. It made it far easier to part on amicable terms.

He detected some of the truth in the way she evaded his eyes. "Is it someone else?" Although he was happy to be free again, Peter was not sure if he liked being stood up. He had decided that Claire was far too unadventurous and quiet, but he thought she was enamoured of him. That was why he had felt himself caught in a trap. He thought the blow would be too hard for her to bear, after what had happened to her before.

She drew a breath to deny it, then decided that he deserved to hear some honesty, after she had strung him along for such a long time. She nodded her head. "Yes, but nothing will come of it. It's Michael Quinlan's brother."

Peter's eyebrows shot up. "The one in the wheelchair? He's married, isn't he?"

"Michael has two brothers. This one is a little younger than Sean. He's a repairman." None of her family ever mentioned Blake and Claire realised that after all this time, Peter was unaware of his existence. That seemed incredible, when Blake's existence meant so much to Claire.

"Does he know that you were... what happened to you?" Peter laboured awkwardly.

Claire felt her face flame and hoped he could not read the truth in her face. "He knows," she said briefly.

Peter suddenly squeezed her hand. "I'm sorry, Claire. You're in a real bind. You've never had much luck, have you? I hope that things will work out for you, someday."

Claire's mind whirled. She did not piece together what Peter meant until she saw him climb into his car. He was wide of the mark entirely. He assumed that Michael's brother spurned her because she had been raped by another man. She wondered what Peter would think if he knew the unthinkable truth, that Blake could not contemplate loving her because he had raped her himself.

With Peter gone, her thoughts turned obsessively to Blake. Almost ever since she had known him, Claire had felt either desperate to forget him or desperate to hold onto him. When she closed her eyes, images of him ran riot in her head. The way his slow grin spread over his face when he was caught off-guard in a moment of humour. The way he walked, with his hands upon his hips and his eyes cast down to the floor. The fine, striking figure he made when he stood to his full height.

Each day, Claire went through the motions of going to work. She listened to Michelle and Tara chatter about their boyfriends and prepared herself for a long, fruitless life, for there would be nobody for her but Blake. She knew that now. It was as if he had actually put his stamp on her by his violent action so long ago.

The only distraction in her week had been a brief visit from Janine Turner, the troubled teenager who had attended her tapestry class. Smiling broadly, Janine had brought her little girl in a stroller. The sight of the dimpled, bright-eyed cutie had been enough to make Claire blink away tears. That had been a little embarrassing, but Janine understood. She'd told Claire all about the parenting course she'd attended at the counselling centre.

Maybe I could learn something like that someday. I could volunteer or even study counselling. I could really make a difference. Claire knew she'd be doing it for her own baby, too. She would never know if her child would have been a boy or a girl, but she could make its brief, flickering life count. Even if Blake never wanted to see her again, she could still do some good in the world.

At last she knew him well. Sometimes she felt so angry with him for his scruples that she longed to shake him until his teeth rattled. Other times she would give anything to hold him in her arms and never let him go. She wondered if he cared for her at all. If he did, she felt hurt that he doubted her offer of friendship. It was frustrating to imagine that he might long to see her too, but refused to come near her.

Claire prayed that she would accidentally come across him at Sean and Angela's flat. It had happened twice before, but never any more, probably because Michael still lived there and Michael still despised him. Once she saw Blake's old car parked in their driveway. Claire walked into the flat with thumping eardrums and barely returned Angela's greeting as her eyes scanned each room for him.

"He isn't here, Claire," Angela said quietly. "He's gone to watch Sean's hockey match. They took our van."

Disappointment crushed her like a tonne weight and she wanted to weep. She felt embarrassed because Angela could read her so easily.

Angela gently took her wrist and led her to an armchair. She sat in an opposite one and scrutinised Claire's face. "You like him, don't you? Don't be too shy to admit it because I can tell you, he loves you. He's head over heels in love. Don't give up on him, Claire. Blake will never make the first move, and you can understand why."

Claire's spine shivered. She knew now that Blake cared for her, at least. She let some of her own carefully bottled feelings seep out. "I've made the first move already and he refuses to see me anymore. What else can I do, Angela?" She briefly described Blake's attitude the last time she saw him and Angela pursed her lips, annoyed.

"That's the problem with Quinlan men!" she pronounced. "They're as stubborn as mules. I took months to wear Sean down after his accident and I'm afraid both Blake and Michael are tarred with the same brush."

Claire managed a wan smile. "Well when you see him, will you tell him I still feel the same and always will?"

"I certainly will!" Angela thought back to a time, not so long ago, when the same girl pleaded with her to keep Blake away from her.

Angela's mind grappled with the problem long after she should have been asleep in bed. Waking Sean and letting off steam only made her feel worse. She stared up at the dark ceiling.

"Do you see I was right? They're crazy for each other. Think how wonderful it would be for Blake to have a girl like Claire. Not only did I read it in her eyes, but now she's admitted it." Angela squirmed and punched her pillow. "I'm itching to do something for them, but what?"

"Leave it to God," Sean yawned. The problem whirled through his tired mind too, but he could not see how it would ever be solved if Blake's mind was set. He feared Angela was trying to fan a cold coal.

"But if God doesn't use me to help, I can't think how He'll work!" she wailed.

Sean stroked her cheek with his knuckles. "Remember your old problem? God doesn't rely on Angela Quinlan to help Him do anything. Don't limit Him."

Angela groaned, and turned limp against his shoulder. She had been a Christian for far longer than Sean, yet he often counselled her so wisely. She rubbed her face against his shoulder.

"What would I ever do without you? Sean, sometimes it's so hard."

For the first time ever, Michael was glad to see that his father was not home. He leaned against the gate of his old home for a long moment, psyching himself up for what he intended to tell Blake. Michael had rehashed his talk with Angela over and over in his head. He was sure he had come to the right decision but he was unsure how to broach the subject.

He found Blake in the laundry, dumping damp clothes from the machine into the hamper. The load was as huge as ever. After Mum's death, everyone forgot the washing until they ran out of clean shirts and underwear. Blake was always the one who ended up caring enough to do something about it. Michael hung back and watched him while the magazine he had bought dangled from his fingers.

"G'day," he croaked, at last. "I'm here to look for my black denim jacket." That was his bluff for being there. He did not know how to tell Blake that he forgave him without backing down or becoming emotional. He hoped Blake would latch onto the fact without needing it to be spelled out.

"It's hanging up in your wardrobe." Blake did not turn around. The last few times they met, Michael always had some abuse to sling at him.

Michael fetched his jacket and loitered in the kitchen, wondering what to say next.

"See you, Mike." Blake expected his brother to leave quickly. He had so much to say, if only Michael would calm down enough to listen. Blake did not want to open his mouth yet because Michael was still so riled up that he would hurt him, whatever he said.

"I'm not going yet," Michael said, with an edge of irritation. Blake was making it so difficult for him. He would not even look at him. For the first time, Michael noticed how studiously his older brother avoided eye contact.

Blake set down the washing basket. "Are you wanting a lift somewhere?" He guessed Michael must have been fuming to find him home instead of Dad. Wherever he is off to it must be pretty important for him to consider lowering his dignity and asking me, Blake thought to himself.

"No," Michael sighed. "There is a party on but I'm not goin'. It'll be full of dope and grog. I opted out, 'cause I knew you wouldn't like it."

For the first time, Blake's heart beat faster with a wild possibility. He dared to raise his eyes and look at Michael. "That's never stopped you before."

"Well I think you're probably right. That stuff is bad for you. I'd be better off without it." Michael remembered the magazine and proffered it stiffly to Blake. "I was at the newsagency, and saw one of these fix-it magazines you like. Looks like a load of rubbish to me but I bought it for you."

Blake felt himself smile. He did not hesitate to reach out and accept the magazine for the peace offering it was intended. "Thanks for that." He tried to keep his husky voice casual. Blake was as reticent to display his feelings as Michael but if his brother had made one move toward him, he would have sniffled like a baby.

A cloud suddenly lifted, lightening Michael's world. His big brother cared for him. He read it in Blake's face. It felt good to forgive him. Michael understood that Blake's action had not been pre-meditated. He had seen his own friends totally befuddled when drunk, as Blake must have been when he raped Claire. Once, Michael had woken up on Mrs Clarke's lounge room couch the morning after Jamie's wild sleep-over and he could not remember a thing he had done since ten o'clock the previous evening. For all he knew, he might have raped somebody, if given the opportunity. At least, Blake had been strong and wise enough to avoid alcohol and drugs ever since. Michael understood far more about the older brother he had always taken for granted. Anyway, if Claire was prepared to forgive Blake, he had no reason not to.

"I broke my MP3 player," he heard himself say. "I dropped it on the bathroom tiles. Will you take a look at it?"

Blake shoved the laundry aside, unheeded. "Sure. Have you got it with you?"

Michael had been hoping he would ask. He fished the separate pieces out of his backpack and sat at the kitchen table, leaning his chin in his hands, to watch Blake work.

"What have you been up to?" Blake asked.

"Not much. I've been looking for work. On Wednesday I sat a Public Service exam and last night I stayed home and watched a movie with Angela and Claire." Michael instantly coloured and peered anxiously at Blake. He was unsure if he should have mentioned Claire's name.

The very sound of it made Blake's heart ache sharply. "How is she going?" he asked simply. He dreaded to hear that she was still unhappy and hurt with him, but somehow he dreaded even more to think that she had recovered.

"I think she's crazy about you." Michael stated the truth frankly and watched Blake's every move. "Angela says so. Claire told her. And she also said some pretty nice things about you to me when I went to see her a few weeks ago."

Blake deftly continued working but the image of the MP3 player before his eyes was not quite in focus. At last, he looked back at Michael. "I don't understand that," he said honestly. "It doesn't make sense. How could she feel anything for me? It just doesn't compute. I can't understand her, Michael."

Michael shrugged sadly. "Neither can I, but it's true."

Blake pursed his lips and said nothing else. He thought somebody must have got the wrong idea somewhere along the way.

"So are you gonna see her, speak to her?" Michael prompted. "Try to work something out?"

Blake shook his head. "I can't, Michael. I just can't. Do you understand?"

Michael nodded. He did not understand completely, but he understood a little.

Chapter Thirty

S ean braced his arms and eased himself out of his chair. He lay on the warm, sweet smelling grass and stretched his arms luxuriously above his head. Angela had taken Michael shopping for some neat clothes, under protest. It was refreshingly quiet without them. Sean let the sun soak into his bones and lay so still that some small zebra finches swooped down to enjoy their birdbath right beside his feet. Sean chuckled quietly to think how Angela deplored the fact that birds rarely bathed there. She simply could not stay still long enough to wait for them.

He remembered the fast pace of his life before the accident. Sometimes he felt as if he were thinking of a close relative instead of himself. He had been far too active and busy to simply sit and enjoy the beauty of God's creation. He breathed a quick prayer of thanks to God for allowing him to slow down and discover the loveliness of nature. Sean had started his attitude of thankfulness as a type of therapy when he needed it, but over the years it had become second nature.

As it happened, he was happy to have his tranquillity interrupted sooner than he expected. Blake came to visit during his lunch break. Sean sat up to talk to him. It was rare for the two brothers to be together alone and Sean made the most of it. The best part of his childhood had been his closeness to Blake.

Blake was troubled. He tried to hide it but Sean saw through his brother's ruse. Blake talked about inconsequential topics as if they meant the world to him. He was usually the most withdrawn and silent of all, but he chattered non-stop, fit to rival Angela or Michael. All the birds disappeared. Sean suspected that Blake was afraid to be quiet because he would begin to dwell on forbidden thoughts.

Sean listened patiently to Blake's detailed spiel about work. Blake was anxious to convince him that he was happy, but Sean knew that he was really trying to convince himself.

"When's the last time you took a holiday from work?" he asked, when he could get a word in.

"I don't need a holiday," Blake said quickly. "Mr Phillips has offered me holidays many times, but I'll save 'em up for one big one. I still want to visit Ireland. How about you? We were going to do it together. How would Angela feel about a trip to Ireland? It'd be fun."

Sean had almost forgotten their old ambition. He felt sad to reflect that his own life had changed so dramatically while his smart and gifted brother had remained in the rut of his youth. Blake still spoke and thought the same way he had at sixteen. Suddenly Sean felt strange being alone with him, as if he had stepped into a time warp.

"Why don't you consider seeing Claire and starting something up with her?" He blurted it out because he had a swift intuition that Blake might open up to him, for the sake of the closeness they had shared.

Blake gaped as if Sean had spoken a foreign language, yet he could not disguise a flicker of hope. "You can't be serious. Not now. Her father hates me. I never want to hurt her again."

Sean carefully plucked a stem of grass. "I think you're afraid to love," he said quietly. "Have you really got Claire's welfare at heart, or your own?"

Blake flushed and tilted his chin. "I don't deserve her. She could do far better than me."

"She loves you," Sean cried. "Angela saw it weeks ago and now I've seen it too."

Blake obstinately shook his head. "Not after what I did, Sean. It'd keep coming up to haunt us."

"Claire knows what you did. She was there, remember."

Blake's eyes kindled with resentment. He said nothing, but if it had been anyone else he would have got up and walked away.

Sean sighed. He hated to sound so brutal but he was tired of watching Blake cheat himself out of any happiness that might come his way, year after year. "I'm not tryin' to be cruel. It comes down to this. Of course you don't deserve Claire's love, but she loves you anyway. Do any of us deserve to be loved? You didn't deserve Jesus' love either, but He loved you enough to die on the Cross for you."

Blake was clearly torn. His chest rose and fell. "If I... let myself love Claire, she might come to her senses and stop loving me. Then I'll be worse off than I am now." He flinched as the truth hit him. Michael, Claire and Sean all spoke the truth. He was a coward. He wanted to avoid being hurt. He had cleverly convinced himself that his sacrifice was all for Claire, but now he understood that his motives were not what he thought they were.

Sean did not seem to think any the less of him. "That's the chance you have to take, for love. It's hard to risk giving yourself so completely to another person. You feel vulnerable. Do you think it was easy for me to trust Angela's love for me, when I felt like a broken shell of a man?"

Blake scrambled to his feet and began to pace along the gravel path with his hands jammed into his pockets. He always had to be moving when he was overcome with emotion. He admitted something he never thought he would ever tell anybody, even Sean.

"I don't deserve Claire because... I keep having all these feelings about her... you know, physical things. And she'd probably be shocked to know how I feel when I look at her... but I can't stop them."

Sean stared, astounded. He could not believe his smart brother could be so dumb. It was only with sheer willpower that he kept himself from hooting. "That's only natural, Blake. Gee whiz, all fellows feel the same about the women they love. Do you think I don't have those feelings?"

"But do you and Angela... I mean is your marriage... do you feel..." Blake raked a hand through his hair and turned away. "Don't worry. Forget it," he broke off, lamely.

Sean couldn't help laughing now. He knew exactly what Blake was getting at all along but refused to rescue him. Occasionally, even after so long, Sean still felt wistful when he watched Blake stride it out, so straight and tall. *Let him squirm!*

"I'll answer your question," he grinned, "on one condition. Don't breathe a word to Angela."

"You know I wouldn't," Blake cried.

"Marriage is pretty good," Sean told him. "Sometimes I'm amazed just how good, but I find myself wondering if it could be even better if I could move my legs. I have nothing to compare it with, after all."

Blake shook his head. "It probably wouldn't make any difference. It's great that you're enjoying marriage, Sean."

"I want to see the same for you. I'd hate to see you grow into a lonely and frustrated old man like Dad, just because you were too chicken to take a risk." He watched his brother carefully. "I'm sure Mum would have loved to see you with Claire," he said softly.

Blake struggled with the unmanly tears that always threatened when he least wanted them. However, he'd had enough practice to control them now. He longed to run to Claire, longed to see her clear blue eyes gaze straight into his heart again. Perhaps she thought him too pathetic now. She had been so angry with him for his cowardice. Blake was not really frightened of her father. If only Claire was willing to take a chance on him, what William Parker thought simply did not matter. He had to see her.

Sean said, "After the way you hurt Claire so long ago, don't you think you owe it to her to launch out and risk being hurt back? Life is too short to turn your back on happiness, Blake. You're an OK guy. Claire would never fall in love with the guy who raped her if she didn't see something in him to love."

Blake knew it was time to cut his visit short. He had to know how Claire truly felt about him. "I'm going to find her now. If she's not at home, I'm sure she'll be at work. See you later." He turned as he reached the corner of the flat. "Sean, thanks man."

Sean smiled and raised his hand in a gesture of farewell.

Blake almost collided with Angela and Michael as he sprinted down the side of the flat.

"Watch where ya going!" Michael hollered.

"Are you going to stay for lunch?" Angela called.

"No thanks," Blake flung over his shoulder. "I have something important to do."

Angela had rarely seen Blake so fired up, and she hurried to Sean. "Where is he off to?"

"To see Claire," Sean announced.

Angela threw back her head and whooped with joy and wonder. "What changed his mind?"

Sean was not often in a position to crow over AngeaQla and he could not resist the opportunity. "I had a word with him and he's taking my advice."

"You're a wizard! I've been advising him to see her for weeks and he's never listened to me!"

Sean shot her a smug smile. "You did your best, Sweetie, but some things are outside a woman's domain. It takes another man."

He found himself flat on his back again, laughing up at the blue sky. After so long, Angela was still the only person who dared to be rough with him and who didn't treat him like delicate china. He loved it.

————

Kate Parker was called from her cooking by a knock at the door. She dried her hands, humming, but when she gazed through the window and saw who stood there, the tune died on her lips. It was the young man who looked like Rowena. She opened the door and greeted him very calmly, considering how her heart had fallen to her boots. How incredibly he resembled his mother when she saw him at such close quarters. He had Rowena's hair and skin tone. He had her expressive mouth and her beautiful dark eyes.

"Hello Mrs Parker, I've come to visit Claire," he said politely. It was clear that Claire was home for her car stood beneath the carport. "Do you think she would see me?" he asked.

On the spur of the moment, Kate was at a loss to know what to do. She was glad William was not home. Kate knew that Claire was pining for him, but she thought it unwise to throw the cat among the pigeons. She had a duty to support her husband.

"I don't think so, Blake," she said firmly. "It would really be better for you and Claire to stop seeing each other."

Blake squared his shoulders and worked his bottom lip between his teeth. He regarded Kate with deep, sad eyes, which did not appear the least surprised.

"I'm sorry." Kate was flustered to find herself apologising. Now that she had spoken, her words caused a heaviness in her heart. She feared that she had done the wrong thing.

"I understand, Mrs Parker." He gave her a startling smile and Kate caught her breath. It was Rowena's smile all over. She wanted to retreat to her bedroom, bury her face into her pillow and weep. Blake's smile made her feel how sharply she still missed her best friend.

She watched him walk away and then returned to her cooking but her enthusiasm for it was gone. The pit of her stomach felt as heavy as lead and the aroma of chocolate muffins did nothing for her. *Why did he have to come?* She felt as if she had let down her only daughter and dishonoured Rowena's memory too. Well, the deed was done, and she would have to forget about it.

A few hours later, Kate trudged up the stairs to tap on Claire's bedroom door, as she had suspected deep in her heart she would do all along. William would be home in twenty minutes and the time to act was now. Kate agreed with William in wanting to shield Claire, but she had no right to keep Blake's visit from her. Claire was a young woman who had to make her own decisions.

Claire sat bent over her tapestry stand, stitching industriously. She raised her eyes as her mother entered.

"You've had a visitor," Kate told her.

"Who was it?" Claire asked, without much interest. Pam had promised to bring her some new patterns from work and Claire expected that was it. She resumed her work.

"Blake Quinlan." Kate pressed her back against the wall and waited for the reaction.

Claire dropped her needle and bolted up, almost knocking over her tapestry stand. It wobbled precariously and righted itself but Kate believed at that moment, Claire wouldn't have cared if she had broken it. "Where is he now?" she demanded.

Kate sat on the bed and explained slowly, urging Claire to keep her head. Claire wriggled her feet into her shoes long before Kate finished talking. Her eyes sparkled. She looked more fired-up than she had at the age of fourteen when she'd auditioned for her school production of Romeo and Juliet.

She paused to squeeze Kate's shoulders. "Mum, thanks for having second thoughts. You did the right thing. I have to see him. Please try not to remember what he did anymore. Believe me when I say he's warm and generous and funny. You'd love him."

"I just want you to be happy," Kate said huskily.

"I am happy now, Mum. Happier than I've been for years."

Kate's useless warning, "Be careful," followed Claire's flowing purple dress down the stairs.

She sat on the bed long after her daughter had driven away, knotting her fingers together and preparing herself for what she must tell William. Kate hoped she could feel friendlier toward Blake some day. Claire had her heart set on him. She reminded herself that he was

Rowena's son and tried to forget that he had raped Claire. She was sure she had done right, now. Claire would have found some way to see Blake with or without their approval. It was far better this way. She was sure that someday, even William would come to understand that.

Kate cast her eyes up to one of Claire's beautiful tapestries. "Have I not commanded you? Be strong and courageous. Do not be terrified; do not be discouraged, for the Lord your God will be with you wherever you go".

Kate could not hold back a few tears. "Lord, you're in this somewhere. I don't know where. Please take care of her. She's so precious to us. I love her."

———

The sky was beginning to darken when Blake returned home from work. No sooner had he parked than somebody tapped eagerly on the passenger side of his car. Blake whipped his head up to see Claire standing there. Several strands of hair had found their way out of her hair-tie and blew across her face.

"Let me in!" She compulsively worked the door handle up and down, although she could clearly see that the door was locked.

He leaned across and flicked up the switch with a shaking hand. He could not help thinking back to the terrible night when she had pleaded to be let out of his car. Now here she was, anxious to be let in! He had intended to pay her a visit at work tomorrow, but here she was.

She plumped into the bucket seat and filled his small car with vibrant colour. "Why did you come to see me today?" she panted.

"To tell you I can't get you out of my mind," he said slowly. "I probably could live without you, Claire, but not very easily. I changed my mind about what I said and I hope you still feel the way you felt before." He paused to steel himself for a possible knock-back. "I wanted to ask you if you would like to come on a date with me? To the pictures, or out to dinner?"

Blake clutched his steering wheel and swallowed hard. It would be only the second time she had ever been asked to date him, and the first time, his mother had asked her.

Claire's thick lashes flickered. When she was able, she managed to say, "I'd like that, Blake," in a near whisper.

Then he saw that it was true. She cared for him. The wonder of it burst through him like a wave.

Blake took one of her hands in his and softly rubbed the back of it with his thumb. He wanted her to understand that he would never consider doing anything that would make her uncomfortable. Claire promptly obeyed her instinct and threw her arms around his shoulders. He had to believe that she trusted him now. She felt a tremor pass through Blake's body and then he responded. He gathered her into his arms and kissed her hair. Claire felt her insides turn to water. This was what she had wanted for so long. Whoever would have guessed it would be him all the time?

Chapter Thirty-One

Never had Claire felt so happy, yet so sick at the same time. She knew there was nothing wrong with her but anxiety. The restaurant food was delicious but the butterflies which whirled through her stomach destroyed her appetite. Looking across the table at Blake was enough to fill all her senses to overflowing. She read admiration for her in his eyes too, but for the first part of the evening they did not dare discuss themselves and their future together. They left it hanging tantalisingly in the air and spoke of Sean and Angela, instead.

"Angela is so terrific," Claire said warmly. "She told me if she stopped helping Sean through his exercises, his muscles would begin to waste. She's helped to make him a great wheelchair athlete."

"He never could have done it without her, that's for sure," Blake agreed. "Angela is pretty special."

"If I was in her place, I'd never manage," Claire said. "I wouldn't know the first thing to do."

Her lack of confidence surprised him. "I think you would." Blake thought Claire was so courageous and resilient, but perhaps, like him, she had grown up doubting herself. "If you were married to a paraplegic like Sean, you'd learn to be just as good as Angela at looking after him. Don't forget, she was a nurse to start with. She had a head start."

The waiter arrived with the crisp side salad Claire had ordered and she gaped at the size of it. She had not expected such a mountain of raw vegetable, croutons and bacon pieces. The thought of ploughing through it made her nervous stomach cramp worse than ever. Even Blake laughed at her expression of total shock.

"Too much for you?" he asked.

She nodded ruefully. "You're welcome to dig in and help me out. In fact, I'd be grateful if you would."

"O.K." Blake was not feeling terribly hungry either but he was prepared to make an effort. He took some celery and carrot sticks. "I wouldn't have been able to eat this rabbit food ten years ago," he grinned, anxious to keep up a steady flow of conversation. "I had two sets of braces on my teeth. Man, they were uncomfortable. While I was adapting to them, I only ate soft food like custards."

She smiled and her dimple popped out. "I've seen a photo of you from back then in Sean and Angela's photo album."

"Have you?" He was astonished.

Claire nodded. "You were with your brothers. Michael was just a cute little boy and Sean was wearing his football clothes. You had a mouthful of metal," she teased lightly.

"Gee whiz, I think I remember the shot you mean." Blake felt sheepish to think of Claire seeing him look so goofy. Her description of him and his brothers filled him with more sadness than he had expected. Sean had been such a talented football player, and Mike was small and cute. Blake had tried so hard to avoid his father's contempt for being an all-round letdown, but nothing ever seemed to work. He was glad those days were over.

It dawned on Blake with some surprise that his family circumstances had not changed much at all. His father's opinion of him was still rock bottom. It was Blake's own perspective that had slowly altered since he became a Christian. He knew now that God valued him the way He had made him and that was the only way he ever had to be. Gerry's rejection still stung at times, but it was no longer as devastating as it used to be.

It had been a mind-blowing moment for Blake to discover that the mighty Creator of the heavens and earth would always love him, no matter what he did. Although he had known that for six years, it had never properly sunk in until just recently and Blake knew who had helped him to see it clearly: the beautiful girl who sat across from him. Not with her words, but with her actions. If Blake did not believe it now with all his heart, he would never have summoned the nerve to invite Claire on another date. Never in a million years! He watched her appreciatively, still hardly daring to believe that she was not just a mirage.

She raised her orange juice with a pretty, slender hand, and took a sip. He could drink in the sight of her all night long. She caught his eye and smiled at him. Blake thrilled with the amazement of it. It was the same sweet, friendly smile she had given him early on the terrible evening of their first date. His heart raced.

"Your teeth are nice and straight now," Claire commented. The tone of her voice made the simple compliment sound like a caress, as if she'd said *I'm crazy about you.*

"They ought to be." He was quite impressed by the steadiness of his own voice. "Mum and Dad paid a fortune for 'em." Gerry never let him forget it, either.

"Did it hurt?" she asked.

"Only a bit. I'd already been in hospital several times when I was much younger, and had a few operations. Going to the dentist to have braces was no big deal after that."

"Why were you in hospital?" Claire asked.

Blake thought of his appendectomy, kidney operation, broken arm, measles and pneumonia. He laughed, "Do you really want to hear about all that?"

She nodded. "Yes, tell me."

So he told her. As he spoke, he felt like an adolescent trying to impress his girl instead of a man of twenty-five. He didn't really like to dwell on his painful past and hoped to steer the conversation back to the present as quickly as possible.

Claire listened quietly. She already knew more of Blake's family history than he had any idea of. Angela had told her how the boys had suffered at the hands of the drunken Gerard Quinlan. Claire had heard how Gerry would roar home and round the two older boys out of bed when they were small, to lash into them. Angela told her how Sean and Blake had taken turns to bait their father when they were teenagers, to protect Rowena and Michael. She told Claire that Blake had always been Gerry's particular scapegoat. Angela even repeated some of the verbal abuse Gerry had slung at Blake in her own hearing. She wanted Claire to thoroughly understand the complexity of the man she had set her heart on.

As Claire watched Blake, a flame flickered through her. It grew steadier and warmer the longer she studied him. How handsome he was. He bowed his head for a moment and candlelight from the centre of the table shone on his dark hair. He raised his glowing eyes again and something deep and primeval inside of Claire responded. He was a dream. His slow smile was like something from out of this world. The butterflies in her stomach fluttered like eagles, and she laid her cutlery across her plate. She knew she could eat no more.

It was not only his physical presence that thrilled her. A certain depth of character radiated from him, without his knowledge. Like her, Blake had once been in a pit of despair. Not only had he abused her, but he had been constantly abused himself from the time he was old enough to stand. Every movement he made showed her that at last he had overcome. Each gesture spoke of quiet steadiness and a calm strength. He was so much more intriguing than he had been seven years ago. Claire wanted nothing more than to draw closer to this new Blake Quinlan, to learn how he had overcome. What had finally prompted him to shelve his past and move on?

She longed for the words to tell him how much she admired him but did not know quite how to choose them yet. She would work on it and select them carefully, so they would mean something special to him.

He finished talking of his own experiences and asked her a disconcerting question. "Have you ever had an operation, Claire?" He thought he was still making small talk.

Her face instantly flushed. It was the most unfortunate question he could have asked. She still did not feel quite ready to entrust her secret to him but the thought of lying to him or hedging the point was even worse. Their relationship was just beginning to blossom like a delicate flower. She did not want to sully it at the outset with any more cover-ups or deceit. There had been more than enough of that already. "Yes, just once," she heard herself reply. Claire's voice felt tight like a taut elastic band, and she had to force the words past her aching throat. She could not bear to look at him. She stared into the candle flame instead. "I had an abortion."

There was total silence for several seconds. She finally raised her burning eyes to his face. "Say something, Blake." He was staring at her, stunned and pale.

"Oh, Claire," he breathed at last. His face was etched with ragged despair.

Like an uncorked wine bottle, her words spilled out with tears. "After that night with you, I got pregnant. Dad made me have an abortion and I did nothing to stop him." Claire's eyes streamed, and she pressed her serviette against them. She battled to control her shuddering shoulders and wondered if the other diners were witnessing her plight.

Blake reached across the table to clasp her other hand in both of his. "Claire, would you like to leave here?" he asked gently. "You wait in the car. I'll pay for the meal and be right with you. If you don't want to talk about it, I'll understand."

She wordlessly accepted his keys and left the restaurant. She dried her eyes in the car, ashamed of her outburst. *Poor Blake!* She thought. *I wanted him to see that I've forgiven him for raping me. Collapsing into a storm of tears is a poor way of showing it.* She took her brush from her handbag and ran it through her hair. She would apologise to him for over-reacting. He took a long time and Claire guessed that the waiter must be busy.

Finally the restaurant door opened and he stepped out into the darkness. He was only a silhouette, but she knew his slender, wiry height and his way of walking with his hands jammed into his pockets and his head bowed. Tears welled in Claire's eyes again at the sight of him. She could not control herself.

He slid nervously beside her and enveloped her hand with his again, not taking his eyes from her face. "I'm sorry it took so long." His voice shook too.

Claire drew a deep breath. "I do want to talk about it. I've bottled it up for seven years, and tonight I am going to let it out." She poured out her story from start to finish. "I wanted to keep the baby. I knew that what happened between you and me was not the baby's fault... Dad shouted at me. He threatened to drag me to the hospital if I refused to go. When I lay there with that horrible rubbery mask over my nose, I knew my baby was still growing inside of me where it was supposed to be safe. I wanted to scream. I could've tried to leap up and race out of the theatre even then, but I was too scared. So I let myself go. I listened to Dad. It would have grown up to be somebody special, but I killed it. I killed my own baby." She pressed her face against the sleeve of his shirt. "I killed your baby, Blake."

He felt the pain of her disclosure roll over him in waves. He did not know what to say so he acted instinctively instead. He pulled Claire even closer to him and held her in his arms. It hit Blake like a brick that she had battled with the same emotions he had. The same loneliness and guilt, alienation and fear of God. He kissed the top of her head and stroked her hair.

"I'm sorry, Claire," he said hoarsely. "I'm so sorry you went through that."

She made an effort to pull herself together again, but he whispered, "You don't have to stop crying. I don't expect you to. You cry as much as you like."

She let herself relax in his arms and rested her face against his chest. For seven years she had longed for somebody to hold her while she cried. Although her grief was still intense, it felt good to release her secret, as if she had removed a heavy overcoat on a sweltering day.

"What sort of mother would kill her own baby?" she sobbed. "How could God ever forgive me?"

Blake knew that she was asking for answers now and his skin prickled. He did not know if he knew the right things to tell her, but he desperately needed to try.

"God had that little one in His hands all the time," he soothed. "God knows he was tiny and innocent. He's safe with God, now."

Claire made a small movement to look up into his face. "He?" she repeated.

Raw heartache struck him and Blake turned away momentarily to rest his forehead on the steering wheel. He clenched his jaw tight to control his own tears for the small child that had never had a chance to live. He managed to explain; "I think it probably would've been a boy because Quinlan men have had mostly boys for several generations." He did not know whether it would help Claire if he broke down too, or if it would make her feel worse.

She hesitated, then rested a light hand upon his shoulder. "I have hardly ever mentioned it to anyone. I never told Angela because I was certain she'd hate me, having tried so hard to have a baby herself. It isn't fair, Blake. Angela and Sean would have been wonderful parents." Claire's voice rang in the stillness.

"Do you hate me now?" she ventured tremulously when he did not answer. "I hated you for raping me. Do you hate me for not being strong enough to say no to my dad? I let him force me into something I didn't want to do, but my innocent baby was the one without a chance to live. I let him be murdered. I killed my own baby. I killed your baby, Blake. Don't you hate me? "

He spun back to face her, with a thundering pulse. If that was what she thought, she had the wrong idea entirely There was no way he could hate her. Suddenly, Blake knew exactly what God would have him tell Claire. Who better than he, who was familiar with the type of shame and guilt she was dealing with? As Claire had helped him, he was, incredibly, in a position to help her in return. Blake softly raised her chin with his thumb to search her eyes and be certain she understood.

"Listen to me, Claire. I love you with all my heart. Do you know what you've done for me? You showed me the heart of God through your actions. You made Him feel real in my life." He spoke slowly, groping for the right words to use. "Who but you would ever forgive me for raping you? After the cruel, brutal thing I did, you're sitting beside me, willing to give me another chance. I find that awesome, Claire. You blow my mind away. That's God's unconditional love at work in you. For six years I understood it in my head, but I never understood it in my heart until you came back into my life and showed me. I can see how immense His love is because of you. I can see how it will cover over the blackest of sins. Before I met you again, I still felt depraved and condemned whenever I thought of what I did to you. Now, because you've forgiven me, I feel truly forgiven by God at last." He touched her eyelid gently with his lips and felt her lashes flicker. "I'll always love you, Claire."

She heard him loud and clear. He could tell from the way her tense limbs turned to jelly that his words were striking home. Blake felt God's love pulse through the car, and fill each of them.

"I'd like to help other girls who are pregnant and don't know what to do." Claire cleared her throat and rubbed her damp cheek against his shoulder. "I'm thinking of volunteering at a pregnancy crisis centre, or studying counselling."

"I think you'd be wonderful." Blake's voice was husky. "You've helped me more than anyone else ever has, so I'm certain you could help many other people. I'd support you completely."

For a moment she was lost for words. He pulled her close while her shoulders trembled. Finally Claire pushed the wet hair back from her face and gave him a shaky smile. "It means a lot to me to hear you say that. I've spent seven years feeling that I did something completely unforgivable."

"God forgives you, Claire," he breathed. "He knows what happened, what your dad said, what you went through and how you felt. He knows you have a heart set on Him. He know's you want to follow Him and listen to his call. He's offering a fresh chance to both of us right now. Shall we take it?"

Claire drew a deep breath and threw her arms around his shoulders. "I love you, Blake." She buried her face in his neck and her hot tears of joy ran down his shirt collar. She breathed in the clean, exciting scent of his skin and his shirt as if he were a sea breeze. Now she understood where his strength and dignity came from, and her heart sang. She should have known she had to look no further than God.

"I love you more than I've ever loved anybody else in the world!" she cried.

Then she was in his arms. They both wept freely, now. He could control himself no longer but he knew instinctively that she would not think him unmanly. He bent his head to kiss her cheek and she wrapped both hands around the back of his neck to pull his face down to hers. Claire sought his lips with hers and felt him tremble in response to the flames of desire and emotion that shot through her. She raised his hand and caressed each of his strong, calloused fingers. She longed to show him that she would give him the love he had craved.

"Let's do it right, this time," she breathed, and felt his head nod against her. "Let's work together and follow where God leads." She thought briefly of the times she had helped others, including Janine Turner the pregnant teenager, and wondered if there was a calling on her life. No matter what, she knew that Blake would be with her for it.

"I want to make you happy," he mumbled huskily when he could speak.

"Making you happy will make me happy," she replied.

All at once, Claire knew that this tenderness, thinking of each other and deep understanding was the type of love God had always intended between a man and a woman.

Also from Even Before Publishing...

A Design of Gold, Paula Vince

After drama and loss Nicola's life introduces her to Jerome,
Michael and Casey. As their lives intertwine they grow,
learn about themselves and find out that true discipleship
can even start at home. Romance and drama from the
author who brought you *The Risky Way Home.*

Another page-turner! If you have never read Paula Vince,
do! *Meredith Resce*

ISBN: 978-1-921633-03-4
$19.95
Available from your local Christian bookstore.
www.evenbeforepublishing.com/adesignofgold.html

Also by Paula Vince

Adult fiction

A Design of Gold

The Risky Way Home

Young Adult fiction

Quenarden 1: The Prophecies

Quenarden 2: The Castle of Light

Quenarden 3:The Dark Secret

If you would like to contact the author you can do so
from her website: www.appleleafbooks.com

Support groups and information

If you, like many before, have found yourself in a situation like those depicted in this book we would like to offer you some direction for support or healing.

Pregnancy support groups are listed on the website:
www.pregnancygiftideas.com

Other support references are listed on
www.evenbeforepublishing.com/ pickingupthepieces.html

We hope after reading this book, not only will you understand more of the challenges that face our young people each day, but if you have ever been through anything like what was depicted we hope that you find strength and healing.